Fifty Thousand Years

Dylan Casa Lobos

Formatting by Polgarus Studio

An Introduction

An historian without an imagination is like a sailboat without wind. The historical novelist has more freedom, but the facts he relies on tend to change with time. If you obtained an education over thirty years ago, you can appreciate the concept of changing facts, especially in prehistory. However, the history of the past few centuries is continually rewritten to reflect well on certain political philosophies and history becomes historical fiction through malfeasance. Usually, the historical fiction or romance writer begins with a purity of purpose; a story within a relatively accurate framework of historical accuracy is the author's purpose. If it is a good story and awakens historical interest for the reader, the author has probably written a good story.

Fifty Thousand Years covers a lot of material and readers may find some terms to be unfamiliar. Therefore a glossary is included with simple explanations of many uncommon terms. There is also an alphabetical list of characters and relationships if you need to reference a character, rather than paging through many chapters. I hope you enjoy the book.
http://natural2thman.wixsite.com/author-blog

Acknowledgements

I had some help and encouragement before and during the writing this book. Two of my helpers are customers, dear friends, and authors. Kathryn Rishoff has been a big help. She read many of my short stories and told me it was time to write a book. Her latest book, "The Weight of it All," will be available soon. Maggie Carpenter was available to explain many of the technical aspects of writing a book and told me about things that will not work. She is a prolific writer and publishes a new romance novel every few months.

A long time ago, my freshman English instructor and the head of the Journalism Department asked me to meet with them in the head office. I was apprehensive and worried they wanted to throw me out of school. My instructor told the class, we could write on any subject, and my stories dealt with life in the raw. I was 17 years old and had never seen so many pretty girls in my entire life. I worried that I may have crossed some invisible line, but I started laughing when they asked me to be an English major. I told them I wanted to major in something I could make a living at and it was their turn to laugh at me. They were exasperated and told me to take Creative Writing every semester and I would receive an A, if I did the work. I accepted, but later, I noticed the classes were three and four hundred level courses with several prerequisites. I didn't take the prerequisites and I caused a lot of resentment among more serious journalism students. Their snide remarks and sour looks didn't deter me; I took the courses, and even attended the parties for journalism majors. I'd like to thank those two guys, I'm sorry; I don't remember their names, but they have surely passed over the divide by now. In the twilight of life, I wish I would have taken their advice, and learned to be a better writer.

I'd also like to thank my friend, Dale Jeffrey dalejeffrey@equinedentistry.com. He has read my short stories for decades and let me know which ones were worth developing. He runs an equine dental school in Glenns Ferry, Idaho, and is a 19th Century man who works in front of two different computer screens. The Navaho call him, Half Horse, a great compliment for an exceptional man, but perhaps, the name Two Computer Screens might be more appropriate.

I also want to acknowledge my formatters at. www.polgarusstudio.com They have been extremely helpful in guiding me through the intricacies of creating a professional novel.

Shannon Passmore info@shanoffformats.com created this beautiful cover. She is a professional, who listens to ideas, and she is quick.

Curt at http://www.floppingaces.net took me on as a staff writer in 2010. Writing as a political writer was a challenge, but Curt managed to keep me from making too many mistakes. I tried to use my stories to teach moral lessons to a bunch of hard-core political debaters. I learned a lot from that job.

Prologue

We modern humans are smug about our progress through time. No longer do we hunt, kill, and build a fire to enjoy our dinner. We don't make love in desperation and hope we live to see the sunrise; however, we have retained certain behavioral patterns and personality traits from those early days, and they remain ingrained in our personalities and cultures. Yes, we advanced and changed everything around us, making it possible for the weak and silliest among us to thrive. Yet, despite our advances and pretenses of modernity, we are the same basic creatures who sought shelter in caves and worried about having a meal the next day. These were our ancestors and it is who we are.

During a glacial maximum of a more recent Ice Age, fifty thousand years ago, there was massive drought throughout the world. The ice fields covering most of North America, Europe, and Asia, were a mile high, and had a great thirst for the earth's water. Thus a large percentage of the world's water was locked in ice. Oceans were one hundred and forty meters more shallow and the coastlines of the continents extended a hundred to three hundred kilometers farther out. The lush, green valleys of North Africa, home to many of the earth's ten thousand people, were becoming deserts. Faced with migration or starvation, the human race was on the move.

There were rumors of great rivers with rich bounties of fish, vast sources of edible plants, and many animals to hunt on the Mammoth Steppe. One of the world's greatest biomes, this vast grassland was south of the ice, for several hundred kilometers, and stretched from Spain to the Yukon. Many tribes had already left Africa; some of them were capable of hunting the mammoths and mastodons and other large dangerous animals that thrived on the Mammoth Steppe. Over generations, these hardy Stone Age people enjoyed a protein-rich diet, and became virtual giants. As dangerous as the animals they hunted, they were territorial and known to kill intruders. There were also Near People or Neanderthals, who could effortlessly crush a man's chest with beastly power. Water and life was near the ice; to survive the changing climate of a harsher, colder world, people had to adapt or die.

This story follows the migration of a family through the maternal line, by tracing a strain of mitochondrial DNA. This particular strain of DNA was unique because it gave a few women uncommon intellect and creative abilities, beginning with the skill to sculpt magnificent tools from flint. These well-made tools became valuable trade items and often kept tribal members from starving, by trading tools for meat with the unpredictable mammoth hunters. These gifted women also provided ideas and creative solutions during times of crisis. We, the readers, get a realistic view of life during the primitive eras and an appreciation of how fragile our veil of civilization is.

Our ancestors explored the earth, in a desperate search to find reliable sources of food. To eat, make love, have children, and watch them mature—these were measures of success, in a world of frequent tragedies and brief moments of joy. The story begins 50,000 years ago and follows these women as they walk through time, and into the modern era, facing adversity and feminism as providers and problem solvers.

Chapter 1
A Place in the Country

Seamus was an enigma and a local legend in the Omineca/Peace Region of Northern British Columbia. He was a horseman among horsemen; although, he chose a different path than the other boys who grew up on the hardscrabble ranches of the Canadian foothills. Most of the lads try the rodeo game, and in a few years, drift into packing and guiding. They eventually grow old and live on memories and a government pension check. Seamus created indignation among the old horsemen when he migrated into the US and worked for the wealthy horse owners of the English horse culture. The old-time horsemen complained that Seamus wanted to be famous, but that wasn't true; he just wanted to see the world, and horses were his passport and his vehicle. His backwoods horsemanship worked well on the expensive horses, and he became moderately wealthy during a long career.

He inherited a registered Canadian trap line during his youth and still owns the lease. Technically, he is a government-licensed trapper, but he has been a professional horseman for fifty years. He tweaked the rules to keep the trap line by paying royalties on fur that was never trapped. For him, the trap line is a means to escape modern life for two weeks every year and return to his roots.

Seamus employed philosophical reasoning and viewed life and his successes differently than most men. He figured modern city life grabbed him by the back of the neck, decades ago, and dragged him into civilization. He liked the money, and it was nice to have people asking him to work with expensive, well-bred horses, but there are prices to pay for these shallow pretenses of success, and Seamus has paid his share.

The first two weeks of every January, Seamus left his Angus ranch in Central California and went out on his trap line in Northern British Columbia for a holiday. He would stay in the trap cabins and ride a snowmobile through the forests and over the hills. He was there to relax and think about what might have been and the life he had wasted away.

During the winter of 2013, about twenty miles west of Williston Lake, when the temperature couldn't get above forty below, Seamus saw Lolo, an old friend, waving at him in the distance. Lolo was a Laplander, a serious trapper and a unique man.

Seamus was in his sixties, and Lolo had been a grown man when Seamus was a teenager. Lolo had no use for a snowmobile; he traveled on snowshoes, walking in deep snow with a backpack piled way over his head, his shirt and jacket open to the cold, and chewing coffee grounds like candy. Lolo was several miles from his trap line, and Seamus assumed Lolo wanted to tell him something important. He drove the snow machine a little closer; Lolo was walking toward Seamus, faster than most people walk on a sidewalk.

Lolo was brought over by the government, to teach Canadian ranchers about caribou. Everyone figured the men of the Orient were going to pay big money for Canadians to saw off caribou antlers in the velvet (the growing stage, when they are covered with short, silky fur). Apparently, ground-up antlers can put lead in your pencil, and recapture the libido of youth.

Like most government programs and pipe dreams, everyone except the politicians went broke when the market cratered. Lolo became a trapper, a good trapper, and he became popular among the women of the reservations. He had none of the metrosexual personality conflicts; actually, Seamus often wondered if Lolo was a throwback to an earlier form of man. He certainly could have survived the Ice Age without a care in the world.

He didn't build or sleep in cabins; yet, Lolo stayed on the trap line all winter. When the temperatures dropped between thirty-and-fifty below, he would burrow into the snow, wrapped in a canvas tarp. Seamus had never met another man as tough or as strong as Lolo.

Seamus stopped the snowmobile and let Lolo walk the last thirty feet. He was walking so fast, Seamus thought he might run over the snow machine. At five foot eight, his bow-legged stride on snowshoes was almost comical, until you realized how fast he was traveling.

Lolo stopped right next to Seamus and put his hand on Seamus' shoulder to brace himself against the momentum of his packs.

In heavily accented English, Lolo spoke without moving his mouth, to keep from losing his coffee grounds. "Seamus, woman wants you, North Fork cabin."

Seamus was trying to decipher what Lolo had said, when Lolo turned away and said, "See you in the later."

By the time Seamus said, "Who is she?" Lolo had already covered thirty feet and was gaining speed. After a few seconds, he turned to wave goodbye and disappeared in the gray-and-white void.

Lolo was never one to waste time with idle chitchat, but Seamus was bewildered. The trap line was approximately thirty by forty miles. Creeks and rivers defined the borders, and Seamus had the exclusive right to trap fur and live on the trap line in his cabins. He was only obligated to pay a royalty to the Crown for the fur trapped on the line. There were no roads, and the country would be considered uninhabitable by city dwellers. The chances of a woman finding one of his cabins and knowing to tell Lolo to give Seamus a message, were slim to none, but who was in the North Fork cabin, and why?

Finding someone on twelve hundred square miles of wilderness was almost impossible for anyone but a bush ape like Seamus or Lolo. In the old days, when Seamus was a teenager, he might see a hunter or a seismic worker once a year, but no one came to visit, and there had never been a woman visitor.

Seamus gave up being a serious trapper over fifty years ago, and by rights, he should sell the trap line. But he doesn't need the money, and he enjoyed being alone in the wilderness and living close to the animals.

The North Fork Cabin was essentially a horse camp. In his youth, Seamus subcontracted to guide hunters for an outfitter and paid grazing leases to the Crown to keep his horses in the meadows. The meadows can keep a pack string alive year round; in the winter, horses paw through the snow to get the grass, and they eat snow for water, unless the creek has water running. They are better at this than people realize; actually, they did it for eons before man started riding them, instead of eating them.

People often say horses are stupid; unfortunately, this is usually because a horse is out of his natural element, and a human is failing to communicate effectively. When Seamus had a good string of mountain horses, he was always training young ones to become part of the string or to be sold. The horses had to learn to cross fast rivers and traverse steep mountain grades with packs or a rider. They had to develop confidence in Seamus and believe he could turn a grizzly or an enraged bull moose on the trail. Eventually, they learned or believed that when he walked forward with his rifle, they were safe.

It was a long process that began when the colts were yearlings. Seamus started them in small groups, because they would need to work as part of a team the rest of their lives. One of the first obstacles to overcome was the fresh bear hide. Horses love oats, so Seamus always started by feeding a pail of oats in a trough by the fence line. After a few days, he laid a fresh bear hide down in front of the trough, and the colts had to stand on it to eat the oats. There was always one or two who ignored the scent of the bear hide, as if to say, "I don't care. I am going to eat the oats." They happily ate the oats, while their friends stood back in shocked indignation and went hungry.

The next day, the reluctant eaters would be standing on the bear hide, waiting for the oats. It's important for horses to overcome the mortal fear they have for the animals that can kill them. Later on, they will be expected to be calm in the face of danger. Horses can recognize the three North American predators who can kill and eat them (timber wolf, grizzly, and cougar) with an extraordinary sense of smell—a sense of smell much greater than our hunting dogs. This can be proven on any given day in the North Country. When you cross a creek bed, tracks of one of the three predators will often be visible in the soft mud. When the dogs cross the scent they begin yelping and take off in hot pursuit, but they go in the wrong direction about half the time. This gives them only the performance of the simple law of averages; when there are only two choices, anyone can be right half the time. Animals can't read sign, but a human can't tell you about the track if you blindfold him and put his nose in the center of it. A horse, on the other hand, recognizes the scent early and always knows which way the predator is headed. Each of them will stare in the direction of the predator, even the youngest colts on their first trip.

To get the horses used to the rifle, you fire the .22 while they are eating and move up to the larger sporting rifle when they become familiar with the sound. From that point forward, all target shooting is done next to their pasture, and, eventually, they accept the noise as part of life.

In the early fall of their second year, they are trained to the ropes. They learn to be caught with a lariat, and they learn what it feels like to have ropes on every part of their body. When they become familiar with the ropes, the horses are packed light, and they follow the older packhorses, darting from one side of the trail to the other, hitting trees and causing their own misery. They soon learn how to negotiate a trail by watching the older horses.

These are simple lessons, and most of the time, the horses are their own teachers; unfortunately, too many horses and people miss out on the basic lessons for life and survival.

By the next hunting season, the colts have seen a lot of territory and crossed fast rivers. Again, they must learn to trust a human's judgment while crossing fast water. A mistake on a fast river means the bears downstream will have a nice dinner.

The young horse would be expected to carry a light pack of eighty to a hundred pounds, depending on the colt's strength, size, and stamina. The young horse should not be expected to pack meat or carry antlers and hides, but he needs to be present when the older horses are loaded with those things.

By the end of the hunting season of their third year, a horse should be ready to become an all-around ranch horse, including: working cattle, working in harness, and roping.

Of course, there are many ways to train horses. Seamus was lucky and had worked for many good horsemen around the world, from several different disciplines. He learned many things that influenced his riding and horsemanship, but the basics have been the same for thousands of years: never ask a horse to do anything beyond their abilities. A good horseman will design a progression of tasks the young horse can understand and build upon; when horses or humans miss the natural progression of learning, they often appear stupid; although, the problem often relates to a failure to teach and communicate effectively.

At ten years of age, a mountain and ranch horse has spent large segments of eight years living in primitive conditions with humans and is often smarter than the average rider and can be a serious opponent in intellectual games like checkers. The well-trained horse has acquired intelligence, honesty, trust, courage, balance, and common sense. Sadly, many humans are missing the same traits we try to develop in mountain and ranch horses.

In the mountains, without the artificial restraints of corrals and fences, the rider needs to be a more effective teacher, and when you are a hundred miles from a road, there are no ambulances to save you after making a stupid error. Living with horses in a natural habitat helps a rider understand the horse, and tends to make the human a better horseman.

Seamus often thought of the first people to domesticate a horse and the intelligence it took to see the possibilities. He visualized a group of nomadic hunters capturing a herd of wild horses in a blind canyon with a fence and gate at the mouth. This simple trap was used for millennia and would have worked well for horse and caribou herds. The animals survived off the feed and water in the canyon and were slaughtered, as they were needed.

Inevitably, a Stone Age child would have made a pet of one of the foals, against the wishes of parents and other adults. When it was time to move, the remaining animals would have been turned loose, but a curious thing happened, the now much larger foal didn't leave; he stayed with his friend, the child.

During those Stone Age migrations, early man carried his earthly possessions on his back. When the child tied his twenty-pound pack on the back of the colt and the horse accepted the load, a whole new world opened to people with imagination. The backbreaking drudgery of carrying all your possessions could now be accomplished with a packhorse, and people were free to hunt on the trail or defend themselves during migrations. The trained packhorse soon learned to carry a human, and the horse tribe gained a tremendous advantage over those who walked. From this humble beginning, advances in mobility, agriculture, war, and hunting were waiting down the trail. When the science of the wheel was realized, the payload of the horse was increased by ten. The practical ratio of riding a horse is one-man to one-horse, but with the technology of a cart or wagon, one horse can effectively transport the man, his wife, kids, and a half-ton of supplies.

These thoughts took Seamus back in time, not so long ago, to the time of primitive man.

Chapter 2
The Story of Nancy

Across the valley, Seamus saw eight horses grazing in the meadow. His visitor was obviously a horsewoman; the mystery was solved. He had known thousands of horsewomen, but only one who could make it to the North Fork cabin during the winter with a string of horses. Nancy Larkin, a woman who began life in a hovel on the reservation, traveled the world in luxury, to end up back in the mountains, living like a nomad with her horses.

If she needed the cabin for the winter or the rest of her life, it was okay. Seamus liked Nancy; she was a vagabond and offered no apologies for her life to anyone. She was not that much different than Seamus, except he found a decent way to make a living in the horse world.

There was a whiff of smoke from the chimney; the fire was nearly out. His 'guest' was napping. In the gray light of early evening, the thermometer on the porch read forty-two below and the flickering light of a candle was visible through the window.

He stood to the side of the door, with his back against the log wall and called, "Hello, it's me, Seamus." He opened the wooden latch and swung the door open to look inside.

Nancy was in the bed and looked frail and weak. She motioned with one hand for him to come in.

Seamus stepped in and said, "Let's get the fire going and warm this place up."

Nancy nodded her head up and down, and Seamus loaded the stove. The embers were hot, and the fire was blazing within a few minutes.

Nancy said, "It's a good stove. Did you make it?"

"Yeah, a long time ago," Seamus replied, with a smile.

Nancy smiled and said, "It's good to see you again, old friend. How are you?"

Seamus looked at Nancy; she was a beauty of the North Country. She was small, with delicate features. Her hands and fingers were graceful, like you expect to see on an aristocratic lady. Her color was slightly darker than the red clay color of the local natives, although some natives were whiter than Seamus. They were the Metis, European, and Canadian Indian cross. Nancy was no Metis.

Seamus smiled and said, "Nancy, I turned around one day and I was old."

Nancy laughed a frail little laugh and said, "Seamus, you are funny. Look at you, handsome, young-looking, and stronger than most forty year-old men—and most of them can't make love to a woman."

Seamus didn't want to hear details, real or imagined, about his romantic life. The moccasin telegraph is a powerful means of communication that white people don't understand, but natives often know things that are unexplainable. Seamus changed the topic. "What's going on, Nancy? What are you doing here with your horses?"

"Seamus, I came here to die."

Seamus pulled up a chair and sat next to the bed. "Nancy, I can put you in the sled behind the snowmobile and haul you to town. We can be there in less than eight hours."

Nancy laughed and said, "Seamus, you and Charles were the only men who could make me laugh."

"I wasn't trying to be funny."

"Seamus, I need some favors."

"I am listening."

"I am asking you because of what you did for Barbwire Johnny. He would have been miserable for all eternity in a graveyard with a bunch of city people."

Apparently, everyone knew Seamus had buried Johnny on a hill above the Peace River, over forty years ago.

"Do you know the old graveyard on the hill, behind the cabin, with all the blueberries?"

"Yes."

"I want you to bury me with my ancestors."

"Nancy, the ground is frozen for at least four feet down," Seamus said, without thinking.

"No, I want to be buried in the trees, like the old days, before the white man."

"I can do it, but it is against the law."

"A lot of good white man's law has done for me. It's like being thirsty and having nothing but a bucket of warm piss."

"Okay, Nancy, but breaking the law is not easy for me. I need to think about this 'favor' you are asking of me."

"I know you, Seamus. You are barely civilized, a brown man in a white body. You have never faced rejection and heartache you didn't bring upon yourself. If you had been born a brown man, your life would not be so damn pretty."

Seamus changed the subject. "Why don't I fix some dinner?"

"Seamus, I have a moose roast in the panniers (pack boxes for a pack saddle) on the porch, and all the fixin's for a grand meal. Bring in both pairs of panniers and cook your best meal."

Everything was frozen. Seamus laid the roast on the butcher block and used an ax to cut it into smaller pieces and let it thaw by the fire. They had yams, corn, turnips, butter, and flour for biscuits.

In a few minutes, the roast was in a Dutch oven on the stove. Seamus loved cooking, but he cooked for himself most of the time. Cooking for someone else was more fun.

The roast and biscuits were nearly perfect. Nancy only ate a few bites, but said her last meal was wonderful. Seamus wished he had a bottle of Cabernet; he didn't like to drink in front of Indians, but he would have made an exception on this occasion.

Nancy pointed to a blanket roll in one of the panniers and asked Seamus to get it for her.

The smell of smoke-tanned moose hide filled the room when she unrolled the leather blanket. There were pictures of Nancy and her beloved Charles Larkin, the polo player.

Seamus knew him well. He had worked for Charles during the early years. Nancy smiled at the photos and held some of them against her bosom. There was another roll of moose hide. Nancy unrolled it to reveal a beautiful native dress of white moose hide leather, trimmed with lynx over the shoulders and beaver on the cuffs and the hem, with beadwork portraying an eagle over the breast area. There were tiny moccasins trimmed in beaver and a new pair of white cotton socks.

Seamus helped her put the dress on and slipped on the socks with the moccasins. She seemed much happier with the dress on, and she told Seamus she had made everything but the socks.

It was a beautiful dress, and she looked like a princess as she stroked the lynx fur.

She touched the moose hide blanket and said, "Seamus, this is my burial shroud. I want you to sew my body into this blanket. Put the photos in the shroud. Leave my rifle and saddle with a bridle up on the bier, with the rest of this meal, and it will be perfect. Are you okay with this? I have an awl and thread. I know you respect the old ways."

"I can do everything, Nancy," he said, but his voice quaked.

"Seamus, I knew your mother. She became a white woman, and took up the white man's vices of tobacco and alcohol and died early. She was never meant to be a white woman.

"I was born too dark to be a white woman. It didn't bother Charles. He loved me, despite my dark hide. He was a good man."

Seamus said, "I remember Charles. He was my favorite polo customer. I rode the mare Madness, and trained her so she wouldn't kill people."

"Yes, Charles told everyone about you riding that mare and civilizing her. She won best polo pony several times at different clubs, and many men offered to buy her, but Charles never sold her."

Seamus smiled and said, “Those were good days, Nancy; we were young and strong.”

“Seamus, the young horses are yours. There will be a couple of foals in the spring. They all go back to the mare Madness and the sire, Hickory. I kept the maternal line through Madness crossed with Hickory, and brought in new stallions over the years. It’s always seventy-five percent the mare. You can have the best stallion in the world, but if your mare is no account, your foal will be worthless.”

Seamus enjoyed hearing about the horses of the past and was excited to have their offspring. “I liked Hickory, but I often wondered what happened to his skull. His forehead was caved in an inch or more.”

“He earned his name. Charles was playing at Oakbrook in Chicago. A Pakistani man was riding a black stallion, and the horse was running away with him from one end of the field to the other. He asked Charles to ride the horse, to see if he could control him.

“Charles could control and play him, but they were way too fast. However, Charles always said, ‘They aren’t running off with you if you ask them to go faster,’ so he went to the whip and asked for more speed. The horse became enraged and headed for the wooden bleachers. The spectators ran, but Charles and the horse hit the bleachers at full speed. The horse had terrible head injuries, and Charles was bruised up. He told the Pakistani, ‘If this horse lives, I want to buy him.’ That’s how he ended up with the name Hickory.”

“I can see it happening, having known Charles and Hickory. Madness and Hickory liked me. We were kindred spirits.”

“Seamus, all the horses like you. I want you to put down my old horses, after I cross over. I’ve already told them. They had good lives, and don’t want to go on without me.”

Seamus remembered the package he picked up at the post office as he was leaving his ranch in Central California. He had read about the recent advances in DNA blood typing and how science can now trace your ancestry after you provide a DNA sample. He picked up the DNA sample kit at the store/post office and planned to read the information in the cabins at night, take the samples, and mail them off when he returned, but here was an opportunity he would never have again. Seamus asked Nancy, "Do you mind if I take your DNA samples and have your ancestry traced? I think it would be interesting to look back fifty thousand years and see where your people came from."

Nancy smiled and said, "Let's do it, but my relatives have been here since the first days. The old people told the stories of creation, when I was a little girl."

Seamus read the instructions and information aloud and Nancy enjoyed hearing about the science of DNA. He used the swabs to brush the cheeks of her mouth and sealed them in the envelopes. The results would arrive six weeks after being mailed. Being polite, he asked Nancy about the story of her life, a story he knew well.

She smiled, and told her story for the last time, "Charles was the love of my life. We met when I was sixteen. I was attending a school in Vancouver that specialized in turning native girls into white girls; some of us were forced to attend. We studied home economics and spent a lot of time baking bread.

"We had Sundays off, and several of us liked to ride the bus to watch the polo games. We were fascinated with the horses, and some of the men. Charles noticed me from the field, and our eyes locked onto each other. He rode over after the game and invited me to the clubhouse for dinner.

"I never went back to home economics school. Charles swept me off my feet; we had a romance for twenty-four years and traveled the world.

"You may wonder why we never married; it was his family and my heritage. They were English aristocrats and Liberal to the core, but they drew the line when it came to me. His family threatened to cut him out of the estate if he married beneath his station. I was not good enough to eat at their table. He received a generous remittance each month, from the estate; without it, there was no fairy tale for us. He was a horseman, Seamus, no different than you, except he had a wealthy family. Of course, his family liked to talk *mucka mucka* (Canadian native expression for meaningless and endless talk) about shouldering the white man's burden, but they didn't want their son to marry a native girl.

"There was no way he could make a living and maintain the polo lifestyle, so we continued on for twenty-four years, living in sin and loving it.

"All good stories come to an end. Charles was playing at the Brandywine Polo Club in Delaware, and there was a terrible collision on the field. Charles died of a broken neck. All horsemen think they are immortal, and Charles didn't plan for an accident, but his time was up that day. I was left with $30,000, a truck and trailer, and a string of horses. His family wanted everything, including his body.

"I couldn't keep his body. They flew it to England, the first night. The next morning, I loaded up the horses and drove back to the land of my ancestors, and here I am."

Seamus held her hand and told her it was a sad, but beautiful story.

Nancy drifted off to sleep, and Seamus studied her features. She was small, about five feet one and maybe a hundred pounds. Her eyes were so dark they were almost black, and her long thick hair was soft and silky, still as black as the raven, with only a few streaks of gray. She was breathing regularly, in a deep sleep. Seamus grabbed a blanket, made a bed on the floor, and fell asleep.

Chapter 3
The Funeral

The next morning, Seamus woke up, wondering why he was on the floor; until he looked on the bed and realized Nancy had passed away.

Seamus sewed Nancy into the moose hide blanket, along with her pictures, and tied her to a six-foot by four-foot piece of three-quarter-inch plywood that would serve as a toboggan and a burial platform. He rode the strongest old horse up the hill, while towing Nancy and all the gear on the plywood. The other two old horses followed along, like they understood what was happening.

On the hill, Seamus found three poplar trees growing in a triangular formation, and they each had a good size fork about ten feet off the ground. Seamus cut down two pine saplings to use as rails and wired them into the forks. He stood on the rails, and used the rope to pull up Nancy while she was still tied to the plywood. He nailed the plywood to the rails and he was finished in a few minutes. The three old horses supervised the work.

After securing the food, saddle, and rifle, Seamus said a prayer:

"Dear Lord, this is Nancy Larkin. I humbly ask you to not judge her harshly. She did the best she could. She was good at teaching kids to ride, and she took excellent care of her horses. Whether she goes to sit at the fires of her ancestors or some other special place, I am asking you to show her kindness. Life wasn't always kind to her—partially because of the way you made her—and you should take that into consideration. She was a beautiful person on the outside, but she had inner beauty as well.

"These old horses will be crossing over in a few minutes; it would be nice if you could help them meet up with Nancy.

"I reckon I have a few more years on this earth. If you have any questions, we can discuss them at length, when I see you in person. Amen."

Seamus poured out three piles of oats in the snow, and the old horses had their last meal. They ate slowly, and when they were almost finished, none of them looked up as he walked from horse to horse and sent them to be with Nancy.

Seamus mailed the DNA samples after crossing the border and forgot about them, but the results of the DNA analysis caught up with him a few weeks later.

Nancy's mitochondrial DNA story was fascinating; Seamus decided to learn everything about her people and the world around them, from the time her ancestors walked out of Africa, fifty thousand years ago, to the present.

Seamus enjoyed the intellectual study and began writing stories about Nancy's ancestors on the Internet. Ignoring the moral qualms about writing in Nancy's name, he wrote to honor a woman who was shunned and humiliated; using her name became a moral equivalence. People wrote complimentary commentary and encouraged Seamus to write more. In the cyber world, he became Nancy Larkin.

Chapter 4

A Primer on the Ice Age

We are currently in a glacial retreat of an Ice Age that has been active for two million years. Our most recent glacial maximums occurred at fifty thousand years BP (before present) and twenty thousand years BP. The current Ice Age has been active for one hundred ten thousand years, and started a significant glacial retreat at ten thousand five hundred BP. There have been countless glacial (formation of ice) periods and glacial retreats (melting of ice).

When snow accumulates for longer than a year, or when the summer isn't warm enough to melt the previous winter's snow, the accumulated snow is a glacier. The weight and compression of accumulated snow creates ice. The addition of snow and the increasing compression creates more ice, and the process can continue for hundreds and thousands of years. Eventually, the accumulation of snow and ice reaches a point when it can no longer support its own weight, and lateral expansion or spreading occurs. Extreme pressures cause the bottom layer of ice to melt, forming a thin layer of water to lubricate the movement of ice over the earth's surface. Loose soil and sand also facilitates the movement of ice. A moving glacier becomes a river of ice, when the lower layers of ice are under extreme pressure they are pliable. The upper layers are brittle and prone to cracking, causing crevasses. The crevasse makes traveling on the surface of a glacier dangerous, especially when the crevasses are hidden by snow.

There have been innumerable periods of glacial advance and glacial retreat, with countless regional variations. During the peaks of the last glaciations, summer temperatures were four to eight degrees Celsius cooler, and winter temperatures were ten to fifteen degrees Celsius cooler. Consequently, the weather of the southern states would have been similar to the western Canadian provinces of today.

During the most recent glacial maximum, the ice covered nearly all of Canada (except for the Yukon and a strip running the length of British Columbia). Most of the northern states were covered by ice, but Alaska had no ice. Northern Europe and Asia were also covered with ice. There was a continuous glacial steppe existing from Spain to the Yukon, known as the Mammoth Steppe.

People visualize the surviving glaciers when thinking of these glaciations, but the ice sheets were up to a mile deep and thousands of miles wide during the peaks. The ice sheets preempted much of the earth's water; the oceans were one hundred forty meters shallower than they are now. Depending on the depths of the coastal waters, the coastal shorelines extended up to a hundred kilometers into the ocean. The Mediterranean was reduced to a series of lakes, and it was possible to walk from North Africa to Italy or from France to Ireland. There was a continental landmass connecting Siberia to Alaska, referred to as Beringia; it was an ice-free savanna, and measured one thousand miles north to south. Herds of horses, rhinos, mammoths, mastodons, camels, and many other animals migrated back and forth over Beringia for thousands of years. The ice-free areas of Beringia, Alaska, and the Yukon and a corridor running north to south through British Columbia, allowed early man to migrate into the Americas approximately twenty thousand years ago. It was also possible for early man to travel from Europe to America using fairly short boat trips from one land mass to another.

Every school child knows Columbus "discovered" the New World in 1492, while trying to access the riches of Kublai Khan's Court, but this 'discovery' was a rhetorical exercise. The Stone Age hunters of Asia were the explorers who discovered America, over twenty thousand years ago, and Europeans probably discovered America during the same era.

The ice sheets had a great thirst for moisture; consequently, the rest of the world existed in perennial drought, with only fifty percent of normal precipitation. Life and water was near the ice. During the winter, everything was frozen, but the weight of the ice on the earth's crust forced ground water out of the earth, forming warm springs and warm spring-fed lakes near the ice. The heat of summer caused a partial melting of the ice, with massive runoff that formed the great rivers and river valleys of today and the Great Lakes.

During glaciation, there are pulses of cold or glacial periods (glacial maximums or ice ages), and intermittent warmer phases, termed inter-glacial. Technically, because the ice sheets of Greenland, Antarctica, and Arctic exist today, we are in an interglacial that began ten thousand five hundred years ago. It is part of an ice age that began 2.6 million years ago, at the beginning of the Pleistocene epoch.

The most recent glacial maximums were at twenty thousand and fifty thousand years ago. The fifty thousand-year glacial maximum forced a major migration from Africa, and the twenty thousand-year pulse coincided with the human migration into the Americas.

Chapter 5

Modern Science and Archeology

The science of blood typing has allowed us to trace the migration routes of early man. The DNA recovered from human fossil remains (primarily from the molar root stems) aid in tracking the migration of the human species and many other scientific facts.

DNA evidence has illustrated the incidence of cross breeding between ancient man and Neanderthal, but the Native African has no DNA links to the Neanderthal. These romantic interludes were confined to Europe and Asia. In the past, it was assumed early humans killed off the Neanderthal; however, our DNA suggests we bred them out of existence.

It is easy to imagine the mammoth hunters as robust human specimens, especially when compared to the common hunter-gatherer, who lived on a narrow margin of life and death, or having a full belly and starvation.

Man acquired the bow during the decline of the mammoths and mastodons and began to include himself in the artwork of the caves. The brilliant artistic realism of the past gave way to crude impressionism. Every man was hunting smaller game with the bow. The bow wasn't an effective weapon for the mammoth, but it was deadly for smaller game and men. The competition for hunting territories increased, and the killing of men became primary art subjects. Wounded and dead stick men were portrayed with multiple arrow wounds. No longer did the noble hunters of the mastodon and mammoth rule the hunting areas of the glacial steppe (the savannah that existed between Spain and the Yukon); modern man had the bow, and every man was potentially a dangerous enemy.

Chapter 6
Sylvie

This story begins with a specific DNA genetic marker or mutation occurring within a tribe of hunter-gatherers living north of the Sahara, fifty thousand years ago. Because there were only ten thousand humans, the gene pool was small, and early man was on the precipice of becoming extinct. A mutation within the mitochondrial DNA was a significant event, because it provided dynamism to the DNA pool. Every species has a critical number of organisms that must be maintained or the gene pool is no longer diverse or viable enough to ensure survival of the species. Complex organisms require a more diverse gene pool.

Sylvie begins this specific journey of maternal inheritance. She is remembered because her mitochondrial DNA created a new genetic marker that came with a variety of artistic and creative skills. She was limited by the technology and necessities of her era, and only her stone working skills could be applied. Later generations would build upon those skills and apply them to the technologies of the day, but Sylvie and her maternal line of daughters applied their artistic genius to making superb flint knives, scrapers, and projectile points for the next forty thousand years.

Sylvie's precision stone working skills became the standard for the world, and her genetic coding gave a phenotypically similar appearance to most of the females in Sylvie's line. They tended to be small people with delicate features and nimble fingers. The hair color was borrowed from the raven, and her eyes were a sea of darkness. Their skin tone was often dark as well.

Her tribe had no idea of the unique qualities of Sylvie's DNA or how it contributed to their gene pool, but her craftsmanship at making flint knives enabled her people to eat, when they might have perished, by trading sharp flint tools for meat from successful big game hunters.

The artistic skills she possessed and passed on were transmitted through mitochondrial DNA, and even though her sons and the sons of her daughters might possess the skills, the sons could not pass them on. These artistic skills were passed on over the millennia, solely through the maternal line because they were embedded in mitochondrial DNA.

Each male child inherits the mitochondrial DNA of his mother, but he can't pass it on to his children. An exact replica of the mother's mitochondrial DNA continues on, from mother to daughter; although, there were a few more mutations in the mitochondrial DNA and eventually these mutations expanded the flint-working skills to include remarkable mechanical, artistic, and design capabilities.

Because of the glacial maximum, and the accompanying drought, Sylvie's tribe and many other tribes elected to leave the once fertile valleys north of the Sahara to try their luck in the North. There were rumors of gardens of Eden in the North. Unfortunately it was their destiny to suffer through periods of starvation and near starvation during the migration. Sylvie died in the area that was to become the Sinai, during an unending quest for a home. Her body was left for scavengers, but two of her children lived to be adults, a boy and a girl. Her daughter, Ariel, acquired Sylvie's remarkable skills for shaping flint tools; in fact, her skills were greater even than her mother's. Everyone who saw her tools agreed that she was the best in the world, these critics may have been correct.

Ariel's craft kept her tribe eating during periods of starvation. Her flint tools were highly regarded by the more aggressive and successful hunters, who were always anxious to trade meat for a well-made flint knife, scraper, or spear point.

Chapter 7
40,000 Years BP (Before Present)

Ten thousand years later, a small tribe of Sylvie and Ariel's descendants, the Diggers, was losing a way of life on the coast of the Indian Ocean, near the Indus River Valley. They dug shellfish and fished the coastal waters, but the shellfish and shallow water fish were dying.

There were rumors of edible plants and freshwater fish upstream, along the Indus River Valley. It was frightening to think of deserting their homeland, but they were starving. They had lived on the coast for thousands of years, but the Ocean seemed poisoned.

The North was supposedly a land of plenty, with fruits, nuts, and a variety of edible plants, and excellent hunting and fishing as well. Unfortunately, the temperatures were colder, and the hunting tribes were dangerous and unpredictable. The chief, Mud Cat, and his wife, Soft Shell, considered the options of migrating north. The Diggers would lose half their tribe to starvation in less than thirty days if things continued the way they were; however, if they moved north, a warlike tribe might kill all of them, but at least they might die with full bellies. There was food to the north, or at least, they had heard rumors of good hunting, edible plants, and good freshwater fishing. There was no real choice; they had to move north or die. Mud Cat told the tribe they would be moving the next morning, and there was a lot of crying. An old couple said they were staying to care for the graves of their ancestors. Many Diggers were hysterical at the thought of leaving their ancestors, but Soft Shell explained there were no longer any options—they must migrate or die.

The next morning, the tribe started north on the west bank of the Indus River. Their journey continued for five hundred years, and they traveled upstream for over six hundred miles.

The Diggers were tiny people compared to the meat eaters of the north; a Digger man was considered huge if he was five feet tall. Up North, some of the women were six feet tall and thick with muscle. It was hard to imagine people so huge, but the mammoths and mastodons were huge, and these people killed and ate these dangerous animals.

The river tribes had no warrior or aggressive hunter culture; the tribes respected each other's fishing areas, and there was good fishing along the river. It was unusual for two men to fight, and usually, it was over a woman.

The Diggers maintained a tribe of twenty people. They managed to survive by fishing, hunting small animals, and gathering edible plants and berries. They migrated slowly and lived in constant fear of the big game hunters. There was a group of former coastal tribes living near the river, and it was these groups of freshwater fishermen who kept the tenuous river culture alive.

People of similar cultures usually married people from tribes within their culture, and the newlyweds could live with the bride's tribe or the groom's tribe. With small tribes, it was important to keep the numbers balanced, because of limited food stocks.

The maternal line of Ariel and Sylvie kept the knack for working flint through many generations. Most of the descendants of Soft Shell could study a piece of flint and see the finished tools inside the stone, and instead of haphazardly making semi-functional crude stone tools, they created extremely sharp knives and projectile points with a bare minimum of strikes. Newcomers, who married into the tribe, learned to work flint better than most, but without the artistic skills of those from the genetic line of Sylvie.

The successful big game hunters wanted the best knives and scrapers and were willing to trade meat and leather for sharp tools. It was a precarious existence, and the Diggers were careful not to provoke the unpredictable big game hunters.

The Diggers tried to impress upon others their value as fine toolmakers. Without these basic tools, a hunter's life was far more difficult. Think of butchering a twenty thousand-pound animal with a butter knife, instead of a sharp kitchen knife, or scraping the hide with a round river rock, instead of a sharp scraper. This simple fact helped keep the Diggers alive in a hostile and dangerous world.

Thirty-five generations after Mud Cat and Soft Shell, a new leader emerged among the Diggers; his mother named him Mad Horse. During his birth, a stallion was protesting the loss of one of his mares to a Digger Hunter, and he was threatening the Digger camp. The camp cowered at the stallion's rage, but Mad Horse's mother, Summer Snow, saw the bizarre episode as an omen. In her mind, the stallion was heralding the birth of a new chief; a great leader, who would lead the Diggers to a new life of prosperity, free of intimidation.

Chapter 8
Lavender

Like most visions, this one was wrong. Mad Horse became a tribal chief; however, his younger sister, Lavender (from the line of Sylvie), was born with a mutation within her mitochondrial DNA (H1W1), and she became a significant genetic marker for the entire human race.

At sixteen, Lavender was an attractive girl. This was an age when Stone Age girls were thinking about a mate and forgetting the carefree aspects of childhood. Unfortunately, a deadly flu virus struck the Digger Clan and every tribe along the river. It was Lavender's mitochondrial mutation that gave her and her descendants the ability to resist two of the great killers of mankind: the flu viruses and cholera.

Within a week, Mad Horse and the rest of the tribal members were dead or near death. After watching her people die in agony, Lavender could take no more; she left the sick and the dead to fend for themselves. She followed the river upstream for a week and found several tribes that had succumbed to the virus. Thinking the disease might be in the river, she followed a smaller tributary to the northwest.

Still alone after several weeks, Lavender analyzed her future. She knew the edible plants, and she could build fish traps to stay alive until winter, but she was ill equipped to survive a northern winter.

Five weeks later, Lavender was picking blueberries and saw a young mammoth hunter. He had stopped alongside the trail to urinate and didn't see Lavender. She took the opportunity to observe this incredible specimen of a young blond mammoth hunter. He was handsome, over six feet tall, strong, and well made, with wide, powerful shoulders, but Lavender was cautious. The Diggers considered mammoth hunters to be uncouth barbarians.

The Digger men always walked away from camp to relieve themselves. She had only seen little boys relieve themselves till this moment, but this was different and extremely interesting. Lavender was amazed at the volume and strength of his stream, and in her mind, she said, "*He must have a bladder the size of a melon.*" Inwardly, she chuckled at her crude joke. When he was finished, he shook his member vigorously and stroked it to shed the last drops. *He's enjoying the shaking of dew from his lily too much,* she thought. He dropped his leather skirt-like wrap and patted his little friend two times. She nearly burst out laughing.

He saw movement in the bushes and quickly raised his flint-tipped spear while staring into the brush. In desperation, Lavender yelled, "No, no, I am Lavender."

He couldn't understand a word she was saying, but when she stepped into the light, he smiled, lowered his spear, and motioned for her to come forward. Most Diggers would have run when he lowered his spear, but Lavender was bolder than most. She walked forward, and he laughed at being intimidated by such a tiny girl. They communicated in sign language, the accepted means of communication between strangers. Language was rudimentary; even among tribal groups, communication consisted of two thousand words, along with clicks, grunts, facial expressions, and hand signals.

The young man indicated his name was Rhino Horn, and she said with voice and hand signals, that her name was Lavender.

"Lavender," he said the name with eyebrows raised, and, using sign language, he communicated, "A pretty name, a pretty girl."

She felt wonderful, after being complimented by this handsome man. Smiling shyly, she asked about his tribe. "We are the Mammoth Hunters. The best hunters to walk the earth," he said with pride, then asked, "Who are your people?"

"We are the Diggers. We fish the river and make tools. The best tools in the world." She smiled and pulled a small flint knife, carved in a crescent shape, from her pocket. She made the sign for gift and handed the knife to Rhino Horn.

His eyes grew large, and he admired the well-made knife. "Did you make this?" he asked.

"Yes, silly," she signaled.

Lavender picked up a large piece of flint along the trail and then picked up a granite rock the size of a man's fist. She studied the flint carefully for several minutes and suddenly struck the flint with surprising speed and power. A large flake fell to the ground. Rhino Horn thought she was done and reached for the flake.

Lavender shook her head no, and struck the rock again. A thin flake slid to the ground. This was the piece she wanted. It was razor sharp and among the best Rhino Horn had ever seen. Lavender considered the flake to be a blank waiting to be turned into a sharp knife. She dropped to her knees and picked up the flake with her left hand. To keep from being cut, she used her leather skirt to hold the flint. She was exposing her thighs and pubic hair to his eyes. *Oh, well, I have seen his man parts*, she said to herself. She tapped the edge to make a serrated edge on one side. She gave Rhino the finished knife.

Rhino Horn was excited. He made signals that she should come to his camp and he could repay her and her family with a pack of meat (the amount of meat a man can carry on his back).

She smiled and nodded her head in agreement. Feelings of excitement and fear warred within her, but Lavender realized she needed a home where people knew how to survive the harsh winters of the North.

The two teenagers walked toward Rhino Horn's camp, while making funny hand signals and laughing at silly jokes. He asked if she had seen him urinating, and she said, "I saw you put away your little man and pat it."

They both laughed, and she asked, "Why did you pat your little man twice?"

He answered, "I don't want to lose anything, along the trail." They laughed and had a merry time, but when they walked into the camp of the Mammoth Hunters, the banter ended.

Lavender was scared. She had never seen so many large, dangerous-looking people. Their hair color varied from pure white, to red, to yellow, and black. Many of the men and some of the women had hair covering their entire bodies, and many women had facial hair. Most of the big people smiled and asked Rhino, with crossed wrists, if they were married, and he would answer, "No—friend," with a closed fist in an open hand.

Some of the hunters were "Near People." She had heard of them, but had never seen one. They were not as tall, but looked much stronger, had alabaster skin, with a variety of lighter hair colorings. They had huge hands and feet, bright blue eyes, and low foreheads, but they were friendly, and went out of their way to welcome Lavender to their camp by taking one of her tiny dark hands in their huge hands and patting it gently and bowing to touch it lightly with their cheek. Lavender was overwhelmed with the kindness and sincerity the Near People showed her.

Rhino pointed to an impressive lodge and said, "My father's lodge. He is a hunting chief and builds traps to kill mammoths." Suddenly, a muscular blond man in his mid-thirties walked out of the lodge, followed by two younger blonde women. They greeted Rhino, and the women made over him in an affectionate manner. Rhino used hand signals to introduce his father, Camel Track; his mother, Gander; and his wife, Jumping Tiger.

Camel Track had some of the Near People characteristics. His jaw was heavy, his nose was wide, and his eyes were the color of the bluest sky. He had a disarming smile, and Lavender thought he was the most handsome older man she had ever met. The two women were considerably different; not in their appearance, for they were all fair-haired large people of mixed heritage, but in their approach to Lavender.

The women wanted to know if Lavender was to become a wife of Rhino. They stood on each side of Lavender with their hands touching her in an intimate manner. Lavender was uncomfortable. Gander put her hands on Lavender's hips and asked Rhino Horn if there was enough room for a Little Rhino.

This comment brought about a round of laughter, but Lavender didn't laugh. The women were twice her size; their hips were large, they were white like snow, had white hair, and blue eyes. Lavender was considered attractive among her own people. Here, among these white giants, she felt alone, different, and intimidated.

Jumping Tiger cupped one of Lavender's breasts and said, "These little plums would never be enough to feed a baby Rhino."

Lavender pushed away the hand and backed away from the women. Her eyes were suddenly aflame, and the women knew it was time to quit tormenting the girl.

Rhino Horn reached in his pocket and pulled out the exquisite stone knives Lavender had made for him. He said, "Look at the knives Lavender made." Rhino Horn's family gathered in closely to look at the knives and hold them.

Stone Age culture relied on the knife. Without a knife, they would be reduced to eating like scavengers and beasts, but these knives were different. They were so sharp; you needed to hold them in a piece of leather to keep from cutting your hand. Suddenly, Lavender became an important guest.

Camel Track asked if Lavender could make another knife for him. She smiled and nodded.

He guided Lavender into the lodge and told his wives to prepare a meal. He handed Lavender a flint rock, a little larger than a man's fist.

She said, "Wait, I need a good striker." She walked outside with Rhino Horn and found a piece of round granite, about the size of a baseball, to use as a striker.

They walked back inside the lodge, while Lavender examined every facet of the flint rock for several minutes. She asked for a piece of leather. Camel Track handed her a thick piece the size of a handkerchief. She grasped the flint rock in her left hand with the leather and held the granite rock in her right hand. She delivered a precise and powerful strike to the flint rock, and a thin flake of flint slid to the dirt floor. The first strike was followed by five more rapid strikes, and five thin flakes soon lay on the dirt floor. Each of these flakes were better than a knife, the typical Mammoth Hunter could make after working all night; yet, she picked up each piece of flint and worked it until there was a serrated edge on one side and a sharp, knife-like edge on the other side.

Camel Track watched in silence as the girl's tiny fingers moved quickly over the stones.

He was witnessing a profound advancement in technique that could revolutionize life in the Stone Age.

The butchering of a large animal is a massive job with several steel knives, but if modern man was tasked with butchering an animal weighing ten tons and given rocks to use as tools, he would consider the job to be hopeless. Prehistoric man labored relentlessly to make crude, semi-sharp knives from stones to process these huge carcasses. If someone could make a knife with the precision of a surgical instrument, in a matter of minutes, that person became a valuable member of society.

Camel Track examined the knives with the knowing eye of a man who had butchered many large animals. He stopped Lavender's work and put a hand on her shoulder; he put his other hand on Rhino Horn's shoulder. He lifted his hands at the same time and patted them both on the shoulder. This was a signal, meaning, 'the two of you.' He then crossed his wrists in a low position. His signal was clear; he was advising the two of them to be joined as a couple. A daughter-in-law like Lavender would be an asset to the tribe and Camel Track's lodge.

Lavender had not considered the possibility of marriage with Rhino Horn, but Rhino was handsome, and Camel Track was gracious. The Mammoth Hunters were rich in comparison to tribes like the Diggers. She looked into the blue eyes of Rhino and was drawn to the young man. He crossed his index fingers, the primitive proposal of marriage, and she responded with the same sign and accepted the proposal. They were married.

Camel Track saw the marriage; he cleared an area in the back of the lodge and laid down a new mammoth hide with hair. He folded it, with the hair on the outside, to fashion a marriage bed. He announced to his clan that Lavender and Rhino Horn were married. Everyone in the lodge cheered, everyone except Jumping Tiger, Rhino Horn's first wife.

Jumping Tiger glared at the tiny dark woman and wondered what a strong, handsome man like her husband could possibly see in such a dirty-looking, tiny girl. She could make excellent knives, but her teats were tiny, her hips were straight, she had a butt like a boy, her eyes were dark and evil, and her hair was so black, it could never be clean. Her husband was acting like a fool, and she felt humiliated. It was made worse by the fact that she had not produced a child in two years of marriage and her husband was losing interest in her.

Events were moving quickly for Lavender. Her life was like a dream. A few hours ago, she had been a homeless vagabond, and now she was married to a handsome man and part of a rich lodge.

The marriage night was an overwhelming experience. She wasn't exactly sure what happened, but it felt like the two of them were flying through the night sky. In fact, Lavender was frightened of falling and excited to the point of screaming out loud. She held tightly to her husband with her eyes closed, hoping he would not drop her and let her fall to her death.

Jumping Tiger spent the night in anguish. Lavender's moans and screams of sexual abandonment and passion infuriated her. The next morning, Jumping Tiger met with Horse Tail, the shaman, who was furious at not being consulted before the wedding of a chief's son. He provided Jumping Tiger with information to sow the seeds of doubt in the mind of an immature young man.

Lavender slept through the morning meal; she was exhausted, and her muscles ached from the vigorous coupling, but Rhino Horn awoke with a voracious appetite. He smiled when she refused to wake up for breakfast and kissed her cheek.

At breakfast, Jumping Tiger sat next to Rhino and began weaving a tale of deceit. "Horse Tail told me interesting things about your new wife and her people."

Rhino wanted to hear about Lavender and her people. Her wild responses to his lovemaking had reinforced his image as a virile young man to the rest of the tribe, and more importantly, to himself. His reputation had suffered after being married to Jumping Tiger for over two years without children. His couplings with Jumping Tiger had become more like work than a celebration. She was cold and boring between the leather blankets, and he was only going through the motions.

"Horse Tail says the river tribes of dark people are serpent worshipers; their shamans gain control of the future and the weather by making their people worship serpents and getting the women to have sexual intercourse with snakes. Apparently, one of the women made a pact with the serpent, and all the river people died, except her."

Jumping Tiger saw Rhino had swallowed the hook. "You know, I have dreams of the future. Last night, I saw Lavender standing on a hill above our village. She was pointing at the village and laughing. Her long black hair had turned into a swirling mass of black snakes. The snakes were biting each other with long white fangs. Their eyes were glowing like the embers of a campfire, and they were eating a white baby. Lavender held a large black snake in her hands and was having sex with the snake, while the snake told her he loved her."

The images in Rhino Horn's mind were repulsive. He threw down his wooden plate with its half-eaten meal and walked over to Lavender's bed. He shook her shoulder to awaken her and asked, "Do your people worship serpents?"

She barely had her eyes open. She smiled and signaled an answer, "Yes, we worship many animals, but I am a Mammoth Hunter, now." She closed her eyes and fell asleep.

Rhino Horn went straight to Horse Tail's lodge, to say, "Tell me everything about Lavender and the Diggers."

The shaman glared at Rhino Horn. "You rush into a marriage with a dark savage, without consulting me, and now, you want to know why your world is falling apart. Always consult me before making important decisions. Unfortunately, you made a commitment and consummated a marriage to a serpent worshiper."

In desperation, Rhino Horn asked, "Can I tell her to go away, back to her own people?"

"Only if she commits adultery; otherwise, she is yours until one of you dies. Don't consider killing her, either. She is a Mammoth Hunter. If you kill her, you will be executed or banished. This is our law. You must feed her and care for her; hopefully, she won't drop a tiny Mammoth Hunter in nine months. If I were you, I would think with your big head, instead of letting your little head make your decisions. Now, leave my lodge, and remember to consult me first before making important decisions."

Rhino Horn was seething in anger.

The women left to look for berries and mushrooms to cook with caribou for the evening meal. They neglected to tell Lavender and let her sleep.

Several hours later, Lavender heard the noise of a trap being built and thought she might find her husband among the workers.

Rhino Horn wasn't with them, but Camel Track saw Lavender and waved her over to the trap. He showed her two heavy spears that were far too big for a man. The shafts were three inches thick and had been hardened in the fire.

Camel Track drew a spear point in the dirt. The figure, done in actual size, was huge. It was a large, elongated triangle, with a notch near the base on each side for mounting to the two spear shafts with rawhide and processed pitch. This was standard among the top flint strikers of the day, but Camel Track had an idea that would revolutionize tools all over the world: with his thumb, he made a half round groove in the dirt model, running half of the length of the stone, from the center of the base toward the point.

Lavender was impressed. She called the groove a flute and pointed at it while nodding her head, "Yes." The flute would make mounting the projectile points on spears easier and more secure, and they would be lighter. Lavender studied the dirt drawing with a critical eye, and was oblivious to what was happening around her.

Camel Track ordered his hunters to find several flint and granite stones. The other men had no idea about what was happening, but they could tell by the concentration of Lavender and Camel Track, this was important.

The men laid several stones and a piece of leather next to the drawing. Lavender examined the different stones and picked out a large flint stone and a granite striker. She studied the flint stone from several different angles, like a modern-day diamond cutter. With speed and power, she struck a flint stone and eliminated one-third of the stone, leaving a smooth face on the base rock. Again, she studied the rock and delivered two more rapid strikes and two flakes slid to the ground. She dropped the base stone and, with the leather, she picked up one of the flakes. The flakes were six inches long and three inches wide. With dexterity and speed the men had never seen before, Lavender chipped the two flakes, until they formed the classic spearhead formation. The finished points were five inches long, and two and a half inches at the base.

Camel Track told a couple of the men to shave down the mounting ends of the shafts, until they were two inches thick. The ends were then split the length of a man's middle finger.

Holding the tip downward, Lavender tapped the base with precision. A long, narrow half-round channel of stone slid away, and the men all said, "Oh," in unison, when they saw the practical advantage of the flute. Without thinking, Lavender turned the point in her hand to strike the other side. Now, there was a groove on each side. The men said, "Oh," once again, and reached out to pat Lavender on the back and shoulders. She was being acknowledged as an equal, among a group of elite hunters. The men soon had the deadly points mounted to the shafts.

They piled fresh poplar branches and leaves, along with valley grass, in the V-shaped corral. The opening was several hundred yards wide, and the sides were logs tied to trees, so that the bull followed the ever-narrowing fence lines. The men would imitate the call of a female mammoth in season, with a birch bark megaphone. The amplified sound traveled for miles. If a bull were in the rut and in the mood for fighting or breeding, he would come on the run. The men used the urine from cow mammoths in season to entice and enrage the bulls to the point where they ignored common sense and tossed caution aside. This elixir was always saved and used sparingly, when a cow in season was killed. A mammoth hide was draped over an eight-foot rail and hung from a sapling that was pulled over with ropes at the far end of the corral. The hide was given movement, like a matador's cape, with the ropes, to entice the bull to walk into the trap.

There were two simple mechanical spear throwers, a horizontal launcher and a vertical model. A downed thirty-foot pine tree provided the power for the horizontal spear thrower. Its base was wedged and secured between three trees. The tree at rest was lying alongside the corral. To get the thrower ready, the top was pulled back and away from the corral by almost twenty feet. Another thirty-foot log was split lengthwise and placed horizontally, split-side-up, so that the arc of the striking log would be guided and partially controlled. The spear was placed in a semi-circular groove cut into the last few feet of the split log, and the heavy spear would fly forward at an extreme rate of speed when struck by the striker log. The second spear was set into a spherical hole, dug into the ground, with only the tip of the spear protruding. The butt-end of the spear rested in a small leather cup, tied to a rawhide rope attached to the top of a thin pine tree that had been pulled to the ground, about twenty feet away, and secured to a manual trigger mechanism.

The spear-throwing machines were tested with shafts of the appropriate size, and each spear flew forward at an amazing rate of speed and force. The traps were loaded and set. The two callers, standing behind the mammoth hide, used the birch bark megaphones to begin calling with the anguished sounds of a mammoth cow in estrus.

The mammoth herd was a matriarchal society, including immature bulls, under the age of fourteen. A cow remained with her natal herd during her lifetime. The mammoth or mastodon cow was like the modern African elephant; it came into estrus every six to nine years for three to six days, without regard to a particular season. The mature bull, at fourteen years, was kicked out of his natal herd, and joined a bachelor herd.

Nature had to have some bulls prepared for the rut at any time and bulls started the rut at indiscriminate intervals. The rut started with musth, a brown, odorous, discharge of the temporal glands indicating to other bulls and cows the onset of the rut. The rutting bull leaves the bachelor herd and begins seeking cows in estrus. The bull in rut quit eating and attacked other bulls and anything standing in their way. Musth and a continuous dribbling of urine are powerful scents used to attract the cows. The bulls folded their ears over the glands and pushed their tusks against the ground to relieve the pressure on the temporal glands and release the musth discharge. The rut lasted thirty days, but the intensity of behavioral and physiological changes were so intense, the bulls didn't always survive.

Without the rutting behavior, and the indiscriminate timing of the rut, the early traps would have rarely been effective, but in an area with multiple herds, there will soon be a bull looking for love and those bulls were vulnerable. Musth is the Urdu word for intoxication, and like the moose, elk, and elephants of today, the bull loses all common sense when the powerful chemicals for the rut are released. He is overcome with aggression and will attack anything, even inanimate objects. It was this behavioral trait that made the bulls vulnerable to early man's keen hunting instincts. Living near the ice made storing the meat easier; guarding the meat was another matter.

A large bull walked into the chute and was answering the cow call with his trunk pointing upward and roaring loudly. His powerful call was answered with the hunter's artificial challenge call of an immature bull. The weaker response made the old bull's eyes glow red with blood. He charged the phantom in a rage.

Camel Track released the horizontal spear. The release of the horizontal spear was the signal to trigger the vertical spear. The spears, with their razor-sharp flint points, struck the beast instantaneously. The bull roared and tried to continue the charge, but the pain of the imbedded spears had him nearly paralyzed. The bull trumpeted a deafening roar of increasing anger. The phantom hide was raised, and the bull charged the mammoth hide at the far end of the corral. He hit the corral at a full charge, and the stacked logs flew apart like kindling, but the exertion caused the spears in his body to inflict severe internal damage. The bull stopped, when his lungs could no longer take in enough air. In a forlorn effort, the big bull dropped to his knees and tried to defend himself from the men gathering around him. A killing spear entered just behind the last rib on the right, and a strong man rushed forward to push it toward the heart and lungs. The bull fell to his left side. He looked one last time at the blue sky and tried twice more to breathe, before departing this life with a deep death rattle in his throat and a shudder of his powerful legs.

The hunters cheered the mammoth's demise. There was no sense of compassion for the passing of this magnificent beast, but there was a sense of respect. They celebrated because the tribe will avoid hunger or starvation for several months and no human had been hurt or killed.

Artists often recorded the animals on the walls of caves and canyons. The reasons for painting the beasts were varied, but the art portrayed the respect they had for the animals. Many of these paintings still exist, and many more are waiting to be discovered.

With a big smile, Camel Track turned to Lavender. "Daughter, you are a Mammoth Hunter, one of us."

Lavender felt proud to be recognized by a chief, as part of an elite mammoth hunting team. She smiled and started making knives for field dressing the bull. The hunters were like children when they were given the razor-sharp knives to evacuate the internal organs, skin, and cut the flesh into manageable pieces.

Chapter 9
The Last Supper

At Camel Track's lodge, a great feast was being prepared for the tribe with fresh mammoth and mushrooms gathered by the women and children. When Lavender walked into the lodge, several teenagers were fawning over her; they had heard about her projectile points and how well they worked.

Lavender smiled and promised to teach them how to work the flint and saw her husband, sitting with Jumping Tiger. Jumping Tiger had her large breasts exposed and on each side of Rhino Horn's right arm. She was kissing Rhino Horn and looking at Lavender to see her reaction.

Lavender started to sit on Rhino's left when she noticed another woman had already taken that position. This woman had her legs open and her skirt was up on her hips. Rhino's hand was on the inside of her thigh, but he lifted this hand to signal Lavender to go away.

Lavender picked a large piece of wood from the fire and walked outside to build her own cooking fire. Three young girls and a young hunter, Turtle, followed her outside and helped her build a fire.

When the fire was burning well, Lavender cut a limb about three feet long and an inch thick. She trimmed the branch, except for two forks in the middle. These were about ten inches apart, and Lavender left them sticking out from the branch about an inch. She cut off a large steak and cut a hole in each end of the steak. The stick was stuck through the holes she had made, and the steak was placed between the two forks. Three smaller sticks pierced the steak horizontally to keep the meat from curling. Lavender sprinkled the steak with salt and braced the stick in a vertical position next to the fire with various stones. The teenage girls asked Lavender to help them make a similar cooking grill. Lavender laughed and helped them. The young hunter managed to make a decent grill on his own.

The five steaks were cooking next to the fire, and the juices were dripping onto the rocks and sending a smoke flavor back into the meat. After a few minutes, Lavender stood up and turned her steak to cook the other side, and the other young people turned their steaks as well. Soon, Lavender reversed the vertical stick; now the bottom of the stick was pointing upward and the top was now the bottom. The steak was cooking much faster. In a few minutes, Lavender turned her steak 180 degrees and soon, her steak was cooked.

The young people laughed at how simple this method of cooking was, compared to the often-disappointing methods they used. Lavender told them that the Diggers cooked fish like this for a thousand years, but it worked well for steaks too. The young people agreed. Her new friends complimented Lavender on the flavor of their food.

After dinner, the young people sang songs and told stories about their ancestors. They all laughed when one of the girls tried to sing one of Lavender's songs. They made jokes using hand signals, and had a good time, before drifting off to sleep in their blankets.

The night air was cold, but Lavender felt an intense heat next to her face. She looked up to see Jumping Tiger waving a long burning stick close to her face. Jumping Tiger used hand signals to warn Lavender to stay away from her man and made the universal sign for cutting a throat. She stabbed the burning stick into Lavender's lower belly for emphasis, and Lavender was burned through her leather skirt. Jumping Tiger threw the stick into the fire and walked away.

Lavender was horrified. She had never been treated like this. Jumping Tiger was twice her size; there was no way she could stand up to her. Lavender was frightened and homesick. She pulled up her skirt and looked at the burn. It was a serious wound and would leave a lifelong scar. She reached in her medicine sack and took out a small leather pouch of grease from the mountain sheep. The grease took away the burning sensation and let her sleep.

Just before daylight, the five young people were awakened to screams of madness. Most of the tribe was vomiting and had bloody diarrhea, and some of the members were hallucinating and screaming in madness. Lavender recognized the symptoms and walked over to look at the leftover mushrooms. The mushroom pickers had found several poisonous varieties: the Fool's Mushroom, the Death Angel, and the Deadly Galerina. Any of these mushrooms would have been enough to poison the whole tribe, but they had combined several of the most deadly mushrooms and made soup from them. Some of the people might not become sick for twelve more hours, but anyone who had eaten the mushrooms would soon suffer a painful death from kidney and liver failure or madness.

Lavender instructed her new friends to wander among the survivors and ask if they had eaten the mushrooms last night. Anyone who had resisted would live. The rest would die. They found several children and a mature hunter, Broke Toe, who didn't like mushrooms and liked them less now.

Lavender had her small following ask the stricken tribal members if they wanted to end the agony. Half of the people were ready to cross over, and they were stabbed upward through the solar plexus for an instant death, avoiding the inevitable agony and lingering death.

Camel Track asked to speak with Lavender before being euthanized. She held his hand and said, "Camel Track, it is Lavender."

He looked up at her and said, "My beautiful daughter, I wish things were different. We work so well together. Take the survivors and start a new tribe. The world is yours." He squeezed her hand with the little bit of strength he had left and said, "Now, send me beyond the mountains, to the campfires of my forefathers, and I will tell them about you, my lovely Lavender." He gave her his spear. She stood up and readied the spear, while he raised his shirt to reveal the area beneath his breastbone. She angled the spear and placed the stone tip against his skin. He smiled at her once more and nodded his head. She plunged the spear deep into his chest and pierced his heart. He raised his hand in farewell, and his heart stopped beating.

Lavender walked past Rhino Horn; someone had already put him out of his misery. She felt nothing for him and walked on, when a hand grabbed her ankle. A strained voice pleaded to her, "Help me. I hurt so much, please."

Lavender looked through the gray morning light to see the contorted face of Jumping Tiger, holding her belly and grimacing in agony. Lavender positioned the spear low and missed the spot.

Chapter 10

Lavender Leads Her People

Lavender assumed control of the survivors. Declaring the camp diseased, she let the scavengers claim the dead and dying. They packed the meat they could carry and traveled east for a few weeks before they needed to make a kill. Thankfully, there were mammoths in the vicinity.

Broke Toe found two pine trees that had fallen in a windstorm. The trees were eighteen inches at the base and thirty feet long. The men made two ax handles with a slot for the blunt side of a flint ax head and set stone ax heads in the handles with a pitch glue and a rawhide wrap. The axes were used to cut off the root balls, and slab the butt to fit tight against the three trees being used as a base for the thrower. They cut away the branches and topped the tree at six inches diameter. The butt end of one log was fitted and wedged between three trees, so that the side with the lone tree or middle was close to the corral fence. They had to flatten the log a lot, but the log was wedged into position so that the free end was suspended five feet off the ground and next to a mammoth trail. The next log was cut at thirty feet. It was split lengthwise by driving in flint and wooden wedges until the log groaned in protest and suddenly split apart in two equal pieces. The flint axes were used to smooth the split surfaces. Broke Toe and Turtle the teenager pointed out, in the past only one half was smoothed out, but Lavender had an idea: she wanted a three foot long channel carved into both logs, and each channel would cradle a spear.

A forty-foot pine, pulled to the ground, would throw the vertical spear; it was about sixty feet away from the horizontal launcher. The top of the tree was pulled to the ground and secured with a rope trigger mechanism. Another rawhide rope was tied to the top and stretched out to the hole, where it was attached to a leather cup holding the base of the spear. When the tree was released, the spear would fly up out of the hole and into the belly of the mammoth.

Lavender knew they had built a good trap and hopefully, they would have a mammoth in a couple of days. In the meantime, they had to watch over the trap to make sure a curious animal didn't spring it by accident.

Lavender's tribe was small, but once they killed a mammoth, displaced people and vagabonds would be begging for a meal. She could build a tribe with these people, but she would need to be a good judge of character.

The next morning, Broke Toe woke Lavender before daylight. There were at least two bulls rutting near the trap.

She told him, "Use the birch bark and call from the front of the trap. When a bull starts coming, walk slowly toward the phantom and continue using cow calls. If the bull hesitates, call like a young bull. We will be there in a few minutes."

Broke Toe left with determination and a grin on his face. He was a real hunter. Lavender needed twenty more just like him.

There were two teenagers on each trigger mechanism. Turtle and a girl were on the horizontal launcher: Lavender and another girl were on the vertical launcher. Turtle could provide the extra strength for the horizontal launcher, in case the trigger mechanism jammed. A boy is quicker to adapt to another plan like hitting the trigger with a club to release it. The sexes are different and have different strengths; Lavender had to use her people effectively to make this trap work.

Broke Toe was the most experienced and he had the most dangerous job, luring the bull toward the phantom. He needed to be quick and anticipate the bull's moves, and be able to run like a deer if the plan went awry.

Every hunting trip was different; tonight, they had too many mammoths. There was a cow in front of the trap, or Broke Toe's calling was so good, you couldn't tell if it was real. Suddenly, Broke Toe came running into the trap at a dead run. He stopped about midway in the trap and looked behind him. He shook his head and called once again. This time two young bulls answered and charged each other at the opening to the corral. Broke Toe looked at Lavender and shrugged. She motioned for him to try the cow call again.

The bulls roared and crashed their great tusks into one another. Unfortunately, the fight might go on all night, and the bulls could end up miles away before they were done.

Lavender decided to work the rope holding the phantom to try to entice one of the bulls away from the fight. She was barely big enough to get the phantom moving.

There was a narrow log tied to the rope, and the hide was draped over this log to give an appearance of form.

An older bull decided it was time to join the melee. He ran out of the dark and smashed one of the younger bulls in the hip, crippling him by breaking his pelvis. Without slowing down, the older bull ran into the corral to trumpet his breeding intentions with his trunk pointing straight up and screaming a shrill roar. The older bull had no interest in the bravado of young bulls; he wanted to breed the cow. When he saw the dance of the phantom with Lavender being pulled off the ground by the strength of the leaning tree, he roared and charged.

The horizontal launcher was heard first. *Whack!* The log struck the twin spears and sent them deep into the mammoth's side. The tree that was bent over arced upwards, and sent its spear upward into the belly of the mammoth.

The bull showed no outward signs of injury. Lavender and Broke Toe ran to escape his fury.

The bull ran to the phantom and tossed it with his tusks. His brain was not equipped to deal with a female he couldn't mount. In frustration, he thrashed the trees in the area.

This hunt was unusual. They had two injured bulls, but one was dragging his hind legs and the other one was walking away, with three spears imbedded deep in his body.

Lavender yelled for Turtle and the girls to kill the crippled bull. Finishing the bull was a dangerous job and would normally require several seasoned hunters, but this group was short-handed, and they would need to do the job alone. The other bull was walking away at a rapid pace, and Lavender knew that if he wandered onto another tribe, they might lose possession. She yelled for Broke Toe to get a rawhide rope from camp, while she followed the bull.

When Broke Toe returned, the bull had walked two miles. The two of them ran ahead and tried to guess the path he would follow. They found a twenty-foot tree that had fallen and made a snare for the bull's head. If they picked out his path, and if the bull managed to get the snare around his neck, and if the rope didn't break, maybe they could slow him down enough to get another spear into his body and finish him.

Normally, the bull would not walk into a snare, but he was distracted from the rut and hopefully, from the pain of three spears in his body. The bull walked into the snare and ignored the rope tightening around his neck. The tree was supposed to slow him down, but it was soon bouncing behind him like a child's toy. Finally, the log got caught between two trees; the mammoth was pulling against the rope and roaring his frustration.

Broke Toe ran up and stuck the killing spear behind the last rib, but before he could drive it home, the rope broke and the bull took off once again, with four spears now imbedded in him.

A group of hunters saw the struggle between the bull and a hunter with a girl. They admired the courage of the pair, but the bull was going to win this confrontation. They ran down the hill to even up the odds and claim a fair portion of this bull.

Surrounding the bull, they threatened the huge animal with their spears. It was a dangerous tactic; the bull was swinging massive tusks with an eight-foot curl, tusks that could crush a man into formless pulp. While the men were attacking the bull on one side and the bull was on the defensive, a strong, athletic hunter rushed in to drive Broke Toe's spear forward, through the diaphragm and into the lungs.

The big bull released a call that sounded more like a wail than a roar. He spread his legs apart to brace against the pain and turned to feel the offending spear with his trunk.

The desperate struggle was over, and the hunters waited for the great beast to die. When the bull tried to roar, the sound was muffled with a frothing rush of blood from his trunk and mouth. The bull was defenseless and rocked back and forth before falling over with a groan.

A hunter and a tiny teenage girl had a wounded mammoth bull, but couldn't kill it. Twelve strong men kill the mammoth; who claims possession?

The two tribal chieftains were both examining the bull, while the bull was coughing and drowning in his own blood.

Lavender was at a major disadvantage, but she had just killed two mammoths.

Unfortunately, they were over two miles apart, and her tribe consisted of three teenage girls, a teenage boy, an adult hunter and a few toddlers.

The stranger spoke first. "I am Poplar Bark, chief of People of the North. Who is your chief, girl?"

"I am Lavender, chief of my people. This is my second mammoth kill today."

Poplar Bark didn't expect this answer. He had a look of shocked disbelief on his face, before he smiled. He looked at the hole in the belly and the two deep holes behind the ribs, and turned to look at Lavender for an explanation.

"The bull was running fast. We were lucky to hit him."

It was obvious the wounds were deep and lethal, but Poplar Bark had many questions for this tiny, dark girl who was leading an experienced hunter.

"How many tribal members do you have?" Poplar Bark asked.

"We are six," Lavender answered without hesitation.

Poplar Bark was stunned. How could six expect to bring down a mammoth?

"Lavender, you can stay with the People of the North, for a while. We can share the mammoths, and you can be chief of your own people. You will be much safer. Some tribes will kill for a prize like this mammoth."

Several of Poplar Bark's hunters had stripped down and were already evacuating the internal organs. They soon found the spears and brought them to Poplar Bark. He looked at them as if they were exotic treasures.

Lavender looked up at Poplar Bark, and signaled, "We stay with People of the North."

Poplar Bark wanted to know how the spears were imbedded in the mammoth. "How, how did you do this?"

"Bring some men to carry the other mammoth and I will show you," Lavender answered.

Poplar Bark yelled for one of his men to gather up twelve men with packs from camp. The man disappeared and came back a half-hour later with the men and packs, as requested.

Poplar Bark said to Lavender, with skepticism, "Take us to the other mammoth."

Lavender smiled and took off at a run. Poplar Bark's men could run, but this little female was jumping over logs and running the length of downed trees, and jumping creeks like a deer. He and his men couldn't keep up this pace and needed to slow down or stop for a rest, but the little girl kept running, and they had no choice but to follow.

Finally, they arrived at the trap. Two of the men collapsed and were wheezing to catch their breath, and the rest, except for Poplar Bark, sat down in exhaustion. He was breathing heavily, but when he saw the traps, he began to study the mechanisms.

The teenagers were glad to see Lavender. They had a large amount of the meat cut into fifty-pound sections, and they were sitting on the grass next to the carcass. The three kids were crawling around the carcass, and the hyenas had almost decided it was time to rush the humans and take over the meat.

Poplar Bark was still studying the trap. He pulled back on the striker log and let it go to admire its deadly power.

Poplar Bark's men could keep the hyenas at bay, but this was a losing proposition. There was also a cave lion growling in the brush, and he expected his fair share.

Poplar Bark had each of his men load up one hundred to one hundred twenty-five pounds of meat, and made a pack from the hide so the teenage boy could carry his share. The girls carried the toddlers, and the group took off for the other carcass just before the hyenas and the lion started fighting over the remnants.

Poplar Bark imagined building another trap in an area that would be closer to home and easier to defend against the hyenas and other scavengers. He looked at the tiny girl leading her own tribe and shook his head in disbelief. She was doing the best she could, but she didn't really stand a chance. Most of the tribes would just take over her little group and steal everything. Those who resisted would be killed. The world was changing faster than he could keep up with; still, it was a good thing Lavender had fallen in with his tribe. He could see she was a talented girl and would be a good role model for the young girls of the People of the North.

Poplar Bark's tribe was glad to have Broke Toe, since experienced hunters were always appreciated. The teenagers were welcome as well, but when the tribal members learned of how Lavender led the small group and was trying to kill two mammoths in one day, she was an instant celebrity.

Lavender helped Poplar Bark select a good spot to build a trap and soon, they had plenty of meat. Lavender and Poplar Bark worked well as a team, but she could feel the life starting to form in her belly. The swelling had started. Although her brief marriage had been a disappointment, she hoped to have a strong boy who would grow into a powerful man and lead his tribe and protect his mother, a man like Camel Track or Poplar Bark.

Chapter 11

A Story Borne of Desperation

Lavender developed a story about the upcoming birth. If the child was a boy, the right story could make it easier for him to become a chief. It was a fantastic story, but if she was convincing, the tribe will believe her. She thought her story was believable; actually, she began to believe the story herself. Her story was wild and exciting, and she enjoyed going over it in her mind. It became better and better with practice. Besides, she wasn't really sure what had happened during her one night of passion.

After a nice dinner, storytellers entertained the tribe with fanciful tales of creation, love, sex, hunting, and other subjects of interest among Ice Age hunters. Lavender knew the basics of every story, but she was going to unleash a story they had never heard before. She stood before the tribe. "Several men have asked me to be their wife. I have refused every offer, and I must refuse every offer in the future, until the Great Mammoth Hunter instructs me to take a husband. It is not my choice. I have been instructed by The Great Mammoth Hunter not to take a mortal husband, until he releases me."

The tribe stopped all other activities to listen to Lavender's story. The lodge was without noise; even the children were quiet.

"The Great Hunter came to me during the night, when I was a young girl, and taught me how to make the best knives and projectile points in the world. He taught me many secrets of stone tools and of building the traps to kill mammoths. The same secrets I am sharing with you.

"After I began the cycles of womanhood, he came to me when I stepped from my bath and wrapped my naked body in his cloak, against his own naked body. In an instant, he harpooned me with his man spear. Once he was inside me, he stopped the normal rutting movements. His manhood was deep in my belly and I couldn't move. There was an intense heat in my nether parts, but I lay beneath him and we flew through the night sky." The tribe was spellbound.

"The Great Hunter said he would give me a son, by touching his finger to the outside of my womb. His touch was so hot, it left a scar." She lifted her leather wrap to reveal the burn scar, left by Jumping Tiger, just above her pubic hair. There was a collective gasp of wonderment, when the tribe saw the scar. "He said if he unleashed his seed, I would be consumed in fire. Yet, his member was so hot in my body, I thought I might catch fire at any moment. He assured me as long as we were flying in the cold night air, I would be safe. We flew above the mountains of ice, and we flew behind the moon and saw the sun having sexual relations with his wife, the moon. We touched the stars and floated among the clouds.

"He told me not to take a husband, until our son is strong. The scar marks me as his first and only lover on Earth. I will be his earthly wife and the mother of his son, until his son is on his way to being the chief of a great tribe. His son will be a great leader and teach people to live free of hunger. He will teach us to hunt better and build a strong tribe, the strongest tribe on Earth.

"I know you have questions. I will answer them, but for now, I want to be alone."

Lavender picked up a leather blanket and walked out into the night.

The tribal members looked at each other with shocked expressions on their faces. They lacked the sophistication to doubt such an outrageous story, and even the members who came with her from Camel Track's tribe were shocked. They had forgotten about the brief interlude with the boorish Rhino Horn.

Everyone had seen Lavender making stone tools and knew she was different, if not magical. They knew she had a vast storehouse of knowledge, and she had to have acquired this knowledge from someone. It seemed logical that the Great Mammoth Hunter had given her these gifts.

Man was barely beyond a level of subsistence, and death was always waiting on the trail ahead. Over half the infants died before they could walk. If the Great Hunter had given Lavender his son, there must be hope for the future. The story of Lavender was compelling and fascinating, but more importantly, it gave them hope. The Great Mammoth Hunter sent them Lavender and his son. There was hope for the future and the future of their children.

Lavender spread her leather blanket on the ground and lay down outside the lodge. It was a dangerous place to sleep; the hyenas, wolves, lions, tigers, and bears all liked to eat the scraps people threw away, but within a few minutes, a young hunter threw his blanket on the ground, a few feet away from hers. Several more young hunters and young women followed him.

One of the young men built a fire and sat down in a guard's position next to it. Lavender was surprised by the dedication of her followers. She knew many believed her story. Tomorrow was a new day. She would be tested every day, and she must meet every challenge for the future of her son.

A few months later, Lavender had a baby boy. The tribe was excited, and she was never alone while caring for her newborn son. She named him Raging Bull, after the wounded mammoth that brought her to Poplar Bark's tribe. How lucky she was to be with a strong tribe of the future. There were more mammoths than there were stars in the sky, and the meat of the mammoth made your children big, strong, and blonde. She was so lucky to have known how to work flint and to have Camel Track teach her about building the traps. She was now a person of status in the tribe. She had once hoped to be a chief, but she was happy to care for her son. She always had at least one young hunter guarding her, and a teenage girl was always ready to help with the baby.

Raging Bull grew and survived the critical period of infancy. He was a strong boy with a smile for everyone. He had his mother's dark eyes and black hair, but his skin was fair, and he was already big for his age. The young girls liked to care for him and pretend he was their son.

One day, while Lavender was visiting with the other young women and girls, she noticed Raging Bull was missing. The women began calling and searching. Lavender was becoming desperate when someone said, "There he is, up on the cliff, above the cave."

Lavender and the other women looked up to see Raging Bull sitting calmly on a ledge about thirty feet above the entrance to the cave.

They called to him, but he was unconcerned and playing with rocks. Everyone was asking, how did he climb the cliff wall, and how was he going to climb down?

One of the young hunters walked into camp, and the women begged him to rescue Raging Bull. He smiled and walked into the cave and came out with a basket women use to gather honey while hanging from ropes over the cliff walls. He tied the basket on his back, smiled and winked at Lavender, and turned to climb the cliff wall.

His name was Sturgeon, and he was an athletic young man. He climbed the wall as if he did it every day. When he reached Raging Bull, he picked him up and put him in the basket. The return trip was much more difficult because of the extra weight, and Sturgeon had to feel his way down the tricky wall with his feet. Raging Bull was unconcerned about the possible danger and waved to everyone. The women cheered when Sturgeon finally made it back down with Raging Bull safe in the basket. Sturgeon reached behind his head to lift Raging Bull and hand him to his mother. Lavender was so grateful that she hugged and kissed the young hunter.

It might have been her contact with Sturgeon's powerful muscles, or maybe it was the kiss, but Lavender was attracted to this young man. She gave him a knife and spearhead for his gallantry.

Sturgeon told Lavender the gifts were of far greater value than his efforts to rescue Raging Bull, but she said, "No, I owe you more than these tools. Raging Bull is my life."

Lavender admitted to herself, *Sturgeon is handsome, and he has a nice smile.* Rhino Horn was a boy in a man's body, and she was little more than a girl back then. Now, Raging Bull was nearly four years old, and she no longer needed to watch him every second, despite the fact that he climbed the cliff wall and scared everyone.

Raging Bull was a boy and would find excitement and adventure. This was part of being a boy, but Lavender was twenty years old and considered a mature woman. It was normal for her to desire a man, a man to hold her and make her feel complete.

Sturgeon was handsome. He had wide shoulders and a narrow waist. His eyes were a dark green color. They seemed to sparkle when he smiled and were different shades in different light. He seemed shy around women. He answered suggestive comments and questions from women, with a wholesome smile. He could have many girls and women, but seemed to be saving himself for someone special. Lavender decided it was time to set her trap for this young hunter with the innocent smile and sparkling green eyes.

When he was close by, Lavender made sure to make eye contact with Sturgeon and always offered him a view of her legs and bosom to try to get his attention. It was obvious he was shy, but there was no reason; most men would give anything to have Sturgeon's good looks and muscular body.

The hunters had bad luck one day. They were smoking a giant cave bear from its den and waiting at the exit with spears. Instead of emerging slowly, the bear came out fast; the men barely saw him before he was among them. The bear was stabbed with several spears, but he managed to slash five of the men with the claws of his front paws.

The hunters carried in the wounded, and Lavender yelled at them to leave Sturgeon with her. They laid Sturgeon down on Lavender's bed, and she ran to the spring for clean water.

When she got back to her bunk, she cut away the shredded wrap covering his thighs. When she cut the blood-clotted clothing away, she gasped at the severity of the wound. There were four cuts that were as deep as her index finger, and she could see the femoral artery. It was a miracle the artery wasn't severed or his private parts weren't cut away, since they were lower than the uppermost cut. Without thinking about the sexual aspects, she cleaned the wounds while holding his sexual parts in her left hand. She made a flint needle and stitched the wounds with hair from a horse's tail.

An older woman stopped by Lavender's bunk and told her to keep his man parts clean and gave her salve for the wounds.

His wounds were serious, and the dangers of infection were going to be even worse. Four of the hunters received catastrophic wounds, but Lavender was only worried about Sturgeon.

Lavender's friends helped care for Raging Bull, and they kept a continuous vigil for Sturgeon over several days. On the fourth night, one of the wounded hunters died from infection, and two nights later, another one died from infection, but Sturgeon fought on with the help of Lavender's crew. A week after the accident, Sturgeon's fever broke and he ate solid food. Lavender and her close friends were giddy over his improvement. He had lost most of his muscle tone, and half his body weight, but he was improving. Poplar Bark assured the nurse crew he had seen this before, and once men recover, they regain their strength.

Sturgeon realized he no longer had secrets from Lavender or her friends. They had helped him with everything, and knew everything about his body. He still needed help to relieve himself, since he could barely walk, and Lavender bathed his wounds and his manly parts every day.

Eventually, when she lifted his manly parts, there was a reaction. His maleness pulled away from her hand and lay hard against his belly. Lavender looked into his eyes for a second and went back to cleaning his wounds as if nothing had happened.

Lavender wondered if he was attracted to her or if his reaction was normal. After that, Sturgeon began holding his own male parts while Lavender cleaned the wounds. He was embarrassed over a now-automatic hardening of his male organ, as soon as she even looked at his wound. Lavender's older friend, Jasmine, demonstrated a different way to clean his member, and a few seconds later, he erupted. Jasmine said he would sleep better and be more relaxed if she washed his member every day or two in this manner.

Lavender thanked her friend and told her, a few days later, "Your technique seems to provide a great relief to Sturgeon."

He no longer held his man parts for the cleaning, and she looked forward to helping him achieve his relief at least once a day.

He shared her bed, and she wanted to share more, but his wounds were still healing, and she was afraid of hurting him. Sturgeon was getting stronger, and eventually, the wound no longer needed to be cleaned. Sturgeon left the cave to go hunting small game for a few hours each day, and his lameness decreased with each day, but he returned to Lavender's bed each night.

On a cold night, Lavender backed up in bed, until she felt the sleeping form of Sturgeon. His maleness sprang to life, and its hardness was warm against her lower back. She had on a leather nightgown, but it was exciting to feel the hardness pressed against her back. Instinctively, Sturgeon reached out in his sleep to pull her closer. His right hand was on her ribs beneath her breast, and she marveled at his strength as he pulled her hard against his body. She moved his hand to her breast, and he began to softly knead the soft mound. Lavender was in a mild euphoric state and enjoyed the erotic sensations for twenty minutes before deciding she needed more. Pulling her nightgown above her waist, she positioned herself to direct his member into the flower of her femininity. Her moistness increased when the hardness of the head touched her outer lips, and she felt another wave of moistness lubricate her passage when she pushed down on his manhood. She had about half his member inside her, when she felt him wake up. He seemed confused for a few seconds, and suddenly, his hands grabbed her hips and rammed the full length into her in one fast and furious moment. She gasped and put her hand against his hip to slow him down, but the storm was unleashed.

At first, Lavender was scared, but his raw passion quickly began to consume her. She bit into her blanket to keep from crying out, before two intense climaxes made her groan in a deep voice she had never heard before. Her body tensed and then relaxed. She felt heat from her inner core. The intense feelings began once again, but before she reached the climax, he gripped her tight and drove hard into her very being, unleashing three bursts of hot liquid against her womb. He drifted into a deep sleep with his semi-hard member still imbedded in her body.

Lavender didn't want to pull free of his member, but it was enough of a distraction, she couldn't sleep. If she moved to get comfortable, the member began to harden, but she didn't want another session right away; she forced herself to remain still.

Lavender suffered through a sleepless night to enjoy the feeling of Sturgeon's member resting within her and didn't fall asleep until just before daylight.

Morning came early for Stone Age people, and Lavender awoke to the noises and smells of breakfast. She felt Sturgeon pulling himself free with a small *plop* sound. She felt an emptiness and sadness at losing her masculine companion, but Sturgeon jumped out of bed with enthusiasm, and Lavender wanted to sleep a few more hours.

Lavender and Sturgeon formalized their relationship and were unconcerned about expressing their carnal relationship in the communal lodge. Their daughter, Tadpole, was born nine months later.

Chapter 12
The Mighty Tadpole

The children modeled their behavior upon the behavior of their parents. Tadpole admired her older brother, and Raging Bull protected his younger sister, treating her like a tribal princess.

At twenty years of age, Raging Bull became a natural leader in his tribe and was in line to become a chief. He was an excellent flint worker and a superior tracker, and because of his mother's encouragement, he believed in his abilities. Raging Bull already had two wives and was looking for another; unfortunately, he intimidated other men and kept potential suitors away from Tadpole.

She didn't mind being alone. Tadpole was an artist; she mixed and created her own paints from mineral oxides and painted animals on the walls of caves they lived in during their migrations. The tribe always lived near the entrances of the caves. This was a matter of safety—there was a real possibility of becoming trapped in the cave by another tribe, a cave bear, hyenas, or a pack of wolves, but Tadpole always disappeared into the darkest recesses of the caves after dinner. She would build a small fire for light, and using brushes she made from the bristles of boar hogs and the mane of horses, she painted the animals with such realism, many who saw the paintings wondered if the animals became animated at night.

During her early years, she painted the animals as she saw them. Later on, she thought of the constellations her father, Sturgeon, had shown to the children on starlit nights and began to paint the different animals to fit within various constellations. The paintings were positioned relative to the locations of the constellations. Using her mother's stories of migrations from the Indus River, she tried to convey those stories within the context of her art.

The People of the North migrated with the herds, and Tadpole had the opportunity to paint in many different caves. Sometimes, upon returning to a cave after an absence of months or years, there would be a new painting by an unknown artist. Tadpole was always intrigued to see the work of another artist. She would study the unknown artist's work carefully. Some of the artists had great skill and others were crude, but to Tadpole, they were kindred spirits, with the same passions that drove her to paint every night.

By the time Tadpole was nineteen, she had constructed scaffolding and was painting a stampeding herd of horses across a ceiling while lying on her back. Raging Bull began to worry about his sister. She was a beautiful, intelligent young woman, but the suitors were no longer begging for a chance to visit. It was well known throughout several tribes, she only cared about her painting, and soon, she would be considered a spinster, too old to start a family. Raging Bull already had four wives and nine children. It was time for Tadpole to take a husband.

A few weeks before freeze-up, one of the scouts found several large herds of mammoths and a cave, to the west, thirty miles away. This was going to be their winter home and their winter's meat supply. Raging Bull told his tribe they were moving in the morning. The tribe trusted his decision, and no one complained, but when he told Tadpole of the plan, she said, "I will be there in a few weeks. I want to finish the ceiling."

Raging Bull looked at her in shocked disbelief. "You can finish the painting when we return. Besides, how will you find us in a few weeks? We will be over thirty miles away, and the snows might come early."

Everyone knew Tadpole was intelligent. The scouts always consulted her, when they were using their rudimentary system of celestial navigation. She had memorized the daily, monthly, and yearly movements of the stars, sun, and moon. She was never lost and could tell you their approximate relative position to every landmark the tribe had ever encountered. She asked Raging Bull, "Do you think I will get lost?"

Raging Bull was losing another argument to his sister. "You might not get lost, but what about us? Who will keep us from getting lost? What about the deep snow? What about food, and what if another tribe abducts you?"

"If I don't make it to your camp this fall, I will be here in the spring. I need time alone."

"How will you feed yourself? You are not a hunter. You are a navigator and a painter."

Raging Bull loved his sister as much as he had loved his departed mother. Several years earlier, he had asked his mother about marrying Tadpole, since she was only his half sister, but his mother said it was against the laws of nature.

He didn't want to leave his sister, but what could he do with this headstrong woman? She was like her mother. She would do as she saw fit.

Raging Bull's problem was partially solved when Blue Cat volunteered to stay behind and watch over Tadpole. Raging Bull thanked him and said he would ask Tadpole.

Blue Cat was twenty-eight years old and considered the best hunter. He had suffered a grievous eye injury as a boy, during a raid by an outlaw tribe, and lost the sight of his left eye. The injury left him with a large scar on his cheek and a white eye. He had been found wandering the countryside in pain and starving. The People of the North took pity on the vagabond and adopted him. It was a wise choice; Blue Cat had an uncanny ability to find game when no one else could. Tadpole was less likely to starve if Blue Cat was with her.

Because of his eye and his scar, Blue Cat had never considered himself worthy of a wife.

He was a quiet man, confident in his abilities. If someone had to stay to watch Tadpole, Blue Cat was an excellent choice.

Tadpole agreed after her brother reminded her of the real possibility of starvation and being snowed in all winter.

The tribe left the next morning. Raging Bull was still aggravated with Tadpole and said just enough to qualify as an obligatory farewell. Tadpole smiled to herself; deep inside, she knew her brother was worried about her. However, if she left the cave and her mural on the ceiling, she might not ever finish her masterpiece.

It was very quiet after the tribe left. Blue Cat only wandered back to the work area to watch the painting once in a while. He hunted and cooked two meals a day, and if Tadpole didn't smell the food, she would never know when a meal was ready. Blue Cat rarely said anything. He would smile and then look away as if he was embarrassed whenever she was near, and Tadpole was happy to work without interruptions.

Blue Cat was an excellent cook, and it was a good thing since Tadpole had never learned to cook or perform any of the jobs of a wife, and she certainly didn't know how to hunt.

Blue Cat always carried two spears, and one day, he was visibly upset. He had missed an elk and the spear's flint point hit a rock. The top one-third of the flint spear point was gone, and the spear was useless.

Tadpole looked at the broken point and said, "Well, my quiet friend, here is something I can do for you. Follow me."

They looked among the rocks and found a dozen good flint rocks and several granite rocks about the size of a baseball. He gave her a piece of leather, to protect her hand while she held the flint, and they sat down in the light at the opening of the cave.

Blue Cat watched in amazement as Tadpole's nimble fingers moved so fast, he could barely follow them. She made two new spear points and a two-bladed knife for him.

She smiled to see him so happy. It was the first emotion she had seen from him, since he became her guardian. He looked up to say, "Thank you," and immediately looked down again.

Tadpole put her hand under his chin and lifted his face so that he had to look at her. She leaned forward and kissed his forehead. He opened his eyes to look at her and realized her leather-covered bosom was only inches away from his face.

Holding his face with both her hands, she said, "Always look at me, when I talk to you or you talk to me. We are friends, and we respect each other."

These were the kindest words anyone had ever said to Blue Cat, and he felt wonderful. From that moment on, Blue Cat would give his life to help Tadpole. She had no way of knowing how deep Blue Cat's commitment was, since he would never talk about it, but it was real and honest. The snow started coming down at that moment, and the two of them looked into the white void and wondered about the weather. "I will finish tonight, and if the weather is right, we can leave tomorrow," Tadpole said, without conviction.

"Yes, Miss Tadpole, we will leave when the weather is good," Blue Cat said. His words sounded hollow. He knew they had missed their window of opportunity.

Blue Cat had been an orphan his whole life, and no one had ever loved him or been kind to him; spending the winter with Tadpole was not intimidating for him. It would be a long winter, but at least he could hunt, and she could paint. And now, with his newfound confidence, they could talk. Blue Cat had always taken what life had to offer and made the best of things, but since Tadpole had shown him kindness, he looked forward to each day.

The winter hit hard that afternoon, and the snow continued for three more weeks. When the snow quit, the temperature dropped to forty below. Blue Cat's meals were only once a day now, and the servings were small. It was hard to hunt in the deep snow, and Blue Cat was worried about the possibility of starvation.

He came home after another unsuccessful hunt to hear whimpering from the back of the cave. He called out to Tadpole, and she cried for help. Blue Cat ran to the back of the cave.

Tadpole had fallen from a ladder, and her right lower leg was broken. The bones weren't protruding through the skin, but the leg was crooked. He knew if he didn't straighten the leg, she would never walk again.

He picked her up and carried her to the entrance of the cave, where the light was better, to assess the damage and plan the correction. He laid her on his bed and looked at her tiny leg bones. *They will be easier to correct*, he said, to himself. She was shivering from the pain. "Miss Tadpole, I need to align the broken bones. It will hurt."

Blue Cat had seen a broken leg set once before, and he was the only bonesetter they had.

He gave her a rolled-up piece of leather and told her to bite into the leather and scream. Once he started, he would continue, until he was done. He pulled up her leather skirt to her hips and slid his body underneath the broken leg until the leg was resting on his chest. He brought his right foot to rest on her pubic arch and braced his left foot against her right hip. Holding her right foot with his right hand, he felt the broken bones with his left hand; with increasing pressure, he began to straighten his legs and Tadpole's broken leg as well. Tadpole was screaming, but Blue Cat continued until he felt the bones click into place just before Tadpole passed out from the pain. With great care, Blue Cat slipped out from under the leg and wrapped it with a piece of moist leather about three feet long and a foot wide. When the leg was secure in the wrap, he secured the leather with thongs above and below the break. He put a splint on each side and wrapped the leg once again. There was nothing else he could do. Broken leg bones were often fatal in the Stone Age; now, he could only hope for the best. He needed to hunt, but he didn't want Tadpole to wake up alone and in pain. He sat by the opening of the cave with the forlorn hope of an animal walking within range of his spear.

Tadpole woke up in the middle of the night. She was in pain and bravely fought the urge to cry. She thanked Blue Cat and asked if he could make something to eat.

"I have enough soup for a few more days, but in the morning I must start hunting again. If you wake up alone, I will be out hunting."

After a small bowl of soup, Tadpole fell into a deep sleep.

Chapter 13
The Wolf

Blue Cat didn't tell her, but the only way he could give her soup was by going hungry. In the early morning hours, he left the cave to hunt. Just as the sun was rising, Blue Cat saw a young bull elk sleeping at the bottom of a small hill.

He threw his spear with accuracy and struck the elk in the right shoulder. It was a crippling wound, but the elk stood and looked like he was ready to run. Blue Cat threw his second spear hard, and it pierced the ribcage, delivering a fatal blow. Blue Cat waited. He didn't want to spook the bull and have it run a mile before dying and decrease his chances of getting back to the cave with the carcass. Finally, the bull staggered a few steps before collapsing in a heap.

He finished field dressing the elk and was taking a few bites of the heart for the strength he needed to drag the carcass to the cave, when he realized he wasn't alone. There was an animal in the bushes. He started to drag the carcass to the cave, when he heard a low growl to his right. He turned and aimed his spear at a starving wolf with a grievous head wound about four feet away. One eye was gone, and the fur was torn away from half his skull. Blue Cat pointed his spear at the wolf's good eye, but he knew his odds weren't good with the wolf so close. Blue Cat threw the half-eaten heart at the wolf, and it was swallowed instantly. He picked up the liver and threw it as well. It was gone in four quick bites. He picked up a leg bone and threw it, but when the wolf caught it, he dropped the bone and lunged past Blue Cat to fight a Cave Lion, sneaking up to take the carcass. It was a spirited fight, the wolf was lunging in and jumping back, but a lone wolf was no match for a 660-pound Cave Lion.

Blue Cat stabbed his spear deep into the lion's back, the cat screamed in pain, and decided he didn't like the odds. The Cave Lion left while snarling and spitting at the mismatched pair.

The wolf began to eat the gut pile, while Blue Cat lugged the carcass toward the cave. In a few minutes, the wolf was walking alongside Blue Cat as if they were the best of friends. Blue Cat shrugged his shoulders and continued pulling the carcass toward the cave.

It was noon when Blue Cat showed up with the elk carcass and the wolf. Tadpole had built a little fire and resisted the urge to scream a warning to Blue Cat, when she saw the half-starved creature next to him.

Blue Cat looked at Tadpole and smiled. "Don't worry, we are friends. We fight lions."

Tadpole looked at Blue Cat as if he had lost his mind, but she said nothing.

The wolf ran back and forth across the entrance to the cave before lying down just inside.

Blue Cat started roasting three steaks. When the food was cooked, he threw a steak to the wolf, and the wolf swallowed his dinner in two bites.

"Why did you feed the wolf?" Tadpole asked.

"He earned it, that and much more. He saved my life, and he saved your life as well, because you would soon starve without me."

The next morning, Blue Cat worked with the wolf to get it to stay in the cave, instead of following him. He was only gone for two hours, but when he returned with a small deer, the wolf jumped up and down with excitement when he saw Blue Cat.

The wolf got the bones from the evening meal and seemed happy with his share.

Later that night, the hyenas were in front of the cave and wanted to steal the rest of the elk carcass. The sight of Blue Cat and the wolf was enough to scare them away, but they were an extremely dangerous threat.

After watching the wolf stand by Blue Cat, Tadpole began to have faith in the one-eyed wolf. The next morning, the wolf seemed to realize Tadpole was helpless. During the night, he dug out a small depression in the hard ground near Tadpole's bunk and seemed to be guarding her.

Just before daylight, loud growling from the wolf awakened Tadpole and Blue Cat. The wolf was running back and forth across the twenty-foot entrance to the cave. Blue Cat picked up a spear and stood at the entrance, but he couldn't see anything in the darkness. Eventually, the wolf quit running back and forth and sat next to Blue Cat. He was still growling under his breath, but he didn't act like he was ready for battle. When the sun came up, the two of them walked out together and found the tracks of a large cave bear. The width of the bear's paw prints were wider than one and a half times the length of Blue Cat's foot, and Blue Cat knew it was probably twelve feet tall when it stood upright. The wolf had proven himself worthy of trust once again. Blue Cat cut off a large steak from the elk and threw it to the wolf.

The bear probably wanted to dig a winter's den in the cave, and without the wolf, Tadpole and Blue Cat would've been defenseless. During the winter, the wolf took it upon himself to guard Tadpole, especially while Blue Cat was out hunting. When she struggled to go outside to relieve herself, the wolf whimpered and circled her, until she came back into the cave and lay down once again.

The wolf slept closer and closer to Tadpole's hand, and seemed to want the touch of his adopted human. One evening, Tadpole moved her hand until it was resting on the wolf's head. After several minutes, she began to pet the wolf, and he tried to crawl even closer. Tadpole slowly overcame her fear of the wolf, and the wolf pledged his loyalty to her. The wolf understood; it was his job to guard Tadpole. Occasionally, Blue Cat used the wolf to track a wounded animal, and the wolf considered himself an important member of this human pack. They named the wolf, 'Dog,' their word for guard.

A much larger Eurasian Wolf had taken over Dog's pack and driven Dog away. After three days of starvation and loneliness, Dog came crawling back to his canine family. The Eurasian Wolf immediately jumped Dog and tried to crush his skull. Dog fought for his life and pulled his head from the jaws of death as he heard his skull starting to crack. He lost an eye and there was a terrible wound, but he was still alive. Dog was looking for a new pack, when he saw Blue Cat, who had just killed a bull elk. He was overjoyed when Blue Cat shared the feast instead of fighting over every scrap.

Life with the humans was good. They were never aggressive with him, and the male was glad to have help facing a bear or a tiger. The female was crippled, but he was proud to guard her when the male was hunting. He was happy living with humans.

Winter turned into spring, and the humans were always looking to the west, as if they expected someone to arrive, but no one came.

Late in the spring, Dog heard noises in the distance. The humans could tell he was excited, but they couldn't hear anything. Suddenly, Dog ran into the trees at a high rate of speed.

Dog was gone for twenty minutes. When he returned, he had a large female wolf pup in his mouth. Blue Cat noticed the facial markings of a Eurasian Wolf, with the coloring of a Grey Wolf and knew the pup was a crossbreed. The pup was docile, and Dog was cleaning and caring for the pup as if it were his own.

The humans had no way of knowing the pup was from Dog's former pack. A female companion of his had given birth to two pups that were sired by the Eurasian Wolf that had nearly killed Dog. The Eurasian Wolf bred the female and then forced her out of the pack. Normally, there is only one breeding pair in a wolf pack, but the Eurasian Wolf bred the unwanted females and drove them away. She had two large pups, but the pups were too large for her pelvis, and she never recovered the speed she needed for hunting. After six weeks, she and the pups were starving. She was crying over the death of one of the pups when Dog heard his old friend.

In the way of the canine, she asked Dog to take her surviving pup; she had given all the nutrients she had received from a few rabbits and ground squirrels to her pups. She was too far-gone to recover, and the best she could manage, was to ask a favor from an old friend.

Dog nudged her neck with his muzzle and licked her forehead to comfort his friend. He picked up the surviving pup, and looked one last time at his dying friend before taking the pup to the human pack.

Tadpole saw that the pup was starved. She chopped some caribou steak and fat into a small pile of food, and the pup ate it in a few bites. She laughed at the pup's swollen belly and named her Pup, the Stone Age word for big belly.

After eating, Pup staggered a few steps and collapsed to fall asleep instantly.

Blue Cat cooked steaks on the fire, and while they were eating, Pup woke up and began to terrorize the humans and Dog. Her teeth were like sewing needles, and she liked biting human toes and Dog's ears. It was funny at first, but Pup was on a rampage, and everyone was a potential victim. Suddenly, Pup fell asleep again and there was peace in the cave. Things were going to be much more lively in the cave, with Pup.

Blue Cat removed Tadpole's cast, but he didn't like the way the leg looked. There was excess bone formation around the break, and the leg wasn't straight. He apologized and agonized over the leg.

Tadpole was lame, and would be lame for the rest of her life. It was pointless to blame Blue Cat. He had done a remarkable job, considering he had only seen the procedure one time. She was lucky to have survived such a terrible break, and she loved the man who cared for her during the long winter.

Tadpole had survived twenty winters; she had no children and assumed her tribe may not have survived the winter. She longed to have a child, and the antics of Pup increased her desire to nurture children of her own. Tadpole loved Blue Cat, but he was so shy, they might die of old age before he made a move.

A warm summer rain gave Tadpole an idea. She lay down, nude, on a large, flat rock outside the cave and found it to be exhilarating. She asked Blue Cat to join her; of course, Blue Cat was reluctant to lay nude in the rain, but Tadpole was insistent. They were enjoying the bath when Dog and Pup joined them. Dog lay on his side, but Pup rolled on her back and enjoyed having her belly washed by the rain.

When the four of them walked into the cave, the wolves shook themselves, and the humans received another shower.

They were enjoying the warmth of the fire, when Tadpole offered to rub Blue Cat's overworked back and shoulders. Her soft touch awakened the desire that had been lying dormant in Blue Cat, and after a few minutes of the feminine massage, he turned around to look at Tadpole's beautiful face. He leaned forward to kiss Tadpole and within a few minutes, they consummated their relationship and became a loving couple.

Chapter 14
The Twins

The next spring, Tadpole gave birth to twin girls, Hawk and Wren. Tadpole and Blue Cat were overjoyed to have the babies, but they were scared. Life in the Stone Age was designed around tribal life. They had no tribal support, and Tadpole would never be a strong walker and able to migrate again.

Pup had the size of a Eurasian Wolf and was four or five inches taller than Dog. At one year, she started chasing Dog and biting him. Blue Cat assumed she was coming into season. Sure enough, the next morning they disappeared and didn't return until the following morning.

Pup's puppy days were over. She was more subdued and extremely protective of Tadpole and the twins. She would growl aggressively at Blue Cat if he carried firewood or a knife towards Tadpole and the girls. Blue Cat learned to deal with this personality trait, and instead of trying to change the wolf's personality, he let Pup guard her family.

Fifteen years is a long time in the life of a human. The girls were young women, but they had never seen another human, other than their parents. They were small, clever girls with dark features, and Blue Cat thought they were the most beautiful girls in the world.

Pup and Dog had both passed on six years earlier, and now, three of their pups were getting old after producing pups of different lineages.

Tadpole was aging fast, and at thirty-five, it was obvious, she was not going to survive another winter. The girls, Hawk and Wren, had provided great joy to their parents. They were both artists and painted many different animals on the walls of the cave. They each had their own style, and it was fascinating to watch them paint. Hawk was more adventurous, and she liked to hunt with her dad and the wolves. Wren preferred cooking exotic meals and was always inventing new methods of food preparation. In the evening, the family would tell stories and sing the old songs of their ancestors.

Sometimes, a wolf would try to sing harmony, and the other wolves would soon join in and drown out the humans.

Life in the cave brought many years of happiness to the humans and the domesticated wolves, but one day, Tadpole lay down and said she was never going to get up again. She was dying, and there was nothing her family could do for her. She wanted to be buried in the room where she had spent her life painting. She asked that her grave be covered with big rocks, so the bears would not eat her body. Tadpole waved goodbye to her loyal wolves that had protected her for so many years and were now gathered by her deathbed. She kissed Wren and Hawk goodbye and smiled at the only man she had loved. He smiled back with his shy smile and with tears on his cheeks as Tadpole passed away.

The wolves howled when she died, and the girls started crying. Blue Cat built a fire in the room with all the art. He thought of how fortunate he was to have loved this kind and talented woman. He worked all night to dig a grave in the rocky soil of the great room.

The next morning, Blue Cat laid Tadpole in the grave with several flint knives and spear points near her hands. He cried with huge sobs, when he covered up his true love, the only person who had shown him kindness in this world. He pushed a huge slab of slate over the grave. When he was finished, Blue Cat sat at the opening of the cave, thinking of all the happiness they had shared in their home.

In the spring, he would take the girls and the wolf pack to find good humans. He would be content to spend the rest of his days in the cave, near Tadpole's grave, but the girls deserved a future.

The girls had been born with a genetic mutation in their mitochondrial DNA. Twenty-first century scientists would designate their line as H1W2.

This new form of mitochondrial DNA was tremendously beneficial to mankind, because it increased the natural resistance to some of mankind's terrible diseases: polio, measles, and smallpox. H1W2 caused confusion among the blood type analysts of the future, when the new DNA mutation spread in two different directions at the same time.

Blue Cat was forty-five years old when he set out to the northwest to find a friendly tribe. The girls were excited, but homesick and grieving for their mother. They moved like their ancestors had migrated for thousands of years, eating plants, fruits, nuts, and vegetables that were available, and setting up camp after killing a caribou, elk, camel, horse, moose, or deer and moving on, when they could carry the remaining meat and after processing the leather with the brain of the animal, or the smoke of their campfires, or the tannin residues of leaves.

They traveled over three hundred miles that first summer and could have traveled farther, except for finding an excellent cave with a freshwater spring.

The cave had provided shelter for many vagabonds for tens of thousands of years. There were fascinating paintings, drawings, and etchings on the walls, and the flint workers had left piles of discarded flint flakes over thousands of years, and these were often rummaged through by others when they needed a sharp edge.

Blue Cat and the girls knew it was best to stop early in the season, upon finding a good cave, and hang as much meat as possible from the ceiling of the cave, before the snows become too deep.

The wolves had changed over several generations; most of the pups were docile and required no time getting used to humans. Sometimes a wolf would disappear for days or weeks at a time. They often returned with the scars of fights, and sometimes they never returned. The wolves protected them at night, and some of them helped with hunting, but they still lived on the periphery of domestication, and sometimes they answered the call of the wild.

Two years later, the girls were eighteen years old, and Blue Cat's hair was gray, but he was one of those men who get stronger rather than weaker with age. From a hill above the joining of two rivers, Blue Cat and the girls saw a large encampment. It had been almost twenty years since Blue Cat had seen a tribe, and the girls had never seen other humans. Blue Cat saw the fear on the girls' faces. He smiled and said, "This is what we have been looking for. Let's go down and say, hello."

As they walked toward the rivers, a group of teenagers started following Blue Cat, the girls, and the four wolves. The twins and wolves intrigued the youngsters, but the teenagers kept a respectful distance. However, a group of older boys were standing in front of Blue Cat. Anxious to assert their masculinity, they were trying to intimidate Blue Cat, and possibly steal the twins. The ringleader was standing in front, and was flanked by five of his friends. He was trying to engage Blue Cat in the boring conversation of boys acting like men. Blue Cat brushed him aside. The wolves were nervous; the hair was standing up on their backs, and they were growling.

Blue Cat was not going to waste time talking to insignificant nobodies, but the teenage leader reached out to grab one of the girls. A yearling pup lunged forward, and everyone heard two large snaps as the pup tore the boy's arm off. The boy screamed, and the wolf shook his head twice before dropping the severed arm to the ground.

Blue Cat ignored the screaming boy and held his spear toward the faces in the crowd. He looked them all in the eye, one at a time, and said, "Stay back, or the wolves and I will kill all of you."

A chief pushed his way through the standoff and looked at the pathetic boy with his arm torn off below the elbow. The boy was whimpering and trying to stop the bleeding. The chief looked at the one-eyed, gray-haired hunter with rock-hard muscles, his wolves, and the beautiful twins by his side, he said to the hunter, "What happened?"

"He tried to grab one of my daughters. The wolves protect the girls," Blue Cat said, in a calm voice.

The chief raised his eyebrows and walked up to Blue Cat. He touched the tip of Blue Cat's spear with his finger and held out his open hand, after nodding his head one time. He was asking for the spear.

Blue Cat handed him the spear, after a few moments of hesitation. The chief handled the weapon with confidence and spun around to strike the injured boy across the nose with the shaft of the spear. The boy went down to the ground on his back, but before he could move, the chief plunged the spear point through the boy's heart and he was dead.

The chief turned back around to hand Blue Cat his spear, but noticed one of the girls had already handed him another. The chief smiled and said, "You will have dinner at my lodge tonight. We have many things to talk about." He reached with his right arm to grasp Blue Cat's right arm below the elbow, and they held on to each other's forearm, the ultimate sign of respect between hunters.

The chief yelled at the tribesmen gathering around, "Stay thirty paces away. These wolves are not used to silly people who live in villages."

Chapter 15
Mother's Son

At dinner, the two men talked many hours about hunting and their travels. The chief's name was Mother's Son, and he was a totalitarian dictator. Mother's Son had faced six challengers, who fought to the death for control of the tribe; he killed them all.

Mother's Son looked at Blue Cat with exaggerated seriousness. "I hope you haven't come to challenge me."

Blue Cat looked at the chief and laughed. "I raised two daughters and trained many wolves to hunt and guard us at night. I have had enough leadership." They both started laughing, but Mother's Son stopped laughing and looked Blue Cat in the eye.

"I need a good hunting chief, a man like you," the chief said, with a serious tone.

Blue Cat leaned in close to Mother's Son. "I need to find good husbands for my daughters. That is why I am here. When they are married, I can teach your hunters how to track and hunt with wolves."

The chief smiled and said, "We need to marry these girls as soon as possible. Forget my hunters, *I* want to learn how to hunt with wolves. Now, tell me about your beautiful daughters."

"Their mother was a great cave artist, maybe the best in the world, and she could make knives and spear points faster and better than anyone I have ever seen. She taught the girls her skills, and they are almost as good as their mother was. Wren is a great cook, and Hawk prefers to hunt with me and the wolves."

Mother's Son looked at Blue Cat with shocked disbelief. "Is this true? These girls would be considered the most valuable women of my tribe."

Blue Cat asked Wren to make a knife for the chief and asked Hawk to make a spear point. The girls looked through their flint pack, and each one selected a good rock. They were not in a race, but their hands were moving at an extremely fast pace; yet, they were relaxed as the flint flakes were flying away and two works of art were beginning to appear. Within a few minutes, they each handed a finished tool to Mother's Son. He looked at their tiny forearms, and each of them had specks of blood where the flying chips had cut them. Hawk had a nasty cut on her left hand from the surgical sharpness of the stone that had cut through the leather.

Chief Mother's Son held a tool in each hand and turned them over and over to admire the craftsmanship, and soon his hands were bleeding profusely from several cuts. He called to one of his wives. "Take these, woman, before I hurt myself." His wife laughed at his joke and held the tools in leather to show them to important members of the tribe, who responded with murmurs of approval.

Mother's Son said, "These girls can paint? Painting will be much safer for me."

Blue Cat looked around and saw a large horse clavicle on the ground and asked, "Can they paint on that bone?"

Mother's Son told a teenage boy to bring the clavicle, but the wolves began growling, and the hair stood up on their backs, when the boy picked up the clavicle and took a step toward the girls.

Blue Cat waved for the boy to stop; he walked to the boy and brought the clavicle to the girls himself. The wolves were still growling, but softer; it was obvious they considered the girls to be their responsibility.

Blue Cat asked Wren to paint a mammoth. She reached in her pack and pulled out a palette of several dry mineral oxides. She added a minute quantity of oil to reconstitute the colors and painted a mammoth in less than twenty minutes. The portrayal of the mammoth was realistic, with long grayish-brown hair and white tusks. When Wren finished, Blue Cat asked Hawk to paint a cave lion on the same clavicle. She mixed some black and yellow colors and painted a lion on a cliff, watching the mammoth from above.

The girls gave the painting to Mother's Son. After studying the painting for several minutes, the tears were rolling down his cheeks. He looked at the girls and said, "This is beautiful. I will cherish it forever."

Blue Cat looked at Mother's Son. "Would you like to see them hunt and cook?"

"No, I will believe every word you tell me, for as long as we are both alive," the chief replied. "I have many sons. Some of them might appeal to your daughters."

"It will be their choice, not mine or anyone else's. That is the way I raised them," Blue Cat replied.

Because of the wolves and their distrust of people, Blue Cat and the girls made a camp away from the rest of the tribe. They only had a few visitors, and most of those were young men wanting to marry one or both of the girls. The girls were intelligent, and men who were slow or stupid seemed boring; finding husbands for these girls would take time.

Mother's Son and Blue Cat became best friends and hunting partners, and the girls were popular in the tribe. Wren married one of Mother's Son's many sons. She had two girls and a son. Unfortunately, the boy caught pneumonia and died soon after birth. Hawk married a nephew of Mother's Son. He was the chief of a small tribe, and they migrated to the east. They had two girls and two boys.

The mutation that became the H1W2 genetic marker of the girls' mitochondrial DNA continued on for tens of thousands of years and was responsible for a strong line of women who were influential in the history of the world.

The line of Wren settled in the coastal area of Southern France and often wintered in the valleys of South Central France. The line of Hawk followed the herds as they migrated east, following the Mammoth Steppe into Asia and beyond.

Chapter 16

The Salmon Tribe

The Salmon People, descendants of Wren, wandered east to west and back again, over thousands of years, following the mammoths on the edges of the ice that are now part of France and Germany. During a migration, Chief Blood Eel and his tribe were caught out in the open during a blizzard, and prospects were grim for survival. His people were exhausted and hungry. The temperature had dropped to forty below, and the wind created a whiteout condition.

The tribal members were at the end of their endurance. The snow was four feet deep, with a thin crust of ice on top and loose powder beneath the ice. The ice broke like glass as they tried to go forward, and it was cutting through their clothing and leaving people with gashes on the legs, arms, and hands. There was a blood trail for the tigers, bears, lions, hyenas, and wolves that hunted humans.

Blood Eel realized he might lose half or all his tribesmen in the blizzard. The Salmon Tribe had sixty adult members. They were caught in the area that was to become Lascaux, in the southwest of France, in the region of Dordogne, when the blizzard struck, about 20,000 BP.

Blood Eel walked back through his sixty people and told them to burrow in the snow until the weather broke. This was a last-ditch option for survival. His people knew some of them would be dead from exposure by morning.

Yellow Hair was five. His mother, Bird Song, estranged wife of Blood Eel, was nearly twenty. Blood Eel had traded 100 pounds of mammoth meat, two spear points, and two flint knives for Bird Song, when she was fourteen. It was an uncommon price, but Bird Song was considered an exotic beauty.

She was from the H1W2 line that had migrated east and west for thousands of years on the steppe, following the mammoths and mastodons. The tribe had acquired blonde blue-eyed traits and the Asian eye with its epicanthic fold by trading for young females and adopting vagabond hunters and children. They were considered handsome people, and their young girls commanded a high price for marriage. Bird Song had the Asian eyes and blonde hair; she was clever verbally and good at expressing herself with her hands. A female like this excited Stone Age hunters, who appreciated beauty and women who could entertain them at night with stories and song.

Blood Eel treated Bird Song like a princess for eighteen months, until she began nursing his son Yellow Hair. For Blood Eel, she was no longer exciting and intriguing. Like a bird dog, he started looking for another young girl to impregnate and to ignore nine months later. He collected a group of young women, who ended up sad and lonely, aside from having one of Blood Eel's children. The other hunters were aware of his strange habits, but because he was a chief and prone to violence, they rarely asked if he would trade one of his neglected wives.

Bird Song accepted her lot in life with quiet dignity and devoted herself to raising Yellow Hair and making the flint tools that were so important for the tribe's survival and for trade. She was a good flint worker with above-average skills and taught her young son to make the precision tools as well.

Yellow Hair was an intelligent and athletic boy, like his father, but Bird Song tried to emphasize the importance of loving a woman. They sang together, and he listened to the stories of her culture. He and his mother fished together and hunted small game. She tried to be the perfect mother and father. Yellow Hair grew up loving his mother and treating women with respect.

It was ten degrees warmer under the snow, and being out of the wind helped as well. Bird Song started building a snow cave and lining it with a leather blanket. She and her five-year-old son, Yellow Hair, could survive for a day or two, until the storm subsided. Yellow Hair was playing while his mother worked to make the snow cave comfortable. When she finished and turned around to talk to Yellow Hair, he was gone. In desperation, Bird Song screamed for her son and crawled to the other end of the dark snow cave. There was a small circular hole in the floor, and warm air was rushing out of the hole. She stared into the dark void of the hole and called, "Yellow Hair! Yellow Hair! Are you there? Answer me!"

Suddenly, she heard her boy's tiny voice, "Mom, it is a cave, a big cave, and it is warm." Bird Song crawled for forty feet through the narrow, dark passageway and pulled their packs and leather blanket behind her.

The temperature was sixty-five degrees Fahrenheit, over a hundred degrees warmer than the temperature above the snow; it felt like a hot summer day. She built a small fire with the Birch bark kindling she had in her pack and told Yellow Hair to manage the fire carefully, while she told the others and looked for more wood.

It would be hard to find the others, but she found several small groups and a dry spruce tree for wood. The other tribal members found more people and told them about the cave and to bring firewood.

The tribal members crawled through the small opening and the long passageway, and into the warmth to see Yellow Hair smiling while he tended the small fire. The people congratulated Yellow Hair, and many of them rubbed the pile of yellow hair on his head. Yellow Hair was a hero.

Blood Eel crawled into the cave and looked at his son and wife with new respect. The light of the fire revealed many paintings on the walls, many of which had been painted by Tadpole, their distant relative. The paintings were five thousand years old. Blood Eel's tribe was in the front room of the cave, where Tadpole had given birth to Hawk and Wren, where Dog and Pup frolicked, and where the H1W2 DNA originated.

During the Ice Age, the drought conditions created vast deserts with massive deposits of silt and sand. There were often windstorms, and the wind carried dust from these deserts, all over the world. Over the eons, the wide entrance to the cave was buried by dust and sand until there was only a small opening at the top, the one Yellow Hair found. It was barely big enough for a man to crawl through.

Chapter 17

The Lascaux Cave

The small fire revealed the art of Lascaux. The sixty members of the Salmon Tribe saw the most beautiful paintings in the world on the walls of a great room.

Blood Eel studied the paintings; he knew the style of different artists and recognized some of the artists from other caves in Europe. He explored several more rooms and realized these works of art were the result of many different artists, including Near People.

The smoke disappeared into the folds of the stone ceiling and indicated natural ventilation. This was important if they were going to have light and heat in the cave.

The rest of the tribe was content to marvel at the beauty of the animal paintings, but Blood Eel studied the paintings through the night and into the next day. His hunters woke up at mid-day, and Blood Eel sent them out for food. They killed a caribou calf before dark. The calf was devoured in one meal. Blood Eel ate only the minimum, just enough to stay alert. He was still studying the paintings when the sun began to set; suddenly, the cavern was illuminated with the sun's final rays of the day. This was the winter solstice, and the tribe remembered this rare event, for this was the only day the sun offered these brief moments of natural visibility within the cave. It became the first holiday to be celebrated annually by the Salmon People or any people.

Blood Eel called his tribe and began to explain the drawings in the main room. He held the meeting in front of the bull auroch (a large prehistoric feral type of cattle) and the dead man. He began his speech, "The dead man is dying after being gored by the bull, but when he dies, his manhood is erect and indicating the direction of travel to escape this world. The position of the bull represents the migration route his tribe and our tribe has followed over generations. His spear points to the North Star, and the other animals are in the positions of the constellations during the Winter Solstice. The Near People painted the bull and the dead man. This artist and his tribe have always been a few years ahead of us. I know him like a brother, by his art. We have the chamber of felines, the painted gallery, a chamber of engravings, the horses, a rhinoceros, a jackal, and, most surprisingly, a horse painting by an artist from the Far East. There are two thousand figures depicted in these paintings, and they are in several basic groups: animals, antlered deer, and abstract symbols, but there is also a bird, a bear, four large bull aurochs—one that is almost eighteen feet long—bison, and wild cattle. There are also images that have been carved into the stones." Blood Eel looked at his people and said, "The sum total of all the knowledge of the world, is drawn and painted on these walls. The keys to escape our world are painted on these walls. It is the dead man, his phallus, and his spear. They tell us if we are to escape, we must travel northwest, then west, and then south."

Blood Eel was rarely wrong. The Salmon People were perplexed with his findings; although, who but Blood Eel could recognize a map of the ancient migration routes and see the constellations in the paintings? It was hard to imagine the Near People were capable of painting such beautiful art, but everyone had seen their magnificent flint pieces. The people who made the finest spearheads were incapable of throwing a spear with accuracy, but they could thrust a spear through the spine of a giant moose or brown bear almost effortlessly.

The Asian horse was another problem for the Salmon Tribe. There were hundreds of horses painted on the walls, but one of them was painted like the horses of Asia; was it possible that one of these master artists copied a painting of an Asian horse, or did an Asian come all this way to paint one horse?

How did these people from the past find this cave, when little Yellow Hair only found it by accident?

The Salmon Tribe spent the rest of the winter living in the cave. In the spring they migrated west to the coast and found a microclimate teeming with wildlife. Warm water from the equator flowed northward along the coast, bringing fish, especially salmon. The coastal area grew grass and lichens, and the herds of horses and caribou followed the grass. The warm water warmed the air, and when the warm air currents of the equator met the cold winds of the ice sheets, there was rain and a greater supply of plant foods. The Salmon People lived in a feast and famine situation with the fish, until they began to use boats and long fishing lines to catch fish offshore.

Blood Eel was the intellect behind fishing beyond the shoreline. He used the technology of navigation that was advanced and passed on to the hunters by his relative Tadpole, five thousand years ago. With this basic knowledge of the heavens, the early navigators made it home after fishing offshore for several days.

The preservation of fish and meat by smoking and jerking (sun drying) had been used for almost ten thousand years, but Blood Eel developed a method of preserving fish by burying them in the sand in an anaerobic situation that preserved the fish for months at a time. They dug a pit the depth of a man, about five or six feet, and with the same dimension for length and width, and lined the walls with mud made of clay, lime, sand, and water. When the lining hardened, they would build a fire in the pit and let it burn for a day and a night. When they had a good catch of salmon, they would line the bottom of the pit with the fresh leaves of the maple tree. Several tons of salmon were stored in the pit, and the pit was sealed with multiple layers of maple leaves and several feet of dirt. The fish fermented over the months and became a tasty delicacy.

The Salmon Tribe gave up hunting and migrating with the mammoths and remained sedentary in their coastal home for the next twenty years. The young people grew taller and stronger because of the consistent sources of protein, without periods of starvation, but Blood Eel noticed a lack of aggression and toughness among them as well.

The culture of the Salmon Tribe grew when the struggle against starvation was not as critical; a major portion of the cultural growth involved the treks to the cave near Lascaux. Blood Eel liked to make the trips to teach the children what it was like during the migrations, when they followed the mammoths, but the main reason was to teach the clever children the fundamental sciences of astronomy and navigation.

Blood Eel made sure the children were in the great room for the winter solstice. Here they witnessed a religious experience, when the natural light of the sun illuminated the room. Everyone was in a state of awe, even the adults, who had seen the event many times.

In the late summer and early fall, most of the tribe traveled to the cave again, for the mushroom season. The Salmon Tribe gathered the wild mushrooms and hung them to dry. There were thousands of different mushrooms appearing during this brief time, but only a few hundred of them are edible; the rest causing insanity or death. It was important for the tribe to learn which ones were poisonous, the technology or science of mushroom gathering had been accumulated over thousands of years. Survival was dependent on knowing which mushrooms were safe.

Vagabonds and beggars were used to test mushrooms, especially those who came to the tribe without skills and tended to be parasites. The tribe acquired several of these people every year. They often arrived in a state of starvation and threw themselves upon the mercy of the tribe. It was customary to feed a stranger if you had the resources, but they often refused to leave or work, and became an extra noncontributing mouth to feed. Only a few survived the mushroom season.

Blood Eel oversaw the mushroom collection. The children began learning to recognize the most obvious mushrooms like the Morels and Shaggy Heads. Blood Eel and a few tribal leaders tested specific mushrooms on non-contributing vagabonds, and noted the results. Some of the mushrooms brought on violent sickness and death in a few hours; others would take as long as a day. The tradition of collecting mushrooms was learned over eons, and those lessons are still with us.

Blood Eel taught the children the secrets of celestial navigation and how to judge the relative time of day by the sun, moon, and stars. Knowing the basic facts helped people find their way home, whether they were on the ocean or in the mountains. These lessons literally came to light for the children when the setting sun illuminated the cave paintings in the great room for a few minutes; it was a magical time for the children and the adults.

The lessons instilled a sense of unity and uniqueness among the tribal members. They considered themselves the most advanced tribe in the world; they understood the secrets of creation, the world, and the heavens. Their intellectual pursuits isolated the Salmon Tribe from many of the other tribes, who seemed little more than ignorant savages. Because of their advanced culture, the custom of adopting lost hunters or starving adults was often considered impractical, but they accepted exceptional individuals, strong men and attractive women, as underlings or informal slaves without official tribal status. If these people hooked up with tribal members, they gradually became accepted as Salmon tribal members.

The tribe still traded flint instruments and food for children, and if desperate tribes had excess boys, the Salmon Tribe was now large enough and strong enough to accept these boys as payment. These foreign children of many different types enriched the Salmon with diverse DNA and contributed to a dynamic gene pool.

With a steady source of food, the Salmon Tribe had a much better survival rate among infants; the adults were healthier and began to live longer. Their numbers increased from sixty-to-two hundred. They were the elite tribe of Western Europe and envied by everyone, but with envy, there is danger.

The other tribes assumed the advantage Salmon People had over the rest of the tribes was due to their access to food supplies, but the advantages were far more complex. They had obvious advantages, like the ability to sail into the wind with seaworthy canoes capable of holding a large catch of fish, and they learned how to divert portions of the migrating caribou herds into blind canyons and butcher the caribou, as they were needed. The tribe fished in the winter, but if they came back without fish or if the weather was too dangerous to go out, they could open up one of the pits and feast on fermented fish.

Keeping caribou and horses in a blind canyon with steep walls and a log gate allowed the tribe to butcher animals whenever they needed fresh meat. If the captured animals ran out of feed, they butchered all of them and smoked the meat.

The protein sources were consistent, and the Salmon Tribe began to plant gardens and orchards on soil that was once the ocean floor. The sand was rich in organic material, and the rivers and creeks of nearby glacial water were easily diverted for irrigation of these early agricultural experiments if the rains stopped.

Trade brought almonds from trees that produced nuts without cyanide; these trees thrived in the climate and produced nuts that were used as a staple food. They also acquired pulses (beans), melons, and berries.

The variety of food sources made the Salmon Tribe even stronger. However, the most profound contributing factor was educating the children and opening up their minds with the information on geography and astronomy. It was not just the information: it was the complex gymnastics of the mind that were required to absorb these abstract concepts. The Salmon Tribe became a tribe of intelligent people.

Blood Eel impressed upon Yellow Hair the importance of keeping the people strong and vigilant; this was one of the best hunting and fishing grounds in the world, and many people wanted this land.

Starvation still plagued the rest of the world in winter; if the tribes didn't kill several animals every month, they starved. Starvation forces people to take desperate actions, and one of those actions might be to attack people and rob them of their hunting and fishing grounds. The competition for food was intense among the animals, but not nearly as intense as the competition among humans.

Chapter 18

Chief Yellow Hair

Yellow Hair's fathers were chiefs going back nine fingers, or generations. He assigned a finger to each of his fathers and could count his lineage back to the beginning of time. He often joked about a future great-grandson and of how he would need to drop his wrap from his waist to count chiefs of his bloodline. His hunters loved the old joke, and some women shrieked at the idea of a man exposing his private parts to count. The Salmon People began to assume they had always lived in this coastal region between the ice and the ocean; the actual information of their history was lost in the fog of time.

Yellow Hair was an accomplished artist and flint worker. He inherited the ability and learned the skills from his mother. However, the tribe had several flint sculptors who could be considered among the best toolmakers in the world. Within the DNA pool of the Salmon People, some of the greatest artistic and technological advances of western man were waiting to be created, but during the Ice Age, artistic and technological minds were employed in the struggle to survive.

Creativity flourished when the fishing was good, but it was agriculture that gave man the freedom and security to indulge artistic license and creativity. Yellow Hair copied the artistic style of his father, while watching him paint the animals they hunted. Blood Eel and Yellow Hair assumed their creativity and artistic abilities were inherited from their fathers, but they were wrong. Both men had mothers from the H1W2 mitochondrial DNA line.

It was Blood Eel who began building prototypes of the bow with miniature spears he called arrows. His bows started as a means to hunt birds, with sharpened wooden arrows. In time, the bows increased in power, and Blood Eel started placing tiny flint points on the leading end of the arrows, and instead of using arrows for birds, hunters were hunting caribou, deer, and moose. His bows became so strong, the wood couldn't withstand the pressures, and Blood Eel began laminating several layers of wood with sinew and glue. The bow became a lethal killing machine at distances of fifty yards.

Visitors and traders saw this magnificent invention, and the technology spread around the world within a few years. Blood Eel was astonished when he saw the creativity of others applied to his simple invention. Like the spear, the bow could be made by almost everyone, and the man who carried a bow was potentially a dangerous adversary.

Life was good for the Salmon People. Migrating to follow the herds was in the distant past. The Salmon Tribe grew in size as the ability to feed its members increased, but there were problems with growth. In the early days, only the best hunters had multiple wives and the responsibility of feeding several families. However, the abundance of food allowed nonproductive men to have several wives and many children. These children learned slothful habits from their parents and became nonproductive parents as well. At first it seemed like a minor inconvenience to the rest of the tribe, but, in time, the strength and moral fiber of the tribe began to erode. Eventually, productive members worked harder to provide for those who didn't work. Bitterness and discontent soon permeated the tribe. Early chiefs had purged or killed nonproductive members, but when there was plenty of food, members were reluctant to cull the lazy, stupid, and incompetent. Nonproductive members felt entitled to the bounty of the wealthy Salmon Tribe and resented efforts to make them work. Success was weakening and leading to the eventual downfall of the tribe.

The unproductive members relied on a primitive sense of enlightenment and humanism; it was considered immoral to drive away or kill weak and unproductive people. Consequently, the weak and unproductive dedicated their lives to being prolific breeders, the only enterprise they could do efficiently, and the Salmon Tribe was visibly transformed. The tribe became larger, but weaker.

The Salmon People were fortunate, their superior flint-working skills gave them the ability to trade for premium women and girls with specific skills or uncommon beauty. However, most of the tribes they traded with were lighter-skinned, with blue and green eyes and lighter shades of hair. Eventually, darker traits disappeared, and the Salmon People became a predominately fair-skinned tribe with only an occasional child born with dark features.

The culture and mythology of the tribe slowly evolved as well. Of course, nothing was written; everything was recorded mentally and repeated orally during the hours after dinner. Wisdom was in the form of stories with parables, and the stories improved over time. The tribe enjoyed listening to the storytellers. The flint workers often made tools while listening, and lovers snuggled while listening, but the most impressionable were the children. They absorbed everything, and their fertile imaginations improved the stories when they were asked to repeat what they had been told.

Some of the storytellers described the stars and the constellations and how brave mariners and hunters traveled using the mythological beings portrayed in the constellations; the stars served as visual aids, while the children looked at the night sky to see the wild and exotic characters.

Chapter 19

H1W2 In Ukraine

A pair of identical twin brothers was born to a chieftain of the Ice People, Wolf Killer, and his wife, Gray Dove, an H1W2 woman. It was assumed one of the sons might die in childhood or one would display the qualities of a chief. However, the boys were both clever and outstanding physical specimens. They loved one another, and they both wanted to be chief. When Wolf Killer lay on his deathbed, everyone expected him to choose between his twenty-five-year-old sons and name a successor, but he surprised everyone by asking each son to take half the tribe. One son was asked to remain in the Ukraine region, and the other was asked to migrate east toward the sunrise and discern the mystery of the sun and its daily appearance. The old chief loved his sons and didn't want them to ever war against each other.

The sons accepted the requests, and the tribe split. Both tribes were significant in the history of man, but the tribe that remained in Ukraine had a major effect. Like many of the tribes of this era, they liked to trap herd animals in blind canyons and slaughter the animals, as they were needed.

It was a boy and his sister who precipitated a significant change in the course of mankind, while observing a captured herd of wild horses. The children were fascinated with the horse herd and saw a foal being born. The boy, Green Apple, was ten years old, and his sister, Falling Star, who was eight, befriended the foal and encouraged it to come to them at the gate. The foal was curious, and in time, the newborn foal developed trust in the children, during its first few weeks of life. The dam was sickly and ostracized from the rest of the herd. She was barely able to keep the foal alive, but the children brought the choicest grasses for the foal to nibble, and he survived the first few months of life. The foal looked forward to seeing the children with their armloads of grass, and each day, the foal and the children grew closer to each other.

The colt was foaled in January, and by June; it was time for the tribe to follow the mammoths and mastodons. The gate was thrown open to let the surviving horses live another season, but the foal walked with his young human friends and ignored the other horses. The tribesmen were laughing at the strange sight of a foal walking along behind the boy and his sister, but Green Apple surprised everyone and changed the course of history, when he took off his and his sister's twenty-pound packs and placed them on each side of the foal's back and tied them around the foal's neck and under his ribs. The foal bucked a few strides, but quickly accepted the load, and began to walk behind the children once again.

Some of the hunters were mad to see the children without their packs and wanted to punish them, but the intuitive hunters were thinking about the possibility of training larger horses to carry much larger packs.

The idea of using a horse as a beast of burden was slower to catch on than the bow, probably because anyone can learn to use a bow, but there are certain physical abilities and mental qualities necessary for working with horses and using a horse effectively. Horsemanship is learned over time and built upon over generations. Eventually, the science of horsemanship evolved, and horses were trained with predictable results.

Using a horse to serve as a pack animal spread from Ukraine to Europe and Asia, but at some point in time, an adventurous human climbed on a tired packhorse's back and set in motion one of the biggest influencing factors in the history of mankind. Using the horse as a beast of burden, man made the drudgery of migration much easier, but riding the horse made movement much faster. Raiding, warfare, wagons, and agriculture were soon to follow the tracks of that first rider.

Chapter 20
Tiger Paw of Mongolia

Tiger Paw was born on the vast grasslands of Mongolia after a great battle with the copper-colored people. His father, Long Grass, became upset when his newborn son seemed to be stillborn. He carried the non-breathing infant to a stream of glacial runoff and held the baby under the ice cold water for a few seconds. When Long Grass lifted the baby out of the water, he was screaming with indignation. His father laughed and brought the baby up to his face to give him a hug. The baby continued to scream and was throwing his arms and kicking his legs to express his anger. His tiny sharp fingernails raked across the cheek of his father, drawing three faint red lines of blood. His father laughed and said, "He has the claws of a tiger; his name will be Tiger Paw."

The tribe members laughed and congratulated Chief Long Grass on his new son, Tiger Paw. They all agreed that he had the temper of a tiger; none of them mentioned the legend of the first son who drew blood from his father on the day of his birth, and later killed his father when he was grown. Such tales were surely legends, but every legend has its origin within a true story.

Tiger Paw was three when the Ice People walked through the land of the garlic eaters, now known as Korea. During their journey through Korea, Tiger Paw's mother weakened and died. This was life during the Ice Age; people often died young, leaving orphans. Long Grass chose Lotus, a pretty young Korean girl, to be Tiger Paw's surrogate mother. She was expected to take care of him as a full-time job. If he was hurt or became sick, she would be punished or killed.

Lotus was scared and unsure of what was expected of her or how to be a mother. She made up for a lack of knowledge by copying the actions of the hens watching over their chicks. She made sure Tiger Paw was washed each day and that he had the best food at every meal. She slept by his side and held him close during the cold nights. She had an ample bosom for a young girl, and Tiger Paw began to knead her breasts and suck on her nipples during the night, even when he was sleeping. At first the boy's insistent fondling of her young breasts was shocking, but she soon began to enjoy the sensations. In time, her breasts began to give milk, and they both enjoyed the close relationship. Eventually, she began to feel his little asparagus standing at attention during their nights. She laughed inwardly at the idea of a little boy becoming aroused, but she massaged his male member each night, until he drifted off to sleep.

During this period, Long Grass and his tribe saw the sleek sailing boats of the Shark Eaters (Japanese) sailing on the horizon, and they wanted the technology. With the help of local builders, they built canoes with crude square sails to cross the narrow sea separating Korea from the land of the Shark Eaters.

The crossing was uneventful; they had a favorable wind that carried them across the narrow passage very quickly. However, the fact that Long Grass and his hunters survived in a violent culture that hated foreigners was remarkable.

Long Grass was a huge man who carried himself with arrogance, but he was diplomatic and loved to put on shows of pomp and circumstance. Whether it was luck or Long Grass's flamboyant personality is hard to say, but he and his tribe thrived in the land of the Shark Eaters for over a year. Long Grass was losing hunters to farmers and fishermen with beautiful daughters, but he was acquiring carpenters, boat builders, and scholars, who were often vagabonds, in need of a source of protein. The Shark Eaters had a unique class of navigators and pilots who knew celestial navigation and the currents of the North Pacific. Long Grass acquired two of these men through purchase, and another one asked to join the tribe to avoid periodic starvation. Long Grass also acquired several new women for his harem.

When he told his Shark Eater pilots and navigators about his desire to build a big boat and a fleet of smaller fishing boats with the latest technology, they advised him to sail to the coast of Siberia; they knew of a forested area with many mammoths and mastodons and no warlords who would kill them for cutting trees to build a boat.

Long Grass and his reconstituted tribe found the southern coast of Siberia to be a hunter's paradise. There were a variety of trees, and the carpenters could select different trees for the various parts of the boats. They spent three years building the fleet. The tribe grew stronger, with small bands of migrating hunters who joined for the security of a strong tribe and because they liked the flamboyant personality of Long Grass.

The Mammoth Hunters or Ice People as they were sometimes called, had grown from a tribe of sixty people to a tribe of over two hundred when they sailed along the southern coast of Beringia. (The ice-free landmass that was exposed between Siberia and Alaska.)

The carpenters and ship builders used pine and cedar to make the light, strong, fast fishing boats, but the most important features were the fir keels and oak framing. The keel on the biggest boat extended four feet into the water and was eight inches thick at the hull. The mast was eighteen feet and used a gaff rig to maximize the sail's exposure to the wind. The carpenters advised against a taller sail because the trees were only big enough to make a four-foot keel; put up too much sail in a squall and the boat would be upside down. The ballast consisted of small boulders, sand, and gravel on the floor to help stabilize the boat and keep it sitting deep in the water. Tiger Paw trusted the judgment of his boat builders, and he loved the power and speed of the fishing boats.

The food was varied because of the many different herds migrating between Asia and North America, and the fishing was excellent in the protein rich waters of the North Pacific. Beringia facilitated the migration of millions of animals and tens of thousands of humans traveling between Alaska and Siberia.

Tiger Paw turned ten, just before the tribe was scheduled to leave Siberia. In the middle of the night, his father came to his bed and said, "You no longer need a nursemaid, little man. She's mine now."

His father pulled Lotus out of Tiger Paw's bed and dragged her half-naked form to his own bed. He proceeded to ravage her in front of many members of the tribe. Tiger Paw watched with hatred and anger burning deep in his heart.

Tiger Paw was humiliated by his father's actions, but at ten years of age, he was helpless to object. He wanted to kill his father, and if he had the ability, his father would be dead. It was a mistake of leadership and of fatherhood, and Long Grass would live to regret it.

Lotus accepted and appreciated the privileges associated with being a wife of the chief and began to respond to the brutish sexual habits of Long Grass. She acted condescendingly toward Tiger Paw and treated him as if he was still a small child; soon, he learned to hate Lotus as well.

They left Siberia with many new members, including a group of teenage girls. Tiger Paw found comfort in sleeping with the young girls, even though he had not matured sexually; at ten years of age, his smile and loving personality, along with a willingness to please rather than take, gave several of the girls the security they needed. He was popular among the girls, but was actually searching for the love he had lost with the loss of two mothers.

There was camaraderie in the tribe, and for ten years it was a happy group, until Long Grass decided he wanted Tiger Paw's latest girl friend. He made his move when Tiger Paw was outside relieving himself. Tiger Paw walked into the lodge to see his father slap his girl and rip her clothes from her body and pry her legs apart. Tiger Paw grabbed a heavy stabbing spear and swung it hard and struck his father with the sharp edge of the flint across the ear. The top part of his ear hesitated for a moment and then fell on his shoulder, followed by a flow of blood. Long Grass picked up a spear and marveled that his son didn't kill him when he had the opportunity. He looked his son in the eye for a few seconds and then rushed forward with a spear aimed at Tiger Paw's belly. Tiger Paw swung away on his left foot and swung the spear once again and sliced through the throat of his father with the razor edge of the flint spear point. Long Grass dropped his spear and grabbed his throat with both hands. It was a futile effort; there was no way to stop his life's blood from flowing away. He looked at Tiger Paw and said, "You're still mad at me for dipping you in the glacial water."

Tiger Paw stared at his father with contempt. In a few minutes, Long Grass dropped to his knees and fell to the earthen floor, to bleed out and die. Everyone in the lodge was looking at Tiger Paw with shocked expressions. Tiger Paw had killed his own father. Long Grass was a popular chief of a strong tribe. A chief who kept a large tribe alive and well fed in a dangerous world. Tiger Paw looked back with confidence and said, "Get him out of here. I am your chief now, unless someone wants to challenge me."

Several young men dragged Long Grass' body out into a winter storm and left him for the scavengers. In a few days, his bones were scattered and gnawed upon by many animals.

After the noon meal, Tiger Paw called a meeting. He was strong and wise beyond his twenty years. There were several older men who might qualify to be chief; thus Tiger Paw had to assert a right of primogeniture. There were no official rights of inheritance for leadership among these hunters; strong men were often groomed for positions of leadership, but in the end, it was the strongest man to challenge the chief or convince an old man to step aside. It was a precarious time. Tribes could split up with factions, to follow different leaders.

The tribal members didn't want to break up the tribe. There were family members and close friends they might never see again. If the older men were willing to accept Tiger Paw as chief, there would probably be no problems. He would be given a chance to prove himself. If he made stupid decisions and the tribe suffered, he might die a violent death in the near future.

Tiger Paw was not just a hunter; he lived to hunt. He had been the best hunter for several years, but he liked fishing as well. At night, he enjoyed making the women laugh during the call of the wild. He took pride in never failing to answer the call of the wild, if called upon. He had twelve kids who were probably his. They ranged in age from five to a few months. Most of them would live to be adults and produce children of their own. He was proud of producing strong offspring who wanted to survive from the time they started to breathe air. It was not that long ago, babies were born weak and indifferent to life. He took pride in feeding his kids and their mothers; of course, these successful hunters and fishermen were considered a rich tribe, and it was easy to provide food to the women and children.

Tiger Paw believed death should be faced with dignity; he maintained that a human who lay shivering, weak, and afraid to die was one of the most pathetic images in the world. A chief was expected to make hard decisions, and he often euthanized the weak and cowardly. He was not expected to be a smiling politician. It was his job to make sure the tribe survived.

They had several dedicated flint strikers who could select the best flint rocks and begin working them with granite stones to make the various awls, knives, scrapers, harpoon heads, spearheads, fish hooks, and arrowheads the people needed to survive.

The hunters came back to camp with stories of finding small bands of people who were starving and of how they carried inferior stone tools. Their spearheads were bulky and not sharp, and their arrowheads were unbalanced and too heavy. Hunters often found examples of poor craftsmanship in these camps and shook their heads at the absurdity of trying to survive with inferior tools.

Tiger Paw continued the traditions of his tribe by reciting the oral history of the Mammoth Hunters or Ice People as they were also called: In the beginning, when the first men walked the earth, they were always hungry in the winter. They were so hungry, they were too weak to answer the call of the wild, and they didn't produce enough babies to grow a strong tribe. The Mammoth Father saw them struggle and realized how sad the people were. He taught them how to make the best tools and how to hunt the big beasts that live along the frontiers of the ice and how to follow the migrating herds, across the lands of the little dark-eyed people and across the land of plenty called Beringia. The Mammoth Father loved his people and taught them that each animal's brain is large enough to tan its own hide. He taught the women to love the hunters and enjoy the call of the wild at night, so the tribe would always be blessed with little ones to carry on the traditions of the Mammoth Hunters.

The Mammoth Father, in his wisdom, gave the tribe groups of little people, and it was a blessing. The early chiefs had doubts whether the little people were human, when they first saw them. They were tiny and had dark eyes that were shaped differently, but they were ingenious people with nimble fingers. Several of the women joined the early chief's harem, and he considered them to be exotic. He loved his wives and made time for all six of them.

The reasoning was essentially correct, concerning the oral history of the tribe, but their concept of time was incapable of comprehending the enormity of the tribe's migration over generations; they spent ten thousand years on the steppe of Southern Russia and Northern Asia, before migrating onto the southern coast of Beringia.

Tiger Paw needed to adjust his logic, because the science of navigation was in conflict with the old legends. The Mammoth Hunters had believed for thousands of years, the sun refueled and rested every night before beginning its long trek across the sky from East to West. During the winter, the sun was too cold to be out all day, so the nights were longer, with more time to answer the call of the wild with his wife, the moon. The sun was like the hunter; if the sun didn't get enough rest after laughing with his woman, he couldn't function properly the next day. Unfortunately, the moon was making extra demands on her husband or he was getting weaker, since the ice was over a mile high and covering several man strides of new land every day.

The idea of the sun's fuel source being in the east kept the Mammoth Hunters moving eastward. For thousands of years, they kept migrating to the east, always east, following the herds. They often made their lodges from the bones and skulls of the mammoths and packed the cracks with moss and grass and covered the top with the hide of mammoths and mastodons. The smoke from the cook fires tanned the fresh hides and made them waterproof. In the summer they used clay mud to plug the cracks. The length of time they spent at a campsite depended on how long the big animals stayed in the area.

Hunting the big animals was extremely dangerous. Men who were trying to spear them had to get close, and the speed of the big animals was as sudden and fast as the Cave Lion or the Cave Bear. The big tusks would swing, and if a man didn't anticipate the movement, he was broken by the tusks and crushed beneath the feet of the mammoth. Mammoth hunters were considered among the most awesome hunters, since most hunters were afraid to hunt the big animals.

The Mammoth Hunters needed an advantage to kill these big beasts. It was easier to kill a bull that had been injured by the tusks of another bull, but hunters could wait a long time for such advantages. The techniques were old, but they were always being improved upon. The men would find the trails to salt licks and feeding grounds. Here, they would use sharp wooden stakes with a flint barb set into the body of the shaft. Being on three legs slowed the mammoths down, but when the men heard the animal bellowing in rage and pain, they implemented the next phase of the trap. A large tree or log was laid out near the stake, with several lariats tied around the log. The men would rope the legs or tusks and let the animal become ensnared in the ropes. They would then run in with their spears and stab with a forward thrust, just behind the last ribs and into the diaphragm. Once this area was speared, it was only a matter of time before the animal dropped to his knees and the hunters speared the neck area to try to cut through the arteries. A full-grown bull weighed as much as a school bus (twenty thousand pounds) and stood over ten feet tall at the withers; a mammoth could feed a large tribe for several months.

Once the animal was down, the laborious work began. They had to butcher the animal and transport the meat, organs, hide, sinew, and even the bones back to their lodges before the very dangerous scavengers, including other humans, moved in to claim the carcass.

There were hostile tribes and periods of disease and famine, but the Mammoth Hunters kept moving east, to find the mysterious source of energy and heat.

It is a simple concept, but migrating hunters and fishermen were less likely to suffer from the ravages of cholera and dysentery, when following the herds. The herds were searching for grass, and the tribes followed. They often made camps for longer periods in the winter. The frigid temperatures of winter also decreased the transmission of disease.

Sedentary tribes without cultural customs for contending with human waste or garbage were often destined to die of disease. Strong tribes with advanced cultural norms viewed the weaker tribes with inadequate hygiene as being unclean and often killed them to prevent the spread of disease.

During the migration of the Mammoth People, they often acquired the customs of advanced cultures from the women they traded for, and the occasional lost hunter they adopted. Tiger Paw accepted the tribal legends of his father and repeated them when children or adults came to him with questions about life and the origin of the tribe. It was important for him to be recognized as a wise man. He believed the Mammoth Hunters were the only true people walking the earth, but he understood the advantages of learning new technology and customs from the strangers who came into their lives, but more importantly, he understood the importance of vitality derived from the bloodlines of new tribal members.

They continued to migrate to the east, onto the coastline land that was to become Alaska. His people knew and understood the grasslands; life flourished there, but for some reason, the herds were moving into the land that was destined to become the Yukon and south following the ice-free corridor in the center of British Columbia, and on into the rest of the Americas.

For many years, the hunters followed the migrating herds, and the fishermen worked the fertile coastal waters of southern Alaska, but securing food became increasingly harder. The lazy and useless tribal members were considered to be unnecessary mouths to feed and were driven away to perish in a harsh land. The old and feeble were expected to wander away on their own, if they had dignity. The weak died along the way. This was a harsh land, and survival was a continual struggle. Supporting nonproductive people was not an option. Infanticide was sometimes necessary to manage the number of mouths to feed, especially in the winter, when food supplies ran low.

Chapter 21
Mysteries of Life

Nine generations back placed Yellow Hair's first father in the time of Ogalalla, the Great Whale Mother. She gave birth to the father of all men, and all the creatures of the earth.

His distant father was the first and only human to slide through the birth canal of the Great Whale Mother. He swam to shore and began the human race; therefore, Yellow Hair's birthright was one of leadership and semi-divinity. He couldn't explain the first woman, the bloodlines of other people, or even those in his tribe. He forbade people from asking frivolous questions, since some questions complicate the story of the beginning. If you accept the basic premise of the story, everything was logical.

Barbaric tribes with huge warriors and well-made weapons ventured into the traditional lands of the Salmon People and brought many wondrous goods to trade for the smoked salmon that was making the Salmon People famous.

Trade was good for the Salmon People, but Yellow Hair noticed men counting how many hunters the Salmon Tribe could muster. Yellow Hair hoped his strong and healthy-looking warriors intimidated those who were camping dangerously close to the Salmon hunting and fishing grounds.

These interlopers were a constant worry for Yellow Hair, but he needed to be concerned with the day-to-day problems of survival.

Winter storms were unpredictable. Consequently, it was dangerous to fish the salt waters beyond the coastal waters during the winter months. If they ventured too far out on the salt waters, on a warm winter's day, the skies were often too gray to see approaching storms; they had been lucky to make it home on several occasions.

Yellow Hair and his younger half brother, Caribou Calf, were boys when they learned celestial navigation from Blood Eel. The boys could navigate using the stars or the sun and the sun's lover the moon, but the celestial bodies were often hiding during the winter. Yellow Hair and Caribou Calf accepted the logic of the sun and moon making love during the winter to stay warm. The sun and moon had already given birth to so many new baby stars and thrown them out in the sky—it was impossible to count them. They were a lusty couple, always ready to make love and let the resultant storms rage in winter or summer. When the boys grew into men, they couldn't get mad at the sun and his wife, the moon, for making love; however, when storms raged for weeks at a time, they sometimes asked the sun and moon politely to stop lusting and baby-making, long enough to slow the storms of winter and let them catch fish.

They rarely ventured out on the salt waters in winter, unless they saw whales or schools of salmon close to shore. If the windstorms started and they couldn't see the shore, they relied on dead reckoning (an innate sense of direction). If they made a mistake with dead reckoning, while in the gray void, the fishermen might never see their women and babies, and a watery grave would be their new home.

The Salmon hunters knew the migration routes of the caribou because the Whale Mother taught Yellow Hair's fathers where and how to trap them over the generations. However, Caribou Calf had an extra sense for predicting the different migration paths the caribou would use each year.

Most tribes speared caribou in the traditional way, by hunting animals on the outer perimeter of the herd. The hunters always killed a few caribou, but it was extremely dangerous. If hunters misjudged, they could be trapped and ground to pulp by the sharp hooves of a stampeding herd. Migrating caribou are a mindless mass of animals, rushing like the water of a fast-moving mountain stream.

Caribou Calf studied the lichens, (the food of the caribou), checked the depth of snowfall and the depth of the icy streams during several days of concentration. When the herds drew near, he kept his ear to the ground, and next to certain trees he called listening trees. Suddenly, he would start shouting out instructions for the construction of the trap, and logs were tied to trees to gradually force or haze some of the animals into a blind canyon (only one entry) with steep walls. A gate was built of stout logs that could be closed when the caribou were inside the canyon.

The herds numbered a hundred thousand or more; the trap was designed to capture a very small portion of the herd. When the canyon filled to capacity (fifty to a hundred animals), the gate was closed and the Salmon Tribe had a supply of fresh meat for the winter. It was foolish to trap more than the canyon could feed, because the animals would begin to starve and they would need to butcher all of them immediately. It was far better to have fewer animals that remained healthy over the winter.

This year they secured their corral early. The men were happy and joking while they secured the gate. One of the young bulls ran at the gate and tried to jump over the logs and landed on top of the gate, breaking a hind leg.

Yellow Hair and Caribou Calf stayed to butcher the bull and told the young men to prepare the winter lodge. Using his flint knife, Caribou Calf cut the bull's neck. After the bull had bled out, he pulled him off the gate, and into a tree, with a rawhide rope tied to the hind legs. While the bull was hanging upside down, it was eviscerated, and the internal organs were dumped on the ground.

Four young females walked up to the hunters and began begging for food. Yellow Hair motioned toward the gut pile. With crude knives, they hacked at the liver, heart, lungs, and intestine. The women were starving and didn't care if they had blood and gore on their faces and hands; they needed the life-giving nutrients of the internal organs. One of the females had a length of intestine, and while she squeezed the contents out of one end, she was continuously swallowing the other end.

Yellow Hair watched them eat like starving wolves and was thankful he and his tribe had never been reduced to such a pathetic level of existence.

When they had finished eating and their bellies were swollen, the women rolled on the snow and ice with severe bellyaches. Yellow Hair had the young men bring a skin sack of fresh water.

The women were from a tribe that abstained from bathing, which was obvious—they were filthy. Yellow Hair was a stickler for health and hygiene, insisting that everyone participate in a ritual bath at least every seven days.

Yellow Hair instructed his men to strip the women one at a time and bathe them. There was nothing remotely sexual in the procedure; Yellow Hair had to conduct an examination, before the women could be considered for adoption.

There was no need in taking in lost people, if they were going to make his tribe sick. Two of the women were in their late teens and seemed to be healthy enough for birthing. Their bodies were well formed, with wide hips and good-sized teats. The young women screamed in protest, while being washed, but the men continued as if they couldn't hear the anguished cries. An older woman of thirty was dripping a foul discharge from her nether region, and Yellow Hair looked at his brother Caribou Calf and shook his head, no. Caribou Calf stepped forward and swung a club imbedded with sharp pieces of flint into the woman's temple, and her life's essence was gone in an instant. Caribou Calf and Yellow Hair's son, Fast Fish, dragged the dead woman to the beach. The crabs and various sea animals made short work of her body.

Fast Fish admired his father for letting the woman die with a full belly; his father was not only a wise man, he was a kind man, who had compassion for those who are less fortunate.

The next female was an immature girl with exotic features. She kept saying "Ca-bu" instead of the universal word for caribou. She was small, but fought like a brown bear cub to keep her clothes on. The boys stripped her down, and when they bathed her, she elicited primal screams, as if she were being skinned alive. Yellow Hair conducted his physical exam and wondered if she had ever bathed in her life. She had blonde hair, and her eyes were almost blue and almost green. Her facial features were exotic. He looked at her nether regions and surmised that she was an intact young girl. Her legs had a light covering of furry blonde hair, and the blonde hair on her head reached her buttocks. He surmised that she was a result of crossbreeding with a Near Human (Neanderthal). Many tribes would consider her an abomination; the product of an illicit coupling with a being that wasn't quite human. Yellow Hair liked her and smiled at the boys as he handed her the filthy skins she had been wearing, and let her get dressed.

Yellow Hair had no way to know, but the crossbred Near Human girl carried the H1W2 mitochondrial DNA of his early ancestors.

Women had a valuable purpose among these Stone Age tribes, but women didn't survive as well as men, and often the tribes had to trade meat or fish for young, healthy women. Some tribes raided other tribes to steal women and children, but the Salmon Tribe was not a band of barbarians. They had plenty of food and a level of sophistication never seen along the ice. If they needed women, they would trade for them or adopt them.

The boys used sign language, and told the women to help clean up the winter lodge. The females began to trust the Salmon men; however, the younger girl never left the side of Yellow Hair. She held on to the bottom of his parka and walked with him everywhere.

When he hunted or fished, she watched every move he made and copied it in a near perfect imitation of whatever work he was doing. If he was gutting fish, she watched him gut three or four, and then began gutting fish beside him. She was a clever girl, but she would always have a problem speaking. Cabu became her name, and she smiled each time the tribal members spoke it. She was the official shadow of Yellow Hair, even on cloudy days. She slept at the foot of his bed and never covered herself with a blanket, even on the coldest nights.

Four years later, Cabu had matured and was helping a work party of women gather firewood, when three teenage boys accosted the group of twenty women with plans to steal them. The Salmon men were out on the salt water, towing in a whale they had killed. They left two old men to guard the women, but the boys stuck the old men with several arrows and stabbed them with spears to finish them. The boys were scared and moving quickly to get the women's hands tied, connecting them all as a group with a rope around their necks. When one of the boys stooped to tie Cabu's hands, she reached beneath her shirt, pulled out a stone war ax (they weren't sharp like an iron ax, but had rounded edges for delivering a lethal blow or crushing nuts and roots), and slammed it into the skull and brain of the teenager. He fell dead without knowing he was dying. A second boy was standing a few feet away, holding his spear in a vertical position; he was shocked when he saw his friend die and was unable to move. Cabu stepped forward to bury the ax in his forehead and he died with a shocked expression of disbelief. He dropped to his knees, and Cabu struggled to free the ax from the dead boy's skull. The third boy turned to run, as Cabu jerked her ax free. He was thirty feet away, when Cabu threw her ax. It struck him in the spine, and he fell to the ground in agony. He looked up to see Cabu running toward him with a piece of firewood in her hand, a piece big enough to brain him, he jumped up and ran.

When the men towed the whale to shore, they wondered why the women weren't on the shore celebrating.

They found the women cowering in the lodge, with Cabu standing guard outside with her ax. Yellow Hair listened to the story and looked at the dead boys. He shook his head at the audacity of the boys and the courage of Cabu.

Yellow Hair told his warriors to take the dead boys off shore, and tie rocks to their feet and necks, before throwing them to the sharks and turtles. Yellow Hair got ready to run the third boy down before the boy had a chance to tell his tribe how the Salmon Tribe had mistreated him. Yellow Hair knew the third boy was hurt from Cabu's ax, and he planned to track him and kill him by nightfall. He told the rest of the tribe to start butchering the whale and yelled at the women to stop cowering in fear and help the men.

Yellow Hair turned to leave and found Cabu holding onto his shirt. "Do you think you can keep up?" he asked her.

It was easier to nod her head than to answer.

"All right, but remember, I don't slow down for anyone."

She smiled and nodded again.

Without another word, Yellow Hair took off running, following the tracks and signs left by the boy. He would point at every sign or track along the trail. Cabu was behind him, running fast and easy.

The boy was in pain and couldn't travel in a straight line. Yellow Hair was a powerful runner, and little Cabu managed to stay with him, but more importantly, she was learning how to track and follow sign.

It was nearly three hours later when they found him. The boy had built a fire and was hoping to get his stiff and aching back to relax with the heat. Yellow Hair signaled to Cabu to wait, and he began sneaking up on the boy. Cabu lost sight of Yellow Hair, and she held her stone ax to her chest, just in case she was needed. She could see the boy's head in the firelight, and he looked like he was stretching his back, trying to get the spasms and pain to stop.

Suddenly, a shadow moved, and the boy was no longer visible. She heard the sound of a quail calling, but quail don't call at night; she jumped up and ran to the fire. Both the boy's arms were broken. The elbow of his right arm was bent the wrong way, and the bones, above the left wrist, were protruding through the skin of his left arm. He was in pain and crying softly next to the fire.

Cabu looked at the boy and then at Yellow Hair; she admired her hero even more. Cabu smiled and wondered what would happen next. Yellow Hair opened up his right hand toward the boy and nodded. Cabu stepped forward and swung her ax with a powerful right hand, and the boy's life essence was gone. They buried the fire under dirt, and Yellow Hair carried the dead boy to a cliff above a cave occupied by a family of brown bears, and dropped the boy's body over the cliff in front of the cave. The bears heard the noise and walked outside to investigate. The body would be eaten before the sun finished making love to his wife, the moon.

When they arrived back at the lodge, they had a tasty meal of whale blubber steam-cooked with fish and onions in a caribou stomach. The tribe wanted to hear the story over and over, and Cabu seemed to enjoy it as much as everyone else, but deep inside, Yellow Hair knew his tribe was in trouble. If the other tribes were sending boys to steal women, it wouldn't be long before they would be challenged for possession of their hunting and fishing territory. Caribou Calf and Fast Fish were strong and smart, but they lacked the killer instinct a warrior needs. The old men who had been killed that day had been strong hunters, but for the last few years, they were nearly useless. Yellow Hair wondered what had happened to his tribe. The young boys often talked and acted like girls. When they killed an occasional mammoth, the mature hunters sometimes acted like boys who were becoming men. His men were strong, and they liked to rut at night, but that is only a small part of being a hunter. A hunter should be fearless, strong, and capable of responding to immediate danger without becoming excited. When he was a young man, he grew tired of the tyranny of his father and challenged him to a fight to the death for control of the tribe. He killed his father, Blood Eel, but his father seemed glad to give control to a son who was brave and capable. None of these young boys would challenge him to fight to the death; not until he was frail like the two old men who were killed today.

After the story time was over, Yellow Hair cleaned his teeth with a wooden pick and went outside for a walk. He climbed up on a small glacier to get a good look at the countryside. He heard noises and braced for an attack, but it was only Cabu, following him. He held out his arms, and she rushed into his embrace. They had a deep bond of affection.

Yellow Hair said, "I am so proud of you, Cabu. You saved our women, and single-handedly, you killed two warriors. You are a good little Salmon woman."

Cabu didn't like to be reminded of her short stature, but Yellow Hair was her hero, and he could do no wrong in her eyes. She looked up at him with a big smile and said, "Cabu, goo waryer too-day."

Yellow Hair looked at her and smiled. He had heard the Near People couldn't speak well. He and everyone in the tribe understood her speech, but visitors from other tribes often made fun of her and the probability of her tainted blood. Yellow Hair's stern expression always stopped the hateful derision; especially after the insensitive person realized they might die, in the next few seconds, for making fun of this crossbred person.

The tribe only needed a few thousand words and a few different clicks and grunts, but when it was combined with sign language, their language became a complex and effective system of communication.

Yellow Hair held Cabu next to him and said, "Cabu, do you see the lights from those campfires? Each campfire has warriors who would like to steal our land and take you away from me. I am getting old, and we must make plans for the future."

Cabu's smile disappeared, and she looked down and started crying. "Don't cry, Cabu; I was thinking out loud. We will work this out and everything will be good." He was lying, but he hoped Cabu believed him.

Yellow Hair kept his thoughts to himself. *The tribes are encroaching on our hunting and fishing grounds. They are unfit to live on these fertile grounds. Many of them have light blue and green eyes and suffer from the rays of the sun bouncing off the water in summer, and they don't have bathing rituals in the freshwater streams running off the glaciers. Their ignorance of the traditions of his fathers made them unworthy. These strangers were weaklings, but they hunted the mammoths, and they were dangerous.*

Yellow Hair knew he was different. He carried the seed of the first human, but it was this first human's lusty ways and weakness for the women of the forests and mountains that had produced the excess humans, the people who wanted the rich resources of the Salmon Tribe.

Yellow Hair hated weakness and had little sympathy for anyone who showed signs of weakness. He had seen weakness in his father and challenged him to a fight for leadership of the tribe and for possession of the princess his father had just married.

He killed his father, claimed his father's possessions, and his wives as his own. His father had been physically strong, until his last day, but it was his moral weaknesses that irritated Yellow Hair.

His former stepmother, who was now his wife, was beautiful and inflamed Yellow Hair's libido to the point of madness, but after the fight, it became obvious she was carrying his father's child. She gained too much weight during the pregnancy and never lost the fat after giving birth. Yellow Hair lost interest in her, though she had been the main reason he challenged his father. Yellow Hair acquired new wives among the other tribes, often trading a caribou carcass for a healthy wife. Many wives died in childbirth or from the cold; it was hard to find a durable wife who was attractive, could tell stories and sing at night, and survive childbirth.

Yellow Hair thought of Cabu. She was tougher than most of his young men. She was indirectly from the tribes called Near People. They were probably born from the early men coupling with some kind of animal. In the early days, some men hunted them for sport, but the Near People were gone now.

Cabu was probably a quarter Neanderthal; she had the traits. Supposedly, the Near People couldn't speak words like a normal human. They mainly used grunts and clicks to communicate. Their language was complicated and nearly impossible to learn, so they weren't stupid. The men ran like pregnant women, and they couldn't handle complex weapons like the bow or the atlatl (spear thrower), but they could crush a human by using their bear hug. They made excellent flint knives and scrapers, and their spearheads were works of art, their cave paintings were some of the best, but their spear shafts were heavy and designed for stabbing the big animals.

He had heard it was best to shoot arrows or spears into them from a distance; they died slowly, with dignity, but if they managed to get ahold of you before they died, you would pass over the divide ahead of them. Cabu proved all the old theories wrong; she could do everything as well or better than the rest of the tribe, everything but talk.

Yellow Hair adopted Cabu into the tribe because he thought she was cute, but now she was becoming a mature woman, and needed a mate. This wasn't going to be easy. Yellow Hair was her hero, and she had never been interested in boys her own age, but Yellow Hair thought nature would take its course and she would find a strong young man.

In the middle of the night, Yellow Hair awoke to one of his wives exploring his nether region. He was exhausted after running down the boy and then walking over the glacier after dinner, but if one of his wives wanted to have a little fun with his root, he didn't care, as long as he wasn't called on to do any work, not tonight.

For a few seconds, he thought of the early days when he was a boy and the tribe asked why he called his male member his root. He told them it was because a man's member was like the root of a plant or tree that reaches into the earth for security and sustenance, and when everything is right, a beautiful seedling will grow. The tribe laughed and called him a storyteller and a poet, but he handled the kidding well. He remembered those early days; today, no one laughed at Yellow Hair—no one dared.

Yellow Hair drifted off to sleep, to be wakened by a noise like the purring of a lion or tiger. A woman had impaled herself on his root and was riding up and down the length while making this strange noise. The fire had gone out, and the cave was in total darkness. The woman had her back to him, and he didn't know who it was, but this was not good. They all lived in the same lodge and they coupled in front of each other, but changing mates caused problems, and usually the woman was traded to another tribe if she wanted a different man.

Yellow Hair reached up and grabbed the woman by the shoulders and pulled her down to see who was making the strange noises.

Her noises became louder and more desperate as he pulled her back against his chest. The change of angle and pressure excited her past the point of no return, and she began a powerful series of orgasms. A hot liquid ran down Yellow Hair's belly and between his thighs, and he began his orgasm as well, while looking into the strained face of his beloved Cabu.

When the spasms were over, she began a slow rocking movement and lifted herself to her former position. It felt wonderful to Yellow Hair, but he had to think about this new development. He made her stop and signaled her to move down to her usual place at the foot of his bed.

Cabu didn't listen this time; she stood up, naked, and walked outside. She swam in the icy waters of the creek and came back into the lodge, soaking wet. She lay down at the foot of the bed, but a few minutes later, she crawled under the covers to hug and kiss the legs of her hero.

He felt her against his legs, hugging him tightly, breathing on his belly, and he had to admit her warmth felt good, but he was the moral guide for the tribe and he was in a dilemma: he was too old for Cabu, and he had always considered himself as her guardian, not her lover. She was different, and it was doubtful any of the younger men would choose her as a wife, but what kind of future could an old man over forty offer a young woman, and what if she had a child?

He had ruled with a flint fist since he was twenty-five, and he alone, decided all questions of morality, but this time, the chief was stumped. Few men lived to be forty-five; yet, Yellow Hair was the strongest man in the tribe. Most men were useless old men after forty and were expected to wander away during the next period of famine. How could he expect to care for a child born through the seed of his root to the essence of Cabu?

These questions bothered him, but right now, she was using her fingers to play with his root and touching it against her lips. When she sucked it into her mouth, it attained its full strength. He forgot his problems and enjoyed the sensations of the moment. When his hips began to move automatically and he started to breathe deeply, she moved up on him and sat down slowly on his root. When it was fully imbedded, she hesitated to savor the intensity of being filled completely with Yellow Hair's root. She leaned forward and placed her hands on the bed next to his shoulders and began a movement of just her hips, a back and forth motion that caressed the length of his root while she began making a cat's loud purring sound in the back of her throat.

Yellow Hair closed his eyes and entered the unknown; a realm not unlike sailing into the thick fog, where nothing else matters. Cabu felt the searing heat of his copious emission wash over the entrance to her womb; she felt the life force of his body enter hers and knew they had started a child. With both hands, she embraced his back to begin her orgasm. After one more hard downward thrust of her hips, an eerie, high-pitched sound began deep in Cabu's throat. It was a primal scream you would expect to hear from an animal in the final agonies of death. It woke up everyone in the lodge; the men, children, and non-sensual females thought Cabu was having a bad dream, but the sexually aware women knew Cabu was locked deep in the throes of passion, dancing on the edge of the cliff between life and death.

Yellow Hair heard the noise but was more concerned with the possibility of Cabu crushing his chest with the grip of her powerful arms. He knew women were often more powerful than men during passion, but had never thought one might crush his ribs and squeeze the life out of him.

The height of her passion lasted for just over a minute and it was over, but

Yellow Hair would show the signs of purple and black bruising on his chest and back for several days.

The next morning, Cabu was happier than ever and seemed to have more confidence, but Yellow Hair was distracted and deeply conflicted in a personal crisis.

Over the next few days, the tribe accepted the coupling of Cabu and Yellow Hair, but his other wives asked that the two of them confine their sexual activities to the glaciers and the forests; the rest of the tribe was losing sleep because of Cabu's passion.

When the days were the shortest and the winter storms were getting ready to blow, Cabu started to show a swelling of her belly. The tribe had another corral of caribou, a pit of fermented salmon, and a supply of smoked salmon, but the barbarians were watching.

Chapter 22

A Severe Winter

The Mammoth Hunters often made temporary winter camps near the carcass of a mastodon or several sea lions or maybe several camels. They needed to camp near the meat to protect it from, lions, tigers, bears, ravens, buzzards, bald eagles, and coyotes. The scavengers were all thieves, and if the Mammoth Hunters didn't stand guard over the carcass, it would soon disappear. It was not as easy as it sounds; they also needed to guard their fleet of sailing canoes from theft and from being damaged by storms.

Killing a large mastodon could mean survival through the winter, but unless the animals were mired in a bog or suffering from a severe lameness, it was far too dangerous to try to kill a healthy animal; even when they were mired in a bog, it took hours to kill a mammoth, and sometimes hunters were killed in the process.

Sea lions were also dangerous to kill; despite their appearance, they can move much faster than a man can run, sometimes faster than the eye can see. Many a fisherman has been killed carrying a stringer of fish along the salt-water sea. A sea lion will watch from under water and suddenly run up on shore to kill the man and steal the fish in less than an instant.

The best way to hunt the sea lion was for a group of hunters to sneak up on him while he was sunning himself on a ledge beneath the hunters. The hunters would send a fusillade of arrows at the heart and lung area. The best spear throwers would throw the heavy spear with a flint tip at the same area, and a javelin thrower would toss the smaller, lighter spear with a smaller tip, hoping to get deep penetration through a tough hide and layers of blubber. If the spear throwers weren't accurate, the animal would run for the ocean and disappear with a fortune in flint arrow points and spear points. Sometimes the sea lions would turn to fight, they had no fear of humans; the spear throwers would run closer for a better chance of throwing another lethal spear, while the bowmen unleashed a steady stream of arrows. If someone rushed the sea lion too soon, figuring the creature was crippled, the man could be crushed by several tons of enraged sea lion or have the long ivory tusks, used to work the ocean floor for mussels and clams, rip into the man and tear him apart as fast as the cave bear or cave lion.

Wild horses were among the most dangerous animals because of their frantic resistance to being caught. In their panic, they would jump over obstacles and run over men without hesitation. If a man was too close, they could kick or strike with any of their four legs and bite with a force strong enough to break bones, or throw a man into the air, or slam him against a tree.

Hunting was always a balance between acquiring sustenance for survival and being killed by the animals. The Ice People understood the risk, and they enjoyed the hunt, but this winter was different. The winter was pushing the animals off Beringia and deep into British Columbia. The animals were migrating south, and the hunting tribes had to follow or die.

Fishermen faced dangers, from monsters of the deep and the weather. They sailed in open boats on a sea of frequent storms. Sometimes they were blown out to sea for several days, but these intrepid fishermen usually made it home. In its last storm, the big boat made it home, only to be thrown against the breakers. The boat was destroyed, and all twelve men were drowned; during the same storm, one of the smaller boats was blown out to sea and never seen again. Five more men were lost.

The death of seventeen men was a tremendous loss for the tribe. It meant widows and a small herd of children had no direct providers. Young men weren't usually interested in older women, especially when they had children, and in fairness, older women weren't interested in young men as husbands.

Tiger Paw would try to coerce some of the older men to take on another wife with children, but it wasn't easy. Providing for others was a big responsibility for a hunter and a matter of pride. He would need to hunt or fish longer to be sure his large family was fed. Most men enjoyed hunting and fishing, but when the winds howled and the temperatures dropped to forty below or colder, there was no fun.

In Tiger Paw's band of hunters, everyone had to contribute with meaningful work or be banished, or possibly executed, by Tiger Paw. Life was a precious gift, but the nature of living next to the ice made it imperative that everyone must work to ensure survival of the tribe. When the fish got lost and didn't return to their rivers and creeks in sufficient numbers, or the caribou were tired and decided not to migrate, the old, frail people were expected to walk alone into the night and not return. Infanticide was practiced to keep the numbers of the tribe down when food was scarce, and to help keep the nutritional requirements low. There were always hard decisions to be made, but the Mammoth Hunters realized they must be ready to sacrifice during times of famine.

Tiger Paw's maternal grandfather, Chief Four Fingers (so named after losing a thumb to the savage bite of a horse) taught Tiger Paw the advantages of adopting new people into the tribe when he was a small boy. He told him, "These adult orphans often come with unique skills that can help the tribe secure food. The women usually make good wives, and they always have different cooking skills, and new stories and songs, these are the little things that make life more enjoyable."

When Four Fingers was young, his tribe, the Ice People wandered through western China and found a small band of silky-haired little people wandering without purpose or direction. Barbarians had annihilated their tribe, and the survivors were starving. The Ice People adopted all of them.

The kindness shown by Four Fingers was rewarded many times, in many ways. Several of the women became excellent bed warmers for Four Fingers, but more importantly, they were excellent river fishermen and boat builders. They taught the Ice People how to sail with a short gaff rigged mast, a keel, and a rudder on the rivers of China. Learning to sail against the wind and across the wind was a lesson so valuable, it made the Ice People rich beyond measure.

During the migrations, the Mammoth Hunters and Ice People merged. They lost their blue and green eyes, and the blonde and auburn hair dominance; they developed dark hair and almond-colored eyes, traits they inherited from the DNA of the many orphans they absorbed and the wives they acquired. Every hundred births or so, a blue- or green-eyed child with auburn or blonde hair was born. The parents received a great amount of goodhearted kidding, but the Mammoth Hunters and the Ice People were kind-hearted, and the child was always loved.

Many tribes had the skills and technology to survive, but if they lacked a strong leader, they were doomed. Four Fingers, Long Grass, and Tiger Paw were strong leaders. They ruled with totalitarian authority. They settled all disputes. If someone didn't measure up, they could be driven from the tribe (a fate that often meant death), or they might be killed outright.

The early Mammoth Hunters and Ice People had managed to keep the number of hunters and fishermen at about one hundred. There were over two hundred women and too many kids to keep track, but women and children died from exposure much faster than men. They traded for women and children; tribes facing starvation were always willing to trade a few women and kids for smoked salmon or a camel carcass. There were few tribes that were as successful as the Mammoth Hunters, and Tiger Paw looked at trading as a means of sharing the bounty.

Unfortunately, this winter was harder than any winter Tiger Paw could remember. The seasonal snow was piling up and pushing the herds and tribes away from the Mammoth Steppe, onto the continent of North America. There were food thefts by the other tribes, and some hunters from other tribes were acting aggressively and making threats at kill sites.

The Mammoth Hunters or Ice People were still well fed; their women had meat on their bones and produced children every year or two. They were successful, but the other tribes were envious of this good life and of how well they were eating.

The Mammoth Hunters or Ice People had a simple formula for success. It required keen observation of nature, and a willingness to work tirelessly to secure food; everything about life was easier if you secured food. Excess food, like dried and smoked fish and meat, could be traded for tools, weapons, furs, and women.

Tribes who weren't successful, had to trade their women and girls for food to live, and eventually, the men became despondent and angry. They looked at the wealth of Tiger Paw's people and wondered why their own tribe wasn't rich with the bounty of the earth. After all, the bounty was put on Earth for everyone—all the tribes should have healthy women and dried fish. They rationalized that the Mammoth Hunters were acting like bears; they took their share, and everyone else's share as well.

Blue Duck, the only son of One Eye, chief of the Muskeg People, was consumed with envy and hatred. He and several companions watched as a small band of Mammoth Hunters brought down a giant moose with several well-placed spear throws. He was incredulous that women accompanied the men on the hunt. Within the mythology of his tribe, it was taboo for women to hunt beside men, especially for a noble animal like the giant moose. This fact alone made his heart burn with hatred and anger; these people had no respect for the ancient customs of his people and now, they were going to enjoy the tasty internal morsels of this magnificent animal, an animal that rightfully belonged to the Muskeg People. Blue Duck decided it was time for the Muskeg People to assert their authority over the greedy tribes of the world, and take what was rightfully theirs.

The Mammoth Hunters had the moose deboned and cut into roast-sized pieces that were packed into six large backpacks, while the women prepared a feast of the heart and liver cut into small chunks and stuffed into the stomach with dried blueberries, onions, and edible poplar branches the moose had eaten on his own. The stomach was roasted over the coals until it swelled and pressure-cooked the contents into a nutritious feast for the three couples.

Blue Duck devised a plan; they would sneak up on the camp and attack the group when they started to eat. They would kill the men and capture the women; if the women fought, they would kill them as well. They would eat the feast and pack the meat back to their own camp. It was a momentous decision. The men were reluctant to resort to murder and theft, but their stomachs had been empty for a week, and they had not known a woman for months.

Blue Duck had five men to attack three men and three women. It was almost dark by the time they had crawled close enough to hear the hunters laughing and talking. The stomach had the entrance and exit tubes tied with a knot at each end, and it was under extreme pressure from the steam and heat locked inside. One of the men split the top with a flint knife, and the delicious aroma made the people cheer and laugh.

The Mammoth Hunters let their meal cool for a few minutes, while they waited with their wooden spoons, ready to dig into the stomach. Blue Duck had his right index finger in the air to remind his men to wait for his signal, before beginning the attack.

When the Mammoth Hunters started to eat, Blue Duck and his men attacked with fierce savagery. The Mammoth Hunter men were killed with multiple spear wounds. An older woman jumped on the back of one of the attackers and killed him with a knife, through the neck, before a spear pierced her lungs. A second woman was hit in the mouth with the butt end of a spear and fell backwards in an unconscious state. The men devoured the meal like a pack of ravenous wolves, and then had turns coupling with the unconscious woman. It was an hour later, before Blue Duck realized a woman was missing. He tried to get his men to leave, but once a leader encourages his men to break the cultural laws of civilized man, discipline and authority dissipates. Besides, their bellies were distended after eating like starved wolves, and they were exhausted from having their way repeatedly with the woman, who was now lifeless. They wanted to sleep and leave in the morning; Blue Duck realized it was hopeless to argue, and he fell asleep.

Blue Duck had been right about the escaped woman; she found a group of Mammoth Hunters led by Bear Killer and Ivory Tusk, sons of Tiger Paw. Just before morning, this well-disciplined group of hunters descended on Blue Duck and his men, and within seconds, two of the Muskeg men were dead. Blue Duck and another were wounded, but still alive. The Mammoth Hunters tied the hands of these two men behind their backs; they wanted them alive.

Bear Killer and Ivory Tusk brought the wounded men back to Tiger Paw's camp and tied them to a tree. Tiger Paw was in a rage after hearing the story, but showed no emotion. He used his serrated knife, with an edge as sharp as a surgeon's scalpel, but far more durable, to cut away the fur clothing from the Muskeg men and let them shiver in the cold.

Blue Duck was screaming threats and insults, but the Mammoth Hunters ignored him. The Mammoth Hunters noticed the silhouette tattoo of a right hand on Blue Duck's chest. It was a well-known and often used symbol of a chief's hand, designating his choice for leadership; it was a black tattoo done with ashes and a bone needle.

This was big medicine for the Mammoth Hunters. It could mean war; the Muskeg Tribe was a large tribe with oversized people, who were often starving. Tiger Paw knew this was a crucial and defining moment in the leadership of his tribe. His sons and their hunting party had been correct in their method of revenge on this chief's son and his raiding party. Blue Duck was screaming for mercy. Tiger Paw yelled for a wooden gag to be placed in the captives' mouths and tied behind their heads with a leather thong. He skinned the tattoo from the chest of Blue Duck and tied it with a thong to the neck of the other captive. Tiger Paw made an incision on the front of the sack holding Blue Duck's testicles, reached in with his fingers and pulled out the testicles. He sliced through the cords that connect them to the body and pierced both testicles to run a thong through them. Tiger Paw tied the thong tight around Blue Duck's neck. He scalped the Muskeg hunter and tied the scalp around his neck. The two Muskeg men were tied back to back so that only one could walk forward.

Tiger Paw used sign language to tell them, they were free to go home. The big question was: would they make it without clothing, and with their hands tied behind them? They staggered away as the sharp ice began cutting their feet almost immediately.

Tiger Paw watched them walk away like a lame crab, and said to his hunters "If they are lucky, they will make it back to the Muskeg campsite, but they haven't had much luck today."

Tiger Paw knew from other tribes, they had reached the northern end of the coastal ice strip. They could no longer follow the coast on land. They were in the area that was to become British Columbia and Alaska. Because of the coastal ice formation, he could either abandon his boats or split his tribe. Tiger Paw decided he would lead half his tribe down the ice-free corridor of British Columbia, and Ivory Tusk would sail south along the coastal ice. They would meet in the south, at the end of the ice, in six months to a year. Ivory Tusk had good eyesight and sailed the boats as well as anyone, and he was strong and fearless. Tiger Paw had picked Ivory Tusk to succeed him as chief. The boats could handle about twenty people.

It seemed like a good plan, but the two men had no idea how difficult the journey would be, or how vast the distance was. Ivory Tusk battled storms off the coast of British Columbia and had to stop on multiple occasions to rebuild the boats. Tiger Paw had struggled with treacherous mountain passes, wild rivers, and deep snows; it had been a hard trip.

Against all odds, they met again in the area of Puget Sound, five years later. By this time, Tiger Paw was a white-haired old man who was at the end of his life, and Ivory Tusk was showing his age as well. The two men were glad to see each other, but realized they were no longer the strong tribe of a hundred fishermen and hunters. They only had twelve strong men between them.

This new area was rich with hunting and fishing, but the other tribes in the area were hostile toward Tiger Paw and his beleaguered tribe. They had to leave, before the warlike tribes decided to kill them. They traded some flint knives and spear points for a few weathered canoes and sailed the fleet of leaking boats for their final voyage down the coast of Washington to the Columbia. With favorable winds, they sailed upstream on the river for two hundred miles. The old boats were no longer seaworthy, and they unloaded them to continue on foot.

They marched east, on the north bank of the Columbia. There was game in this area, and the local tribes weren't so belligerent or dangerous. They eventually crossed the Snake and traveled another hundred miles, until they reached an uncommonly good bed of flint and obsidian (volcanic glass).

Tiger Paw enjoyed watching the people of his tribe working the flint and obsidian. He was happy. A young girl brought him some meat soup with berries. Tiger Paw thanked her and wondered why he had never seen her before. He asked who she was, and she said, "I am Magpie, your great-granddaughter."

He laughed and said, "I didn't know I had such a pretty granddaughter. You look like Lotus, my stepmother."

She smiled and walked away. Tiger Paw slowly ate his soup and fell asleep. He didn't see the next sunrise.

The tribe spent nearly twenty thousand years working the flint quarries of Southern Idaho. Their hunting, fishing, and boating skills evolved, and they adapted to life on the River of Many Fish (Original name of the Snake, before the sign language was misinterpreted by a white trapper in the early 19th Century), but the nimble fingers of the little people made flint pieces that were among the best in the world. Traders came from every part of North America to trade for these exquisite pieces of flint. People who could afford the prices recognized these flint pieces all over the continent.

Chapter 23
The Raid

The enemy tribes approached the Salmon camp during the night and were in place to attack at dawn. The guard watching the caribou gate had already been killed.

A Salmon man came out of one the two large lodges to relieve himself at first light. He noticed the caribou guard was missing and saw a slight movement in two different spots. He acted like everything was normal and started walking toward the lodge when an arrow flew through the cold morning air and struck deep in his back. He ran screaming into the lodge as two more arrows flew into his body.

Yellow Hair jumped up, wrapped a fur skirt around his hips with a leather belt, and grabbed his bow and a quiver of arrows. The hunter was writhing in pain, with arrows protruding from his body, when Yellow Hair yelled, "We are being attacked!" He tied the quiver of arrows to his belt and stuck a war ax next to it. He ran out of the lodge, into a storm of arrows, to protect his tribe.

The enemy tribes planned to kill the Salmon men, steal their salmon, the caribou, their women, their children, and their home. They outnumbered the Salmon people by five or six to one, but these raiding killers knew they were in for a fight. There were several archers in a stand of trees by the second lodge. They were hitting the men as they came out to fight. Yellow Hair sent an arrow into the neck of the closest bowman and charged three more with his war ax. Yellow Hair ducked one arrow, and it flew over his back; he ran straight at the man to bury his war ax in the attacker's face. Another enemy archer was aiming an arrow at Yellow Hair when a yellow blur appeared; suddenly, the archer's head burst open with powerful blow from a war ax. It was Cabu. She killed the archer and the man next to him, who was frozen in disbelief after seeing a tiny blonde woman kill his friend.

Yellow Hair picked up a quiver of enemy arrows and made a stand behind a pile of large boulders. His brother Caribou Calf joined him and together, they unleashed a steady stream of lethal arrows.

Yellow Hair held a handful of arrows in his left hand with the bow and was unleashing a steady torrent of six lethal arrows a minute. His uncanny accuracy was slowing the enemy attack, but he was soon running out of arrows. With his last three arrows, he killed three more attackers. Yellow Hair could see that his people would soon be overrun if they didn't move. He ran forward to pick up another quiver of enemy arrows and began his lethal assault again before yelling, "Head for the boats!"

Sea Otter ran to his uncle, Caribou Calf, and they covered the retreat of the survivors with well-aimed arrows as the tribal members ran toward the boats. Several Salmon men joined Caribou Calf and his nephew; they fired their last arrows with the concentration and accuracy of desperate men who are not afraid to die. In a few minutes, Caribou Calf and Sea Otter were the last Salmon men covering the retreat. They withdrew into the trees when they saw the Salmon tribe had reached the boats.

Hopefully, the enemy's lack of critical thinking had kept them from disabling the boats; the boats would provide an escape, if they could survive the half-mile run and the enemy arrows.

The attackers followed the Salmon Tribe, except for three warriors who stayed to kill the Salmon wounded. They used spears to kill those who could not run with the rest of the tribe.

Caribou Calf and Sea Otter crept up on the ghouls and fired their arrows into two of the three men, from twenty feet. The third one heard the screams of the other two and threw his spear at Sea Otter, but when you see a man throw a spear, it is easy for an athletic sixteen-year-old to jump clear.

Caribou Calf sent his arrow into the man's belly, and Sea Otter's arrow flew seconds later to land in the man's neck. The arrow cut through the man's esophagus, missing the carotid arteries, to lodge in the man's spine. He was destined to die a long, agonizing death, unless one of his tribesmen put him out of his misery.

Caribou Calf and Sea Otter couldn't follow the rest of the tribe without running through the enemy warriors, and even if they fought through the attackers, by the time they reached the beach, the surviving Salmon tribesmen would already be sailing away. They slipped into the trees and disappeared into the shadows.

The boats were undamaged. The Salmon warriors set up a defensive line along a small sand ledge and an old tree that had washed up on the beach. The women, old men, and children struggled to launch the canoes under the direction of Cabu. She had a bow and a handful of arrows, and she was shooting the invaders while the boats were being launched. Yellow Hair and the last Salmon men ran past her and got the boats in the water. Yellow Hair yelled for Cabu when the boats were underway, and only then did she quit firing her deadly arrows to run through the surf and swim to Yellow Hair's canoe.

Yellow Hair did a quick count; he had lost two-thirds of his tribe. Sadly, there was nothing he could do for the wounded and the brave ones who were still fighting at the lodges. They launched five of the six seagoing canoes, after taking the sails and paddles from the last boat.

After losing such a big portion of the tribe, they would barely have enough strong men to paddle five of the six big seagoing canoes. The enemy appeared en masse, on the beach, when the boats were underway and out of range. They looked at the sixth canoe, but the paddles and sails were gone, and any thoughts of following were forgotten.

It was a horrible day for the Salmon People; everyone had lost family members and dear friends. There was no way they could take back their winter's supply of food, or traditional hunting and fishing grounds. They would need to find a new land and rebuild their tribe over generations, an area with no campfires.

When the shock of the morning was worn away by hours of sailing, the men dropped fishing lines over the side. It wouldn't be easy to feed this many people with no food in storage and no way to haul fresh water. They paddled into deeper water, a little farther out to sea, and began to catch bigger fish.

Yellow Hair saw his oldest son, Fast Fish, in one of the other boats, and he looked bad. The two boats came together, and Yellow Hair changed boats to see what was wrong with his son.

Fast Fish had been hit with an arrow in the thigh, and the arrowhead was still imbedded in the femur. The wound was already infected and discharging a terrible-looking and vile-smelling liquid.

Yellow Hair assumed the invaders used poison on their arrows, since the wound had infected so quickly. He knew his son would soon die in agony. Fast Fish was lying in the bottom of the boat. His father looked into his son's face and said, "Soon you will leave this life to visit the Whale Mother beneath the sea. You can wait until you cross over, or you can see her while you are still alive."

The young man nodded. Yellow Hair found one of the skins they used for a sail and laid it out next to Fast Fish. He scooped up sand and rocks from the ballast on the bottom of the canoe, about twenty pounds worth, and spread it over the sail skin. Yellow Hair wrapped his son in the sail and tied a leather cord around the sail so that only his son's head was showing. He lifted Fast Fish over the side and looked into his son's face. Yellow Hair said softly, "Tell our fathers and the Whale Mother, I will be there soon, but first, I must make the tribe strong once again, in a new land."

His son nodded his head, 'yes' as Yellow Hair laid him into the water. Just before Fast Fish sank beneath the surface, Yellow Hair said, "We will sing of you at the campfires, and I will soon see you in the spirit world, my son." Yellow Hair looked into his son's eyes, until Fast Fish disappeared into the depths.

Several more were lost to the poisoned arrows, and Yellow Hair thought of the many enemy warriors who had their own arrows fired back at them and were dying of the same poison. There was no satisfaction, but those warriors must be questioning the use of poison by now.

The Salmon People were deeply saddened by the human losses and the loss of their traditional home, but what could they do? They sailed and paddled away their grief through the day and camped where there was a freshwater stream and no campfires.

The wind came up after midday, and they used their sails. Always on the lookout for freshwater creeks and rivers, they worked their way north along the frozen coastal regions of France, Britain, and Ireland. (It was possible to walk from France to Ireland because of the diminished ocean depths during the peaks of the Ice Age.) The ice often left small strips of beach. Sometimes there were miles of forest, and sometimes a massive wall of ice extended into the salt waters for miles with no beach to land on. The men hoped they wouldn't hit a storm in these areas, because there was no place to land, and they would surely drown. Luckily, they always found land when the storms began to blow, and pulled their large canoes up on a dry beach and made shelters by covering the area between the canoes with the sails.

They often waited in these temporary camps for days to sit out winter storms or "Her Canes." The Whale Mother's husband was a womanizer and was known to disappear for days at a time. When he came home in a state of exhaustion, she beat him with the spear he used as a cane. These beatings caused the terrible storms and at these times his cane was her cane, The Salmon People called the Whale Mother's storms "Her Cane," a term that became synonymous with violent storms or the temper tantrums of the Whale Mother and all females with philandering husbands. They saw several "Her Canes" over the next months and began to wish her husband would behave.

They used this time to make harpoon points, knives, and fish hooks from flint. Cabu and some of the women were the best flint workers. Working the flint had evolved and the women coined terms for the tools they used. They studied a rock for several minutes before striking it with a granite stone they called the hammer against a larger piece of granite they called the anvil. With several precise strikes the new instrument began to take shape, and the final lighter taps produced a precision cutting instrument or projectile point. The women could see cutting edges in flint stones and start flaking off large pieces that often made smaller and smaller pieces, until they were making tiny arrowheads, no bigger than a woman's smallest fingernail, for grouse and ptarmigan.

The hunters used the down time to kill several seals. They smoke tanned the case skinned hides to serve as fresh water containers. Without these water bags, they couldn't have made the longer sails of the North Atlantic.

Yellow Hair had tried making projectile points and knives, but they were ugly and clumsy looking. The women made tools that looked like works of art and sliced through the wild animals with a minimum loss of momentum.

Yellow Hair counted heads: after losing several people, there were twelve hunters, including him, eight fertile women, including Cabu, three old men and an old woman, near the end of their days, and six children, not counting the child Cabu was carrying. The tribe would need to change and accept a new lifestyle.

Yellow Hair was relying on the maps in the cave to find a new land. The paintings indicated a great land to the west, and if they continued to follow the ice, moving west, they were sure to find this new land. His tribe had nearly been wiped out, and he was taking them on a trip into the gray void. Maybe the maps were wrong and they would wander forever, without finding a new home. Yellow Hair began to have self-doubt, for the first time in his life.

Chapter 24

Sea Otter and Caribou Calf Escape

The enemy tribe celebrated their victory with an orgy of gluttony, and while they slept off their indigestion and exhaustion Caribou Calf and Sea Otter prepared to escape. The men surveyed the abandoned canoe; they knew the boat was left without sails and paddles, or the enemy would have tried to follow.

They needed paddles; they found a ten-inch pine that had fallen at least a year earlier. Using wooden wedges, they started two parallel splits about two inches apart. The tree creaked and complained before giving up a two-inch by ten-inch board from its center. They cut two lengths four feet long and used their flint scrapers to plane the flat paddle area of the board, until it was less than an inch thick. They used their knives to whittle the shaft of the handle until it was a two-inch shaft, with a four-inch handhold at the top. Within three hours the paddles were finished. At one of the summer lodges, they found some older caribou hides and sewed them into sails. There were also two leather water bags that could keep them at sea for a week or more. They hurried to launch the canoe before daylight.

When they tried to drag the canoe to the surf, they realized it was too heavy for two men to do alone. That's when they noticed Lucinda, an H1W2 teenage girl from the tribe. She might just have enough muscle to help get the twenty-foot canoe with its gravel and rock ballast into the ocean.

She was dazed and disoriented, but when they motioned for her to help with the canoe, she came forward and started pulling. Together, after throwing out some of the bigger rocks, they managed to launch the canoe. They raised their gaff sail and picked up a good breeze. It felt good to be leaving the scene of the tragedy, but there was a question: should they sail north or south to find the survivors? Within a few minutes, the question was academic. A brisk northerly wind started to blow, increasing in force until it was gale strength; they lowered their sail to run with the wind and tied oiled hides across the gunwales to keep the boat from filling with rain and seawater.

They hoped Yellow Hair and the other canoes were sailing with the wind to the south. The wind pushed them farther out to sea and the waves were up to fifteen feet high. Using the tiller, they remained positioned on top of the waves, until they rode down the big hills of water at an angle to the trough below. If they rode straight down the wall of water, the bow would cut through the bottom of the trough, and their lives would be over. At the bottom of the troughs, there was relative calm, until another wave lifted them up on a hill of water, and they were in the full force of the storm and preparing to take another wild sleigh ride once again. If a wave of water broke over them while they were in the trough, it would be the end.

They continued in this series of sleigh rides for a day and a half of sheer terror. On the morning of the second day, they awoke to a day of peaceful calm, with clear skies and a light wind from the west.

They sailed through the Strait of Gibraltar. Because of the Ice Age, the ocean had lost one hundred and forty meters of depth, but Gibraltar is normally nine hundred meters deep. The rest of the Mediterranean was reduced to a series of large lakes. Caribou Calf, Sea Otter, and Lucinda sailed into a huge bay, and realized they would never see their friends and family again.

Chapter 25
New Land

By using the elevation and relative positions of the North Star and the sun, Yellow Hair knew they were now traveling south. Unfortunately, the ice sheets extended into the Salt Sea, and it was becoming harder to find a suitable beach to land and rest, and cook. They continued to sail south along the eastern border of the ice.

Eventually, they found a good place to land on the western bank of a large bay. It would later be named Chesapeake Bay. Upon landing Cabu walked into the trees and came back an hour later with a baby girl and a baby boy. Yellow Hair inspected the babies and held them up to the North, South, East, and West to introduce them to the basic directions of navigation they would need in this strange land.

Yellow Hair named the babies Tigress and Wolf, before wrapping them in tanned sealskin. Tigress and Wolf were the first H1W2 babies to be born on the eastern seaboard. Tigress was named for the Sabre Tooth tiger they saw in this new land.

The Salmon People camped on the bank for a few days, using their canoes for shelter. Yellow Hair sent out scouts to find a spot to build a base camp, and he settled on a small hill about a mile from the shore and the boats. They would have camped closer, but so much of the ground was low, swampy, and plagued with mosquitoes.

The Chesapeake was a rich source of fish and crabs, but the tribal members wanted to explore inland, and within five years, they had become excellent hunters of several types of deer, including the red deer or elk.

Chapter 26
A New Life

Lucinda, Caribou Calf, and Sea Otter landed in the northeast corner of the bay; there were plenty of fish and game signs. They decided to try and make a life in this new land. They were tired of the sailing canoe, and glad to be on solid ground.

They pitched camp in the tree line and slept a much-needed rest until morning. Sea Otter sensed something was different, and he crept to the edge of the trees. Several Near People men were examining the canoe and handling the paddles, the sails, and the mast.

He woke up his uncle and motioned him to be quiet. They crawled to the tree line to see the strange beings looking at the canoe.

Caribou Calf wondered what they were doing. Were they curious, or getting ready to steal the canoe? He decided to wait and see if they would just leave. They didn't look like they had the mental acuity to sail, or even paddle.

The four men picked up the canoe like it was a toy and walked to the water. Sea Otter wanted to stop them, but they had only one serviceable arrow and a spear; in a close quarters fight, the Near People would destroy them. With hand signals, Caribou Calf urged his nephew to wait.

There were only modest one-foot waves when the heavily muscled Near Men put the boat in the water. Watching them get into the boat would have been funny if they weren't stealing the canoe. Instead of squatting down on their knees in the boat, they stood in a type of crouch, while two of them tried to use the paddles. Normally, tidal forces don't affect the Mediterranean, but the bay represented less than ten percent of the normal Mediterranean, and it was very close to Gibraltar—the ocean waters of the Atlantic were ebbing. The canoe was being pulled farther and farther away from shore, into deeper water. One of the men sat on the side, and when another joined him, the boat spun like a top, and the four men were struggling to stay afloat. Like all people new to boats, they didn't realize the boat would stay afloat after dumping the ballast, despite being semi-submerged. They struggled in the water, until they all drowned.

When the men quit struggling, Caribou Calf and Sea Otter swam with the current to retrieve their boat and worked hard to tow it back to the beach. Sea Otter developed even more respect for his uncle. If they had tried to stop the theft, they might have been hurt or killed.

Lucinda seemed to recover from the shock of the raid and began working flint stones to make projectile points, knives, axes, and adzes.

They now realized they had to find a place to hide the boat; it was obvious there would be trouble if other people saw the boat and decided they could handle a boat on the big water. They decided to fish during the day and explore this strange coast. For several weeks they caught enough fish to come in early and explore different beaches and the land beyond the trees.

They found more wildlife and freshwater streams while exploring the northern beaches. After paddling up one of the rivers a short distance, they built a camp for the coming winter.

On a dry sand hill of fire-killed pine, they dug a twelve-foot by twelve-foot hole with a depth of two feet. They pushed over a stand of ten and twelve-inch fire-killed pines, cut them to length, and dragged them to the dugout. They stacked the logs four feet high and notched them in the corners.

When the walls were up, Caribou Calf started constructing a hearth from clay, sand, rocks, shells, and sticks. After the hearth had dried for three days, they started a small fire and baked the clay mortar.

Sea Otter built the roof using logs split in half and extending out from the north and south ends by two feet. He packed wet clay, sand, shells, rocks, and Birch bark between the logs.

A passageway was dug underneath the southern logs for an entry, and a sealskin hide was hung from the bottom log to block the elements. They filled the gaps with clay, sticks, and bark.

The little home needed to have the mud patched every year, but it lasted several generations.

During an early blizzard of the first winter, they were eating fermented fish when they heard a woman's voice calling from outside the dugout.

The two men crawled outside and found a raven-haired woman with two small children. They were starved and nearly dead. The vagabonds were invited inside, and Caribou Calf gave each of them a small fermented fish.

They weren't sure the fish was edible, until they saw the men and Lucinda eating it. Once they were sure the fish was food, they ate until their shrunken stomachs were full.

Caribou Calf knew from experience that feeding a starving person too much was a waste of food. The woman and the children lay down next to the fire, after the woman made signs to indicate they were grateful for the hospitality.

Sea Otter, Caribou Calf, and Lucinda looked at the vagabonds and wondered what was going to happen. They had plenty of fish, and they were successful hunters as well, but the woman was older than the two men. Both of them dreamed of young women with lithesome figures, women with no children. They shrugged and said it would be good to have another woman for the domestic chores, and the children would be a big help in a few years.

During the night, Caribou Calf was barely aware of the woman crawling in between his hide blankets. She was warm, and her huge milk paps felt good against his back. He drifted back to sleep to be awakened by a soft, knowing hand exploring his private parts. It was over in a few seconds. Months of pent-up emotion were released, and his body straightened from his sleeping position, and Caribou Calf began to realize the advantages of accepting women vagabonds.

Lucinda watched the woman move under the blanket with Caribou Calf and saw him achieve his relief. A few minutes later, she climbed between Sea Otter's blankets to relieve his frustration.

Chapter 27
Cabu's Map

Cabu enjoyed watching her children grow strong and seeing the strength and kindness of Yellow Hair in their personalities. When the kids were sixteen, the tribe met some warlike tribes from the north, and Yellow Hair decided to take the advice of an old vagabond who gave vague directions to the west by a circuitous route. They were in the area of what was to become Wadkin's Ferry on the Potomac and traveled south to Berkley County, West Virginia. They continued south to the future town site of Winchester, Virginia, Frederick County. As the old vagabond predicted, they found the Great Trading Path, a trail that had already been used for centuries. This trail led through the Shenandoah Valley, through the future towns of New Market and Staunton, and across the James River. The path now angled to the southwest to the headwaters of New River. The river was fast and dangerous, but there were various boats on both shores that traders had been using for years, but for people who had sailed the North Atlantic, the crossing was a mere inconvenience and the hills were uneventful.

Tigress and Wolf helped the now-frail Yellow Hair up the mountain and through the gap, which was a surprisingly easy path. They camped in the gap (Cumberland Gap) that night, and Yellow Hair asked Cabu, Tigress, and Wolf to walk with him to the western precipice. They looked out over the vast land before them, and Yellow Hair said in the feeble voice of an old man, "There are no campfires."

His children looked at him and were puzzled, but Cabu understood the significance and saw the gleam in the old man's eyes. Yellow Hair died in his sleep that night, and the Salmon People buried their beloved leader with kindness on the edge of a New World.

After leaving the Cumberland Gap, they crossed the Cumberland River and followed a well-used path to the northwest. They found the head waters of the Green River and followed the river until they came to three trees that had blown down. They worked the trees by burning out the interior and shaping the interior and exterior with flint adzes. It took two months to build three canoes.

The Green was a deep, narrow river with a slow current. The fishing was good, but Cabu worried about an ambush. The trees were thick, and there were lots of places for an enemy to hide. A few days later, they left the Green and paddled into the Ohio, the biggest river they had ever seen.

They used their sails to cross to the north shore and make camp. While dinner was cooking, two large canoes with six men came into view, paddling upstream. The young people ran to hide in the forest, but Cabu, Tigress, and Wolf waited in camp for the strangers to land. Their camp was visible from the river, so there was no need in being afraid. Cabu figured she and her children could handle six men, if it was necessary. The rest of the Salmon People were apprehensive or maybe cowardly, but Cabu and her kids had stone war axes in their belts, and their bows by their sides, they were ready for battle.

The men walked into camp. Cabu was unconcerned; Tigress and Wolf learned from their mother's quiet composure how to maintain confidence in the face of danger.

The men used sign language to explain that they were traders and had many valuables to trade.

Cabu made the sign, "Show me."

The leader of the traders unrolled a small leather blanket with a variety of projectile points and knives. Cabu looked at the finely made pieces and acted indifferent. She threw down two arrows with small exquisite bird points and pulled out two pieces of stone she had picked up recently. With a few well-aimed strikes, the flint pieces began to take the form of two extremely sharp knives with multiple projectile points taking shape. The traders looked at each other in amazement. They had never seen anyone work flint so quickly and effortlessly.

The traders all gathered in close to handle the pieces she was producing, and to watch her nimble fingers work the stones.

When she was finished, the leader pulled out a balanced black glass knife with an extremely sharp edge. Cabu asked what it was made of, and the leader said, "Obsidian."

She lost interest in her own pile of tools and made the sign to trade her six flint stones for the knife. The leader couldn't believe his luck, but to Cabu, this new knife was invaluable. If she could find the raw material, they could have the sharpest knives in the world.

Cabu pulled out several sacks of flint stones, and serious trading started. Cabu obtained many exotic articles, like shells, furs, and pemmican, and the traders obtained a small fortune in flint pieces.

Cabu asked about people in the New Land and where she could obtain obsidian.

The leader, who identified himself as Talon, liked this strange woman with blonde hair, who was an artist with stone. He instructed one of his men to cook some venison and pemmican, while Talon communicated with Cabu.

Talon cut a two-foot by two-foot piece of tanned deer hide and painted a map of the rivers of North America. He made an "X" where there were villages and "XX" where there were cities. If the cities were peaceful, he used black ink. If they were warlike, he used red ink. He painted a circle at their present location; downstream from a waterfall across the river he called O-hi-yoe. (The waterfall disappeared when the river was dammed, twenty thousand years later.)

He drew the location of the obsidian quarry on the north bank of the River of Many Fishes. He made the sign of both arms weaving in an undulating motion; the same motion a trapper would misinterpret as the sign for the Snake River, when told the name of the river by an Indian, twenty thousand years later.

The man was an artist and he painted a miniature illustration of the North Star with the Little Dipper and Big Dipper, so the map could be calibrated with the stars and used correctly.

Cabu laughed when she saw the constellations and told the trader about the cave at their old home with the celestial navigation points painted on the walls, in the form of animals and other symbols.

Cabu and the trader became friends, and they agreed to try and meet at the confluence of the Ohio and the Mississippi in two weeks. The trader indicated that the river current was strong and the distances can be covered quickly. Cabu told him, they use the wind and they travel very fast, much quicker than with paddles.

The trader asked to see how this invention worked. Cabu asked Tigress to take a sailing canoe into the middle of the river and demonstrate the art of sailing with the wind and against the wind. The traders were amazed at the technology and said they were going to start building sails the next day. They parted company with promises to see each other again.

Cabu and her children studied the map for hours and considered it to be one of their most valued possessions. Cabu was especially happy, because she could carry on with Yellow Hair's dream of finding a safe place for his tribe, and his last son and daughter.

The spring winds were brisk easterlies, and the current was with them. The map lacked accurate perspectives, and Cabu thought they might reach the Mississippi River in two more days, but they found the Wabash the next day. Talon had neglected to paint or mention the Wabash. The river was nearly a mile wide with the runoff from the melting ice and the spring rains. They sailed upstream on a due north course against a series of rapids. The river was thick with freshwater mussels, and after fighting the current for half a day, the Salmon Tribe stopped to cook some of the shells. There were several different types, and they tried a variety, but when cooked, the mussels gave off a pungent odor and had a disgusting taste. They had to leave the site of the meal to put the smell behind them.

The glacial runoff made the current of the river extremely strong, and, judging by the straight southerly direction of the river, after five days of sailing upstream, they determined this was not the Missouri.

Just when they were ready to turn around, they noticed groups of mussel-eating warriors on the high banks of both sides of the river, and there were great piles of shells, over fifty feet high, as well. The stench of the village was horrendous. The warriors were naked and covered in the foul smelling grease of the mussels.

The Salmons were safe from arrows while they were in the middle of the river, but if the mussel eaters launched canoes, the Salmons would be overwhelmed.

Cabu told her people to land on a sandbar near the eastern bank. The mussel eaters all had arrows in their bows, but the bows were of poor quality and didn't look strong enough to send an arrow over 30 feet. The men looked dangerous; even though they were pointing their arrows at the ground.

Cabu wrapped some pemmican, venison jerky, and two flint blades in a tanned beaver hide and walked toward the bank on a gravel bar to offer the gift. She backed away, without turning her back on these belligerent warriors. She was about twenty feet from the gift, when she turned and walked toward the canoes. She heard several warriors struggling to be the first one to recover the gift, but an old man started yelling, and the warriors quit fighting.

The Salmon People pushed their canoes off the gravel bar and continued upstream. Cabu looked up to see a naked old man eating the pemmican with a smile on his face.

The Salmon People made camp upstream about ten miles from the mussel eaters and within sight of the wall of ice. Cabu was wishing they had turned around instead of continuing northward; the mussel eaters were going to want more exotic treats and gifts on the return trip. They could hear the groaning and grinding of summer ice. Cabu decided it was better to slip by the mussel eaters during the darkest of night, just before the gray mists of morning.

During the night, they heard a faint clicking noise that grew louder and louder, until it became a roaring noise like the summer ice. Cabu remembered the sound; it was similar to the sound the hooves of the caribou made while migrating over frozen ground. Cabu yelled at everyone to break camp, load the canoes, and pull the canoes upstream to the ice. This noise was many times louder than Cabu remembered.

The women were paddling upstream and the men were pulling the canoes with ropes when the first buffalo plunged into the river. The Salmon Tribe struggled upstream under a ceiling of ice, where the river was running. It was a dangerous spot, but it was much safer than being in front of the buffalo crossing the river just downstream from the ice. They tied the canoes to rocks and shivered in the cold ice cave with the river running beneath them. One of the young men slipped in the shallow but fast-running water sand was washed away with his canoe and two young women. The canoe and passengers were ground into red pulp, beneath the churning hooves of the buffalo.

The ice projected outward on the bank and provided sanctuary from the millions of buffalo crossing the river. The Salmon Tribe would be okay if the ice didn't collapse on them. The buffalo crossed all day and into the night. The next morning, stragglers in herds of fifty to a hundred buffalo were still crossing the river.

The Salmon men floated up on one of the last ones and speared it from the canoe. They towed the buffalo to the bank and used the tongue and the hump to make dinner. They cut the hindquarters and placed one in each of the canoes and packed them with ice from the glacier.

When they felt sure the main herd had crossed the river, they let the current carry them back toward the O-hi-yoe River. They passed the camp of the mussel eaters. The sand bar was gone, and the steep banks of the river were now ground down until they were level with the water. The great shell mounds were gone, ground into white dust. There were no survivors; the mussel eaters were wiped off the face of the earth, and no one would ever know they existed, until university archaeologists excavated the village, twenty thousand years later.

The few remaining Salmon People were thinking about how fast death comes, and how lucky they are to be alive. The tribe made camp at the mouth of this river of death, and Cabu drew the river on her map, with ink from poisonous black berries, and made the sign language symbol for death and remorse next to the river. From that day to the present, the river was called Wabash, their word for death and remorse.

The spring rains and warm temperatures were much more intense than normal and melted vast sections of the southern ice sheets, and huge chunks of ice or icebergs floated down the swollen rivers, until they began to back up on the Mississippi and the Ohio and Missouri Rivers, and the rivers overflowed their banks for a hundred miles. Many tribes thought the massive flood was the end of the world, but the Salmon Tribe had been migrating for years and they had seen many catastrophes. They were not afraid and assumed the floods were part of the natural world. To the Salmon Tribe, hardship was a part of life, and a better life was just beyond the horizon. Using the tops of trees as a guide, Cabu, Tigress, and Wolf guessed the channel of the Missouri and continued their migration upstream toward the obsidian source on the River of Many Fish.

Approximately one hundred fifty miles beyond the mouth of the Missouri, the Salmon Tribe saw the most bizarre tribe they had ever encountered. A tribe of naked barbarians lived on a big hill overlooking the river. They survived on the buffalo that drowned while crossing the Missouri River upstream. When a drowned buffalo was seen floating down the river, the men swam out to the carcass and towed it back to their camp.

There were several carcasses on the shore in various stages of decomposition, from fresh to past the point of being swollen with gas and the hair slipping off. They didn't appear to have the technology of cooking; they ate the carcasses raw, in total disregard of the decomposition of the remains. They were human carrion eaters. They lacked the technology of flint knives. Their fingernails were infected from tearing at the rotten flesh, and looked more like the claws of animals than the fingernails of humans. Their hovels were made from buffalo skulls arranged haphazardly with un-tanned segments of hide stretched over the horns and skulls. The strong stomachs of the Salmon People revolted when they saw and smelled these wretched savages.

The Salmon Tribe pushed past these degenerative people and continued on to the Great Falls of Montana. They abandoned their boats and followed the migration trails of the elk, deer, and buffalo, through the mountain passes to the Southwest on a former game trail that was already an ancient trail. During the twentieth century, the trail would become the roadbed for Interstate 15 from Great Falls to Pocatello.

The last of the Salmon Tribe met the last of the Mammoth Hunters in the flint and obsidian quarries on the north bank of the Snake. The Salmon Tribe would become part of a new tribe, and the H1W2 line was refreshed.

Cabu lived a few more years. Her blonde hair was now white. She enjoyed playing with her grandchildren and reminiscing about the great days of the Salmon People and thinking about her loving husband, Yellow Hair, during her last years. She was glad to see her people doing well, but she dreamed of trading all her tomorrows to just live one day of her youth with Yellow Hair.

Over thousands of years, the remnants of the tribes that were once the Salmon People of Southern France and the Ice People or Mammoth Hunters of the Steppe combined and disseminated their females to become part of many diverse tribes, including the Comanche of Wyoming and the Cherokee of North Carolina.

The Comanche of Wyoming were hunter-gatherers, who loved to hunt the buffalo; they hunted them on foot, diverting the herds over cliffs with fire and by spooking them with wolf hides. There were no horses for thousands of years, until French Canadians or the Courier du Bois came down from Canada and the Spanish rode up from the South, along with a modest supply of horses arriving from the Eastern Seaboard, during the early seventeenth century.

Just before the appearance of the horse, the Comanche migrated to the Llano Estacado (Staked Plains) and drove out the Apache. The Comanche was a group of tribes of only a few thousand, occupying the greatest native grassland of North America in an area about the size of Indiana. The Comanche was so fierce in the protection of this vast domain, known as the Comancheria, it was never fully explored by white men until after the Civil War. The Llano Estacado included parts of Colorado, New Mexico, Oklahoma, and much of North and West Texas; very few people entered the Comancheria and survived. Many of the native grasses were shoulder high and the country was devoid of features. There were only a few sources of water and they were nearly impossible to find without knowledge of the terrain and a keen sense of direction.

When the horse arrived, the Comanche quickly learned to hunt and kill the buffalo on horseback. They became efficient horse raiders in a short time. From Mexico City to the Canadian border, the Comanche raided with impunity. They specialized in acquiring gold, horses, cattle, children, and women. These items were traded to the Comanchero, the only traders who were allowed in the Comancheria. The Comancheros were primarily renegade Mexicans who knew how to gain the trust of the Comanche. They provided the metal cooking kettles and skillets, weapons, knives, and clothing the Comanche desired from the white man's world.

The horsemanship genes must have been hidden deep in the DNA of the Salmon People and the Ice People, or else it was acquired from other tribes, but never has a group adapted so quickly to the culture of the horse and gone on to become the greatest mounted warriors of the world, according to equestrian experts of the era.

Chapter 28
Pirates of the Mediterranean

When the ice began to melt over thousands of years, the Mediterranean slowly refilled, and the rest of the world began to receive normal precipitation. The descendants of Caribou Calf and Sea Otter adjusted to the rising water and the prevailing winds. The original dugout that housed several generations was under a hundred meters of water and forgotten. They sailed eastward over generations, until they landed on the coast of the Levant (the Holy Land) seven thousand years ago. They were among a group of enterprising and creative people on a fertile, well-watered strip of land on the coasts of modern-day Lebanon, Syria, and Israel.

The sailing and navigation technology of the Salmon Tribe evolved into a more modern science and facilitated fishing, trade, export of preserved fish, and the distribution of bulk-dyed cloth. The technology became the basis for the first dynamic economic system of the world. Specialized in the preservation of fish, (probably using forms of smoke and fermentation technology), they sold cedar logs to Egypt and all over the Mediterranean. They also specialized in being the middlemen to facilitate trade in precious metals and agricultural produce. They were the only sailors of the region who could navigate accurately, and the only ones who could harness the wind with precision.

The people of the coastal Levant considered themselves to be citizens of the individual walled cities: Byblos, Sidon, and Tyre. They shared a culture and an economy, but not a national identity. The early Greeks described them as the Phoenicians or 'Phoinikes' (Red People); this probably refers to the reddish-purple bulk cloth they exported. It is impossible to know whether they were actually stained from the production of the cloth or if the name refers strictly to the cloth, but the name stuck.

The port cities became a balance of power between the great powers of Egypt and Mesopotamia (The Fertile Crescent between the Tigris and Euphrates Rivers) to the east. The Phoenicians were identified in 1100 BC, but were referred to as the Canaanite people for several thousand years before 1100 BC.

The earliest Canaanite town was Gebal, known today as Byblos. On the coast of Lebanon, Byblos has been occupied for over six thousand five hundred years and is one of the oldest continually occupied settlements in the world. Records and archeology indicate Byblos was shipping cedar from the mountains of Lebanon to Egypt earlier than 3000 BC. From 2500 to 1200 BC the Canaanite towns of today's Lebanon, Tyre, Sidon, Sarepta, and Beirut were all prospering.

Pirates raided the port cities of Canaan around 1200 BC; shiploads of desperate men raided, plundered, raped, killed, and destroyed everything in their path. They were from a variety of places, but primarily from the Aegean, east of Greece.

The DNA of Lucinda and the women of H1W2 thrived in the Levant. Her descendants were traders, craftsmen, sailors, and fishermen, but when the pirates descended on the Levant, they killed nearly all the men except for the most skilled craftsmen. The women and most of the youngest children were allowed to live as slaves. In the year 1200 BC, Janus, of the line of Lucinda and Sea Otter, was seventeen when a fleet of pirate ships raided Tyre. The island and its people belonged to the pirates within forty-eight hours.

Captain Ogram was from an island in the Aegean. Born into a family of pirates, his world had been a life of violence and poverty. He was thirty years old and the captain of his own ship of miscreants, cut throats, thieves, and murderers.

A crew is critical to the survival of a pirate captain, but a pirate crew becomes bored when there is no loot to be taken, and a bored crew of cutthroats is always open to the option of mutiny and a new captain. Like all pirate captains and sea captains in general, Ogram ruled his ship with the iron fist of discipline. His men followed him because of an iron will, seamanship, and a fearless nature.

Being a pirate captain was his life, but he dreamed of something else. He had already achieved the dream of every lad from his culture, but there had to be something more.

Janus was the daughter of Artemis and Saphis. She was beautiful, a mirror image of her mother, with auburn hair and blue eyes. Her father had accumulated extreme wealth in the precious metals markets of the Mediterranean. The family lived on a large villa in the countryside on the island of Tyre, a few hundred meters from shore.

Janus had a continuous line of suitors, from noble families, who wanted her hand in marriage and a share of her father's precious metals business. At seventeen, she was bored with the attention of so many young, and a few not-so-young men, who seemed more interested in her father's business than her as a person. They were so conspicuously obvious with their intentions; she detested the sight of them. This was creating a problem for her parents; it was improper for a young lady of seventeen not to be married or betrothed. Family friends kept asking about Janus and her matrimonial prospects, and her parents became defensive. Men were approaching Artemis and inquiring about an arranged marriage, but Janus was too independent to consider such a proposition. Artemis loved his daughter and wanted her to have the freedom to choose her husband, but Janus was difficult and moody.

The pirate navy consisted of over a hundred ships. They arrived during the night, and by first light they controlled the north and south harbors of Tyre. By noon, they were in control of the walled city.

The pirates had never seen such wealth, or even imagined there might be so much wealth in the world. Without discipline or leadership among the pirates, the first day of occupation was an orgy of looting and debauchery. Captain Ogram saw the beginning of the senseless violence and destruction, and bought three good horses. He asked First Officer Leonis and his lover, Pirogue, to accompany him on a trip through the countryside.

Leonis trusted his captain and knew lives would be sold cheap as pirates drank wine and admired the loot of other pirates.

The three men were unfamiliar and uncomfortable with horses, but they were intelligent enough to learn from the horses instead of making demands the animals didn't understand. Soon enough, they were getting along with the horses and covering a lot of ground quickly.

On the western coastline, Captain Ogram saw what he was looking for: a large country estate with cultivated fields, an olive orchard, carved marble statues of gods, and a huge country manor house. Pirates had not looted the estate. Leonis remarked that the gods must live in a place like this country estate. Captain Ogram and Pirogue agreed.

An older white-haired man, Artemis, ran out of the estate gate with a spear, a shield, and a sword. He was soft and dressed like an aristocrat. Four slaves with swords followed him, but they had no training in warfare, it was obvious by the way they held their weapons. The pirates slid off their horses and slowly walked forward, without drawing their weapons.

When they were within range, Artemis ran forward and threw his spear. He had determination, but lacked the strength to throw a spear with speed and power. The pirates stepped aside to avoid the impotent attack and ignored the spear's potential. Artemis rushed forward again to attack the captain with his sword, but when the sword of a trader meets the sword of a man who is hardened by a lifetime of work and fights to the death, the result is predictable. The two swords met with a loud clash, and the sword of the soft aristocrat flew from his hand. In fact, the explosive force was so great; Artemis thought his wrist and hand were broken. He grabbed his right wrist with his left hand and grimaced in pain. Captain Ogram grabbed the aristocrat and spun him around; now, Artemis was on his knees with the captain's blade at his throat. Whispering in Greek, Captain Ogram said, "Tell your slaves to throw down their weapons and you will all live to see tomorrow. If they want to fight, you will all die in the next few minutes."

Artemis said to his slaves, "Put down your weapons. You have shown bravery and loyalty; I thank you."

The slaves dropped their weapons and two women ran out of the estate.

The pirates assumed they were mother and daughter. They looked alike and the age difference was appropriate. The women fell to their knees about twenty feet away from Captain Ogram and began to plead for the life of the man. "Please, please don't kill him."

The captain had no intention of killing him. His vague plan was unfolding well. The captain told his men to gather up the weapons, and he let his sword drop from the man's neck. When the weapons were collected, he sheathed his sword and grabbed the man by the shoulders and effortlessly lifted him to his feet.

The captain looked at the two attractive women and said, "We have not been introduced. I am Captain Ogram, and these are my officers, First Mate Leonis and his lover Pirogue. We are not here to rob and kill; we are looking for a home, and you have such a nice home, we thought we might live with you and protect you from the rape and pillage of the other pirates. If you want us to leave, we will be gone in a few minutes; otherwise, I think we can come to a compromise."

The women were speechless. A few minutes ago, they expected to see Artemis have his throat cut by a pirate, and now the same pirate was offering them protection from the pirate horde.

The young girl looked at the pirate captain, who could have killed her father so easily; she was intrigued and excited to see this man whose muscles rippled beneath a loose shirt and faded purple loincloth. The pirate captain had thick black curly hair reaching nearly to his shoulders, and he looked as strong as one of her horses. He smiled after saying every sentence and looked directly into the eyes of her mother, her father, and herself the whole time he spoke. She thought of all the men who came to beg for her hand in marriage—none of them looked directly into her eyes. To Janus, they seemed dishonest and up to no good. This man seemed honest. Obviously, he was capable of great violence, but he wasn't trying to intimidate her family. He was being calm and friendly.

The owner of the estate spoke, as if he had met a business acquaintance, "Captain Ogram, let me welcome you to our humble villa. I am Artemis, and this fair lady to your left is my wife, Saphis, and to her left is Janus, our daughter, an accomplished equestrian and poet. Let me show you our guesthouse. I hope it will be up to your standards. My grooms will take care of your horses and tack."

Artemis took a hold of the captain's hand, in the custom of the day, and led the three men to a smaller building. A building the pirates would have considered a palace.

Leonis and Pirogue looked at each other and smiled. Their captain was up to something, and they were along for the ride.

Artemis led the men into the guesthouse. "Make yourselves at home. The baths are in the back; the servants are warming your bath waters. Dinner will be served in two hours." Artemis turned to face Captain Ogram. "Captain, I know we got off to a bad start, but I was trying to protect my family. I did not expect to meet a gentleman among pirates. We are at your mercy, but at dinner, I think we can discuss plans that will be beneficial to both of us."

"I admire you for defending your family, and I hope we can build a future together, Artemis. It's obvious we both have skills that can work in tandem," Captain Ogram said. He put out his right hand and grasped the forearm of Artemis, and Artemis returned the gesture. Artemis felt like he had grasped a large tree limb and realized the raw power of the man who held the lives of his family in the grasp of his hand. For some reason, he trusted this barbarian, but he had no choice.

The three men were ready to enjoy a bath, but the captain warned his sailors to think of the servants as spies.

The two gay sailors were dedicated to each other, but the captain didn't ask questions about their relationship, nor did he expect to divulge his personal life to them. However, on this occasion, he wanted no problems caused by out-of-control libidos.

The captain was right; the male servant was a handsome, muscular lad of eighteen. He asked if the men were ready for their baths. Dressed in a revealing outfit meant to accentuate his male features, he seemed disappointed when the captain offered no encouragement. Leonis and Pirogue were polite, and measured the young man's assets with prolonged gazes, but told him to heat the water and lay out some towels. They would not need him to bathe them, dry them, or give them a massage. The young man was pouting when he tended the fire heating the bath water.

The baths were two stone and mortar pools about four feet wide, four feet long, and three feet deep. They were built almost next to each other to share the same heat source, which was a wood furnace under the floor with a clay and stone chimney to vent away the smoke.

When the baths were of a suitable temperature, the gay sailors climbed into one, and the captain climbed into the other. The men were unashamed of their nakedness or their sexual habits. Such things were considered natural in life, and they accepted most behaviors without question or judgment.

A sultry black-haired teenage girl walked up to the baths, wearing a simple wrap around her hips, with her luxurious hair piled and wrapped on top of her head. She was tiny, with breasts formed like small melons. Her skin was a dark olive color, and the captain thought the back of her neck was especially appealing, where wisps of fine black hair were floating in the light breeze.

She said her name was Alicia and asked the gay men if they needed her to bathe them. They laughed and said the captain might appreciate a good back scrubbing.

She turned to look at the captain with a cheerful smile and asked if he wanted his back scrubbed. She had black eyes that danced in an impish smile and nipples that had suddenly hardened into dark little olives.

The captain said from his tub, "Yes, missy. I can't reach my back, and it would be nice to get it clean."

Alicia walked to the backside of the tub, while the captain leaned forward, away from the edge of the tub. She pushed him forward with her hands on the captain's massive shoulders and urged him to sit on a small ledge under the water. He sat down on the ledge, and the water was up to his armpits. Alicia slipped out of her wrap, climbed into the tub behind the captain, and wrapped her legs around the captain's chest as she slid down his back. He could feel her taut little olives tickling his back and the crinkly feel of her pubic mound as it caressed the skin of his back. When her tiny feet touched his manhood, it came to life and stood strong and proud. She began speaking in soothing terms while she cupped his manhood between the soles of her feet and massaged it with a slow up and down movement.

He could feel his moment coming, but stood up to stop the proceedings. She complained with a falsetto voice, "Captain, I am not finished."

"It's good enough, thank you," he said, and turned around to face her.

The end of his manhood protruded out of the water, and in an instant, she grabbed it and said, "Let me wash your friend." She washed the top of his manhood, and the captain strained to keep from losing his seed. She saw his reaction and slid the washcloth to his testicles and covered the crown with her mouth. That was it; the captain unleashed three powerful surges, and Alicia swallowed several times to keep up with the bursts.

She stood on the ledge and whispered in the captain's ear, "I thought I was going to drown. I could barely swallow each gift before another flooded my mouth. Come into the room next door, and I will massage you with scented oils."

His sailors couldn't really see what had transpired, nor did they care.

Alicia stood up and stepped out of the tub. She dried herself and retied her wrap. "Captain, dry yourself, and I will get everything ready in the room next door."

The captain dried his body and walked into the room. There was a wooden platform with a towel on it. Alicia asked the captain to lie on the platform facedown. With hands that were strong for her size, Alicia began to massage the massive musculature of the captain's back. She thought, *this man's back feels like a horse's back or the trunk of a tree.* After giving his back a good massage, she began running her fingertips over his backside and down the back of his thighs. His hips began to make slight movements to simulate the sexual act. She spanked his buns and asked him to get up.

He stood up, and when he turned around, Alicia was on her knees over the platform. Her wrap was bunched above her waist and her most intimate parts were exposed. She reached back between her legs to grasp his manhood and guide him into her.

He grabbed her hips, and when he felt the head enter into the wetness, he held her and lunged forward.

For the first time in her young life, Alicia felt completely filled. She began to make mewing noises deep in her throat when the captain withdrew slowly and then pushed home hard and fast. She reached back between his legs to grab his balls in a tight grip and pressed them against her clitoris. The spasms came fast, and her oil was hot on his balls and her hand. When she climaxed and pulled hard on his balls, he fired semen deep into her womb.

Alicia wanted to sleep, but she had to get the captain ready for dinner. She washed his private parts and dried him off before helping him dress in new clothes, more suitable for dinner with aristocrats.

When the captain left, Alicia lay down in a state of exhaustion and delirium. She drifted off to sleep while wondering about the captain's seed, deposited so deep in her womb. She had never allowed anyone that liberty, but something deep inside her wanted this man's seed on this special day.

The captain advised his men, on the way to dinner, "Watch them, and eat the way they eat. We don't want to look like barbarians." His men nodded to indicate they understood the instructions. The captain wasn't really worried; his men were aware of the possibilities and advantages of becoming legitimate businessmen, instead of pirates.

Dinner was a unique experience for the pirates, with gourmet foods cooked by a chef. The plates and utensils were silver, and the serving dishes were gold. The pirates didn't know wine could taste so good. They had imagined kings might live in this kind of luxury, but not businessmen. They could take the dishes off the table and retire, but there might be more possibilities, much more lucrative possibilities.

Artemis figured there was no need to hold back; these men could take whatever they wanted at any time. It was obvious the two sailors were gay; they were not likely to rape the women. The captain was a man's man in every sense, but he was more of a thinker than the average pirate. Artemis desperately wanted a marriage; this would ensure the survival of his family and company. He worried that his headstrong and independent daughter might think such a marriage would be an arranged marriage. She could mess up the best of plans. Tonight's dinner should be an indication to the possibilities of uniting a princess and a pirate. One thing was for sure, they needed to move fast; soon the roving bands of marauders would be plundering the countryside, and this pirate captain was the only one who could prevent the total destruction and the loss of everything, including their lives.

The pirates were trying to eat like aristocrats, and the aristocrats were nervous about the invading horde of pirates in the city. The family members each wondered in silence, *will these men be able to stop the pirates, at the gate?*

Artemis started the conversation after dinner by looking at Captain Ogram directly. "Captain, will you be able to stop the pirates? From the smoke, we know some of the neighboring estates have been plundered."

The captain smiled and answered slowly, "We will meet the pirates at the gate. Some pirates respect me: others don't respect anyone. Pirates aren't a disciplined military force, but we are willing to protect you and your family with our lives. Now, the question is, what are you prepared to do for me and my crew?"

Artemis thought for a few moments. "If we survive this attack, it will be because of you and your men. Offering you money that you can take at any time is silly. Instead, I offer you and your men a future. I need sailors who know how to fight; except, that is only a slight elevation from your present position. I would like to train all of you to help me in the precious metals business. If you, Captain Ogram, marry my daughter, I would have a partner. Your sailors are intelligent men; they could easily work in the business as supervisors and live well. We have many men who can handle the technical aspects of the business, but no fighters. We need fearless men, men who can step forward in desperate times."

Janus' face became flushed when she realized she was being used as a bargaining chip with pirates. She stood up and dropped her napkin on her plate. "Excuse me, I feel ill."

She walked away and left everyone at the table wondering about her willingness to be the bride of a pirate.

The captain looked at Artemis. "I can recruit a few good men, I assume they will serve on your merchant ships?"

"Indeed, we can use many good men. I place my trust with you, Captain," Artemis replied, eagerly.

"I will hang my flag over the gate; the flag will stop all but the most ruthless, and those are the ones we need to worry about."

The captain turned to his two sailors. "Get my flag out of my kit, pull down the flag of Artemis, and run up my colors. Artemis and I have a few things to discuss. I'll be out there in a few minutes to check on the mob."

Both men nodded their heads to the captain and then to Artemis. They left in silence.

The captain leaned toward Artemis and spoke in a hushed tone, "As for me, the marriage can take place tomorrow."

"My daughter is the unknown," Artemis said, with raised eyebrows.

"With your permission, I will speak to her tonight," the captain added.

"Absolutely," Artemis said, without hesitation.

The sailors handled some good-natured heckling from friends and former friends, but things became serious, later in the evening, when Captain Tenon showed up with his crew of cutthroats.

Captain Tenon yelled from outside the gate, "Ogram, you think this place is yours. Too bad, it is now mine, and if you don't come down here and talk to me, we will be through that gate, quicker than you can pour piss from your boot."

Odie, a young blond slave boy of the estate, walked up to Captain Ogram and his men, carrying a self-made bow with a quiver of twenty well-made arrows, painted red. "Captain, today, I fight beside you," Odie said with conviction. He was sixteen and carried his bow with confidence.

"Get on the wall, keep your bow hidden, and try to flank the pirates on the road, without spooking them. They will never think you are one of mine, and we will surprise them with an enfilading fire. Don't raise your bow until you see these two releasing their first arrows. Speed and accuracy will carry the day. We are glad to have you with us."

The gate was partially opened; Captain Ogram and his men stepped through. The captain carried a spear and a shield, with a sword on his hip. His two crew members carried bows and quivers bristling with feathered arrows, and swords on their hips. Odie flanked Captain Tenon's pirates and looked out over the wall. His bow was hidden from the pirates below.

Captain Tenon looked at Captain Ogram and his two officers with contempt and said, "Everyone knows, sailors don't know how to use a bow."

"Some people had occupations, before becoming pirates," Captain Ogram replied with a grin.

The bowmen seemed anxious to start using their bows. They each had an arrow ready to fire and a handful of arrows in their left hand, along with the handle of the bow. Captain Tenon had twelve men, and Captain Ogram appeared to have two men with bows. The odds were thirteen to three; Tenon wondered why the two men from Ogram's crew weren't shaking in fear.

Captain Tenon played his hand. "I'll give you twenty minutes to clear out, with all you can carry. No one dies. If you want to fight, you will all die. You have twenty minutes."

Captain Tenon turned to face his men and motioned for them to sit down on the road.

Captain Ogram quickly walked three strides closer, while Captain Tenon was facing his men. When Tenon turned to face Captain Ogram, he saw Ogram's lance in mid-air, just before it pierced his chest and left lung. Captain Tenon tried to give the order to attack, but he was drowning in his own blood, and arrows were flying past him and into his men. A few seconds later, Captain Tenon fell onto his back. He turned his head to see five of his men crawling away from the onslaught of arrows; each of his men had multiple arrows sticking out of their bodies. The rest of his men were dead or in the final agonies of death. Captain Tenon turned to look at Captain Ogram and saw the sword flying downward just before it cut off his head.

Leonis and Pirogue ran past Captain Ogram and decapitated the wounded and the dead. They placed the heads on pikes and arranged them on each side of the path leading up to the gate. Captain Tenon's flag was tied to the pole beneath his head.

Captain Ogram ordered Leonis, Pirogue, and Odie to maintain a continuous two-man guard over the gate and to swap off one man every two hours, until the danger had passed.

Ogram was proud of his men. Young Odie's bow made the difference, and he was going to be rewarded. He had placed several of his red arrows in the heads and chests of Tenon's men.

Ogram walked into the courtyard and met Artemis. Ogram was not in a celebratory mood. He was no stranger to killing, but he didn't enjoy killing men, even men he despised.

Artemis wanted to thank the captain, but Ogram ignored his thanks and walked past him to say, "Odie is a free man today, and a member of my crew."

Artemis said, "Of course. He is yours."

"No, he is a free man, but right now, he is guarding the gate with my crew. Don't let anyone distract him, or they will answer to me, and I am in a foul humor. I have plans for Odie. He is a good man."

Artemis saw the intense wrath of Captain Ogram and decided he never wanted to provoke the man. He told his slaves and foremen, "Odie is a free man. Don't ask him to do a chore ever again, or Captain Ogram will put your head on a pole outside the gate."

He told Alicia he needed a quick bath before seeing Janus. Alicia said, "A bucket bath would be quicker, my captain. It takes too long to heat the big tubs."

Ogram answered, "A bucket bath will be fine." He noted Alicia's phrase "my captain," and wondered if this meant she considered herself on special intimate terms or if she thought of herself as a slave who belonged to him. Those were the two main meanings of such wording. Oh well, worrying over the emotions of a slave girl was not on his list of priorities right now. If his plan was going to work, he needed to convince Janus to consent to marriage. The marriage would be more enjoyable if she was a willing partner, but a marriage was going to take place, with her consent or without it.

Alicia had Ogram lie facedown on the wooden table. She sponged his back, legs, feet, and buttocks with loving care, while wishing the captain were meeting with her to talk of marriage.

She rinsed the captain with a bucket of hot water and had him turn over. She repeated the process again, but paid extra attention to his manly parts. Soon, his member was standing thick and tall, but Ogram put his hand on her shoulder and said, "There will be none of that right now. I need to meet my bride to discuss the wedding."

Alicia smiled and began to dry her hero. Just before she finished, she reached down and grabbed his member. She kissed the head with a loving caress. He felt his balls click in preparedness, and the head swelled even more; suddenly, Alicia rose up while still holding onto the member and talked directly to his manhood, "Good luck with your marriage negotiations." She smiled and shook the member from side to side, before walking away and giggling.

The captain got dressed and was walking toward the main house to see Janus, when he realized Alicia had helped get rid of his depression; he grinned thinking of her tiny features and how she fired up his desire, but right now, thanks to Alicia, he needed a woman.

Captain Ogram knocked on the door and was met by an older house slave, who led him into the flower garden and said, "Please wait, Janus will be here in a few minutes."

The captain waited and waited and waited. When Janus appeared, she was aloof and disinterested. He tried to engage her in conversation, but she ignored him.

Exasperated, the captain said, "I've had enough. I will give your father a bill for my services, and maybe you will be more open to someone like Captain Tenon and his crew."

Janus lost her look of detachment and turned to look Captain Ogram in the eye. "You low-life bastard, what do you expect after moving into a villa and demanding to own everything, including me?" She swung her hand to slap him across the face, but the captain was fast. He caught her wrist and gave it a twist.

"What do I owe you?" the captain asked. "I can take whatever I want. I saved you and your family. If I leave tonight, your riches will be gone tomorrow, and you will be servicing a pirate captain, if you are lucky, by this time tomorrow. Now, tell me how much I owe you and your family."

"Let me go; I will give you what you want. I will marry you, and you can share in our business and wealth. Now, let go of my wrist."

The captain let go of her wrist and watched Janus turn around and pull up her skirt above her waist. She climbed on a stone bench and presented her backside to the captain. "You can have me, but you will never make me respond to you. Make it quick. I am tired."

The captain's member was hard before he could pull it free of his clothes. Despite her rude behavior, he didn't want to hurt her. In the darkness of a moonless night, he guided his member back and forth along her outer lips and between her buttocks, seeking the homeport before the storm. He felt her wetness and positioned his member in the opening of the breech. He spread his legs and bent his knees for a better angle of entry. He pushed upward, and her vulva rose with the pressure, maintaining contact at the correct point of entry, but unconsciously preventing actual entry.

For the next attempt, he dropped down low by bending his knees even farther, and when she spread her knees to follow, he put his hand in the small of her back and pressed down forcefully, while his hips rose up hard and fast. She squealed from pain, but he was lodged halfway inside her, and she had no way to escape this rock-hard intrusion into her most intimate part. She gritted her teeth to keep from crying out. It was painful, but it felt good at the same time.

She was wondering what was going to happen next, when she felt a slight movement deep inside her. The captain had her hips locked between the iron grip of his hands, and he was moving back and forth, but only about a half-inch each way. The slow gentle movement felt good, but now, she wanted more. Suddenly, she felt a radiating heat and gentle waves moving outward from her vagina and into the rest of her body. She began to copy and exaggerate his movement, and her breathing quickened. Suddenly, she locked up and was swept away in a powerful orgasm. The captain used her time of helplessness to drive home fully and increase the movement to the full length of his member, and like a horse seeing freedom through an open gate, he let his member run at full speed. It was a short burst of speed; he had a powerful release and flooded her channel until his discharge filled her and squeezed past his cock to form a pool of fluid on the stone bench. He withdrew slowly, until there was a slight pop when his cock disengaged.

The sensations were exquisite. His cock slid forward and rose slightly to burrow along the crease of her ass. He was overwhelmed and leaned forward to increase the contact and slide back and forth a few times. He moaned, before releasing a small load of semen at the base of her spine. For the first time in his life, the captain felt like he had lost control of his sexual response. His body was shivering and he felt dizzy. He leaned back to see his seminal fluid dripping from her vulva and down her inner thighs.

Janus was weaving on the bench and seemed to be drifting in and out of consciousness. The captain pulled down her skirt to hide her nakedness and to protect her from the chill night air. He started to walk away, but turned toward her buttocks, lifted her skirt and landed a sharp smack to her posterior. He walked away, but he felt like he was on board a rolling ship, after half a bottle of wine.

This wasn't what he wanted, but he wasn't going to be ordered around or controlled by a teenage girl. He was the captain of a pirate vessel and about to become a partner in an international trading company that sailed all over the known world.

Janus was incensed, when she realized the captain was walking away without saying goodnight or giving her a goodnight kiss. She stood up and braced herself to keep her balance. She called out, "Captain, don't ever leave me without a kiss, especially after making love."

The captain liked this new attitude. He walked up to her, spread his legs so that they were face-to-face, and held her in his arms. He kissed her long and passionately, and she responded as if she was swept away by the power of the kiss. She pulled away a few inches and smiled with her most angelic face and closed her eyes for another kiss. When the captain closed his eyes and reached down for another, she bit through his lower lip and ran to her room.

He cursed her audacity and meanness, and then laughed at the situation. It was hard to be too upset about a cut lip, when he and his men had killed thirteen men and cut off their heads, earlier in the day.

He stopped to take a leak in the shadows, when he heard the giggles of Alicia. He finished while she watched with interest. He started walking back to the guesthouse, when Alicia ducked under his arm and wrapped the muscular arm around her.

"Do you need me tonight, brave captain?" she asked.

"No, I am tired, Alicia," he replied.

"You need me more than you know." He looked at her in confusion, and she pointed at the front of his clothing. A spot of blood, bigger than his hand, had soaked his cotton wrap. "Oh my. I suppose I do need some help, Alicia."

"I will help you, my captain."

The captain thought, *this slave girl, is fun. She makes a joke out of everything. If only Janus were more agreeable, like the slave girl Alicia, things would be much easier. Oh well, I have trained bums to be good sailors; I will train Janus to be a good wife.*

Alicia cleaned the bite wound and sewed five stitches on the outside, just below his lip. She gave him a sponge bath and dried him. When Alicia massaged his body, his little friend came back to life. When she was satisfied with the condition of his member, she straddled his hips and slowly lowered herself onto his manhood. She liked being in control, and since he wasn't likely to explode too quickly, she took her time and enjoyed herself on this man who was too tired to move.

The scar from the bite stayed with the captain for the rest of his life. Unfortunately, Janus did not respond well to his wife training techniques.

Captain Ogram woke up late the next morning. The tiny arms and legs of Alicia were wrapped around him, and he had a hard time getting free. He saw his wrap on a clothesline outside and walked out in the nude to get it.

Unfortunately, Saphis was walking up the path with a female slave. She looked at Captain Ogram and said, "Captain, you are lucky to be one of the few men who look better without clothes."

"Excuse me. I didn't mean to meet you out here, like this." He was obviously embarrassed for his future mother-in-law to see him naked.

"Don't worry, Captain. I enjoy looking at a handsome man . . . and his equipment."

The captain pulled his wrap down from the line and covered his private area and was even more embarrassed when Saphis and the slave woman began laughing. "Oh, Captain, trust me, you have nothing to be ashamed of. I am a good judge of men. However, you should dress for breakfast. It is customary in the civilized world." His future mother-in-law and the slave girl walked away, while enjoying a good laugh.

He walked into the guesthouse, where Alicia grabbed a hold of his friend and watched it spring up almost immediately. She put her hands on his shoulders and pulled herself up until she was poised over his member. She let herself down and began to climax, almost immediately, as she slid down his shaft. When she was finished, she gripped him tightly and enjoyed a few moments of bliss. Her breathing quickened and then slowed back to normal. When she opened her eyes, he said, "We need to make it quick, breakfast is almost ready."

She pulled herself off his root and said, "I am done."

He looked down at his shaft and said, "What am I supposed to do with this?"

Alicia poured cold water over his member and smiled up at him; the problem was resolved.

The four of them were outside at a small table for breakfast. Janus sat across from Captain Ogram and stared directly into his eyes, looking down occasionally at his fat lip and the stitches while lifting her eyebrows, and then smiling before winking at him. Saphis sat to the captain's left with her legs crossed; her left leg was over her right, and she was tickling the back of the captain's calf with the toes of her left foot. Artemis sat to the captain's right; he was talking business and wanted assurances that the marriage was going to happen. Artemis addressed the captain, "Captain, can we plan on a wedding?"

The captain answered, "I think we have reached a consensus, but Janus should speak for herself."

Janus glared at the well-meaning captain. He had said something wrong, by trying to be considerate of Janus and her feelings. She kicked him in the shin with the tip of her sandal and tightened her face into a look of rage, for emphasis.

Artemis turned to his daughter. "Are you prepared to marry the captain?"

Janus turned slowly to face her father. Her face was angled toward her plate, and she looked at her father and the captain with only the upper parts of her eyes. She had the appearance of a person with a psychotic mind. With her voice at least two octaves lower than normal, she slowly said, "Yes, I will marry our hero, this son of a bitch, for better or for worse."

Her choice of words made Artemis lift his eyebrows. He reminded himself how glad he was to be handing off the responsibility of his difficult daughter to someone else. The captain could manage a crew of cutthroat pirates; hopefully, he would be able to manage his new wife. Artemis turned to address the three of them. "I think we should have the marriage ceremony tomorrow. The captain and I need to discuss business and how to best get back in operation. How does that sound to you two?"

Saphis turned her chair a few inches toward the captain and had her left foot under his thigh and was soon touching both his thighs, under his wrap, with her toes. His member jumped up to attention, and her foot began to make feather-like touches on his shaft.

The captain decided to speak out first, "I need to, uh, and I want to get married as soon as possible."

Janus stared into the eyes of the captain and said, "I will make time for the wedding in the morning. It's impossible to rearrange my afternoon schedule, so it must be in the morning." She ate a few bites of food and left the table without another word.

Artemis ate his meal and stood up. "Congratulations, Captain. Let's hope I soon have several grandchildren."

He walked away, and the captain wondered if being rich wasn't as grand as he thought. There were gale winds and rough seas on the horizon, problems he had not anticipated.

Saphis said to the captain in a sultry voice, "Do you have a name, other than Captain Ogram? Family members are usually on more intimate terms than crew members."

"Augie—my family and boyhood friends called me Augie."

Saphis reached under the table to grab his root and said, "I like it." She pulled his member back and forth and began a slow up and down movement. "A man's name should reflect his character. Yours is perfect."

She slipped under the table and took the head of his member deep in her mouth and worked one hand up and down the shaft, while the other hand lifted his balls, as if to judge their weight.

He straightened his legs under the table, and several jolts racked through his body, followed by two lesser ones. He was still trying to catch his breath, when she crawled out from under the table to say, "I hope we can be close, Augie. My daughter is difficult, but I am the same woman every day, and don't worry about Artemis. He is inclined to be like your two friends. He barely managed to produce Janus after a bottle of wine, his first and last effort to make love to me." She winked at the captain and walked away.

Captain Ogram was overwhelmed with good fortune and beset by problems. A beautiful slave girl wanted his root at every opportunity, and now the sensual mother of his beautiful fiancée wanted him as her plaything. These were mixed blessings. The women were all sensual and exotic beauties; however, if his betrothed desired him with the passion of her mother or her slave, he would be a happy man. The two women who desired him so much were potential traps that could destroy any chance of a good marriage. He made up his mind to devote himself to his wife and meet the other two with a firm 'no' in the future.

Captain Ogram went to bed, wondering about how fast his world was changing. He closed his eyes and slept soundly before he was awakened to delightful sensations to his manly parts.

Alicia was nursing his manhood while he was sleeping. She looked up to say, "He was hard and reaching out to be loved. How could I deny my new friend?"

The captain acted exasperated, despite the pleasure, "Alicia, it is my wedding day!"

She smiled and said, "There is enough for both of us, and your mother-in-law as well. Besides, you and your little man will be lonely if you depend on your future wife."

He was trying to resist the feelings that were starting to overwhelm him, when she used her fingernails to brush against the crack of his ass. The climax consumed him. He rose up on his heels and shoulders, to hover above the bed. Alicia held on to his thighs and maintained contact with his manhood. The captain didn't notice her extra weight; lost in ecstasy, he balanced in an arc above the bed for nearly a minute. Slowly, he drifted back to the bed and fell asleep again.

In the early morning hours, Alicia began heating a bath for the man she admired. She wished he could be hers, but she was thankful for her time with this man.

Tyronnia was one of the few estates on the island that wasn't destroyed. The rich who could afford the price of mercenary pirates paid dearly for protection. Sometimes it worked, and sometimes the guards pillaged the estate.

The immediate family attended the wedding, along with everyone who lived in the compound. A normally joyous occasion was overshadowed by the devastation brought to the island by the people who had arrived a few days ago, the same people who arrived with the groom.

Of everyone involved, Artemis got the best deal; he managed to divert his two female antagonists on to his new partner. Like many men, he married and realized the female form didn't really interest him as much as the masculine form. He no longer had 'between the sheets' obligations, and his spoiled daughter was married to a man who could strike fear into the hearts of murderous pirate captains.

What a relief, to be rid of the contempt and ridicule from a woman who needed what he couldn't give. Now, she had a man who was near her own age, who had an insatiable taste for women and enjoyed their company.

His daughter was another matter entirely. Like one of the aggressive mares in her stable, she despised the men who desired her, but wanted desperately to be held and loved by a man. Like her mother, she was beautiful, and men acted silly in their admiration; yet, this was the behavior she loathed. Captain Ogram would spend a lifetime trying to appease her complex personality.

Yes, Artemis got the best part of the deal and saved his company as well.

Chapter 29
Nine Months Later

All three women gave birth within the year. Alicia was the first; she had a dark-haired son, and named him Antagoni. Three days later Saphis gave birth to a son, Africanus. Forty-eight hours later, Janus gave birth to a daughter, Aristede.

The three women admired each other's babies, but Janus noticed that Alicia had quit flirting with other men after the captain arrived; her mother also lost all interest in ridiculing and aggravating Artemis. Her parents were never a close couple, but they had drifted apart even more since the arrival of the captain. Janus kept a close eye on her husband and made sure he was never alone when other women came to Tyronnia; she was possessive of his manly charms, even if she rarely wanted or needed them. Having sexual control over him gave her a sense of power, and she used her body to entice, tease, control, and manipulate her husband. She liked to make herself available just enough to keep him always hungry for her. Control over the captain was like owning a beautiful sculpture or painting; after a period of time, the owner rarely looks at it, but enjoys the pride of ownership. The fact that other women desired her husband and stared at his masculine form added to her sense of power, and to have him begging for the occasional sexual favor made her feel omnipotent. Janus enjoyed being married because of the power it gave her, but the captain lived in a state of sexual frustration for thirty years.

Alicia and Saphis lost interest in sexual relations with the captain after their children were born. His good looks and sexual stamina now seemed superficial; the love of their children was real and honest.

When Aristede was born, Janus resented sharing her husband's attentions with their daughter, but his world revolved around little Aristede, a natural manipulator, who knew how to control her father, leaving Janus intensely jealous of her own daughter.

Leonis and Pirogue were both given command of their own merchant fleets with foreign offices, but their success and the many opportunities for infidelities consumed them with jealousy and misery. They drifted into drunkenness and became diseased with the infections so common among men who are popular with other men. Success and excess killed them early.

The three children grew up as best friends, and they loved each other. A retired cavalry officer was brought in from Persia, and he trained them to become excellent riders; soon, they dashed around the countryside like young daredevils. A highly skilled archer from the mainland taught them to use the bow during daily lessons, and every lesson became a competition. An old Greek, Unitas, was hired to teach the children philosophy, literacy, navigation, and math. He was their favorite teacher. Unitas had the rare gift of being able to make the subject matter come alive for students. Instead of dreading each day's lessons, they looked forward to them and discussed what they had learned during and after dinner.

Of course, Alicia wasn't included among the dinner guests; she was a slave, and, technically, her son, Antagoni, was as well. No one thought of Antagoni as a slave. He had the same features as Captain Ogram, but with his mother's silky dark hair, black eyes and warm personality. Antagoni had a quick wit and a disarming smile. Everyone assumed he would be a natural leader for the trading business in the future.

Africanus was as grand as his name. He was quick to fight and wanted to win every contest. He had fair features with green eyes. Strong and reckless, Unitas often counseled him to use discretion.

Aristede was the favorite of everyone. She could brighten up the gloomiest days with an impish smile and a wink. She grew up holding onto her father's finger, and when she was a young adult, she held his arm wherever they went.

She worshiped her father above all things, and was the only one to call him Augie.

Odie, the former slave who picked up his bow and stood on the wall against the pirates, became the captain's right-hand man, and was expected to run the business when Artemis and the captain passed on.

The captain grew older and began to lose the strength and good looks of his youth. Although Aristede loved him and stood by him without question, and the captain felt blessed to have a daughter who loved him above all others.

The Phoenicians began to open up trading colonies in Spain, Corsica, and Sicily. Africanus was eighteen, when he decided he wanted to sail to the farthest outpost, Spain.

Antagoni asked Captain Ogram where he might best serve the company and himself. The captain replied, "We are building a new trading center in Egypt, but there is unlimited opportunity in Spain and Sicily. Spain is rich in mineral deposits, and Sicily is a major shipping port in the middle of our empire. We will control all the precious metals trade of the world in a few years. There will be danger, but if you want to build an empire, Spain and Sicily are the most promising opportunities." The captain handed Antagoni a sheepskin. "Your mother is a slave. This document frees her and identifies you as a free man. You work for the company, and I don't expect problems, but I am your father, and you are technically free, if you are ever challenged."

"You are my father?" Antagoni asked for confirmation.

"Yes, everyone else knows, or thinks they know, but I am telling you, now. You are my son," the captain replied with sincerity.

"Then, Aristede is my sister?" Antagoni asked.

"Your half sister," the captain replied. "Is something wrong?"

"I hoped Aristede would be my wife. I love her. I love her more than life."

"Everyone loves Aristede, but you are her half brother. You can only admire her from a distance."

The captain could see that his son was upset. He tried to console him. "You have lived on an island all of your life. The most beautiful girl on that island is your sister. You need to meet many girls and learn to enjoy them."

Antagoni asked, "Does Aristede know that you are my father?"

"She will know if you tell her. If you want me to tell her, I will. I leave that up to you."

Antagoni began to withdraw, after talking with his father—a man he had known all his life, but without knowing he was his father. The next day, he asked to work in the company office in Spain.

He and his mother sailed to Spain on the next ship, but before he left, he told Aristede the dark secret that prevented them from loving each other.

"Aristede, I have something to tell you before I leave."

Aristede smiled and winked at the young man she loved; she thought he was going to propose and ask her to sail to Spain.

When Antagoni hesitated, Aristede became impatient. "Yes, are you going to tell me that you can't live without me?"

"Yes and no, Aristede. You are my half sister. The captain is my father as well. I love you more than life, and for that reason, I must leave you."

Aristede's cheerful face began to redden. The tears welled up in her eyes, and she placed her palms over her eyes. Deep sobs racked her body. She walked away while Antagoni was still apologizing.

Aristede never forgave her father for his indiscretion, and although the captain lived in wealth the rest of his life, he died a lonely, bitter old man.

Odie, the slave boy who helped Captain Ogram defend the estate, was the glue that held the company together, and he eventually married Aristede. The captain's confidence in Odie allowed him to realize his own potential. He emulated the captain, and Aristede fell in love with the former slave.

The Phoenicians controlled commercial trade on the Mediterranean from the ninth century BC to the sixth century BC. They traded precious metals, wine, and the Cedars of Lebanon. They were gradually conquered or absorbed by other cultures, and their written culture was lost, because it was written on papyrus. Yet they developed our alphabet and spread culture, knowledge, and ideas throughout the Mediterranean, and especially the Aegean. Providing the spark to ignite a cultural birth in Greece, leading to the beginning of Western Civilization.

Chapter 30

Alexander and Hellenistic Culture

Hellenistic is derived from the Greek word for Greece, 'Hellas.' The Hellenistic Culture starts with Alexander's death in 323 BC and concludes with the Roman annexation of Greece. However, the Hellenistic influence on the world didn't end with the Roman occupation.

The maternal line of Aristede and the H1W2 strain were still on the island of Tyre until the time of Alexander and the siege of Tyre, in 332 BC. Tyre was a part of the Persian Empire and the wealthiest port city of the empire. The other Phoenician cities capitulated to Alexander. Tyre surrendered the old city on shore to Alexander, but refused to surrender the island fortress with ports on the north and south coasts. These ports were the real wealth and power of the Phoenician naval and commercial fleets. Alexander was uncomfortable having Tyre with its naval power at his back during the invasions of Gaza and Egypt.

Tyre was an island several hundred meters from shore, and Alexander had no ships to mount a siege. However, there were stone buildings on shore. Alexander destroyed the buildings and used the rubble to build a causeway to the island fortress.

The citizens kept up a relentless barrage of boulders from catapults and arrows from ships, while the causeway was being built. When the causeway was completed at great cost, siege machines, augers, towers, and battering rams were built to destroy and enable a breach of the walls, but fire ships kept setting the equipment on fire.

Alexander called on the other Phoenician cities that had already capitulated to provide ships, and Alexander soon had a navy to stop the assault ships of Tyre.

After seven months of siege, Alexander breached the walls and sacked the city. Those who were wealthy escaped by sailing to North Africa and creating the city of Carthage. The thirty thousand survivors of Tyre were either executed (probably by crucifixion) or sold into slavery.

Carthage became the trading center and economic powerhouse of the world, until Rome destroyed Carthage. Before and during the siege, the wealthy escaped the impending Roman destruction of Carthage (no stone was left standing) by sailing to Spain. Again, some of the H1W2 maternal line barely missed death or slavery by escaping to sanctuary in Spain. The H1W2 line continued for over fifteen hundred years before being caught up in the tumultuous march of history again.

Chapter 31
One of the Last Great Flint Strikers

Snapping Turtle was considered to be the greatest flint striker in the world; although, there were several great flint strikers in the world and they were all considered to be the best. Snapping Turtle owed his skills to a group of people who came from the East and a group from the West, almost twenty thousand years earlier. He knew nothing about Tiger Paw or Yellow Hair, but it was their DNA flowing in his veins. It was their dream of finding a safe home that allowed Snapping Turtle to become one of the richest men in the New World.

When his first ancestors walked through America, there were probably a hundred thousand people in North America. Immigrants were still arriving because of the Ice Age, and the passages between America and Europe and Asia were still being used, but many people were moving south, into Central America and South America. Immigrants had already traveled to Tierra del Fuego. The dreams of new land free from hunger, disease, and war compelled early men to explore, but the dreams of their forefathers were forgotten after a few generations.

Traders, warriors, and hunters came great distances to trade for the precious articles made of flint and obsidian. The rivers were the highway systems of the day, and they traveled wherever there were rivers.

Snapping Turtle had never traveled from the quarry where he was born. The quarry contained the potential wealth of one of the richest kingdoms in the known world. If he left, a strongman or chief might move in and be impossible to dislodge. It was true, he was one of the greatest artisans in the world, but the skill needed to work flint and obsidian was not difficult to acquire. He was content to stay in the quarry that had belonged to his ancestors for countless generations.

He made flint knives, projectile points, awls, axes, and scrapers. It was an interesting time; the bow was considered a recent invention, yet the atlatl or spear thrower was still used by many hunters and warriors. The atlatl spear was a lighter version of the heavier lance. All three weapons required projectile points of different sizes and weights. The projectile points had to be light, sharp, and balanced. If the projectile point missed its target and hit a rock or a heavy bone, it broke and had to be replaced or altered; the qualities that made the projectile points durable also made them vulnerable. Man has always been forgetful and careless, and known for losing knives, scrapers, awls, arrows, and spears. Consequently, men could chip and shape crude tools for replacements or depend on the abilities of Snapping Turtle and his artisans to provide the finest instruments. It was his craftsmanship and that of his workers that supported the community and established trade in the Western World..

The traders came from faraway places to trade for his flint works of art, and they brought wondrous treasures. Snapping Turtle acquired a vast knowledge of the world, and of the goods the world had to offer by communicating with the traders using sign language and a few universal words and grunts.

Women and children were some of the most common trade goods, but Snapping Turtle was open to trade for anything of value. He liked young, beautiful women for his bed and mature women to take care of domestic chores, tending the garden, the orchard, the beehives, and watching over the children. He was fairly certain he had sired over thirty children and had at least twenty slave children brought by warriors wanting his flint pieces. The boys would be raised up to be either flint workers or warriors to guard his empire. He tested the kids when they were young to see if they had the potential to learn the flint-working skills.

They had to recognize the pieces within a rock, and then chip out the instrument with an economy of work to produce a symmetrical instrument that became the tools and weapons of civilization. His work was noted for the flutes down each side of the arrow and spear points. The flute made mounting on arrows and spear shafts easier. Men also looked at the flutes as a mark of status. For if a man owned these instruments, he was considered wealthy. Actually, the flutes were important because they allowed the point to be balanced, symmetrical, and considerably lighter. Snapping Turtle thought the flute style was from his family, but his knowledge of history was limited. The flute was made in several locations over North America for many years before his family arrived. However, these were the characteristics that made his work so well known throughout North America.

If a boy couldn't learn the skills of an artisan, he became a soldier and hunter. The hunters practiced their accuracy with both the bow and atlatl to secure fresh meat. Sadly, Snapping Turtle realized his warriors were not as disciplined or as fierce as some of the tribes that came to trade.

Snapping Turtle liked to trade his daughters (many of whom were H1W2) off to powerful men from other tribes as wives. It was sad to trade off his daughters, but it was vital to maintain a healthy community. These outside marriages made for alliances and protection among neighboring tribes; however, it was beneficial to keep the blood fresh within his tribe if healthy children were to be born.

An early daughter was traded to a group of buffalo hunters, forerunners of the Comanche, from the area that was to become Wyoming. They were skilled at stampeding buffalo and getting them to jump off cliffs. They often killed more than they could process, and thousands of buffalo spoiled beneath the carcasses of thousands more. Eventually, the Comanche migrated into Texas, Oklahoma, and New Mexico to drive the Apaches out of their traditional homeland. They continued hunting the buffalo on foot and driving them over cliffs, until they acquired horses.

The spirits of the mist told Snapping Turtle's forefathers that girls should not procreate with relatives of close blood; the spirits sent imperfect children when their laws were broken. Sometimes one of the boys would fall in love with one of his girls and problems would arise. He raised the slave children with his own children, and over the years it was often confusing to remember which ones were his natural children and which ones were slaves. He knew there were good reasons for people to mate away from their own blood, and those reasons often became painfully obvious through children.

Snapping Turtle had many wives and never lacked for comfort, but his young workers and soldiers needed a wife by a certain age or they became restless and irritable, and the quality of their work was compromised. He felt like he had to spend a disproportionate amount of time securing wives for his young men, but it was best to keep the artisans working and the hunters alert. The responsibilities of leadership were overwhelming.

Women, who were not artisans, were an important part of Snapping Turtle's tribe. They farmed the fruit trees, corn, and melons that grew by the river and gathered the edible Camus roots and various nuts. They would grind the foods and cook them to make them edible. Without hardworking women, his society would fall apart. He appreciated women for the pleasure they provided in bed and for the work they did—of course, without them, there would be no children and the earth would wither and die. Snapping Turtle considered himself a learned man for understanding these complex issues. Most men were content to have a full belly and a woman in their bed. Snapping Turtle had evolved well beyond the basic needs of the common man.

Snapping Turtle's favorite wife was Dancing Raven, an H1W2 woman. She came to him through a trade for a set of four obsidian knives and an obsidian war ax. A warrior, Elk Slayer, wanted the four obsidian knives, but had nothing of value to trade. Snapping Turtle said he would accept the pretty girl he had with him as a fair trade. Elk Slayer became angry and told him Dancing Raven was his wife, and he didn't want to trade her.

Snapping Turtle shrugged his shoulders and rolled up the obsidian knives in a tanned deer hide to put them away. Elk Slayer leaned forward and grabbed Snapping Turtle's wrist. Suddenly, there were three spears aimed at the chest of Elk Slayer.

Elk Slayer had committed a serious breach of trading etiquette; you don't touch the flint traders. The great flint workers always had bodyguards who were ready to kill in an instant. Actually, Snapping Turtle wondered why Elk Slayer was still alive. His father's bodyguards would have killed him. Snapping Turtle stepped closer, stood face-to-face with Elk Slayer, and said, "You are alive because I like you and I think we can make a deal; otherwise, you would be dead and I would keep the knives and take your wife as my own. I will make a final offer. If you don't accept my offer, you are free to leave and never come back."

Elk Slayer looked at the three warriors with contempt. He was not afraid to die. "You must give much more for Dancing Raven," he said in defiance.

Snapping Turtle held up his hand, with the palm toward Elk Slayer, and closed his eyes with a touch of drama. He turned around and walked into his lodge and emerged a few minutes later with an obsidian ax. It was about the size of a man's hand with the fingers extended. It had a serrated blade and a blunt end, and it was mounted on a two-inch piece of hickory a little over two feet long. It was both a piece of art and a deadly weapon of war. Because of the fragile nature of obsidian glass, no one would use it for work. It had only one purpose; it was an instrument of death.

The warriors guarding Snapping Turtle thought he had lost his mind; a weapon like this could buy four or five beautiful girls, and to give away the knives with the ax was insanity. Elk Slayer was holding the ax like he was ready to use it. He was in a rage. He wanted the obsidian tools, but he hated losing his wife.

Snapping Turtle signaled to two of his wives to escort the girl into his lodge. She submitted meekly, and Elk Slayer was escorted out of camp. His sense of loss was compounded by feelings of buyer's remorse. He swore an oath to himself: he would return for revenge, and take back his woman.

Dancing Raven was one of those women men desire beyond reason. Her long black hair was thick and silky. Her teeth were like pearls when she smiled. When she rolled her large dark eyes, she showcased her exotic facial features. She had a sensuous way of moving that accentuated her femininity, more like a mountain lion than a woman. It was these fluid movements that made men lose their senses.

Snapping Turtle moved Dancing Raven into his lodge and treated her as a favorite wife without consummating the marriage. He had two objectives: he wanted to know whether she was carrying the savage's child, and he wanted her to be curious about her new husband, rather than fearing an aggressive personality.

Within two weeks, his wives let him know that she was not carrying a baby. This news pleased Snapping Turtle. He wanted his own child with Dancing Raven. He gave her beautiful clothes with furs to keep her warm and made sure she had the best foods to eat.

Dancing Raven's life had changed from constant brutality and work to a life of luxury. She began to admire Snapping Turtle and wonder why he was not finding her attractive enough to make love to her.

Snapping Turtle was playing a game of seduction with the ultimate seductress. He had time and a multitude of wives to keep him satisfied. He pushed his luck when he treated two of his older wives like queens at dinner. The three of them flirted and laughed until it was time to go to bed. The two wives crawled into Snapping Turtle's bed, and made love until the early morning hours.

This situation caused doubt in the mind of Dancing Raven, and if her husband continued to ignore her, while making love to women who were older and heavier, she would lose the prestige of being married to a chief.

Three nights later, the tribe had a wedding for one of Snapping Turtle's sons, and Dancing Raven made sure she was seated next to her husband, with her hand resting on his thigh or his shoulder throughout the evening. She wore a new white tanned deer hide dress, trimmed with lynx around the hem, over her shoulders, and down her back. It was an expensive winter garment, and Dancing Raven wanted everyone to see how well her husband cared for her. She had small, shiny, white seashells braided into hair, and they clicked together when she put her head back to laugh or turned her head in one of her sensuous movements.

The women noted her actions; Dancing Raven was ready to become a wife. The men envied Snapping Turtle, and wished they could enjoy the beautiful Dancing Raven.

When the celebration ended, Dancing Raven crossed her arms beneath her breasts, as if she was cold, and pushed them upwards to accentuate their modest size. She leaned against Snapping Turtle as if she needed his warmth, and he instinctively put his arm around her shoulders.

She found many things to do before climbing into bed, but made sure the other wives knew she planned on sleeping with her husband. She kept Snapping Turtle waiting to create anticipation, but not long enough for him to fall asleep. After the calculated wait, she walked to his bed and slowly undressed. She stood naked with her feminine form silhouetted by the yellow-colored light of the dying fire.

Her body was perfectly formed; Dancing Raven had confidence in her femininity, but she wanted the other women to see her naked form. After this evening, they would never doubt the power she held over her husband.

However, when she crawled between the covers, she was no longer in control of the situation. Snapping Turtle was nothing like other men she had known. He made love to every part of her, and within twenty minutes she was recovering from the most exciting and powerful orgasm she had ever felt. There was a rippling buildup from the core of her being, until the explosive moment when the sensations made her forget everything else. She was still feeling the receding waves of ecstasy and waiting for her body to recover, when her husband began to make her feel another orgasm. Snapping Turtle seemed to know when her last orgasm was almost over and when to begin another. She lost track of the number of orgasms and drifted out of her body to watch from above. Eventually, her body began quivering, and she passed out. Snapping Turtle rose up over her and slid into her moistness. He let himself spend inside of her after a few strokes; he needed relief, but it wasn't exciting without her participation. He made a mental note not to take her this far the next time. She definitely had her limits.

The next morning, Dancing Raven didn't wake up. She slept through the day and didn't leave the lodge until dinner. She seemed distracted and unable to keep her balance while walking. For the next few days she was quiet and subdued. On the fourth night, she crawled into bed with her husband and asked that he make love to her with less enthusiasm. Her whole body ached after their first session, and her thighs and stomach were bruised from the contractions.

Snapping Turtle promised to be more careful in the future and avoid giving his wife so much pleasure.

Thus Dancing Raven, the woman who controlled men with a smile and sensuous movements, met the man who could control her through her sexuality. Snapping Turtle played her body like a concert violinist tunes and plays his instrument. It was no longer a question of *if* she was going to orgasm; it was a question of intensity and frequency. She no longer worried about how she was perceived by other women. Dancing Raven was exploring a higher realm of ecstasy.

Snapping Turtle and Dancing Raven had a baby girl nine months from the day they first made love. They called her Skipping Coyote. Four years later, she was a charming child who brought a smile to every face in the village with cute antics and funny mannerisms.

Snapping Turtle considered himself to be a fortunate man. Not only did he have all the women and children a man needed, but he had strange shells from faraway rivers and big waters, he had exotic furs to wear in the cold months, he had exotic foods, and he even had the giant tusks of the monsters (the tusks of mammoths were the inspiration for many legends). The traders told fascinating tales of fighting these extinct monsters.

Men came to trade anything and everything for his flint and obsidian knives, and his points for arrows and spears. Many of these men were warriors, and some of them made him nervous, especially if they were belligerent and had almost nothing of value to trade. These men were dangerous and unpredictable.

There were problems. He remembered the warriors of his grandfather's time being more disciplined and intimidating to the traders—the earlier flint strikers were better artisans as well. Perhaps his grandfather was even a better artisan than Snapping Turtle. He was concerned; if the quality of the work was in decline and the ferocity of his warriors was perceived to be weak, his empire was in danger of being attacked, or liable to collapse from within.

Snapping Turtle often wondered about quitting this job of being chief to a tribe of ungrateful, lazy people who worked less and less and wanted more and more. If it was possible, he would travel south with Dancing Raven and Skipping Coyote, to a warmer climate, where he could forget about the crops, the tool making, the bees, and all the problems of a tribe. He tended to spend more time with his young wife and daughter than he did attending to the everyday problems of a large tribe.

Snapping Turtle would never know how the raiders came into camp just before daylight on that fateful morning. He awoke to the sounds of screams and moaning. He grabbed a spear and ran outside, to be struck down with a blow to the side of his head by a warrior whose nude body was painted red and black. The war club was heavy and had multiple sharp pieces of flint imbedded in the heavy end, and one of the pieces of flint had pierced the bone of Snapping Turtle's skull.

He was stunned and watched in horror as his young flint strikers had their hands tied behind them and were bound together in a long line with the young women and girls. Those who put up a fight were cut down with clubs, knives, and spears. He noticed the stone weapons carried by these raiders were not made by his tribe, but they were well made, perhaps as well made as his own weapons. Nearly all his people were captured, dead, or dying.

His storehouse was being raided, and a fortune in stone was being stolen. They were also placing his personal treasures in leather sacks. He stood up and stumbled forward to stop the theft, when he felt a lance impale him from behind. He looked down at the well-made stone projectile point protruding from his abdomen and fell to his knees. He touched the stone lightly with the knowing fingers of a master artist and determined the stone to be of a superior and foreign construction. He marveled at its artistry.

Dancing Raven was draped over the shoulder of Elk Slayer, and he was leading Skipping Coyote by the hand. Elk Slayer had an evil smirk on his face. Snapping Turtle recalled the advice of his grandfather: "Never strip a man of his pride by trading too sharply." Snapping Turtle was still on his knees when Elk Slayer walked up to him, pulled the obsidian ax from his belt, and buried it in Snapping Turtle's skull. Snapping Turtle's world turned black, and his life was over.

Snapping Turtle's life was over, but the skills of the flint artisan were encoded in the mitochondrial DNA of many of his wives, and had been passed on to many daughters. The young slaves and his sons who were learning the skills of flint striking were considered to be very valuable to the raiders. Trading them to tribes over great distances allowed the skills to be disseminated. The girls who were traded over the same distances also possessed the ability to pass on the traits of the artisans to their daughters through the genetic traits within the mitochondrial DNA. By rolling the genetic dice often enough, eventually a child would be born who would pick up the tools and start turning out the superior tools and weapons that were so vital for survival during the Stone Age, but Stone Age skills were soon to be discarded, Europeans were introducing the magic of iron for making knives, projectile points, scrapers, and many other tools. Almost anyone who was good with his hands could make iron arrowheads and knives with a few basic tools. There was no need to trade for artistic pieces made by dedicated craftsmen.

Snapping Turtle's extended family and his tribe were among the richest in the New World. It was difficult to maintain discipline, when his workers and soldiers became fat and lazy, and spent their free time lusting after each other's wives.

Unfortunately, when the tribe became focused on acquiring wealth, pride in community and stone working skills began to diminish. He was one of the few who recognized the decline of the community. He saw his workers meeting clandestinely with traders who brought intoxicating drinks and plants. These workers were hedonists, living solely for themselves. In his grandfather's day they would have been executed or exiled from the tribe. However, so many of his workers were stealing from the tribe to indulge personal weaknesses, he would have a revolt if he tried to maintain the old laws.

Snapping Turtle's goal was to maintain his tribe and their wealth, but, in reality, he was focused on the acquisition of wealth. He knew he was responsible for inspiring the sense of community so necessary for maintaining a strong tribe, but he lacked the leadership of his forefathers and the will to enforce the old laws that could have made his tribe strong for a few more generations.

Snapping Turtle's people were happy; unfortunately, without discipline and loyalty to the tribe, a disintegration of society was inevitable. Ultimately, it was he who failed the tribe.

Elk Slayer had his wife back, but he didn't. She never forgot the sight of her beloved Snapping Turtle with a spear protruding from his abdomen and receiving the coup de gras from the obsidian war ax. Her feelings of disgust toward Elk Slayer were immeasurable. She considered him a stinking barbarian who was worse than a wild animal.

Elk Slayer grew angry and bitter; he owned a beautiful woman who refused to respond to his advances. He decided to trade off Skipping Coyote, to get Dancing Raven to forget her life with Snapping Turtle, but this illogical move made the situation worse. That night, Dancing Raven hid one of the obsidian knives made by Snapping Turtle, and while Elk Slayer was sleeping, she pushed the knife beneath his ribs at an upward angle, just below the sternum. She pierced his heart with the razor-like black glass. He awoke for an instant with his eyes wide open and tried to scream into a large piece of leather that was shoved into his mouth. He thrust his head backwards and there was a death rattle in his throat. He died a few seconds later.

Dancing Raven withdrew the knife and wiped away the blood, and while on her knees, she held the knife to her throat and fell forward.

Chapter 32
Skipping Coyote

Skipping Coyote saw her father killed and never heard of her mother's fate. She traveled endlessly with a band of traders, and was adopted by one of the couples of the small band, Red Bear and his wife Puma. They had no children and enjoyed the lively antics and intelligent conversations Skipping Coyote provided. They were loving parents and gave Skipping Coyote a good childhood.

When Skipping Coyote was twelve years old, famine struck the southwest. The trading band was losing people because of starvation. Red Bear and Puma decided to move south to the mountain areas of northwestern Mexico, to the home of Puma's people. They left in the middle of the night to avoid taking on stragglers. It was a difficult journey, and they were fighting starvation during the trip. Red Bear was more of a warrior than a hunter, but he kept his family alive, until they reached the ancestral home of Puma.

The people of her home village remembered her from fifteen years earlier, and there was a great flowing of tears and many stories of loved ones to hear. Skipping Coyote became a favorite of everyone. Puma's tribe was the Tarahumara, a tribe of runners. Not like we think of runners today, but runners that can run down deer and elk. Red Bear had never seen his wife run, but he was always amazed at how she could walk all day with a heavy pack and never get tired. In fact, he was the one who always called an end to the day's journey.

Red Bear considered these people to be the most unusual people he had ever met; yet, they were modest to the point of being shy about their running skills. They called themselves the Foot Throwers, and they could run up and down the high altitude mountains effortlessly.

Red Bear was also surprised to learn that heredity was traced through the maternal lines of the Foot Throwers, and this was why Puma was so graciously accepted back into the tribe, with a husband and a surrogate daughter.

In a few more years, Skipping Coyote married a chief's son, Dark Moon, and they had two daughters.

The Foot Throwers were a loving and happy family tribe, who sang songs and laughed in the evening. The Foot Throwers had no warriors and didn't train for war. They lived so far up in the mountains, few people wanted to make such a challenging climb; so they existed in peace for eons. Until one morning, a group of Aztec warriors walked into the village and demanded twenty hostages. The Foot Throwers were shocked and didn't respond. The leader of the savages became impatient. He walked up to one of the chiefs and killed him by hitting him in the head with a club imbedded with fragments of obsidian. The soldiers began tying ropes around the necks of people. When the Foot Throwers realized they were being taken captive, they ran in every direction.

The warriors laughed and took out after the runners, but the only ones they could catch were the old people and young children. The chief of the Aztecs became enraged and brained the first warrior who came back empty-handed.

Mountain Waters, the youngest H1W2 daughter of Skipping Coyote, was captured and started back to Tenochtitlan, the Mexica or Aztec capital on the future site of Mexico City. In those days, Tenochtitlan was the sixth largest city in the world. The city was built on an island of Lake Texococo in central Mexico in 1345 AD. Tenochtitlan was the religious center of Aztec civilization.

According to legend, seven tribes migrated, from the seven caves of Aztlán of northwest Mexico, in successive waves to the Valley of Mexico. Science and archaeology contradicts the legend: a series of severe droughts in the

Southwestern United States and Northern Mexico forced the migration of many cultures to the Valley of Mexico, between 1100 and 1300 AD.

The purpose of the migration was to find the best location to build a city. The priests carried a large idol, Huitzilopochtli, who whispered instructions to the priests. Apparently, Huitzilopochtli promised great wealth and prosperity, if the people obeyed his instructions. During the migration, he named the people Mexica and/or Azteca to give them an identity.

Unfortunately, the gods had a serious falling out during the migration.

Huitzilopochtli's sister, Malinalxochitl, had a son, Copil, who fomented a rebellion among the Mexica. Copil felt the Mexica had abandoned his mother, the goddess Malinalxochitl. Huitzilopochtli was disgusted with the senseless violence and moved to defeat Copil. Huitzilopochtli instructed the Mexica to rip Copil's heart from his chest and throw it as far as possible into Lake Texcoco. The point of landing would designate the construction site for the new home of the Mexica.

When Copil's heart was thrown into Lake Texococo, it landed on an island next to an eagle about to eat a snake while perched on a prickly pear cactus.

During the construction of Tenochtitlan, Huitzilopochtli became enraged with his sister, Coyolxauhqui, the moon goddess, because she murdered their mother. He killed Coyolxauhqui, cut off her arms and legs, and threw them around the construction site. Like most moon goddesses, she managed to maintain control during the night, but died again at every sunrise.

Mountain Waters arrived into this violent culture twelve years before its collapse in the early 16th Century. She and about a hundred other captives from the northwest were marched over one of three causeways to an island in the middle of a large lake. Mountain Waters stared in awe at the magnificent buildings constructed of stone and painted in dazzling colors of white, blue, and red. There were frightening depictions of gods and monsters carved in stone and painted in bright colors. An aqueduct supplied a continuous stream of fresh water. Large boats were conducting commerce on the lake. The captives were marched into a walled portion of the city, containing the homes of the nobility and the priests. The city's population of two hundred fifty thousand lived in apartment buildings several stories high. The captives thought the city must have more people than the rest of the world. After walking for over two miles through the heart of the city, the captives were led into a walled section of the city, an even more exotic place. There were stone palaces, monuments, and carvings of monsters far bigger than the hostages could have imagined.

The hostages were brought into a courtyard, and after being examined by several different men, a brisk bidding began on individual hostages. After the bidding was concluded on a hostage, the captive was led either to a large group guarded by men who were assumed to be priests because of their exotic dress and painted bodies, or to private individuals in the crowd.

Mountain Waters noticed that all of these people were giants, and the rest of the people in the city were normal-sized. Being a child made the difference more dramatic and frightening.

The bidding for Mountain Waters was over in seconds, and a priest led her to a young couple. The man was tall and muscular, and his wife was even taller. They examined her mouth and felt over every part of her body. After the examination, they nodded to each other and seemed happy with their purchase.

Everyone began walking through a large crowd, to the base of a huge pyramid, and began to make their way up a long staircase to the top.

At the top of the staircase, Mountain Waters marveled at the beauty of the tranquil scenes around the pyramid. There were lush green fields with lakes and mountains on the horizon. She longed for her home and her family members, but she knew she had to keep her mind in the present, if she was ever going to see her family again.

There were loud horns blowing and shrill whistling instruments; the noise was deafening. Most of the people, including the largest group of hostages, were standing near a large stone altar.

Mountain Waters had no way of knowing, but the priests were about to recreate the symbolic death of Copil.

The first hostage was led to the altar and thrown on his back, while priests held his arms and legs. With an obsidian knife, a priest sliced open his upper abdomen and reached into the victim's chest area to rip out his beating heart. The heart was held high by the priest to loud cheers from the crowd below, while four other priests began skinning the victim. When the corpse was skinned, one of the priests wore the skin like a piece of clothing and walked out to the edge of the pyramid to hear another round of cheers. The body was dismembered, and the parts were thrown down the staircase, to be gathered by workers down below.

The process took less than five minutes; soon, a new victim was chosen and the gruesome act was repeated. Mountain Waters was in a state of shock when the first victim was sacrificed. She remained silent, while all of the little girls and adults who befriended her were butchered.

Mountain Waters hoped she wouldn't be killed, but she decided to shut off her feelings and show no emotion. The wealthy adults who were standing with her were quiet and only nodded their heads with slight smiles during the procedures. A few children and women within her group of hostages lost their composure and started screaming hysterically; they were immediately led over to the priests to be the next victims.

The human sacrifices began in the early morning hours and continued until late in the afternoon. The Mexicas or Aztecs sacrificed over twenty thousand people a year; efficiency and speed were important.

Later that evening, Mountain Waters and her parents attended a banquet for the priests and royalty of Mexica society. There were thousands of people, and again, Mountain Waters noticed that these elite people were all giants.

Slaves who were subservient and respectful served the elite Mexicas, but they were ignored by the elites. There were appetizers of fresh exotic fruit. Mountain Waters was nearly starved after her long trip, and was grateful for the food she was served. She sat between the people who purchased her. They smiled at her, while they talked with friends. They seemed to be saying nice things about her, but there was no way she could know for sure.

While waiting for the main course, her benefactor cut away the noose around her neck and introduced himself as Totla and his wife as Misere. Mountain Waters told them her name and repeated it slowly so the couple could learn to enunciate the strange sounds. Several priests stopped by to visit.

Mountain Waters knew they were inquiring about her, since she could hear the Mexicas trying to pronounce her name.

It was obvious she would need to learn the language as quickly as possible to survive and return home. Mountain Waters decided that her every thought and action from this point forward would be dedicated toward staying alive and returning home.

The main course was served on silver and gold plates. There were large servings of vegetables and different cuts of strange-tasting meats. There was more meat on her plate than she could eat in a week, but her stomach had shrunk on the trip, and she could only eat a few bites before she was full.

A corpulent man across from her laughed at her appetite. He spoke to one of the waiters and was carrying on a lively conversation with Mountain Water's adoptive parents when the waiter returned with six roasted human hands for the fat man. Suddenly, Mountain Waters realized where all the meat came from and why these people were so big and the poor people were so small and skinny.

The Mexica had no domestic animals; therefore, there were minimal sources of protein. The royalty and priesthood within the walled city relied on cannibalism for their protein, and they had an ample supply.

Mountain Waters felt her stomach turn over when the man bit through the tiny fingers of a child's hand, but she willed her food to stay in her stomach. Survival was going to be more difficult than she imagined.

Mountain Waters survived and grew into a young woman, but she remained detached from the Aztecas. She could never accept them. Mountain Waters dreamed of her childhood and the family she had loved. Her Azteca parents treated her with kindness, and she was grateful to them for saving her life, but she remained aloof, an island in a sea of depravity.

Mountain Waters turned sixteen and had shown no interest in the young men who wanted to marry her; the priests suggested she join a convent. Her parents considered this the only option for their daughter, whose behavior bordered on being anti-social.

The convent women never married; however, they were required to have a daughter by a bound captive. Male children were taken from them after two days, but the females were raised within the religious order to continue the tradition. Slave girls attended the Azteca priestesses and they lived in luxury; they had everything but freedom.

A few months after Mountain Waters was accepted into the order, she was expected to breed with a captive. She was told it was simple. He would be bound, and she would control the situation. The captives were specially selected because of their intelligence, and physical features. If they produced weak or sick babies the captive would be sacrificed immediately, so they tried to do their best.

Mountain Waters was grateful it wasn't going to be an Azteca.

She was led into a room after calculations were kept on her cycles and the most advantageous date and time was chosen. She was wearing a green brocade robe trimmed with feathers and gold, and was naked beneath the robe.

There were two young nude women with the captive. The nude captive was laying on his back, on the platform, with his hands tied behind him. The two women were smiling and motioned to Mountain Waters to come to the platform. One of the women had his member in her hand and said, "There is a balance between him being ready and waiting too long." The other woman helped her take off the robe and placed Mountain Waters' knees on either side of the man's hips. She then rubbed a liberal amount of fine oil on Mountain Waters' vagina and on the man's member. Her untried opening was then positioned over the rock-hard head of the man's penis, while one woman directed the penis and the other woman pushed gently on Mountain Waters' shoulders and encouraged her to relax, and let the penis enter her sanctum.

The head slid into the outer opening, and Mountain Waters thought it was as far as it was going to go when the woman who had her shoulders pushed down with all her weight. The penis was now fully lodged, and Mountain Waters was whimpering from the intrusion. One of the women whispered in her ear, "Rise up and down a few times and it will be over." Mountain Waters bent forward and rested her upper body on the man's chest. She began to slowly move her hips up and down. She heard the man moan and felt a hot, searing liquid pouring into her. She let out a soft moan, just before the women pulled her off the captive and rolled her onto her back.

Mountain Waters thought, *how rude, I was beginning to enjoy the ritual, and they pull me away.*

One of the women said to her, "It is important to keep the seed in the proper position as long as possible." She was given cold water and melon pieces while she lay on her back for thirty minutes. The captive was led away by a noose around his neck, and that was the last time she ever saw him.

The priestesses who watched over the cycles was correct on the optimum day and hour for Mountain Waters to conceive, and nine months later, she gave birth to a baby girl. Her mission was complete. Each woman was expected to have a girl to keep the order at the correct size. Baby boys were probably adopted, but no one knew for sure. Mountain Waters named her child Running Girl and secretly hoped they would run off together one day.

When Running Girl was ten years old, she and her mother were ordered to travel north to start an abbey in a new Azteca town. The town was over a hundred miles away, and they would be walking. Mountain Waters hoped the trip would build up the legs of her daughter and they could make their run for freedom.

In the middle of the night, at the last campsite, Tlaxcalteca warriors attacked the Aztecas. The Tlaxcalteca had been waging the Flower War, against the Azteca, for a hundred years, but now they had powerful allies, Spanish conquistadors with horses, war dogs, muskets, and crossbows. The Tlaxcalteca had formed an alliance with the Spanish and they wanted vengeance.

Mountain Waters could tell by the sounds of the battle, the Tlaxcalteca were winning. It was a dangerous gamble, but she decided to make her escape.

With a small pack on her back, Mountain Waters took Running Girl by the hand, and walked into the shadows, until they were well away from the battle. She looked down at her daughter and said, "Now, we run with the wind."

Running Girl looked at her mother and smiled. They ran through the night. The next morning, Mountain Waters replaced their worn-out sandals with heavier sandals the workers wore. They rested throughout the day and drank freely from a stream. Mountain Waters had enough grain and nuts for them to live seven days, but they needed to find water each day.

Near the future city of Zacatecas, they ran into a village of silver workers called The Silver People. Mother and daughter were adopted into the tribe almost immediately. Mountain Waters and Running Girl were fascinated with the skills of the silversmiths and anxious to learn the art. They were fast learners and contributed to the metalworking techniques with the artistic and creative expression of H1W2 women.

They found a home, during a period of monumental change in Mexico. Cortez was destroying the Azteca Empire and laying the groundwork for the birth of Mexico.

Chapter 33
Spanish Horses in North America

The introduction of Spanish horses into North America produced some of the greatest horses to ever drink water. Great feats of endurance and speed, that are incomprehensible to modern horsemen, were once commonplace among horses of the American Plains.

A legend among the Old Spanish horses, was a gray stallion with black ears, he is linked forever with a horseman who turned his back on civilization and, like the white Maya Gonzalo Guerrero, shared his knowledge and skills with the natives. Most horsemen know wild horses are lucky to live for ten or twelve years; yet this stallion or his sons, were seen many times over two hundred years.

Gray horses with black ears are not common, but occasionally, a mare or stallion will "mark" foals with a consistent identifying feature. Usually it is white socks or a bald face. In this case, we should assume the stallion produced exceptional gray colts with black ears.

With feral horses, a stallion rules his herd or harem with iron hooves. Colts are kicked out of the band when they reach sexual maturity, between three and five years, and join a bachelor herd of colts and older stallions.

There is no law of primogeniture, but the rules of succession are simple. If a colt or stallion is ready to challenge the herd sire, the old man will be waiting. It is a fight to the death, but if one of the two decides to quit early, he might be allowed to limp to the bachelor herd with wounds and a broken spirit.

The gray stallion rode over the best grasslands of Texas, Oklahoma, Nebraska, Montana, Wyoming, and Alberta, trying to charm and collect the fastest mares for two hundred years, but no one could catch him or his elusive harem. The gray stallion was too smart, and his mares were too fast to be caught; unfortunately, he was destined to have a confrontation with the world's greatest horsemen.

Chapter 34

Paco Santee, "un Hombre del Tierra"

Julio was born in 1570, to a fifteen-year-old Indian girl who fell in love with a twenty-year-old Mexican of Castilian heritage, Don Onate. Onate was in line to inherit a huge silver mining hacienda near Zacatecas. Julio spent his first eight years learning to ride, learning arithmetic, and learning to read. He and his mother had a carefree life, but his father had a marriage opportunity to a rich and powerful young woman, the illegitimate daughter of Cortes and a granddaughter of Moctezuma. The marriage would provide massive wealth, opportunities, and prestige for Onate. His father advised him to marry as soon as possible. Unfortunately, his mistress and son posed a problem. He didn't want his new wife to think he cavorted with common Indians. To avoid complications, he sold his mistress into slavery, to a friend in Cuba, under the condition that she work as a house servant and not as a field hand with a short life expectancy. He arranged for his son to serve as an apprentice with one of the world's greatest equine matadors, Paco Santee. He paid handsomely to have this opportunity for his son. Hopefully, Julio would make the most of the opportunity.

Don Onate took his son to Mexico City, under the pretense of showing him the city and to see the bullfights. After watching Paco Santee perform, Don Onate asked Julio if he would like to be a bullfighter, and, like most young boys, he answered, "Yes." Don Onate told his son he would see if he could arrange for the schooling.

The fog and early morning chill had Julio shivering during the ride to Santee's rancho in Cuernavaca. Hector, a bodyguard and servant for Don Onate, told young Julio, "Santee es un hombre del tierra." (Santee is a man of the earth) That was all he would say about Santee.

Julio knew Paco Santee was considered to be the world's greatest horseman. An equine matador who killed bulls so gracefully, he was known as "The Dancer." He also knew he raised fighting bulls for the arena, at his rancho near Cuernavaca.

Paco Santee was a master showman and a perfectionist; he wanted precise results in the arena of Mexico City and at home, when he trained his young horses. Julio was to arrive a half-hour before daylight on the Ides of March. He was to be mounted on a well-schooled and well-made horse of good bloodlines, a horse that would become Santee's property, when the boy progressed and moved up to a more advanced horse. Julio was to bring all his possessions on a pack mule that would become Santee's as well.

Hector was to stop at the arena gate and let the boy ride up to Paco, alone. Santee calculated every move for maximum dramatic effect; this morning, the boy was to realize, he had a unique honor to train with Paco Santee, and for the next thirteen years, Paco would be his mother, father, and professor. If Julio had the talent, work ethic, cunning, and intelligence to learn, he would learn the lessons that would make him a man and a caballero (gentleman or horseman).

Santee saw that Julio was riding a well bred, but ill-trained horse. It was a wasted ride for the boy and the horse. Now, Paco would need to ride the horse to see if it was worth the time and effort to train. Hopefully, the boy wouldn't get hurt before a suitable mount could be found.

Santee remained aloof and stared off into the gray mist. Julio rode up to the horseman; his horse saw Santee's stallion and stopped acting like a nervous fool. Santee looked at the horse and thought; *At least the horse has enough common sense to realize he is out-classed.* Santee's powerful stallion ignored the newcomer and stood waiting for the faintest cue. Paco looked at the boy to say, "¿Mi vagamundo para donde vas?" (My vagabond, where are you going?)

Julio recognized the clipped nasal accent of a Castilian aristocrat. With the voice of a hero-worshiping Mestizo boy, he replied, "Mi tío, voy a ir contigo al infierno o al cielo. Tú eres mi professor." (My uncle, I go with you to hell or heaven. You are my teacher.)

Santee looked at Julio with a slight grin. His almond-colored eyes had a gold ring around the irises, possibly a Moorish influence; his intense stare was cold, dark, and mysterious.

Santee thought: *The lad has bravado and intelligence. The bulls and horses will test him, and we will soon learn if the boy's courage is real.* He cursed the poor judgment of the father for sending him on an ill-trained horse. He wanted the boy to gain confidence on a well-trained horse. This horse would be a constant struggle, just to ride, and possibly a waste of time. This is what you expect from a man who pretends to be a Castilian caballero, the type who thinks they look good riding a nervous, ill-mannered horse. If the boy can stay on this horse without getting hurt, there will be many horses, many bulls, and many lessons.

A slight movement caused the tiny spur chains on Paco's boots to swing, and the horse rotated his ears forward and backward in anticipation. His horse's body tightened, and the blood vessels began to bulge on his face and neck. The horse knew Santee was about to ask, and he was poised to spring into action, but he remained perfectly still.

Santee raised his rein hand and tilted the reins backward in a barely perceptible way. Without looking behind him, the horse trotted backwards for thirty feet. Santee tilted his hand slightly to the right, and the horse turned a pirouette to the right. He tilted his hand slightly to the left, and the horse turned a pirouette to the left. He cantered a ten-meter circle to the left and a ten-meter circle to the right. Santee cantered along the fence and picked up a lance off the rail. He stuck it in the dirt, and at arm's length, while holding onto the shaft, he cantered slowly around the lance to the left and to the right. Santee picked up the lance and held it vertically. Santee lifted the reins two times, and the horse stood poised in the classical Levade stance on its hind legs. When he lowered his lance and pointed toward Julio, the horse ran at full speed toward the boy. Santee raised his lance, and his horse slid the last twenty feet to stop directly in front of Julio's horse.

Paco Santee was impressed. Julio showed no fear when Paco's horse ran toward him, and smiled when he slid to a stop. Julio passed the first of many tests on the path to becoming a caballero and an equine matador.

Julio saw five minutes of riding and realized Paco Santee made the horsemen of his past seem clumsy and stupid. Now, he knew why horsemen spoke of Santee with reverence and hushed tones.

Julio's father, Don Onate, wanted to erase all signs of his former mistress and his bastard son; in his mind, selling the mother into slavery and apprenticing his son for thirteen years was logical and humane, compared to the other options available.

Onate was Criollo, of Spanish heritage, but not born in Spain. This was a stain against him in Spanish society. Despite being rich and powerful, he was considered morally, physically, and intellectually inferior to native-born Spaniards. His fiancé was an illegitimate daughter of Cortés and a granddaughter of Moctezuma, a tremendous match of prestige and wealth.

Unfortunately, the friend of Don Onate who bought Julio's mother was killed during a card game, and his wife sold everything before returning to Spain. A bordello purchased Julio's mother and a jealous customer killed her a few months later.

Don Onate distinguished himself as a military leader against Indians of Northern Mexico, and Onate was given permission to exploit vast lands north of the Rio Grande on September 2, 1595. Onate would become the ruler of all the land he colonized in New Mexico, from the Red River to the Pacific Ocean. He was to outfit two hundred men and provide mining equipment, tools, seed, farming equipment, trade goods, medicine, and one hundred head of cattle, a thousand sheep for meat, a thousand goats, and one hundred and fifty mares. Everyone was expected to pay a fifth of all wealth discovered or made on the new land to the king of Spain, referred to as the King's Fifth. The possibilities for corruption and graft were monumental.

Julio learned of his mother's fate at the age of sixteen, in 1586. His father didn't give him the aristocratic name Onate, so Julio adopted the name Campo Santee. He became Julio Campo Santee, a man of the earth, a man like Paco Santee. By this time, he was considered the best equine matador in

Mexico, and many Spanish aficionados of the sport were saying he belonged in Madrid, but the details of his mother's death changed Julio. Previously, he was considered to be the prototype of Paco Santee and the crowds loved him, but suddenly, he changed, and the attitudes of his horses changed, since the personality of a horse reflects the personality of its rider. Julio and his horses now enticed and weakened the bull with precision movements and a careless indifference to the thirteen hundred pounds of violent death waiting to destroy them at the first sign of a mistake. However, Julio and his horses didn't make mistakes. The crowds continued to roar approval. Paco played to the crowd and worked them, but Julio ignored the crowd, like he ignored death. From the poorest Indian hovel to the wealthiest haciendas, Julio's latest performance was the main topic of conversation, until his next sensational performance. No one ever complained of him being an arrogant showoff; indeed, he was an indifferent, coldblooded killer.

Santee realized at this time, Julio was the best student he had ever trained or seen. The student surpassed his instructor, and Paco retired from the arena to watch and help Julio with his horses. Julio's skills in the bullfighting ring were already legendary—fame, fortune, and women were his for the taking, but he chose the austere life of his benefactor and stayed with Santee during his declining years. Santee was his surrogate father; the only father Julio had known. Like the colt that is kicked out of the herd, the rage seethed in Julio. The killing of bulls was only a superficial release for the hatred he felt for his father.

It was Paco Santee, who kept the cold, indifferent killer of Mexican fighting bulls under control, but Julio killed so effortlessly and devoid of emotion, he worried Paco Santee. However, Julio was devoted to his mentor and would never disappoint him with anti-social or lawless behavior. Santee returned the loyalty with the love a man bestows on a son.

They lived in Santee's log and adobe ranch house twelve more years, and Julio continued to kill the bulls from horseback with such grace and elegance, mature men were seen crying in the stands, and women of all ages threw him flowers with messages of love and lust. Santee loved to watch his protégé perform his magic dance of death, but he wished Julio would become involved with the beautiful Mexican women who flocked around him. Sadly, the professor and his student always rode home alone.

Paco Santee passed away in his sleep at the age of seventy-eight, when Julio was twenty-eight. Julio burned the ranch house with Paco still in his bed, and headed north with their gold, silver, cattle, horses, and pack mules in the middle of the night. The rules and laws of civilized men no longer applied to Julio. He felt profound sadness when he left the burning ranch house. He wanted to cry, but Julio had no tears; without knowing why, he tilted back his head and made the mournful cry of a wolf grieving for a lost pack mate. This cry of the wolf became the calling card of Julio Campo Santee, and from that night and into the future, when Spaniards, campesinos, vaqueros, gringos, and Indians heard this mournful cry, they locked their doors and kept a weapon next to their bed.

Chapter 35
Julio and the Llano Estacado

Julio rode north into Texas. He avoided everyone and eventually found the Llano Estacado, one of the great grasslands of the world. He had a mule that could smell water from thirty miles away; so the unmarked and unending topography was not an inconvenience. He appreciated the loneliness of the Llano Estacado. The isolation and solitude fit Julio's personality. He found the buffalo and discovered they could perform like the fighting bulls of Mexico City, except they were faster, with more endurance, and they were more unpredictable. Julio killed them in a sporting manner if they chose to fight, but if a bull ran from death, he ran it down and let the speed of his horse drive the lance behind the last rib and forward through the diaphragm and into the lung and heart area. It was like fighting the bulls without a crowd. Julio didn't need a crowd to enjoy killing.

A Chief of the Quahadi Comanche heard about the Mexican magician who killed buffalo effortlessly from horseback and wanted to meet this horseman. The two men became instant friends, and Julio put on a demonstration of his skills. After the demonstration, Julio was encouraged to live with the Quahadi and teach them about riding, horses, and killing buffalo from a horse. One of the chief's daughters, an attractive H1W2 maiden, brought Julio out of his self-imposed shell, and the Quahadi Comanche soon became the greatest horsemen and horse warriors in the world.

After Julio taught the Comanche the finer aspects of horsemanship, horse theft became a major industry, with Don Onate supplying the best horses. Julio taught the Comanche to leave the best broodmares and older stallions to make sure the Spanish continued to raise good horses for them in the future. The Quahadi Comanche increased their herd size by over ten thousand in two years.

Horses coming from Canada and the US mixed with the greater numbers from Mexico increased the herds of wild horses by hundreds of thousands on the extraordinary grasslands of the American Plains.

Julio lived with the Comanche well into his seventies and died over a hundred years before the American Revolutionary War. He and the Quahadi Comanche developed horsemanship far beyond the level of everyone else, and they conducted their raids with virtual impunity. They were the epitome of the primitive horseman and lived in a horseman's paradise, the Llano Estacado. The wild horse herds are estimated to have been over one million, and the buffalo, their main staple, numbering several times that amount. They considered the theft of cattle and horses to be a game of sport. They also engaged in slave trading and slavery, and their reputation for cruelty to captives is hard to imagine.

They existed in a primitive state of freedom. Two hundred years later, their concept of freedom made an impression on men like Ranger Horn, who saw the inevitable demise of the Quahadi Empire.

Freedom was a vague concept to Julio, but his mother's loss of freedom and unfortunate demise became painfully clear to him during a chase for the gray stallion with black ears.

The stallion had eluded the Spanish, the Mexicans, the Indians, the Americans, the Canadians, and the Comanche, but Julio and a band of hard-riding Quahadi horsemen had been chasing the gray ghost for three days in the canyon country of New Mexico. Each time they thought he was trapped, he knew or found an escape, but he finally made a mistake and led his mares and colts onto a pie-shaped mesa with steep walls over a hundred feet high.

With a herd trapped like this, Julio taught the Quahadi to employ his signature technique for breaking horses, a method that allows a good horseman to train a horse in a few hours.

While the riders kept the herd from escaping, several of them would throw their ropes and catch a mustang around the neck. The mustang would fight, and the loop tightened to became a ligature; soon the horse could no longer get enough air and would collapse. The rope was loosened, and while the mustang was recovering, the Comanche was sitting on the horse's neck, with the horse's head pulled up to the man's chest, with the Comanche breathing into the horse's nostrils. When the horse stood, the Comanche was on the horse's back; inevitably, the horse accepted the rider. Perhaps it was better to have a rider than the suffocating rope, but a wild horse could be trained to ride within minutes. It was a rough technique, and occasionally the horse died, but there has never been a comparable way to break wild horses to ride in a few minutes.

When the Comanche horsemen approached the gray with black ears, he was running wildly around the perimeter looking for an escape, but he had no options. The mares and juveniles were standing together in stark terror as the men and their horses closed in on them. When the stallion realized there was no escape, he galloped around his mares one last time to say goodbye and ran toward the precipice at full speed. Julio heard himself say, "No, no, no," as the stallion jumped into the void.

The Comanches were happy to capture the colts and fillies by the gray ghost, and they were laughing and joking as the breaking process began, but Julio felt sick. He turned his back on the colts and fillies being roped on the mesa. With tears in his eyes, he thought of the magnificent stallion and his unwillingness to compromise freedom. He chose death over slavery, and Julio was the one who made him make that choice. Julio thought of his mother, who had been sold into slavery, and he realized the importance of freedom and how quickly it can be lost. If Julio had not chased the stallion so relentlessly, the horse would still be alive and eluding everyone. Horses were Julio's life, and sadly, he had just killed the finest specimen of them all. He never chased wild mustangs again.

The Quahadi Comanche measured wealth primarily in horses, but their portfolios included gold, silver, and slaves. During and after the time of Julio Campo Santee, the Quahadi Comanche were the richest Indians in the Americas.

Julio's horsemanship was the perfection of thousands of years of accumulated horse culture, a culture honed to perfection during the Moor's occupation of Spain and the age-old tradition of raising, moving, testing, and fighting the black and brindle fighting bulls from horseback. The vaquero (Mexican or Spanish cowboy) used the fourteen-foot blunt-tipped lance to move and test the cattle for the fighting spirit required in the arena. This is the reason our American cowboy, the prodigal son of the Mexican vaquero, was initially known as a cowpoke.

Chapter 36

Exploration After Columbus

Twenty-five years after Columbus landed on San Salvador, three thousand leagues of Atlantic coastline were explored, from Patagonia to the coast of Labrador. Men were seeking passage to Marco Polo's India and the riches of Kublai Khan, but their efforts were in vain. The eventual source of Spain's vast wealth and the last coastline to be explored was also the closest to San Salvador, the Atlantic Coast of Mexico.

The heirs of Columbus tried to maintain control over their claims to the profits of the West Indies; however, maintaining control over greedy and reckless men, on the other side of the world, was nearly impossible.

Diego Velázquez de Cuéllar led the conquest of Cuba, as the lieutenant of Diego Colon. After the conquest of Cuba, Velázquez set himself up as governor and reported directly to the Crown, eliminating the percentage of profit Diego Colon expected.

Velázquez came over with Columbus on his second trip, in 1493, after seventeen years of service in the wars of Spain. As governor of Cuba, he was a man of experience and wealth. He was mild-mannered, but known for being suspicious and jealous; a collision of personalities between Velázquez and Cortés was inevitable.

Chapter 37

Hernán Cortés: Conquistador

Hernán Cortés Pizarro was born in Medellín, the kingdom of Castile, in the year 1485 and died 12/2/1547. He was born into a noble Castilian family of humble means. Known for being intelligent and clever, Hernán caused many problems for his parents. He was considered unfeeling, conceited, malicious, petulant, and preoccupied with the seduction of girls and women.

He attended the University of Salamanca at the age of fourteen to study law; unfortunately, the regimen was difficult for the restless spirit of a conquistador. Cortés quit after two years; however, he managed to learn Latin and become a proficient writer.

Dreams of the "New World" stoked the imagination of young Cortés, and he longed for adventure and riches. He traveled to the port city of Valencia, with the idea of serving as a soldier in the Italian wars, but became preoccupied with chasing the women who are always found in port cities.

He signed on for an expedition to the New World. Unfortunately, the night before he was scheduled to depart, he was climbing a wall for a clandestine liaison with a young married lady, and the wall collapsed. Cortés received substantial injuries, and the ship departed while he lay in a hospital bed.

In 1504, at the age of nineteen, Cortés signed on with an expedition led by Alonso Quintero. Alonso was ambitious, but had limited success in the New World. He was noted for wanting to break formation with his companions and strike out on his own. However, the crown strictly controlled the conquest of the New World, to protect its twenty percent royalty of all wealth extracted from the New World.

On the island of Hispaniola (Haiti and the Dominican Republic), Cortés visited the governor, a friend from Spain, to inquire about opportunities to acquire wealth. The governor's assistant assured Cortés of a land grant, but the impetuous Cortés replied, "I came for gold, not to till the soil like a peasant."

In accordance with the law, Cortés registered as a citizen. This allowed him to receive a building plot and land for cultivation. The governor appointed Cortés the notary of the town of Azuza and awarded a repartimiento (gift) of Indian slaves. He served as a notary and worked as a planter for five years. Although his life was anything but ordinary, he helped suppress native uprisings, and fought several duels over the virtue of girls and women.

Because of sickness (possibly syphilis) in 1509, he missed the disastrous expeditions of Diego Nicuesa and Alonso de Ojeda to the mainland. Cortés recovered by 1511 and signed on for an expedition to conquer Cuba with Diego Velázquez de Cuéllar, who served as an aide to the governor of Hispaniola. Although the natives of Cuba had no military tradition or capability, they fought bravely for their freedom. Cortés was noted for being resourceful during the campaign. He was made clerk to the treasurer, responsible for assuring the king of his one-fifth of all profits from gold, slaves, and commerce. He was rewarded with a repartimiento (gift) of huge land grants and native slaves, and appointed alcalde or mayor of Santiago, the official capital. He built the first house in Santiago, raised cattle and was in the mining business; Cortés had wealth, and power.

After balancing an affair between two sisters, who were sisters-in-law to Governor Velázquez, there was enmity with the governor. Cortés was obliged to marry one of the sisters, Catalina, under pressure from Velázquez. The marriage produced a son, Martín. Cortés enjoyed success for fifteen years, before the quest for adventure and gold overwhelmed him.

Chapter 38

A Christian Knight in Mexico

The Muslims, or Moors, occupied much of Spain for nearly eight hundred years. They were expelled in 1491 after a brutal and bloody campaign. When the war was over, there were thousands of unemployed soldiers, men who were willing to serve as conquistadors.

Pablo Castile was one of the last Christian Knights of Spain. A devout man, he had sworn a vow of celibacy and dedicated his life to ridding Spain of the Moors.

Without war, Pablo faced poverty and a nameless grave; although, he was intrigued by prospects in the New World. This was his last opportunity to acquire a stake in life, and he was ready to gamble everything. Pablo was an accomplished horseman with many years of experience in mounted warfare; he knew cavalry tactics as well as any man alive.

Horses were valuable in the New World, but his horse was twelve years old and might not survive the voyage. The passage had a mortality rate among horses of over fifty percent, and this area of the ocean, near the equator, became known as the Horse Latitudes, because of all the dead horses that were thrown overboard.

Pablo found a noble lady, who was looking for a well-trained horse to ride on trails and trips to town. Pablo let her ride his horse to see if they were a good team. It was obvious the horse liked her. Pablo gave her a few lessons on riding a high-schooled advanced horse. She responded well and the horse loved the lady's well-intentioned but naive attempts to cue an advanced horse. The horse and the lady were an excellent partnership. Pablo decided there was no use in prolonging the agony. He wished the lady well, and kissed his only friend goodbye. The lady gave Pablo a small sack of silver coins. He knew she had included more than a few extra coins by the weight of the sack.

Pablo sailed to Cuba, and was again mired in poverty with no prospects for the future.

Chapter 39
The White Mayan

Francisco de Montejo landed with seventy-five sick and starving Spanish soldiers, on the beach of Chetumal Bay, Yucatan. He was greeted by an overwhelming Mayan war party, ready to attack the Spaniards. Montejo noticed a white, bearded man with tattoos and body piercings among the Mayan warriors. Montejo asked to parley with the white man. The white man spoke Castilian and was a war chief.

The white Mayan told Montejo, to leave or die. Montejo had no options; he left Chetumal, and lived to tell a bizarre story of a white Mayan war chief.

Gonzalo Guerrero, a Spanish sailor from a small village in Andalucía, was the white Mayan war chief. He was a crewmember on a ship sailing out of Panama in August 1511, with a shipment of gold and slaves.

A gale drove the ship onto the Pedro Keys, a reef near the Bahamas. The ship was destroyed on the reef, and a small boat was launched, saving some of the crew and passengers. Unfortunately, the 'lifeboat' was without food, water, or sails. Apparently, the slaves and gold were lost with the ship.

The small boat drifted west for fourteen days, and several crewmembers died, before landing off the coast of Yucatan on the island of Cozumel. The survivors were the first Europeans to land on Yucatan.

The Maya captured the Spaniards and immediately sacrificed most of them. Gonzalo Guerrero and Jerónimo de Aguilar escaped and were captured by another Mayan chief. The second chief was an antagonist of the first chief and was humored by the story of their escape. He offered the men the option of taking a wife and becoming Mayan.

Guerrero jumped at the chance. He married one of the chief's daughters, Zazil Há, and distinguished himself in battle against native enemies and Spaniards as well. His knowledge of Spanish weapons and tactics gave the Maya technical advantages and confidence in the future. They learned the Spaniards, horses, and war dogs were not immortal and the rifles and cannons did not harness lightning and thunder.

Previously, Maya fought to capture the enemy. Warfare was a means for capturing victims for sacrifice. The European concept of total warfare bewildered the Mayan warriors and native armies were often annihilated or fled in terror because of the weapons, horses, and war dogs. Guerrero's information gave the Maya a distinct advantage in warfare against the Spanish.

Aguilar chose to remain a slave and maintain his faith; he refused multiple offers of beautiful women from the chief. He remained celibate and a slave, until he was given to Cortés, as a gift.

Guerrero had multiple opportunities to return to Catholicism, including a letter from Cortés. He refused and stayed with his family. Cortés sent Aguilar to Guerrero to convince him to return to the church. Guerrero proclaimed his love for his family and said, he would never be accepted in Spain because of his tattoos and piercings, and with the Maya he was a chief.

It was assumed Guerrero was killed in a battle against the Spanish; a tattooed white man was found among the native dead, shot through the lungs by an arquebus (early musket). Guerrero was fifty years old.

After teaching the Indians to rush the riflemen before they can reload, and how to wait in ambush with spears to kill the horsemen, Guerrero was considered a villainous symbol of treachery among the Spanish. However, he is considered a hero in Mexico, and the father of the Mestizo. His most notable contribution was to infuse genetic resistance to European diseases among the Mexican people. His children survived the smallpox epidemic that killed half of the Mayan people and the measles epidemic that swept the Yucatan, killing ninety percent of the smallpox survivors.

Strong Bow, Guerrero's oldest son, headed north after his tribe was annihilated by disease, into the future state of Texas. His assets included dynamic genetics and an intense hatred of the Spanish and the white race.

Chapter 40
Cortés Leaves Cuba

The first expeditions to Mexico, Cordoba in 1517 and Grijalva in 1518, brought back minimal amounts of gold, but fantastic tales of gold farther inland. Cortés used his influence with the Governor of Cuba for permission to conduct an expedition to Mexico, on the pretext of exploring and trading with lands to the west.

Cortés was forbidden to colonize, but he coerced Governor Velázquez into writing a clause in his authorization, allowing for emergency measures to be taken without authorization; emergency measures were to be used, "In the true interests of the realm."

Cortés sold or mortgaged his properties to purchase three ships. Multiple investors became factors in the expedition by providing eight more ships.

Velázquez became suspicious of Cortés's intent, because of the size of the venture, and tried to stop the expedition. Cortés heard about Velázquez's change of heart and set sail, leaving Governor Velázquez in an impotent rage on the dock.

To avoid a confrontation with Velázquez, Cortés left the north shore of Cuba without a full complement of men and landed on the south shore of Cuba, to recruit more men.

It was here that Cortés met Pablo Castile. Castile was worried because of his age; he was forty-eight, and his hair was nearly gray. Cortés was thirty-four.

Pablo Castile waited in line wearing a white tunic with the Red Cross on the front and back, signifying a Christian Knight and monk. When it was Pablo's turn, he stood at attention and said, "Pablo Castile, a Christian Knight, I fought the Moors. I want to join your expedition."

Cortés looked at this relic from the past and was awestruck. He had to be one of the last from a bygone era. However, the knights were well trained in warfare and cavalry tactics, and they were certainly the most experienced warriors in all of Spain. Their integrity was above reproach; they would rather die than compromise their honor. They were even celibate to avoid earthly temptations. Cortés weighed the possibilities and asked, "Can you lead my cavalry unit?"

"Yes sir, I can lead with God and honor," Pablo replied without hesitation.

"Good, you will be the captain of my cavalry. You are Castilian?" Cortés asked.

Pablo's cold gray eyes looked deep into the eyes of Cortés, and he said, "Yes, sir!"

Cortés replied quickly to relieve the intensity of this killing machine of the past. "Good, I will expect more from you. Sign here."

Pablo made an X and then the cross, followed by another X. This was more than enough for a Christian Knight.

The Moors were primarily Caucasian Muslims from North Africa. When they needed reinforcements, they usually came from West Africa; these troops were blacks.

During periods of reciprocal occupation, some Muslims became Christian and some Christians became Muslims. Occasionally, whole towns were converted one way or another to avoid being annihilated; consequently, some Spaniards were dark. It was best not to question a devout Christian Knight about his heritage. They were known for being touchy about the minor details of life, and a sharp blade through the throat was often the response to indelicate questions. They answered to a higher authority than those here on Earth, and they had no fear of earthly consequences. Pablo was darker than most Spaniards.

After the recruitment of soldiers was over, Governor Velázquez sent word to the mayor to arrest Cortés and stop the expedition. Cortés heard about the situation and sent his officers to the mayor's office for a conference. They were instructed to delay the mayor until Cortés could get the ships out of the harbor. The officers would board a small boat and meet the armada outside the harbor.

The officers wore their swords and it was a tense situation in the office of the mayor. The mayor insisted he had no choice but to arrest Cortés and stop the expedition. The officers had various arguments for why the order was invalid, and the mayor was impatient with the lame excuses.

Suddenly, Pablo walked forward and drew his sword partway out of its sheath and closed it with a loud clash of metals. In a voice that was little more than a whisper, he said, "Señor Alcalde, if you detain our Captain, we will burn your city to the ground, and we will ride through the countryside and burn every plantation to the ground, along with the crops. When people ask why we are being difficult, we will tell them, it is because their mayor made a poor decision. We will not harm you in any way, but your citizens will have you drawn and quartered. Can we compromise?"

The mayor looked at this killing machine of a monk and knew it was best if he said nothing. He nodded his head, and said he was done for the day. There were important matters to take care of at home. He prepared to close down his office and wished the men good luck on their journey.

When the men began filing out of the office, the mayor called out, "Señor Christian Knight, please take this dagger with you. It belonged to my uncle, a Christian Knight."

The dagger was about eight inches of the finest Toledo steel. The handle was walnut with a silver cross inlay. It was a priceless heirloom.

Pablo held the cross to his chest and said, "I will wear it with pride and honor, Señor Mayor."

Each of the officers wondered what had transpired, why they were not arrested, and how Pablo ended up with a knife worth a small fortune.

Cortés sailed a half-hour later with eleven ships, five hundred and eight soldiers, one hundred sailors, and sixteen horses. The officers left with the armada, and when Cortés heard the story, he had a puzzled look on his face, shrugged his shoulders, and said to his officers, "Pablo might come in handy."

One of his officers said, "He has already come in handy."

The men were responsible for their own weapons and signed on for no pay, but they would receive a share of the loot.

It was a fairly short trip to Yucatan, where Cortés was given the Franciscan priest Jeronimo Aguilar, who was fluent with the Mayan language. Aguilar agreed to serve as an interpreter for Cortés and was a tremendous advantage in dealing with the Indians.

Cortés continued to explore the coastline, until he landed at Tabasco in March 1519. He used his time in Tabasco to gather intelligence from the local Indians. His personality won them over; they exchanged gifts and observed each other's behavior.

Cortés used this time wisely; actually, he let Pablo use the time well. The soldiers learned military discipline and the basics of military maneuvers. The cavalry was drilled and coordinated with the infantry, a unique concept for conquistador armies. Under the guidance of Pablo, a well-disciplined, cohesive army began to emerge.

Indian spies reported to the Azteca, these Spaniards were different from the other Spaniards. Cortés had a real army. The Indians were well aware of the capabilities of disciplined armies and what they can accomplish. The Azteca had some of the most well trained armies in the world, armies of over a hundred thousand troops.

The Indians realized the Spanish leader had a bizarre personality, when Cortés was given a gift of twenty Indian women. Cortés used the event to display his talent for theatrics. Instead of being grateful, Cortés flew into a rage and began knocking over the stone pagan idols of the Indians, while screaming that if his men had sexual relations with pagan women, their God might rain down damnation on the whole world.

At this point, his men began to wonder if Cortés had lost his marbles, but the Indian hosts and Chief Tabasco asked if there was a way to appease this Christian God of vengeance. Aguilar rose to the occasion and told the chief, "If the women are converted to Christianity, they can become mistresses and wives of the Spaniards."

In a peculiar moment of history, Chief Tabasco gave permission for women he no longer owned to be baptized by their new owner, and a priest, who was, until a few days earlier, a Mayan slave. Cortés thanked Chief Tabasco for saving his men; indeed, for saving the world, by allowing the women to be baptized. The women were immediately baptized. Everyone was grateful to avoid the wrath of the Christian God and the madman.

One of his officers took up with Malinche, a beautiful young Aztec girl, who had an uncanny ability with languages. She learned Spanish at an extraordinary rate and was innately clever.

When Cortés learned of the unique abilities of Malinche, he appropriated the girl as his personal property. She became his mistress and bore Cortés a son, Martín.

Malinche became the official interpreter and a trusted advisor for Cortés. She had an intuitive ability to know when chiefs and ambassadors were lying or up to trickery; in both roles, she was invaluable to Cortés and the success of the expedition.

Cortés sailed to a natural harbor on the southeastern Mexican coast and founded Veracruz. This move allowed Cortés to have himself elected captain general and chief justice, after declaring his men the first citizens of Veracruz. Cortés was free of the authority of Velázquez. He had the legal authority to begin the conquest of Mexico. Ironically, Velázquez had used the same legal maneuver to secure Cuba.

Due to the complex nature of the Spanish legal system, Cortés faced imprisonment or death, upon his return to Cuba, under charges of mutiny for ignoring the governor, although a successful expedition would clear him of charges.

He continued to drill his troops and under the direction of Pablo. The army improved and became a powerful force instead a ragged mob.

There was a significant Indian settlement near Vera Cruz called Cempoala, and Cortés marched his troops to the town. Twenty dignitaries and an enthusiastic group of villagers greeted the Spaniards. Cortés used diplomacy to convince the Totonac chief and his dignitaries to be baptized and rebel against the Aztec nation.

The Totonacs helped build Veracruz, and the city served as the staging area for the invasion of Mexico and the conquest of the Aztec nation.

Chapter 41

Cortés portrayed as a god, 1519

Moctezuma II ruled over the Aztec nation in the city of Tenochtitlan (future Mexico City). When Moctezuma heard of Cortés, a man who resembled a god who was scheduled to arrive, he sent emissaries with gold and presents for Cortés. During the visit, Cortés learned he was considered an emissary of Quetzacoatl or perhaps the god.

In the mythology of the Aztecs, Quetzalcoatl was a god-king, who controlled lightning. According to prophecy, Quetzalcoatl would return on a one-reed year of the Aztec calendar based on a fifty-two-year rotation. Cortés was fortunate to show up on 1519, a one-reed year. His odds of accomplishing this were fifty-two to one.

Quetzalcoatl was to come from the direction of the sunrise and float to them on the sea. The god-king had light-colored skin, a beard, short hair on his head, he was expected to have military success, and rule the Mexica people.

When Cortés was ready to begin the conquest, he scuttled his ships, except for one small vessel. While the men watched the ships sink, Cortés told his men, there was no turning back—defeat or mutiny was not an option. They would be successful and build new ships upon the successful completion of their mission or die in New Spain (Mexico).

When the army left, they had forty Cempoalan warrior chiefs and two hundred natives serving as porters and to pull the cannons through the jungle, toward Tlaxcalteca.

Tlaxcalteca was a group of two hundred city-states, without a central government. The Tlaxcalteca had been at war with the Azteca for a hundred years during the Flower Wars, and they were formidable foes for the Spaniards.

Initially, the Tlaxcalteca and the Spaniards engaged in a series of skirmishes, until the Spaniards were forced up on a hill and surrounded. The Spanish were about to be destroyed, when a chief's father remarked that the Spanish would be better allies than dead enemies.

On September 18, 1519, Cortés arrived in Tlaxcala and was greeted with enthusiastic joy by the residents and their chiefs.

The Azteca had imposed an economic blockade of the Tlaxcala, and they were in abject poverty. The Tlaxcala lacked salt and cotton clothing and many other products. Consequently, the only presents they offered Cortés were women and food.

Cortés stayed in Tlaxcala for twenty days, and apparently won the confidence of the leaders and convinced them to be baptized and take on Spanish names. Whether the new converts understood Catholicism or added the Christian God to their own pantheon of gods is pure conjecture.

Cortés went on to fight a brutal war against the Azteca nation. Without his Indian allies, he would have been defeated; as it was, he was nearly defeated on several occasions. He became the governor of New Spain, or Mexico. His rein was a continuous struggle to increase control and wealth, while resisting those who wanted his wealth.

He built Mexico City over the Azteca capital and created several more cities.

He lost the governorship in 1526, although he retained his power base. His political enemies continued to scheme to overthrow his control.

In his mid-fifties, Cortés returned to Spain to fight many lawsuits. He wanted to reestablish his governorship, but was hopelessly mired in the legal system, facing massive debt and legal problems. He decided to return to Mexico, but died of pleurisy on December 2, 1547.

Chapter 42
A Knight Rides Through Zacatecas

Pablo Castile, the Christian Knight, rode through the village of The Silver People. By chance, he looked into the eyes of Mountain Waters, and she looked back at him. There was something between them. They were destined for this moment.

Because of his service for Cortés, Pablo was rich. He had twenty mounted Indian soldiers and a native interpreter with him. He called up the interpreter and asked him to find out the name and status of the young woman.

The interpreter tried several languages before making a connection with Azteca. She was reluctant to answer the questions and insisted on a private council with this strange, but handsome old warrior. She was worried about being driven out of her adopted home if the Silver People learned of her life with the Azteca.

In private, Mountain Waters told Pablo the story of her life and of Running Girl and their escape. Pablo told Mountain Waters he was awarded a large hacienda for his service against the Azteca. He was on his way to claim the land and begin ranching. He was a Christian Knight and had taken on a vow of celibacy, but he had done so much killing against both the Azteca and the Muslims, he no longer considered himself a Christian Knight. He wanted to live in the wilderness, build a hacienda, raise horses, and have a family. He liked Mountain Waters and would marry her and welcome her daughter into his home if Mountain Waters would marry him.

Mountain Waters realized this might be her only chance to rise above the communal life of a small tribe of silver workers. She agreed to accompany Pablo into the wilderness and become his wife.

Pablo asked how long it would take to gather up her possessions, and she replied she could have everything, in ten minutes.

When she left, Pablo had two mares saddled for Mountain Waters and Running Girl. The villagers were astounded to see Pablo lift each of them onto the back of a horse. They were among the first generation of Mexican Indians to learn the culture of the horse.

It was illegal to put Indians or Mestizos (Spanish and Indian) on a horse, but Pablo trained his own small band of cavalry, who served as vaqueros (cowboys) for the hacienda (large ranch). Pablo became lord and master of his hacienda. During uprisings and revolts by local Indians, Pablo served as an indifferent judge and executioner.

Pablo built his hacienda in the Sierra de Sombrerete mountains, in the extreme northwest of the future state of Zacatecas.

Pablo found an ancient mine on the hacienda. When his men dug deeper, they found a major source of silver. Pablo Castile, a man who had lived in poverty most of his life, was now extremely wealthy.

Pablo was an excellent husband and treated Mountain Waters with love and kindness, until he passed away fourteen years later. They had a boy named Hernan and a daughter named Maria. The Castile family thrived on the hacienda for generations.

Chapter 43
North of the Rio Grande

Any geneticist or stockman will tell you, some traits are inherited through generations, and some are discarded with the influence of new bloodlines.

Angel Hermoso was considered a deranged homicidal maniac among a group of cold-blooded killers, the conquistadors of Cortés. It was not just his indifference to killing—they all killed without remorse—it was his curious habit of reciting scripture during the bloodletting. His devotion to God and the church was so intense, the others considered him to be a fanatic; the fact that he could kill for hours without a break in his recitation of the Bible made him seem a deranged fanatic. Angel Hermoso was an efficient and loyal soldier, and he was rewarded with a large land grant, but it was located in the wilderness, a no man's land, west of Santa Fe and far away from those who wanted to distance themselves from this strange man.

The hacienda was three days' ride west of Santa Fe, but it was considered to be so far beyond civilization, young Spanish maidens, especially those from aristocratic families, would never consider the possibility of marriage in such a God-forsaken wilderness. Angel accepted the remote location and began building a hacienda. He wanted to build a dynasty, but he lacked the main ingredient, a wife. Regardless of the location, few women wanted to marry a religious fanatic. Angel was forced to purchase and barter for several wives. He became proficient in acquiring wives, because they kept running away. Eventually, he acquired a wife who was "touched," or psychologically imbalanced. She didn't notice the bizarre habits of Angel and was happy with life on the Hermoso Hacienda. Sadly, his wife's hygiene tended to blunt Angel's passion, and he purchased two more wives from the bordellos of Spain. These wives were happy to have only one maniac to contend with, and Angel was glad to be producing Castilian babies. With the passage of time, Angel evoked a hidden psychosis in his Castilian wives, equal to or greater than Angel's. Through the generations, women with a trace of cruelty and sadism in their personality were given an opportunity to become the wife of a Hermoso man.

The Hermoso hacienda thrived in the wilderness by developing a trade network with the Comancheros (Mixed Spanish and Indian traders who were trusted by the Comanche), specializing in slaves, gold, horses, cattle, cooking implements, and firearms. Angel Hermoso's devotion to God and Catholicism was replaced with self-deification and feelings of omnipotence among his heirs. The remote location allowed the Hermoso Clan to rule with ruthlessness and cruelty that struck terror into the hearts of Indians and Mexicans. They owned the land and the people, and they were the law. The only people they didn't control were the raiding Indians and the Comancheros.

The bloodlust was passed down, along with excessive and cruel carnal desires. Any woman was considered property, to be enjoyed and discarded with indifference. Heredity and inheritance were often decided with poison and assassination, but the family managed to keep their fiefdom.

The indigenous people were subsistence farmers; the concept of working like a European serf or slave and growing crops to give away the largest share to a landlord was alien to them. Consequently, the Hermoso Clan persecuted the Indian farmers without mercy, for being lazy and slothful. Rape, torture, and murder were considered reasonable measures to coerce these slaves, who didn't consider themselves slaves, to be more productive and provide the wealth and prestige the Hermoso Clan wanted.

A few Indians submitted and endured the transgressions; others became hostile and sought vengeance. From both groups, there were many children born of rape. Humiliated and rejected by almost everyone from birth, these outcasts became the nucleus of the Comanchero and they rode from East Texas to Arizona, exacting revenge on everyone as retribution against those who had wronged them.

Chapter 44

The Comancheros, 1843

The Comanchero was the scourge of Northern Mexico and the Southwestern US. Despite a reputation for bloodshed and larceny, they were excellent traders, dealing in guns, slaves, buffalo hides, and whiskey. Although they traded on a wide margin, they were not beyond raiding the people, with whom they had just traded, to steal the goods back and increase their profit margin.

The Comancheros gained the confidence of the Comanche and were the only outsiders the Comanche would trade with.

Comancheros led by Soledad Guerrero, brother to the Comanche and homicidal maniac, Santana Guerrero, both descendants of Strong Bow, and the white Maya Gonzalo Guerrero, were trading with Chief Grizzly Claw and the Quahadi Comanche. The Comanche were camped on the Canadian River on the Llano Estacado. Slaves, guns, whiskey, buffalo robes, blankets, knives, cooking utensils, cattle, and guns brought about spirited barter, but the most spirited negotiation was being waged by Coyote Pup for Cougar, a young H1W2 woman and daughter of Grizzly Claw.

Coyote Pup offered seven horses for the girl, and Grizzly Claw refused. No one offered more than six for a girl, and this one didn't have any meat on her bones; Coyote Pup was incensed.

Grizzly Claw had no intention of trading his daughter; another Quahadi chief wanted her for a wife, and the more horses he was offered, the more she would bring from the Quahadi chief. The marriage to the other chief would strengthen the ties between the two bands. Trading his daughter to a Comanchero for a dozen horses had no political or strategic value. Besides, he had over three hundred horses, more horses than he could ever ride.

Coyote Pup wanted the girl. He offered eight horses, and the chief laughed at him. Coyote Pup pulled his knife, but Soledad aimed his pistol at Coyote Pup's chest and told him, "Forget the girl or die where you stand." Coyote Pup got control of himself. He had fear and respect for the crazy Mayan. He might fight a Comanche war chief, but he didn't want to cross Soledad.

Everyone was happy when the Comancheros left camp, everyone but Coyote Pup. The Comancheros were headed back to Santa Fe to sell the buffalo robes and restock. Coyote Pup and his friend Jose Flores wanted to try some of the new horses, to see which ones would command a higher price. By luck, they saw Cougar riding by herself. They split up and closed in on her from two sides. They were behind her and caught her unaware.

She broke into a gallop and turned hard toward Jose and then back the way she had come from. The two men shot past her and turned their horses to try again. Cougar was gaining ground and would have escaped, but her horse broke through a prairie dog tunnel and broke its leg. Cougar flew off her horse and rolled. She wasn't hurt, but she lay motionless on the dirt. Jose rode up and jumped off his horse to see if Cougar was still alive. When he turned her over, a flint knife cut deep into his lower abdomen and was pulled upwards, until his ribs stopped its progress. He grabbed his belly to keep from losing his intestines, and she grabbed the .54-caliber cap and ball pistol he had in his belt.

When Coyote Pup rode up, Cougar fired the pistol at Coyote Pup, from six feet away. The bullet carried away part of his right cheekbone and the top half of his ear. The force of the bullet nearly knocked him out of his saddle, but he sat up and pulled his pistol before she got to him with her knife. When she saw the pistol, she turned and jumped on Jose's horse. Coyote Pup wanted to shoot her, but he had another idea. He untied his sixty-foot reata (raw hide lariat) and spurred his horse to give chase. He was about twenty feet away when he threw the loop that pinned her elbows to her sides. He stopped his horse, and yanked Cougar backwards out of the saddle. He dragged her, through the rocks, gravel, and cactus until she couldn't fight back. Then he tied her wrists behind her and raped her.

When he was finished, he put the loop around her neck and put her on Jose's horse with her hands still tied behind her. If she tried to escape, the rawhide reata would break her neck.

When he rode up to the rest of the Comancheros, Soledad started laughing and told Coyote Pup he should take help the next time he went out to capture young girls.

With his ruined face Coyote Pup looked at Soledad and said, "Jose is dying back there with his guts ripped out, and she did it."

Soledad grinned to say, "That may be, but pretty girls bring more money if they aren't half-dead."

Soledad didn't want to risk the possibility of Grizzly Claw finding out they had captured and sold Cougar, so he bypassed Santa Fe and rode to the Hermoso Hacienda with this special prize.

Antonio Hermoso saw the girl and wanted to possess her. He offered two horses.

Soledad was livid. "We can get more than that from a bordello. We have children and young women we can sell you."

"I'll give you four horses for the girl. Take it or leave it, but there are eight rifles aimed at you. I will give you four minutes to accept. Each minute you waste will mean one less horse, and if you wait too long, you will all die." There were multiple rifles in strategic positions aiming at the Comancheros.

"I will now give you three horses."

"Okay, okay, three horses and she is yours."

During the exchange, the Comancheros were already planning revenge.

Antonio Hermoso kept the girl chained in the loft of the horse barn. She provided a daily release for rape and assault. However, it was obvious the girl was pregnant after five months. Her treatment changed. Antonio's wife, Estrella, was sterile, but she was ecstatic over the idea of having a child; hopefully, it would be a boy. Estrella stopped Antonio's abuse and began to care for the girl to ensure a healthy baby. Cougar received good food, clothing, and blankets. They compared the estimated due date against the date of Cougar's arrival to be sure Antonio had sired the baby. Estrella cared nothing about Cougar. She would be tortured and killed, after finding a suitable wet nurse; it was the baby she wanted. Estrella unchained Cougar during the last days of her pregnancy.

Chapter 45
Escape

Cougar went into labor about an hour before the Comancheros attacked the Hermoso Hacienda. The baby girl was born and the placenta expelled while the screams of the Hermoso Clan filled the night air. The torture in the yard was hideous, but it provided a diversion for Cougar to make her escape. Suddenly, she heard two men walking toward the barn. She recognized the voices of Soledad and Coyote Pup. They were looking for her. They split up outside the barn. Coyote Pup came in the front door, and Soledad was walking around to the back.

Cougar knew there was a block and tackle pulley for butchering cattle attached to a beam in the loft, and a reata coiled on a peg. She untied the reata in silence and tied it to the pulley rope on the block and tackle. The pulleys would decrease Coyote Pup's weight to thirty or forty pounds. When he walked beneath her, she dropped the loop around his neck and began hoisting Coyote Pup in the air. He managed to get his right wrist through the loop, before it became an effective ligature, but his feet were five feet off the ground, and he was being strangled slowly. Soledad ran over to help, but he could do nothing from the floor. He saw a ladder that stood through a hole in the loft floor and climbed into the loft. When his head appeared through the floor, he received a pitchfork through the neck. Soledad remained perfectly still with two tines of the pitchfork protruding through his neck. He couldn't go down the ladder, and he couldn't come up the ladder because, every time he moved,

Cougar walked left or right while holding the handle, and it felt like his neck was breaking.

Cougar decided to end this game and yanked the fork hard to the right, and she heard the bones in Soledad's neck crack. She used her foot to push him off of the pitchfork, and his body crumpled to the floor.

Cougar climbed down the ladder to take Soledad's knife. Cougar scalped Soledad and climbed into the loft to scalp Coyote Pup. He tried to scream, but it was a silent scream.

Cougar grabbed her baby, and waved to Coyote Pup as he was fighting for his last breaths. She headed northwest, while hearing the screams of Antonio and his wife as they roasted over a small fire. They were no longer a problem, but she didn't want to be captured by the Comancheros and sold into slavery again.

She headed northwest to avoid the Comancheros, since they were likely to ride northeast, to their home in North Texas. Cougar's baby was strong, and she could feel the pressure of the milk forming in her small breasts, but if she couldn't find food, her breast milk would dry up and her baby would starve.

On the third day of walking, she saw a grouse making his drumming noise to attract a mate. She laid her baby down in the grass and looked for a good throwing rock. She picked up two walnut-sized stones, and walked a few steps closer to increase the odds of hitting the bird. The first rock struck the bird in the back. He tried to fly and turned a back somersault. Cougar threw her second rock as he stood to fly again. This one hit him in the head, and his struggles ceased.

She built a fire by striking a flint rock with Soledad's knife and aiming the sparks into a pile of dry grass. She ate one half of the breast and washed it down with cold water from a small stream. After three days of starving, the small piece of meat seemed like a feast. She felt the life-giving energy of the protein and felt pressure from the milk being supplied to her breasts. She would eat the other half later that night, before falling asleep. The days were warm, but the nights were cold. She saved the wings, after carefully skinning the bird to keep the feathers imbedded in the skin. The feathers would help keep her feet warm on these cold nights. She used a length of the intestine to secure the feathers and placed them in a pocket of her skirt.

The baby girl seemed to feel the life-giving power of the grouse. She sucked a little harder and began to thrive on her mother's milk. Cougar and the baby slept through the night, while the feathers helped keep Cougar's feet warm for the first time since the night of the raid.

Cougar slept well, but she was hungry; she needed to find more food to keep her baby alive.

That afternoon, she was weak from hunger, when she saw an old poplar tree that had fallen down with the trunk split down the length of the tree. There was a huge beehive exposed, with enough honey to feed her whole tribe. Cougar broke off huge pieces of the comb and ate so much of the honey she felt sick. She was covering the honey she had harvested from the tree with pine boughs when she saw a horse struggling with hobbles (a leather rope used to tie the front legs beneath the fetlocks or ankles).

The horse's sweat was steaming in the cool mountain air. The horse had a Mexican saddle on his back and a long reata coiled up on the right side. He had been fighting the hobbles and had probably traveled for miles. If she could undo the hobbles and take off on the horse before the owner tracked it down, she could cover a lot of miles.

She broke off several large pieces of comb and walked toward the horse. He was a well-made gray stallion, about fifteen hands. When Cougar was a few strides away, he snorted and pulled back by dragging his front hooves in the dirt. Cougar stopped and took a bite of the honey and held out a large chunk of the honeycomb as an offering. His appetite overcame his fear. The horse ate the honey and looked for more. Cougar gave him another piece and untied the reata and slipped the loop over his head and around his neck and ducked down to slip off the hobbles. She moved slowly and smoothly to gain trust. She used almost twenty feet of the reata to fashion a hackamore and reins, then laced the rest of the reata back on the saddle. The reata would make life so much easier and survival more likely.

Cougar was moving fast; if the owner saw her, a bullet would be the kindest response she could expect.

Cougar looked in the saddlebags and found a honing stone, a flint and iron piece for striking sparks to build a fire, a wooden plate, and a tin cup; life was about to get much easier for Cougar and her baby. There was a blanket and a serape rolled and tied behind the saddle. She made a backpack out of the serape and carried her baby on her back to free up her arms. Cougar was rich, not with gold or silver, but with the means to survive. She swung up on the horse, and he accepted her small body.

She kept heading northwest, but at a much faster rate. She found a creek and walked the horse in the middle of the stream for a half-mile upstream before finding a large gravel bar that would cover her tracks coming out of the stream, in case a good tracker was following her trail. She traveled upstream because most people would travel downstream to save their horse from fighting the current, but she figured the horse was strong enough to handle the current and she might lose her tracker, if there was a tracker closing in on her.

Late that afternoon, she found a large pine that had blown down and had started to rot. The bears had beaten her to every downed tree, but this one was hers. She used her knife to break loose sections of bark to find the succulent grubs and hundreds of black ants. The grubs were an inch and a half long and thicker than one of Cougar's fingers and full of nutrients. She lifted the strange off-white colored creatures from the tree, brushed off the pieces of wood from their worm-like bodies, and ate them like candy. She crushed the ants between her index finger and thumb, and ate them as quickly as she could catch them. She ate for twenty minutes, while letting her baby feed at her breast. The inconsistent sustenance, constant travel, and demands of her child were taking a toll on Cougar's vitality. She was growing weaker, and the baby was growing stronger. Like a good range cow, she was giving all her nutrients to her baby. Cougar's belly had shrunk to the point that she could only eat a small amount of food, but she was hungry within a few hours.

She needed to find out if someone was tracking her. If there was going to be a showdown, it was better to have it now, while she was still fairly strong. The ridge above could provide a view of the open valley she had just crossed. To the west, the ridge tapered down to the valley. She put her horse into a trot and asked him to climb the steep grade to the top. About three quarters of the way up the grade, she noticed a large pine, leaning against another tree.

The top half had broken off long ago, and the upper trunk was barely resting on another tree. It was kept from falling into the narrow path of the trail by a few branches.

Cougar walked her horse carefully beneath the leaning tree and then pushed her horse to trot up the hillside and jumped off to tie the gray at the top along the trail. She looked out over the valley and saw an Indian on a paint mare, leading a pack mule. He looked like a Cheyenne and he was tracking her. Cougar knew she had to get those panniers on the mule. Life was in those pack boxes.

With her reata and knife, she ran back down to the leaning snag to set a deadfall trap. Building a deadfall to kill a bear or man is a risky business; a wrong move can kill the person setting the trap. Cougar used an innate sense of mechanics and leverage to set the trap. She climbed the live tree and cut away the branches to free up the top of the leaning tree, to make sure it would fall onto the trail. The friction of bark against bark was the only thing holding the leaning tree. For the trap to work, the base has to be free enough that the horse will trigger the trap by stepping on the rope. Cougar opened the loop and wrapped it around the base. The rope was then stretched around the trunk of a small poplar tree and then tied to a tree on the other side of the trail. The sun was setting, and the rope would be harder to see. He was a good tracker and likely to see the rope, but Cougar had a diversionary plan. Actually, it was an old battle plan, feigning retreat and springing a trap; Hannibal in Italy, Genghis Khan in Asia, the Muslims in the Middle East, and the Comanche in Texas used it successfully many times.

When the Cheyenne warrior came up the trail, he saw his horse tied to a tree at the top and a woman cooking over a fire, while nursing a baby. He had a smirk on his face, as he got closer. Out of the corner of her eye, Cougar saw when the rider was five strides from the trap and ran to her horse to make her escape. The warrior used his heels to ask his horse to gallop the rest of the way and get to the girl before she could escape. He ran his horse toward the leaning tree, and his horse stumbled. The warrior heard something from above and looked up to see a thirty-foot log with a twenty-four-inch diameter, just before it crushed him and his horse.

The warrior was knocked out and pinned beneath the log. The horse's back was broken, and it was crawling around on the ground with its hind legs paralyzed and splayed out behind her; the high-pitched screams of a horse in agony filled the air. Cougar made sure the warrior was incapacitated and then cut the throat of the horse to put it out of its misery. She stripped the warrior of his clothing and moccasins. Everything was large, but she could wear the clothing over her own to stay warm.

The warrior woke up and discovered he was trapped beneath the log and laboring to breathe with the full weight of the log on his chest and his chin braced against the log to keep it from rolling over his head. His arms were pinned beneath the log, and he could feel multiple broken bones from within his chest. He looked at Cougar and realized she was alone. He marveled at how she had managed to defeat him. Cougar noticed he was still alive and reached over to take his scalp, and let loose with a Comanche war cry. The warrior screamed in outrage, a noise that suddenly turned into a barely audible gurgling protest when Cougar cut his throat. He died when Cougar rolled the log over his face and crushed his head.

Cougar forgot about the warrior and began to survey her new possessions stored in the rawhide panniers on the pack mule. There was at least twenty pounds of pemmican (a sausage mixture of dried ground meat, blueberries, and rendered fat). It was well made and would last for months on the trail. There was also leather, cloth, leather thongs, salt, and bone awls for sewing.

Cougar built a fire to cook the horse's liver and tongue, while she sliced the hindquarters into thin strips and smoked them over the cook fire. A portion of the back hide was salted and packed for brain tanning at a later date. The hind legs were case skinned from the area above the hocks to approximate the length of Cougar's calf and feet. These were turned inside out and mounted on sticks with a sharp angle to dry and smoke tan in the shape of the human leg and foot. Cougar sewed the toe area before the hide dried completely, using the portion that formerly covered the back of the hock joint to position her heel. She trimmed the excess hide to fit her calves, used an awl to poke a double line of vertical holes in the area that would cover her shins, and then threaded the holes with the leather thongs. This allowed her to lace up the top portion of the boot to fit snugly around the contour of her calf. Using water to make the hair of the mane and tail more pliable, she weaved a covering for each of her feet and ankles by turning the loose strands back into a nebulous foot-like form that fit her feet like insulating socks. Within a few hours, she had recreated primitive man's earliest boots and socks.

Using the dead Indian's tomahawk, she cracked open the horse's skull to remove the brain. Cougar secured the brain in a small leather sack. The brain would decompose until it became a tanning agent for the back hide of the horse. She thanked the Earth Mother for making each animal with enough brain to tan its own hide. She ate portions of the liver and stored the dried meat in her panniers. She would eat well, until the meat ran out or spoiled from rainfall. She hoped the weather stayed cold enough to help preserve the meat.

Cougar and her baby left the deadfall camp after two days. She was well rested and better prepared for the snows of fall. Now that Cougar was more likely to survive, she named her baby Montana, the Spanish word for mountains. She liked the sound of the word, and her baby seemed strong like the mountains they were traveling through.

With the warrior's bow, she killed a cow elk whose curiosity of the horses overwhelmed her innate sense of danger and allowed her to wander too close to Cougar and the horses. She made camp for several days while she jerked the meat and tanned portions of the horsehide and the elk hide. From the thicker and tougher horsehide, she made a serape and used the rendered fat of the elk to make it waterproof. The days were getting shorter, and the sun stayed lower on the horizon. Cougar knew she had to find some type of shelter if she was going to survive the approaching winter.

Cougar had heard stories of the Colorado River to the northwest with a rich supply of fish and beaver for the winter. Hopefully, she would find a cave or deserted lodge to spend the winter in comfort. Indians had survived on this river for eons. If she kept bearing to the northwest, she knew the life-sustaining waters of this fabled river could not be too much farther.

Winter came early, and Cougar awoke one morning to find her elk hide tent buried under two feet of snow. Cougar's life on the high plains of the Llano Estacado had left her unprepared for extreme cold and snow. She broke camp when there was enough light to find her horses and set out to find a more suitable winter camp, but that same afternoon, a blizzard blew in from the North, and she became disoriented in the blowing snow. She let her saddle horse lead the way; Cougar was helplessly lost and cold. Later that day, she was so cold and exhausted, only the heat from her horse was keeping her alive. Her horse walked up to a corral and stopped. Cougar looked up to see horses and a log building with smoke coming from a chimney; it was visible as a faint outline in the heavy snowfall. She dropped from her horse and tried to walk to the cabin, but her legs were so weak, she fell in the deep snow, and couldn't get up. Her horse screamed for his human friend's welfare.

Bif Cunningham heard a horse scream, and knew it wasn't one of his. He walked out on the porch and saw a skinny saddle horse and pack mule standing in the yard. He walked over to them and noticed a small human form lying half-buried in the snow. He picked up the body and was surprised to find it was a woman holding a baby to her breast. He carried the two of them into his home and placed them on his bed. He pulled some cotton and woolen clothes from the stacks and pulled the frozen rags from her body. He covered her warmly and put a male infant at her breast to suckle. He fed her a spoonful of chicken soup and washed her body with warm water and lye soap. He rubbed lavender oil with lanolin from mountain sheep on her body and said out loud, "Women and horses fancy the scent of lavender, it relaxes and soothes them."

The only things he noticed about her nakedness, was that she was skinny and small, and her breasts were the size of apples. "Big enough," he said aloud to himself with a smile. He stoked the fire to make the cabin extra warm and set aside food to cook in the morning. He picked up her baby and washed her. He noticed a rash on the baby's bum and smeared bacon grease and lanolin over the redness, and fashioned a diaper from a cotton neckerchief.

His wife had died two nights earlier. In desperation, he tried feeding his baby son with everything he had, but the baby refused to eat. Now, his son was sucking nonstop at the girl's breast. She would be warm and well fed in his house; she had saved his son's life.

Bif meant to watch over her and the children through the night, but the extra warmth of the cabin made him drowsy, and he drifted into a deep sleep in a chair next to the bed.

Bif was big enough to be considered a giant. He was six foot five and weighed over three hundred pounds. Yet, he was known for having a good heart; he treated everyone with respect and kindness.

Cougar was five feet tall and weighed ninety pounds while wearing her winter clothes. She awakened and looked around the cabin, wondering if she had died. She was in a bed, and she had an extra baby, a boy. He was much larger and had blond hair. His hands were reaching for her, and he was making sucking noises with his tongue. His blue eyes and blond curls made her want to hug him. His noises made the milk flow from her breasts. When she put the boy to her breast, she noticed she was clean. That's when she saw the sleeping monster. It was huge, bigger than a bear. It had reddish-blond hair and a full red beard.

This barbarian child nursing at her breast was forming a bond. She might not give him up.

There were pieces of baked chicken on a plate that was placed on a table beside the bed. She ate the meat and the ends off the bones and split the bones to eat the marrow. The food in her belly gave her strength. She put the babies next to each other at her breasts, and the two sucking mouths lulled her into a deep sleep.

Cougar awoke to the aroma of food cooking, but the image that greeted her was from another world. Bif had on his regimental uniform from the Royal Scottish Highlanders, complete with kilt, tunic, and white shirt.

Bif wanted to formally welcome Cougar, but she was scared for the first time in her life. Perhaps it was the kilt. (To her, he looked like a man in a dress.) The long stockings that came to his knees had a jeweled dagger attached to one of the garters, and the massive knees covered in red hair looked like they belonged on an ox. Cougar hid under the blankets to protect her and the babies.

That's when the noises began. She had never heard such noises. Under the blankets, she shook with fear; the babies started crying, and Cougar cried with them, until the noises stopped and Bif laid down his bagpipe.

Bif laid out several dresses on the bed for Cougar to choose from, along with women's underclothes.

From beneath the blankets, she touched the clothing.

Bif smiled and winked at her. He turned to face the stove to dish out breakfast on huge plates. She quickly put on a deerskin skirt and a white cotton blouse.

Bif turned to place the plates on the table, and Cougar fought the urge to eat like a wolf. She wanted the barbarian to think of her as a proper Comanche princess.

The meal was rich beyond imagination for Cougar; there were pancakes, hominy, bacon, biscuits, jam, honey, porridge, and coffee with cream. Cougar ate for a few minutes, and was soon stuffed. She placed her plate of food on the bed and covered it with the blankets, to preserve it for later. Bif smiled; he had seen the effects of starvation many times.

She walked around this strange house and began to explore. The house was more of a warehouse. There were trade goods and furs and buffalo hides by the thousands. Never had she seen such wealth, nor could she have even imagined there was this much wealth in the world.

She wondered if the giant killed people and robbed them. Maybe that was how he acquired the barbarian baby. Cougar had many questions, but they didn't communicate well enough to ask questions.

However, the monster's wealth was partially explained during the first afternoon. A white trapper showed up with a bale of beaver hides, a sack of beaver castors, and several fox and wolf hides. He traded for bullets and gunpowder, tobacco, a blanket, and three #2 traps. He pointed to Cougar, but the giant said, "No." Cougar began to trust the giant, when she realized she wouldn't be traded away. Cougar relaxed her grip on the knife on her hip when the stranger shrugged his shoulders. He noticed the three scalps hanging from her belt and lifted his eyebrows. The story of Bif's scalp-lifting Comanche woman was soon told around many campfires.

Cougar realized the monster had valuable knowledge of things that make life better. She tried to learn everything about the cooking secrets of the iron stove and the exotic meals.

She stood beside Bif when he traded with mountain men and Indians, but unlike Bif, she didn't smile or exchange pleasantries. She glared into the men's eyes to determine if they were up for larceny and mayhem. She learned to grade fur. Some things were simple, like recognizing the difference between winter beaver and spring beaver by the color of the underside. Poorly handled furs were likely to slip the hair and be worthless, and it was important to determine which furs were stretched and dried properly.

Bif was proud of the way Cougar conducted herself during the trading. She only spoke to Bif, using bits and pieces of three different languages, and sign language.

Men always noticed the three scalps hanging next to the knife on Cougar's belt. Her right hand was never away from her knife as she used her left hand to point out the imperfections on each fur to Bif.

Bif and Cougar went for a walk, with the children, on a warm spring day. They came to a large cottonwood, and Bif pointed to the higher branches, holding a funeral bier. With his hand over his heart, Bif said, "Mi mujer" (my wife), and a mystery was solved.

Cougar quit thinking of Bif as a monster—he was merely a giant. She had been careful not to fall in love, in case he had another wife. She would never settle for being a second wife. Up to now, they only discussed business and the children. This new information was important for Cougar. The funeral bier was impressive and showed Bif's love for his deceased wife.

She thought about claiming this blond giant as her own. If she declared Bif as hers, she would never share him. She would own him, protect him, even die for him, but Bif would be hers and only hers, until the end of time.

Cougar asked Bif if he would let her shave his red beard away; Bif was the first and probably last White Man to be shaved, rather than scalped by a Comanche. She loved the smoothness of his facial skin and rubbed her cheek against his cheek. Bif became aroused and was embarrassed, but when Cougar saw his reaction, she wasn't embarrassed.

When Bif and the babies were asleep, Cougar crawled naked from her bed and joined Bif on the floor. Their romance was consummated on the floor of his cabin, and in time, Bif realized how serious his little Comanche was about long-term commitments, their romance continued to blossom for thirty years.

Over the years, the children were inseparable. Their trading business was one of the most successful of all trading outposts on the Santa Fe Trail. Cougar's story of survival and victory over the Comancheros and the Cheyenne warrior were legendary, and the scalps hanging from her belt served as a reminder to skeptics of the ferocity that lurks just beneath the surface. Cougar's silence and her razor-sharp knife struck fear into the hearts of many strangers.

The children seemed to think alike, and often two voices said the same thing at the same time. Sometimes one of them would speak part of a sentence, and the other one would finish the sentence without a break.

Bif asked Cougar if they should find mates for their children. Cougar said they were not of similar blood and if they became a couple it would be fine, but if one were to find another mate and leave, the other one would be destroyed.

When the kids were fifteen, they built several fish traps on the Colorado. Montana rolled her skirt to her waist, and Seamus was nude as they caught the trapped fish and tossed them onto the bank. They were laughing and neglected to see three young warriors walk out of the brush. A warrior grabbed Montana by the arm and jerked her out of the river. Sean objected and received a blow from a war club across the face. Sean fell backwards, and the other warrior jumped on him and held him underwater. The three warriors were laughing while Sean was drowning. Montana reached into the folds of her skirt and pulled out a knife, and in less than a second, she cut the throat of the warrior holding her arm. He let go of her, to stop the spurting blood with both hands; he died with a surprised look on his face, when Montana stabbed her knife into the warrior's temple.

The warrior with the club was in front of Montana and didn't hear the other warrior choking on his own blood. He was too busy laughing at the struggle in the river. Montana stuck the knife deep in his right kidney, and he leaned back in extreme pain as she ripped the blade in a saw-like motion to the right, until the knife came out his side. He fell to his knees in pain, and when he caught his breath to scream, she stabbed the knife through the side of his neck and pulled it forward through the front. He fell forward and was dead when he hit the ground. She jumped from the bank and landed on the warrior who was drowning Sean. She stabbed him three times in the back and took his scalp. He fell helpless into the water, and rolled over to look at her before floating downstream.

Montana knew she should have finished him, but Sean was more dead than alive, and he was her first concern. She pulled Sean to the bank, rolled him onto his belly and stood on his back, until the river water gushed out of his mouth. He coughed several times and groaned. He was alive.

She scalped the other two warriors, gathered their weapons, and pushed the dead men into the river. She yelled at Sean to get to his feet. They needed to leave.

Bif and Cougar listened to the story, while Bif looked at the arrows and the decorations on the assorted weapons.

He walked over to Montana and placed his big hand on her back and said, "You did well, but it is time to move on. The beaver are gone, and the fur market has gone to hell. We can load our freighting wagons and travel to Oregon and cash in. We can trade fur in Oregon with the Chinese and not worry about the Cheyenne the rest of our lives. Let's load the wagons. It's a long way to Oregon."

Cougar knew there were problems of a more serious nature. When they were alone, she asked Bif for the rest of the story.

Bif said to Cougar in a barely audible voice, "Montana took on the secret warrior society of the Cheyenne, the Ghost Coyotes. She killed and scalped two, possibly three. As far as I know, no one has ever killed two of them in personal combat, and none of them have ever been scalped. The third one escaped with several knife wounds and without his scalp lock. They will be out for blood. If the third one survives Montana's knife and the river, they will be here in a few days. I don't know how she did it, but she did it, and now, we must leave these mountains forever."

Cougar looked up at her blond giant with dark, brooding eyes that looked to be on fire. She was silent, but deep in her thoughts, she told herself, *my daughter is Comanche. She knows neither defeat nor fear.* Cougar nodded her head once, to say 'yes,' or signal that she understood, and continued loading the freighting wagons.

Bif planned to intersect the Oregon Trail in southern Wyoming and head west to the Columbia. He would surely get the highest price for his buffalo hides and fur from the international ships trading with China. The fur market had gone to hell in the traditional markets on the East Coast and Europe, but ships trading with the Orient were still paying a good dollar for the best fur.

Bif was a shrewd man in the trading business. He had served with the British military in Africa and India. He learned to trade for inexpensive foreign articles and ship them back to shops in Britain. It was a slow process, but after ten years, Bif built a sizable account in the Bank of England.

His dream was to be a trader in Western Canada, but he liked the idea of being an independent trader, and the only way he could work in Canada was to work at an outpost for the Hudson Bay Company. Like many Canadians, especially the French Canadians, he dropped down into the US to take advantage of the freedoms available to an independent entrepreneur.

A successful trader in the wilderness must have confidence, poise, an eye for value, and a keen sense of how to turn a profit, but more importantly, he must know how to get along with many different types of people.

Bif could be extremely formal and polite when meeting chiefs; he wore his uniform and played his bagpipe, a type of music that never ceased to amaze the most dignified chiefs and warriors. After playing the bagpipe and marching in cadence, Bif gave gifts to all notable people.

Bif made a name for himself as a showman and a diplomat. The tribes considered his show and gifts to be a highpoint of their year, and they traded with him, when others might have given them more value. It was the show and the personality of the man that won over the loyalty of the tribes.

Bif was fifty-one, little Cougar, his beloved and devoted wife, was over thirty, and the kids were both fifteen. It was time to take his family into civilization. He knew he was the only one who could relate to the wildest and the most-tame Indians. Cougar was silent and distrusted everyone outside of her immediate family. Sean was a kind-hearted soul like his departed mother, and like her, he had no idea of how to turn a profit. Montana was a dark-eyed beauty, with an overabundance of confidence and an outgoing personality, but her whole life was based on challenging the world and everyone around her. She loved the mild-mannered Sean above all else, and Bif shuddered to think what might happen if some beautiful girl tried to steal Sean away from her.

Bif was getting older, and the trading post wouldn't be successful without him. He needed to build a store, in a new country, where his mixed race family would be accepted, and where they didn't need to worry about a miscue in protocol.

In southwestern Wyoming, they joined up with the Jessup wagon train, and Colonel Jessup was glad to have this frontier family.

Chapter 46

Selena of Spain, from the Line of Janus

Toledo Weapons were the standard of Europe. Duelists and military men knew inferior weapons cost lives. When your life depended on the quality of a blade, you wanted the best. Most weapons were unreliable. The Toledo blade was arguably the best in the world.

Salvatore was the son of the youngest brother of the Toledo family. He would never inherit a major portion of the family fortune; he was too far down the hereditary line. Most men in his situation chose between the military, or the church; although, some chose a life of leisure. Living off a modest stipend and pursuing the typical pleasures of young gentlemen: drinking, gambling, horse racing, dueling, and playing the games of seduction. All of these endeavors were considered suitable for dilettantes of compromised means, but Salvatore had a different attitude. Although his career path was considered beneath his station, he was learning everything about producing weapons, from selecting the iron ore, to the sharpening and polishing of the finished blade.

His family was incensed when he walked home with a covering of coal dust and dirt. The men laughed at him, and the women rolled their eyes with smirking grins.

Despite the disapproval, Salvatore was becoming a respected craftsman. If someone was missing, Salvatore stepped forward to fill in. He was an important component of production. He took fencing lessons and rode horses like other gentlemen, but he had strength of body and mind other men envied.

Antonio was the one who was in line to inherit the business. He had dedicated his life to drunkenness and gluttony. He was impatient for his father to die and the day he could pursue debauchery without worrying about overextending his monthly remittance.

Salvatore's dedication to the business irritated Antonio and made him wonder if Salvatore had plans to abscond with the business. Salvatore's work ethic was in contrast to Antonio's hedonism and challenged the concept of elitism. Antonio was overwhelmed with feelings of inferiority. He hated Salvatore and made plans to destroy him.

Saturday nights were the social events of the week. During the week, Salvatore thought of Saturday, and his chance to see and talk with the beautiful Selena. She was the love of his life.

Selena's maternal line went back to Aristide and Janus of Tyre and Carthage. Luckily, her ancestors settled in Spain before the Roman invasion of Carthage. Two thousand years later, Selena's family was considered an aristocratic family of a moderately successful shipping and trading business.

On Saturday evening, Salvatore sat at a small restaurant and watched for Selena, and her brothers on the promenade.

This was a formal ceremony for selecting matrimonial partners. Young girls dressed in beautiful dresses to attract the right prospect. They were chaperoned by male relatives. A suitor had to ask the head chaperone for permission to speak to the maiden. If he was given permission, he asked the maiden if he could join her. If she accepted, he engaged in pleasant conversation and tried to make a good impression.

It was fashionable to have many suitors ask, but to walk with only a few. A young lady should be in demand, without being too approachable. If a suitor was considered appropriate, he was asked to Sunday dinner. After three or four Sunday dinners, he was expected to propose. Failure to propose could result in a duel with a brother or cousin of the maiden. Honor and respect were serious considerations, and breaches of etiquette were settled in duels to the death.

Women of compromised virtue and a lusty nature used the promenade to set up liaisons with the men who needed them. An eyebrow raised, a furtive glance, or a slight smile were indications of passion and desires to be settled in another type of duel, to be fought on a different field of honor. These liaisons were also dangerous; husbands and male relatives might take offense if a female family member's honor was compromised.

Salvatore was handsome, and many girls considered him a good catch, but he had been invited to dinner at Selena's and was being considered as a husband for her. There were many opportunities, but he only cared about Selena.

After walking with Selena for fifteen minutes, one of her brothers said it was time to leave.

Salvatore said good night and smiled. Selena's oldest brother said, "Please come to dinner, tomorrow at 3:30."

Salvatore accepted the invitation and was barely able to hide his excitement.

While Selena walked home with her brothers, Salvatore was thinking about the progression of their courtship. He had been invited twice. If he were invited two or three more times, he would be talking to her father and brothers about marriage.

He ordered a glass of wine to calm his nerves and sat in an open-air cantina. He drank the wine quickly without tasting it and decided to ride by Selena's family home to feel close to her. She was dancing in his mind.

Just beyond the lights of town, two men were lying in the road. Salvatore jumped from his horse to help the men; one of the men was dead, and the other was in the final agonies of death.

He recognized Selena's brothers; they had been stabbed and cut many times. The older brother grabbed Salvatore's sleeve and was barely able to speak, "Antonio Toledo." He pointed at carriage tracks. "Selena; go . . . now!" There was a rattle from deep in his throat, and the young man died.

Salvatore jumped on his horse and followed the tracks in the moonlight. The carriage was parked behind a bordello, and three brigands were guarding the back door.

Ignoring caution, Salvatore dismounted and casually walked up to the door, while the three men stood with their right hands resting on the handles of their swords. When Salvatore was close to the door, one of the men stepped in front of him and said, with a smirk, "Use the front door, sport. There's a private party here tonight."

In an instant, Salvatore drew his sword and slashed horizontally through the man's heart and lungs. He was dead before he hit the ground. The second man was drawing his sword, when the sword of Salvatore swept downward through his neck and chest. The brigand dropped his sword and tried to stop the blood loss, but it was hopeless; the man's upper body was nearly cut in two pieces.

The third man hesitated after seeing his friends' bodies cut apart with two sword slashes, and Salvatore thrust his sword just below the man's breastbone. The man pulled his bloody shirt away to look at his wound and failed to see Salvatore's sword cut deep into his skull.

Salvatore kicked in the door to see the obese Antonio thrusting wildly into the unconscious body of Selena. She was bruised and bitten all over her body. Her face was nearly destroyed: her nose was broken, her eyes were swollen shut, and her lips were cut and many times larger than normal.

Salvatore froze upon seeing his beloved Selena being ravaged. Antonio saw the man he hated and jumped off Selena to grab his sword.

Despite his obese body, Antonio handled his sword well. The two swordsmen were evenly matched. After a brief flurry of thrusts and parries, at the same instant, they both thrust. The sword of Antonio hit Salvatore's shoulder and was deflected into his left cheekbone, chipping the bone and leaving a nasty wound. The blade of Salvatore pierced several inches of belly fat, but his thrust was pulled back when he received his face wound. Salvatore was blinded by pain and blood, but Antonio howled in pain from a superficial wound. He pushed past Salvatore and ran naked over the bodies of his hired cutthroats to drive his carriage to receive medical care.

Salvatore overcame the pain from his wound and carried Selena in a blanket to his horse. His horse was frightened by the smell of blood and death, but acquiesced to carry the two riders, after reassurances from Salvatore.

He held her battered body closely, and rode to the home of Esperanza, his cousin. She often watched over Salvatore and took him for walks by the river when he was a small boy. They were close, and he still looked up to his older cousin. She was married to a man who traded clothing and blankets to the New World.

Esperanza asked no questions, but she had a groom hide Salvatore's horse in the stable. She attended to Selena and had a servant girl clean Salvatore's wound.

The two women were the same size, and Esperanza made sure Selena had a nightgown and a variety of things to wear. She sewed the wounds of Salvatore, and when he was finished, she asked, "Who did this to the girl?"

"Antonio Toledo."

Esperanza asked again, "Is he still alive?"

"I gave him a wound in the belly, but I don't think it penetrated the belly lard."

"Who else knows what happened?"

"He had three brigands, acting as sentries. I killed all three."

"The two of you should leave the country. If Antonio lives, he will kill both of you. If he dies slowly, he will send assassins. We have a ship leaving for Lavaca, Texas, in a few days. I will arrange for your passage on that ship. The captain is a family friend."

She asked, "Are you two lovers?"

"No, I admired her from a distance, and her family had me over for dinner. I was planning to propose," Salvatore replied with humility.

Esperanza thought for a few seconds and said, "Things are different now. She will need a long time to heal, and she may never heal, but the two of you are now fugitives and she is defenseless. I will have a driver take you to Andalucía in an enclosed carriage. From there, you will sail with the tide. When you arrive in Lavaca, check with our broker for messages addressed to Roberto from me. In a few months, we will know more about your future. Living and traveling with the girl will be difficult, I am warning you. Remember, you are her only benefactor. Here is a hamper of food, wine, and brandy. Drink the wine to sleep and drink the brandy for the pain. You are in a precarious situation, because of the madman Antonio. He will want you dead, and he will kill us if he learns we helped you. There is nowhere in Spain or Europe where you will be safe. Now, go with God."

A groom drove the pair to the harbor, and they gave the captain a letter from Esperanza. The two of them were given a tiny cabin with one bunk and very little room. Salvatore hung a hammock above the bunk, but he could tell Selena was uncomfortable with the closeness.

Selena stayed in the cabin except for nightly walks, and they both sipped the brandy at night. She always wore one of several veils, to hide her broken nose.

The Atlantic crossing was five weeks of boredom and extreme heat.

The Texans and Mexicans of Lavaca astonished the Spanish couple. No one spoke Spanish well, and sometimes they wondered if the people were actually speaking Spanish. The Mexicans were respectful and polite, but the Texans seemed like barbarians who spoke frontier English sprinkled with butchered Spanish; however, they were extremely polite and believed in liberty and justice under the law. There were no social classes in Texas; there were only Texans, Indians, Mexicans, Spaniards, and drunkards.

Salvatore and Selena stayed at a hotel and began to enjoy their conversations with the frontier Texans. Salvatore liked their commitment to a sense of morality and their rugged individualism. He began to sense that they were like him, but without the Old World formality.

The Mexicans held on to the Old World sense of social class structure, but the Texans held such notions in contempt. The Mexicans considered Selena and Salvatore aristocrats, because they were Spanish born of Castilian blood. The Spaniard born in the New World was lower in the social class structure, but higher than the Mexican, who was of mixed Spanish and Indian blood.

The Texan disregarded these distinctions, paid minimal respect to aristocrats, and respected people who earned respect. Salvatore found their singular attitude and commitment to these principles to be refreshing and humorous, and he couldn't agree with them more. He hated the Old World class system. He joked to Selena that it was easier for Texans to ignore the class system, because everyone was uncultured in Texas.

He laughed, but he loved the Texans.

In time, they learned Antonio had survived, and since there were many Spaniards conducting business in Lavaca, they decided to move away. Salvatore asked Selena where she would like to move, and she said, "Oregon. They will give you a hacienda in Oregon if you move there."

Salvatore thought about the possibility of free land. Esperanza had given them a sack of gold and silver coins, but it would not last forever. Oregon sounded like a place to escape the madness of Old World blood feuds and build a weapons business. "Where is Oregon?" he asked.

"It is in the northwest, near the Pacific Ocean," Selena said with excitement. The first excitement Salvatore had seen, since that terrible night.

"How do people get there?"

Again, Selena was proud of her inside information. "They drive wagons with oxen on a trail they call the Oregon Trail."

"Let me find out if we can get there from Texas," Salvatore said.

Salvatore was glad Selena was breaking free from her shell. She had obviously been talking to someone to know this information, and until recently, she had avoided everyone. The new life growing in her belly made her more self-conscious and withdrawn, but the idea of moving to Oregon made her come alive.

When she told Salvatore about the child, he said, "I will love the child as my own when we are married." Selena couldn't tell him that she could never have a man look upon her scarred body with all the bite marks and her broken nose. She knew she could never marry and told Salvatore to tell everyone they were brother and sister. She felt disgraced and wanted to travel as far away from Spain as possible.

According to the locals, who knew almost nothing about Oregon, the trip was possible, but they would need to cross the Comancheria, and no one except for the Comancheros and the Comanche had ever done that. They stressed the problems associated with the Llano Estacado, an enigma without landmarks and only a few hidden water holes.

Salvatore had killed three men in less than two minutes and fought an expert swordsman to a draw; his ability to fight and his courage were not an issue. His family had always studied the stars and known how to navigate, and they could plot position by using the angle of the sun. He had no fear of getting lost in a trackless desert. However, Salvatore made a major error by underestimating the Comanche and the size of the Llano Estacado, the home range of the Comanche.

Many of the wagons of Texas lacked the quality Salvatore wanted. There was no comparison between the wagons of Spain built with Old World craftsmanship, and the wagons built in the New World. He bought the best wagon he could find and two teams of oxen. He bought two water barrels for each side of the wagon. The oxen and horses would drink a barrel a day. This meant they would need to find water every four days.

An old man, who was dying, sold Salvatore a small mule that was able to smell water from twenty miles away. The old man wasn't interested in money; he wanted someone who would take care of Matilda the mule. She was worth her weight in silver. Matilda found water every two or three days on the Llano Estacado and beyond.

The stories about the Comanche and the Comancheros were not exaggerated. The Comanche raided with virtual impunity from the Canadian border to Mexico City; eventually, the Texas Rangers adopted Comanche tactics and acquired the Colt Walker Revolver, and the federal army began building forts on the frontier. The reign of the Comanche was nearly over. However, the American Civil War was soon to begin, and the federal troops were withdrawn. Texas buried its Indian fighters on the battlefields of northern Virginia, and the Comanche empire established dominance once again.

The Comanchero traded guns and whiskey to the Comanche for slaves, buffalo hides, and horses, and in their own way, were just as deadly as the Comanche.

Salvatore decided to hire three vaqueros to ride alongside the wagon as escorts. He paid each of them a small gold coin and three silver coins from Spain and told them they would be paid again upon arriving in Oregon. He bought each of them a rifle and pistol, and told them they were each responsible for acquiring a well-trained saddle horse. They were overjoyed, and each of them showed up the next morning with a well-trained saddle horse. The vaqueros were excited about the trip and anxiously awaited the adventure.

They would follow and cross the river drainages as they headed northwest, they were the only landmarks in a sea of grass that was shoulder high. The plan would be to keep moving north to the next river and follow it upstream before heading north again to the next river. This would help assure them of never being too far from water.

During the trip through East Texas, Salvatore was glad to have the vaqueros. They rode past many gringos who looked like bandits and miscreants, but the frontier renegades seemed to respect the firepower of his vaqueros.

When they entered the Comancheria, there were no more frontier ruffians. They were camped one evening, when they heard a gringo call to them, "Hello, Ranger Horn coming in—don't shoot."

Salvatore and the vaqueros drew their pistols.

Ranger Horn walked into the firelight with a big grin, and he spoke out in a horrible gringo accent, "Buenas noches, amigos."

Salvatore and his vaqueros said nothing as they looked at the bizarre giant. He stood six foot three and had several pistols and a large knife on his belt. His horse had two rifles and a shotgun in various scabbards.

Salvatore asked in broken English, "Señor Horn, are you alone?"

"Yes, Captain Horn of the Texas Rangers, at your service."

"Captain Horn, we don't need assistance."

Horn looked at the pot on the fire and said, "Can I have some frijoles? I haven't eaten in two days."

Salvatore nodded his head, and said in a voice without humor, "Mi casa es su casa."

Horn smiled and said, "That's neighborly of you. Relax, gentlemen, I am just going to get a bowl and spoon out of this saddlebag." The ranger pulled out a wooden bowl and a large spoon. The tension began to fade away.

He helped himself to a modest portion of beans, and Salvatore asked, "What are you doing on the Comancheria, Capitan Horn?"

"I am tracking a ruthless, bloodthirsty killer. His name is Santana Guerrero. He and his Comanchero brother, Soledad Guerrero, are part Maya and part Spanish and one hundred percent homicidal maniacs. I've been tracking Santana for three weeks, and tonight, I am going to kill him."

Salvatore told his vaqueros the information, and they asked a few questions in Spanish. Horn answered in English, "Yes, he was a Mexican; now, he is the worst Comanche of them all. He will drop by this evening to kill all of you. If you see Santana up close, he has a scar across his face and his nose. The bottom half of his nose is barely hanging on to his face."

The Spaniard and his vaqueros put their pistols away and began discussing the ranger's story. They became quiet, and Salvatore looked at Horn. "Captain, how many are there?"

"I figure there are at least twelve, maybe fourteen. The odds aren't good, but I can't get help, unless I leave you people alone to be butchered. The fiesta is tonight, and I aim to put a lid on the party."

"Captain Horn, we will help you kill Santana."

"Good. You all look like sporting gentlemen and it's for damn sure, I can use the help."

"Is there a plan, Captain Horn?" Salvatore asked.

"This coulee is a good redoubt. We'll roll the wagon in the coulee and stack the supplies on the bank for protection, then we'll tie the horses and mules close to camp, just upstream, with one of your men guarding them. They always try to stampede the horses, before they start their maneuvers. I will be upstream about thirty yards. When the shooting starts, I will move closer with an enfilading fire. Make sure your men know where I am, and tell them not to shoot me. When the Comanches commit, I will have my pistols blazing. With a little luck, we will kill them all, before they kill us."

Salvatore and his vaqueros were impressed with the plan and Horn's confidence. He was obviously an experienced Comanche fighter.

Horn left his horse to be tied with Salvatore's horses and mules, and left his rifles with the vaqueros. He carried the three pistols on his belt and had his shotgun on a sling over his shoulder. He silently slipped away in the darkness. Salvatore and his men unloaded the wagon and stacked the supplies to provide protection from the Comanche bullets. They tied the horses and mules about ten yards upstream on both sides of the dry coulee.

Selena was approaching her due time, but she wanted to be next to Salvatore when the fighting started. Salvatore whispered to his men, "Selena is not to be captured alive." They each nodded in agreement and settled in to wait several hours.

The first Comanche crawled undetected to within thirty yards of Salvatore's group. He charged in a crouching position while screaming a blood-curdling yell. He fired his rifle and drew his knife. Salvatore and his vaqueros all fired at the Comanche, and he died running; his momentum carried his lifeless body to the coulee.

The Comanches began firing and rushing the coulee. Salvatore could see the revolvers of Horn firing into the Comanches to his right. He heard his vaqueros take several bullets, but there was no time to see how bad the injuries were. They were still firing.

Ranger Horn was now walking among the Comanches with his shotgun booming out two rounds at a time. Everything was quiet, until a bullet slammed into Salvatore's knee, and he fell forward onto the lifeless body of one of his vaqueros. Salvatore looked up in pain to see the scarred face of Santana, just before a war ax slammed into his skull.

Santana reached for Selena, but was shocked to see the upward flash of a sword before it disappeared into his belly to emerge through his throat, beneath his chin. Santana dropped his ax to feel the steel blade protruding through his Adam's apple while looking downward, in shocked disbelief, at the pregnant woman who had stabbed him. Santana fell forward and forced the sword upward into the bottom of his skull, when he hit the ground. Selena's water broke. Horn ran up and shot Santana in the head twice.

The battle was over, and her beloved Salvatore and the vaqueros were dead. Selena was going into labor, and the only help she had was an illiterate Indian fighter.

Ranger Horn picked up Selena and carried her to a shade tree, away from the carnage. All day and into the night, Selena tried to give birth, while Horn encouraged her and wiped the sweat from her face and neck.

Selena was getting weaker. At daybreak, Horn told her, "I helped with calving when I was a boy. I know about delivering calves, if you want me to try. However, if we don't get this baby out soon, I fear you will be too weak, and I might lose you both."

Despite her exhaustion, Selena smiled and was comforted when Horn said, "I might lose you both."

Selena said in desperation, "Try, please try."

Horn felt in the birth canal. The head was in a normal position, but a foot was wedged beside the head. It was impossible for the baby to be born. Horn put his thigh under Selena's lower back, and with all his strength, he pushed back on the baby's head and foot. When he felt the baby's foot slip backward, the head slid forward, and the baby was born into Captain Horn's waiting hands, within seconds.

He cleaned up the baby boy with his neckerchief and put him on Selena's breast. Horn laughed at the baby's aggressive appetite. "He must have got hungry, trying to be born." Horn laughed at his joke and noticed the bite marks and scars on her thighs and breasts. He assumed the Comanches had ravaged her. Horn had seen this type of damage on women many times. He was used to it, and it didn't shock him. It was probably when her nose was broken as well. It wasn't a terrible break, the lower half was offset to the left a quarter inch, but it was the only blemish on an angelic face; a face beyond comparison on the frontier, maybe the whole state of Texas.

She was going to need help, and since Horn's ranger contract was officially up with the death of Santana and his boys, he could help Selena find her people.

Horn held the baby when he was done feeding, and the two of them drifted into a light sleep, while Selena slept deeply. Later that afternoon, Horn introduced Selena to her son and served up one of his best meals beans, coffee, and bacon.

Horn laughed at Selena's appetite and said, "My cooking must be improving, but I can see where your son gets his appetite. He hit the ground hungry, and there was no way I was going to stop that boy from getting something to eat. He nearly pushed me outta the way to get his breakfast."

It was hard to understand Horn's frontier English, but after thinking about what Captain Horn had said, Selena smiled and chuckled. It was the first time she had appreciated or even heard humor since that awful night in Spain. Yet, Horn was telling funny stories and smiling after so much death. He was a giant, but he was kind and gentle, and he was trying to make her laugh. He had saved her from Santana and delivered her baby during a difficult birth. Horn was an unusual and talented man, but he was humble and polite. He had seen her scarred body, but didn't ask embarrassing questions she didn't want to answer.

Horn said, "I am going out to gather up as many horses as possible. We need to get moving, and those horses are worth cash money for you and your baby."

Selena watched him walk away and thought to herself, *if Ranger Horn can accept me without a veil, the rest of the world can accept me.* She never wore a veil again.

Horn found the oxen, Matilda the mule, his horse, and nearly all the rest of the horses, including a few of the Comanche horses. He laid Salvatore and the vaqueros in shallow graves and asked Selena where she wanted to go. When she said, "I am headed to Oregon," he told her he wasn't exactly sure where Oregon was.

Selena let out a little laugh and said, "It's, due northwest, silly."

No one had ever called Horn silly, but it sounded okay, when Selena said it. "How far do you reckon it is?" asked Horn.

"I'm not sure, but it's on the Pacific Coast."

Horn was puzzled and wondered what he was doing. He had never heard of the Pacific Coast. He once rode to Santa Fe to shoot a killer, and he had hanged horse thieves in Mexico, on several occasions, but he had never heard of the Pacific Coast.

He knew few white men had ever been this deep into the Comancheria and survived. Selena and her baby would never make it to Oregon without him.

Horn was born on a ranch, sixty miles southeast of present-day Fort Worth, twenty-seven years earlier. He had been in twenty-three skirmishes with Comanches. He learned to ride and fight like the Comanche, and he was an efficient Indian killer. He had hanged many renegades and horse thieves in Texas and Mexico, but he had never been north of Texas. Beyond the Comancheria there were Cheyenne, Arapaho, Kiowa, and many tribes he had never heard of. If they were lucky, they wouldn't get scalped, and if their luck held, they would survive the winter. He heard the snow didn't get too deep on the trail south of the big mountains.

Selena and the baby seemed to get stronger each day, and soon Selena and Horn took turns riding and driving the wagon. She seemed to have a good feel for livestock, and she had been taught to ride at some point in her life.

The Comanche killed Horns' parents when he was ten and he had to make it on his own, until he was old enough to join the rangers. He had started riding packhorses at three, and he had his own pony at five. By the time Horn was eight he was starting young horses. Before the Comanche raided their ranch, he was riding professionally as a jockey against men on Saturdays and Sundays. During the raid, he hid in the brush and saw his mother raped repeatedly and his father roasted over a small fire, while chained between two wagon wheels; yet, it wasn't vengeance that drove Horn. He had a strong sense of morality and believed in right and wrong. He questioned everything; even now, he was questioning what was happening to the Comanche and his way of life.

Between ten and fifteen, Horn survived by working for a blacksmith. He worked at the forge and anvil when there was work and learned many of the secrets of working iron. His hands grew to be exceptionally large and strong because of the work, and his eyes were trained to observe a high degree of detail.

The blacksmith was a drunkard and belligerent to the boy who showed promise and a pleasant smile, but he needed Horn in the shop, when he drank too much and was unable to deal with the public.

Horn saved his pennies to buy a horse, saddle, rifle, and pistol. He dreamed of the life of a ranger in poverty, instead of living in coal dust with the abusive blacksmith.

Horn lied about his age, when he signed on with the rangers at fifteen. He was big for his age, and he rode like a Comanche. The other rangers were teasing the big kid about his lack of whiskers and baby soft face, but while they were chasing a war party, Horn pushed his horse into the fleeing Comanche riders to put his single shot pistol against the spine of a shocked Comanche and killed him. He then proceeded to drag another Comanche from his saddle and cut his throat. Those were the only Comanches they killed that day, and the kidding stopped abruptly. He became a legend among men who were legends.

The blacksmith complained to the ranger captain, about Horn being underage, and how Horn was under an implied contract of apprenticeship to him. He said he was inclined to complain to the political officials of Texas. The blacksmith had been drinking, and the captain sensed the real nature of the problem.

The captain told the blacksmith, "He made his mark. He is a ranger now. I suggest you forget about this. If you barge into my office again, I will put a .54-caliber pistol ball between your running lights." The captain stood up and pulled out an old-fashioned horse pistol from his sash, pulled back the hammer, and aimed it at the blacksmith's head from three feet away.

The blacksmith drank himself to death over the next few days.

By 1859, the Comanche was being pushed farther into the Comancheria, and the white man's diseases, cholera, smallpox, influenza, and syphilis were annihilating the western tribes. Buffalo hunters were decimating the most important source of food the Indian relied upon to maintain his culture. The Texas Rangers had forsaken the typical white man's method of warfare and adopted the Comanche raiding techniques. The Comanche was in decline; however, history would give the Comanche a reprieve, and the Comanche would be free to resume raids in Texas and Mexico, and the intertribal warfare throughout the plains. The Civil War drained Texas of its men and took away the protection of federal cavalries, from posts throughout the West, and Texans would soon be laid in shallow graves throughout the southern battlefields.

Horn was relieved to cross the Canadian River, but he figured they were in the area that had been designated as the official dumping ground for the eastern Indian, the state that would become Oklahoma. There was a lot of bitterness among thousands of Indians, who were driven from their homes and the Comanche still raided in this area. Horn knew they were only marginally safer, but they kept traveling fifteen to twenty miles each day.

It was mid-afternoon when Horn saw two human figures running toward them from the foothills to the west. They were nearly a mile away, running hard and fast.

Horn drew his rifle from his scabbard and said aloud, "What's going on here?" His horse was worried and turning, until Horn asked him to trot forward. A group of six Apaches topped the hill behind the runners and were pushing exhausted horses to run down the two runners. Ranger Horn said, "I don't like the way this looks" and spurred his horse into a gallop toward the runners.

The lead rider was only thirty yards away from the runners when Horn raised his Sharps rifle to fire. His first shot missed, and Horn whispered a curse under his breath. His second shot struck the lead rider in the chest and rolled him off the back of his horse, just as the rider let go of his lance.

Horn watched in horror as the lance arced through the air and struck a young Indian woman. The flint spear point entered her lower back and was now protruding from her lower abdomen.

Horn could see an infant in her arms, and he flew into a killing rage. He draped the Sharps over the saddle horn with a leather thong he kept tied to the saddle. He drew his Walker Colts and began firing the .44-caliber bullets into the other Apaches with a bloodlust he had never felt before. He fired all his pistol rounds and pulled his 12-gauge to fire twice more. He calmly reloaded one of his colts and put a bullet into the head of each Apache. He learned a long time ago not to trust Apaches to die a normal death, just because they had a mortal wound.

He joined the Indian who was trying to comfort his dying wife.

Selena ran up and asked Ranger Horn in Spanish if there was anything they could do. Horn tightened his lips and shook his head no. The Indian mother was on her knees and was holding her newborn to her breast. Eventually, she sat down on her calves and tried to be as comfortable as possible while waiting to die.

Horn and the man were communicating with sign language. Selena asked what the man was saying. "He says his wife can't die in peace, knowing that her baby daughter will starve to death," the ranger replied.

Selena looked shocked and said, "Ranger Horn, you tell her I will feed her baby like it is my own and raise her up to be a young lady."

Horn gave the appropriate hand signals, and the young Indian woman's facial expression took on a look of sublime peacefulness. She held out the baby to Selena and slumped down to die.

They laid her in the wagon and drove to a little hill and buried her at sunset. Selena fixed dinner, while the men dug the grave. They buried her in silence.

After dinner the Indian man, Chico, sang a funeral song in his own language. It was a haunting song and made the hair on Horn's arms stand up. When he was finished, Selena sang a Spanish song of love, life, and death. During the song, the Indian man started crying, and Ranger Horn felt all the emotion of twenty-seven years boil to the surface, and he began to cry as well, not so much from death and sorrow, but from the happiness of knowing a good woman and the expression of kindness she showed by taking on the little Indian baby (an H1W2 baby).

Selena now began to realize why the Texas Rangers were regarded so highly. Ranger Horn didn't hesitate when he saw an injustice. He was not only the peace officer, but he was the judge, jury, and executioner as well. He was a magnificent man, but he was as humble and unassuming as he was brave. She decided that this was the man she wanted to spend the rest of her life with.

The next morning, at daylight, Horn was awakened to the sound of an animal in camp. He jumped out of his bedroll to see Chico cut the throat of an exhausted bull elk. Horn helped the man butcher the animal, but he was astounded by what he had just seen.

When the men were cooking elk steaks, beans with onions, and coffee, Horn asked Chico how he had caught the elk and brought it into camp.

The Indian explained that he was a Tarahumara, and from the high mountains of Northwestern Mexico. They were legendary runners who hunt game by running it down. They usually don't venture away from home, because they are shy of the rest of the world, but they had to leave their home.

His wife was in a contract of marriage to a chief's son. It was arranged when she was a small girl, but she had fallen in love with Chico, and they decided to elope.

They didn't expect the chief to hire Apaches to hunt them down. The Apaches had been on their trail for ten months, and if they had not run into Ranger Horn, he would have died with his wife. Since Ranger Horn had saved his life, Chico was bound to serve Horn for the rest of his life.

Horn had heard of the Tarahumara, but considered them to be legends. It was said; they were able to run distances of a hundred, and even two hundred, miles a day. No wonder those Apaches looked so gaunt. They had spent the better part of a year trying to run down the young runners, who called themselves, "Foot Throwers." It was no telling how many horses the Apaches had stolen and ridden to death, trying to keep up with the runners. The Apaches were legendary trackers, but to run down people who can run over a hundred miles a day will kill horses; you will kill a horse every few days.

The Apaches were relentless and would have considered the pursuit a matter of honor; although, from their appearances, the Apaches were barely alive, and they couldn't have lasted much longer before dying on the trail. The story was even more phenomenal, because his wife ran during her pregnancy and had given birth only a few days ago; yet, they were still running and looked to be in great shape.

He told the tale to Selena, and she began to cry. Horn put his hand on her shoulder and said, "The two lovers were together for a year, and the fruit of their love will live under our protection." Selena spun into Horn and wrapped her arms tightly around his middle and squeezed with unimagined strength. She was five foot eight, Horn was six foot three and an extremely strong man, but her strength was almost frightening. She cried even harder, and Horn patted her back with his hand and told her not to worry, things would work out.

Later, Horn was thinking about the strength of Selena's bear hug. She was visibly upset, but was she upset with him? Had he done something wrong? It was confusing for Horn. He was a fearless Indian fighter and tracker of horse thieves, but he had no experience in affairs of the heart.

Ranger Horn had never considered having a servant and disliked the idea, but Chico was proving himself to be very useful. Every afternoon, he would run ahead to find a good campsite with good water and feed for the livestock. He'd have a fire started and fresh meat or fish cooking by the time the wagon arrived.

One morning, Chico saw a lone buffalo about a mile in the distance. He told Horn to be ready, because he was going to run way around the buffalo and then spook it towards Horn and his horse. Horn tried to tell him the buffalo may turn to fight, but Chico was already running away to flank the animal. Chico was an excellent hunter, and Horn assumed he knew what he was doing.

In the distance, Horn saw Chico run toward the buffalo to spook him. The buffalo took three strides in retreat and then turned to fight. Chico kept running straight at him and slapped the buffalo on the forehead and ran toward Horn. "Well, he don't lack for nerve," Horn said out loud, when the buffalo followed Chico, with a frightening burst of speed.

The distance was soon eaten up by the speed of Chico and the rampaging bull. Chico swung north away from the wagon, to take Selena and the children out of danger, and Horn charged the buffalo at full speed. He saw his first two rounds sink deep into the chest cavity. He was then galloping alongside the buffalo, but the animal did not slow or show signs of distress. Horn put the muzzle up against the animal's back and fired. The bullet destroyed the heart of the beast, and he collapsed in a rolling heap.

Chico let out a war cry and danced around the buffalo in celebration. Horn let out a Comanche war whoop as Selena drove up in the wagon. They were celebrating because of the kill, and because there was meat for the rest of the winter. They could carry all the meat on the wagon, and the meat would be preserved in the cold. That day they celebrated with a day of rest and a meal of tongue with wild prairie onions.

Selena used rudimentary sign language to ask Chico if the baby had a name. He replied, his tribe names a baby after it survives the first few days. At this moment, Selena decided to name the baby Fleet Dove, in honor of her mother's courageous run for freedom.

Later that afternoon, Chico began mixing and cooking a pot of cactus and other plants he had been collecting along the trail. He rendered some of the buffalo fat and mixed it in with the residue of the plants. Once it was stirred well, Chico placed it in the snow to cool.

Two hours later it had congealed into a gel, and he presented the mixture to Selena in a wooden bowl. She looked at him with a question on her face. It didn't look edible. He made the motions of rubbing the mixture on his chest. At first she thought it was meant as a breast salve, but he pointed to a scar on his forearm and put a small amount on the scar.

He had surely seen the scars from the bites on her breasts; they were still vivid red marks on her ivory skin. She thanked him and thought she would first experiment and apply the mixture to the scars on her abdomen. Her breasts were the only things keeping the helpless babies alive, and she didn't want to take a chance of ruining their feed supply.

She applied the salve that evening, and the next morning she looked at the scars in disbelief. They were nearly gone. The angry-looking redness had disappeared, and the scars were faint and hard to see. She was overjoyed and quickly applied the medicine to all the scars she could see and reach. Within days of applying Chico's salve, the scars had all but disappeared. There were only faint traces of the marks.

She thought of the ranger and how good it felt to hug him and hold him to her body. He had been so embarrassed and at a loss to know how to return the affection. She laughed at his naive nature that she admired so much. He was a darling man, and she needed him to hold her.

She devised a plan. When Chico was out on one of his two-hour runs, she called Horn into the wagon under the pretext of rubbing the salve on her back. He was rubbing the salve into the scars, when she pushed the sheet covering her hindquarters to expose a few scars he had never seen. Horn began rubbing the salve into these new scars very dutifully and professionally, as Selena made a low, guttural cat noise in her throat and turned around to embrace Horn to her naked body. Horn started to panic, when he felt the abnormally strong Selena grab him in a fit of passion, but he forced himself to relax and with the utmost care and gentleness he returned her raw passion with a kind and loving touch. His naïve response inflamed Selena's aggressive passion even more.

Selena reached down to open Horn's trousers. Horn wasn't sure how to respond. His manhood was rigid and ready to perform, but he couldn't believe Selena actually wanted him. However, Selena's determined efforts to get his trousers below his hips convinced him that she not only wanted him, she was demanding that he make love to her.

When she grabbed his root, she marveled at the hardness, thickness, and length. She pulled down on his manhood and raised her hips upward until the initial contact and entry was made. With her legs wrapped around his thighs, Selena was getting used to the feel of Horn's member in her most intimate part when she pulled herself up to his ear and said, "Now, move it, now."

Horn didn't hold back. He pushed down and forward to sink his manhood deep into Selena. The sensations caused her to open her mouth in a silent scream. Her eyes were open wide, and she was breathing in great gulps, and holding the air to keep from screaming.

Her hips began a slight up and down movement that she had never imagined possible. The movement increased the sensual feelings, and she whispered to Horn, "Move, Horn—move, damn it."

Horn was shocked to hear Selena use such language, but he began a slow, and precise movement that lifted Selena over the edge. She couldn't get her breath fast enough and she kept saying, "Oh, oh, oh."

Horn stopped and raised up to ask, "Are you okay, Selena?"

A wave was washing through the center of Selena, and she said, "No, no, don't stop. More, more, don't stop."

Horn was confused, but he complied with Selena's request and continued on, until he too lost all restraint.

In less than two hours, they had consummated the passions that had been pent up for years within both these young souls. They pledged love and commitment to each other for the rest of their lives, and a true American love story was born from tragedy and pain.

Chapter 47

The Journal of Sadie Bristol, Oregon Trail, 1860

Call me Sadie. (An H1W2 woman). My husband, Balcer, and I are bound for Oregon. We left Saint Louis by riverboat on the Ides of March, in the midst of a cold snowstorm. We steamed five hundred miles upstream on the Missouri to Westport, Kansas. There were thousands of emigrants waiting to head toward Santa Fe, California, or Oregon. I saw my first Mexicans. They were working for the Santa Fe Traders. There were also many Negroes working on the docks, and hundreds of Indians from a variety of tribes.

The Sacs and Foxes had their heads shaved and their faces painted. The Delaware and Shawnee wore red turbans with calico shirts. Yes, these are the same Delaware who were allies with William Penn. They have become the pirates of the plains and live to plunder, raid, and wage war from Canada to Mexico. They learned horsemanship and became mounted buffalo hunters. The Wyandot Tribe dresses in the fashion of white men and work on the docks. The French Canadians are everywhere, as are the French Indians, who call themselves Metis.

Balcer and I drove to Independence, while waiting to join up with the right kind of emigrants. There were many shops to service the emigrants with necessaries for the trip west, and the air was filled with the continual ring of hammers on anvils as the farriers were shoeing mules, horses, and oxen at three dollars a hoof. It was an unheard-of price, but they were the only ones who could shoe your stock until you arrive on the West Coast or Santa Fe.

There were also wheelwright shops that repaired wagons and their wheels. Most of the wagons had already traveled from the East Coast, and many people wanted the wooden wheels and iron tires tuned up by the only wheelwrights between here and the West Coast.

Balcer and I didn't like the look of many of the emigrants; some had the ne'er-do-well look of mountebanks, ruffians, gamblers, and vile-looking outcasts. My husband said, "Such people cause problems on the trail." He insisted we wait for a group with character and integrity. We found a group led by Colonel Nathan Jessup, a retired cavalry officer and former plantation owner from Northern Virginia. Colonel Jessup was searching for a scout when we joined his group. He told Balcer, many of the mountain men were drunkards and men of low character, prone to fighting and gambling. Eventually, he chose Mr. Toms, a bona fide mountain man with an Indian wife. Together, they speak several Indian languages and the universal sign language of the tribes. Mr. Toms is a rough, coarse man, but he doesn't swear unnecessarily, and he worries over everyone's welfare when he is in camp. I feel safe with Mr. Toms as our scout. His wife, Cocina, and I became instant friends; she is teaching me sign language.

He insists on leaving right away, despite the bitter winds and snow that makes for cold travel. Mr. Toms scoffs at the complainers, "T'is far better to shiver on the prairie in the spring than to starve and freeze in the deep snow of the mountains this winter."

There was a meeting to protest the early departure. Colonel Jessup started by saying, "We shall trust the judgment of our scout in all such matters relating to the trail." Colonel Jessup further insisted that everyone must recognize his personal authority, or they would need a new wagon master.

Balcer stood up and said if we are to reach Oregon, we need a strong leader; a leader who knows how to set up a defensive perimeter, and lead a military campaign is the best kind of leader, and we are lucky to have the colonel. The others agreed, and swore an allegiance to the colonel.

We leave in the morning, and I am too excited to sleep

The colonel is an honorable man. When he heard sabers rattling and the talk of civil war; he resigned his commission, sold his plantation, and gave manumission to his slaves. Family, friends, and fellow officers on both sides called him a traitor, a coward, and a turncoat, but he didn't want to take up arms against his country, nor his fellow Virginians. He served as a scout for the cavalry during the War with Mexico, fresh out of West Point; he is no coward.

Colonel Jessup has a Negro valet and driver, James. His parents purchased James, when he was a small boy. His purpose was to be a friend and playmate for their son. The boys grew up together. It was a custom on remote plantations. When the colonel gave James manumission, James insisted on staying with the colonel as a salaried valet. He is a respected advisor to the colonel, and fought beside Colonel Jessup in the Mexican War.

The cold weather soon turned into cold spring rains. The oxen labored to pull the heavy wagons through the mud, and people began throwing away the heavy furniture in their wagons. Instead of twelve to fifteen miles a day, we were making six to eight. The wagons are developing problems with the wheels being wet and soft. Balcer says the wheels may develop loose iron tires when the wood shrinks in the desert. Mr. Toms is worried about our slow progress, and everyone hopes the rains end soon.

The rains have stopped, and each day becomes hotter than the day before. We are passing the graves of emigrants, and several people have caught the cholera. Every two or three days, someone dies of cholera. It is a devastating disease with no chance of recovery. The only redeeming factor is the victim dies within two days, and their suffering is finished.

Chapter 48

Texas Ranger and Family

Ranger Horn and his family joined the wagon train in the area that was to become Nebraska. Ranger Horn's people were shocked to see the suffering among the emigrants; the wagons are falling apart, and many of the people seem on the verge of starvation, and dysentery is rampant. The Horn wagon is still sound, and they have eaten well on the trail, thanks to Chico, a Tarahumara Indian who can run down deer and elk. The Americans find it astounding that the Horn wagon had been on the trail all winter and the three adults and two babies are healthy and in good spirits.

Colonel Jessup is glad to have an experienced lawman and Indian fighter with him, but he says he has never met a man so obsessed with moral judgments of right and wrong, and the sense of being the law, the judge, and the executioner. Colonel Jessup took time to explain to Ranger Horn, the laws of Texas don't apply to someone who has never been to Texas. Horn was in a state of shock at the concept of jurisdictions. In Horn's mind, Texas was the only law west of the Red River, and the idea that they were in an area with no real law, other than the colonel's jurisdiction over the wagon train, was confusing for the Texas Ranger.

The colonel appointed Ranger Horn as his second-in-command and began instructing Horn in the Constitution and of how America had won its Independence. Thus, from these history lessons, along with reading lessons, the colonel says a brilliant mind is evolving from a rustic frontiersman. Horn now reads every book the people of the wagon train have to offer, and quotes the great philosophers of the past.

Captain Levin introduced Ranger Horn to Plato, Homer, and Aristotle, and they have deep philosophical discussions that leave the old sea captain perplexed at the young man's ability to grasp complex concepts, so soon after learning to read. In the future, Ranger Horn maintained that Plato was the nucleus for his transformation from a rugged Texas Ranger into a judge for the future state of Oregon.

The colonel conducted the marriage ceremony for Selena, a cultured lady from Spain, and Ranger Horn, a few days after they joined the wagon train. Selena was beginning to swell. Selena enjoyed talking to the other ladies and using her newly acquired English with a backcountry Texas accent. She talks about her babies, and her ranger. She was quickly accepted among the women of the wagon train, who admired her for taking in an orphaned Indian baby and her knowledge of the sophisticated culture of Spain.

Chico began working closely with the colonel and the guide, Mr. Toms, to find good forage and water.

Farther west, on the trail, Bif Cunningham and his family joined the Jessup wagon train with two wagons. Colonel Jessup and Mr. Toms figured the Comanche Cougar and her daughter, Montana, might be able to help during future negotiations with hostile natives. They are attractive women, but they both have three scalps on their belts, and in the presence of men, their right hands are always resting on their scalping knives. They never smile at men, except for Bif and his son. They are friendly to us women, but we are scared of them. It is comforting to think of hostiles seeing these women and thinking we might all be dangerous.

Bif Cunningham is a former soldier from Scotland. His wife and daughter are tiny, his son will be big like his father, and he is nearly as big as an ox and almost as strong. He is as friendly and outgoing as his wife is withdrawn and treacherous. They have a close family and love each other very much. I believe the person who crosses this family will have a short lease on life.

The new wagons bring hope and strength to the wagon train, because of their positive attitudes and their abilities to thrive in the wilderness.

Americans are fulfilling these dreams of Manifest Destiny. They are bringing ideas of nationhood and freedom to the Pacific Northwest with resourcefulness and courage. It is their intellect and ingenuity that will tame this new country, making it safe and civilized in the near future.

Chapter 49
The Trail

Since I am half-Cherokee, I have a keen interest in the Indians we see on the plains. My mother was a sixteen-year-old Cherokee maiden, when she survived a raid by murderous white men in North Carolina, and decided to walk north to Canada on a slave trail. She made it to Tennessee, before my father found her in a state of starvation and exhaustion. He nursed her back to health, and I was born a year later and raised in a log house as a white girl. I grew up wearing calico dresses and learned to read, write, and cipher. My father was a dedicated horseman and taught me to ride and train horses. I studied the only book we had, the Bible. My mother taught me about the Cherokee culture. I considered myself much more educated than most because of having two cultures and a loving family.

The first nomadic Indians we encountered on the trail were the Delaware (the former allies of William Penn) returning from a buffalo-hunting trip. Both men and women were riding horses; they had many pack mules loaded with buffalo meat, hides, cooking kettles, and all the necessaries for life on the trail.

An old man rode up to my husband, and in perfect English, asked who our chief was, and what tribe I was from. He made a motion like he was smoking a pipe, my husband gave him a pouch of tobacco and pointed to the colonel and said, "Colonel Jessup." He told the old man I am Cherokee.

The old man seemed impressed and grunted his approval. He gave my husband a casing of pemmican. His pony had a mane and tail full of burrs. His saddle was a wooden Spanish type covered with a blanket, and the stirrups were carved from wood. He then asked if my husband would trade me for some horses or mules. My husband told him we had too many horses for the trip. The old man shrugged, and rode away.

My husband looked at me and said, "Do you think I should have asked to see his livestock?" He was trying to be funny, but I didn't appreciate the humor. These Indians trade young women and girls like livestock and there is nothing funny about the slave trade. I am glad to have been raised as a white girl.

We are taking thirty head of good breeding horses to Oregon, and hope to be raising and selling trained horses in the near future. I am much more aware of horse types and equipment than most people, and I have a good eye for horseflesh.

The Kickapoo are the most colorful Indians. They shave their heads and paint their faces red, green, black, and white in all sorts of designs. They wear blousy calico shirts and colorful turbans. They have leather leggings with a cotton breechcloth and wrap themselves in red and blue blankets. The men have large brass earrings and wampum shell necklaces, and they ride the most bedraggled ponies of the prairie.

One of the most remarkable scenes of Indian life we saw was near the Platte, a band of Dakota were breaking camp to hunt buffalo. The women began by pulling the sewed buffalo hides from the poles that formed the foundation of the teepees and lashing the tops of the poles to the sides of horses by using a packsaddle to support the rails of the travois. Cross rails would be lashed farther back on the rails to add rigidity to the travois.

In a matter of minutes, a peaceful village of lodges turned into mass confusion and chaos. The lodges were folded on the ground, and all their earthly possessions were spread alongside. There were buffalo robes and wooden frames with painted leather sides that stored dried meat, copper kettles, iron skillets, stone mallets, and various objects waiting to be stowed. The goods were placed into baskets and lashed to the framework of the travois, and then the packsaddle was loaded to unbelievable heights.

The women were the packers, and they went about their work of loading the entire camp with stoicism and dignity, and the old women screamed insults and ridicule at everyone.

The men sat around a few campfires and observed the process with an air of indifference. They each held onto the reins of a saddle horse and smoked a pipe. In twenty minutes, the tribe was moving and the men came to life, mounted their horses, and joined in the procession.

There was a group of pretty girls, riding mules and horses. They had smiles for everyone, but they acted shy and bashful when white men looked their way. Little boys with tiny bows and arrows walked along the prairie shooting every bird and animal within range. There were young warriors with paint and feathers racing around on fast ponies to prove their horsemanship, while trying to impress any females who might be watching. Every packhorse had two or three small children clinging to the load, increasing the burden each animal was required to carry.

We never ask a packhorse to carry over one hundred forty pounds, but these horses were carrying at least two times that much.

There were countless dogs running through the exodus, and they kept up a continuous howl rather than barking. I told my husband they sound like their cousin the wolf. He said they were part wolf and nervous about the move. My husband has a way with animals and can often tell you what they are thinking.

There was mass confusion; yet, the Indian camp was moving within twenty minutes. Our slow, orderly, and precise movement is so boring in comparison. The Indians leave nothing, but littered behind us are cracked and shattered wrecks of maple and walnut furniture from Britain and Europe. They were priceless heirlooms a few months ago, but now they are thrown out like rubbish to lighten the load.

The Dakota Tribe traveled beside us for most of a day. At noon, we were treated to the sight of a young teenage boy on a pony, chasing a buffalo bull. The bull ran next to the right side of the wagon train, and the boy was pushing his pony hard to stay with it. The bull was huge and nearly exhausted when he ran by our wagon. His tongue was hanging out of his mouth and nearly on the ground, his tail was stiff and pointing upwards, when the boy pulled alongside and sent an arrow deep into the bull's ribs, from the right side. The bull spun and tried to hook the pony with his horns, but the pony jumped to the right, and the horns missed. The boy had the reins tucked in his belt and was holding onto his bow, his legs keeping him on the horse. The pony drifted back toward the buffalo, giving the boy an excellent opportunity for another shot. The second arrow landed a few inches away from the first arrow. The bull stopped and glared through a shaggy mane with red eyes at the boy on his pony. The blood was flowing from his nostrils and mouth with air bubbles, indicating a mortal wound of the lungs. The bull stood to collect his strength and repeatedly charged the pair. The boy and his pony avoided the charges with effortless movements. After several charges, the bull stopped and struggled to get his breath, with his chin and tongue resting on the ground. Finally, he gurgled a death rattle deep in his chest, and groaned when he fell to the earth and died.

Several warriors rode up and had the bull cut up and processed within a few minutes. They were eating the raw liver, heart, lungs, and brain, and they began splitting the leg bones for the marrow. The boy rode up to our wagon and offered a split leg bone with the marrow exposed as a gift to me. He was smiling a big bloody smile. I thanked him and put the bone on the seat. I pulled a pink ribbon from my hair and offered it to him. He wiped his hands on his pony and held the ribbon between his finger and thumb like it was gold. He rode over to a pretty girl on a mule and gave her the ribbon. She tied it in her beautiful raven colored-hair and waved to me with a big smile. I realized how different I was from these people who are so close to my heritage. I look like them, but I am from a different culture, and I can never go back. I placed the bone under the wagon seat. My dog will eat it later.

Mr. Toms keeps preparing everyone for the dangers of the Snake River crossing. He is not prone to exaggeration; everyone is thinking about the crossing and the possibility of losing everything.

Chapter 50
Balcer Contracts Cholera

The oxen are slowly starving because nearly all the feed has been eaten along the trail; they are reduced to eating White Sage. We have lost thirteen mares; we have no idea whether wild mustang stallions lured them away, or if Indians stole them for they consider horse theft a sport. I was raised as a White girl, and although my mother was Cherokee and taught me about the native culture, I find it difficult, if not impossible, to understand these Indians of the plains.

Our right rear wheel has developed a loose tire. Captain Levin says it is because the wood wasn't quite dry when the wheel was made, and the wheel has shrunk almost an eighth-inch because of the dry desert conditions, leaving the iron tire loose on the wooden wheel. Every night he tightens the wheel with wooden wedges and metal screws, but I don't think the wheel will last until we get to Oregon.

This morning, I rode a horse to find one of the oxen that had quit camp to look for better feed, and I came upon a wretched band of Cheyenne. There were no young men, only women, children, and old men. They were weak from hunger and suffering from the elements. A young girl had died from cholera, and they were digging a grave for her with sticks.

Who knows where the men were, maybe they died from disease or were killed in battle. I knew I had to help them.

I rode back to the wagon and got a shovel and a few pounds of my husband's smoked summer sausage.

The people thanked me and tried to communicate in sign language, but I only know a few expressions in sign language. They ate half the sausage, and an old man dug a grave about eighteen inches deep in the hardpan dirt. I would have preferred a deeper grave, but the old man worked hard to dig that deep.

The girl's mother placed three silver thimbles on the young girl's fingers and wrapped her in a blue army jacket with brass buttons. An old woman made the signs of sewing, and I realized the girl was being marked for the afterlife as a seamstress.

Somehow, this ragged band had lost their men. Maybe it was war, maybe it was disease, maybe it was just fate, but without strong men, they were hopeless and bound to perish.

They returned the shovel, and we said our goodbyes. As I rode away, I realized how the natural scheme of men and women is designed to work and how important it is.

My husband dreamed of owning a quarter section in Oregon, but it is unlikely he will ever see his fabled Oregon or the Columbia River. He has contracted the cholera and lies dying. My oxen are starving, and a wheel is falling apart on my wagon. There is only a narrow divide between success and death. My chances for survival diminish with each passing hour.

We have buried thirty-four emigrants since leaving Independence. My sweet, loving husband will be number thirty-five, in a few hours. He fights bravely to hang on, but no one survives this dreadful disease, and he suffers horribly. A once powerful young man now is a rack of bones. It would be an act of Mercy if God would take him sooner than later.

Thankfully, we have no children. I can't stop and I can't turn around. My situation is desperate.

I am not strong enough to lift the wooden yoke for the oxen, and sliding the bows into position is impossible for a woman who is less than five feet tall and barely weighs ninety pounds. If it weren't for the help of my gentlemen: Captain Levin, Colonel Jessup, Bif Cunningham, and Ranger Horn, I would be left to perish on the trail.

We have seen countless graves from the wagon trains ahead of us, and it is horrible. The graves are seldom dug deep enough to keep the wolves, lions, and bears from digging them up and eating the bodies. We pass ten or twelve half-eaten bodies a day. My husband asked that I make sure he is buried deep enough that the animals wont eat his flesh.

My husband died during the night. He was a brave man and passed on without remorse. He told me to find another man to take care of me.

There is a problem with the time and manpower it takes to dig a grave. The ground is hard and must be chopped with a pick or an ax to dig just a few inches.

Mr. Toms and the colonel helped bury my husband. They dug the grave at least four foot deep and wrapped my husband in a sheet. Mr. Toms built a fire over the grave with grass and brush. He assured me that the scent would be burned away, and the animals wouldn't know there was a body buried beneath. Mr. Toms knows a lot of wondrous things about the country; I trust his judgment and feel my husband's body will be secure.

I have lost my husband and most of the horses I own and wonder if I should go on or just give up.

Captain Levin helps me with my wagon at night so that I have time to check on the horses. He is an Irish Jew who spent his life sailing around the world in search of the Spermaceti Whale. He started as an orphan by stowing away on a Nantucket whaler in Dublin for repairs. He worked his way up until he became a captain. Captain Levin is a learned man who reads passages from the Bible and the Greek philosophers to me in the evening when chores are finished. He helps me find the strength to face the morrow. He also tells me about the wondrous places of the world that few people ever see except for men of the sea like him. He is a kindly man who is strong of character and body. Despite his advanced years, he works harder and longer than most young men.

I am lucky to have my "Gentlemen," Mr. Toms, the colonel, Captain Levin, Ranger Horn, and Bif Cunningham. They help me hitch up my oxen and check in on me to make sure I am safe. I don't know what might happen without them.

We were three days from the Snake River Crossing when the iron tire from my right rear wheel rolled off and continued on its own, passing me and the front of the wagon before coming to rest against a large sage bush. I stopped the oxen, and Captain Levin came over and looked at the wooden wheel. "It's beyond repair," he said.

I asked, "What should I do?"

"Throw away everything, but your most important gear and stow that in the front half of your wagon. I will saw the wagon in half, jam the steering mechanism, and make a cart out of a wagon," Captain Levin replied with a smile.

I threw away a few small pieces of furniture and my husband's belongings. No one else wanted them because of the weight.

Captain Levin cut away the back half of the wagon, made the front wheels so that they wouldn't turn, and fashioned an ingenious drop-down gate with leather hinges. I was moving within an hour and the oxen seemed to appreciate the lighter load.

In the evening, Colonel Jessup came to inspect my cart. He complimented Captain Levin on an excellent job, and asked if he could talk to me a few minutes.

We walked in the cool night air of the high desert, and he told me that I was in a desperate situation.

I agreed, and said, I had no choices, and I had to continue.

He told me, I could become his wife before the crossing, and we could make a life together in Oregon.

I was in a state of shock. The colonel was an officer and a gentleman, and I was a half-Indian widow; I didn't think that any other man would take me for a wife. I told him, "Yes, a thousand times yes. I will be a good wife and I will make you happy."

He took me in his arms and said that it was unusual to propose so close to a husband's funeral, but these were extraordinary times.

I agreed, and he kissed me. My knees buckled and I was breathless. The colonel smiled and started to straighten up, but I pulled him down for another kiss. He is a good kisser.

We walked back to my wagon and told Captain Levin the news. The captain congratulated the colonel and brought out a bottle of Irish whiskey. He poured out a very small amount in two glasses, and the two men drank a toast to our new life and Oregon.

The colonel asked Captain Levin if he would conduct the service on the night before we crossed the Snake and help him with some other unrelated legal papers before the wedding.

Captain Levin said, "I will be honored to help."

I couldn't sleep that night. I was dreaming of the future.

Chapter 51
Three Island Crossing

We drove down a long grade to the Three Island Crossing, and planned to rest a day before attempting to cross the treacherous waters of the Snake.

The colonel held a meeting and asked everyone to write a will. He said he didn't like dividing the goods of deceased people, and he wanted some help. People began to appreciate the dangers of crossing the Snake.

Those who couldn't write had the captain or the colonel help them. The wills were collected by Captain Levin and given to Colonel Jessup.

The Indians brought dried fish and pemmican to trade. The emigrants were glad to add something new to their diets.

Later that night, we had the wedding ceremony. I wore a new dress; I had never worn. Cocina, Mr. Toms's wife, wove flowers from the desert in my hair. Captain Levin read scripture from the bible, but I didn't hear anything. Everyone was happy and refused to think about the dangers of the morrow.

The night seemed to float by as if I was in a dream. I had faith in the future and no longer had a fear of being alone.

The colonel gave the remnants of my wagon to James, his former slave and lifelong friend. James was proud of his new possession and drove the oxen to the river with pride.

I moved my few belongings into the colonel's wagon and felt like I had a home.

Ours was the first wagon to cross. The colonel told me to jump downstream if we tipped over and to hold on to a small barrel with a rope tied around it. He said the water is fast enough to roll the wagon over and over, so I must swim away from the wagon and stay clear of the oxen.

He wasn't smiling when he gave me my instructions.

The pull of the river was frightening. The oxen struggled desperately against the current and barely kept the wagon from being swept away.

After the emigrants saw how hard our team fought to keep the wagon from being swept away, six families decided not to cross the Snake, and headed southwest to California; the rest began throwing away almost all of their goods after hauling them so far.

The wagons started crossing the river. Captain Levin's wagon was swept downstream and rolled over many times. The drowned oxen and the wrecked wagon drifted downstream. Captain Levin's body came to rest on the gravel beach of the first of the three Islands. He was sitting up with one arm waving at us and looked as if he were beckoning. My husband gave one of the Indian boys a silver coin to swim over to the island, and tow the captain with a rope to the north side of the river.

James, the former slave, made it across almost effortlessly in my old wagon. His eyes were as big as teacups while he crossed, but he was laughing out loud when the oxen pulled his cart up on the bank of the river.

There was a large family swept away. Their bodies were never seen again. The rest of the wagons crossed without incident.

The river crossing was the most perilous part of the trip.

Several men dug Captain Levin's grave on the upper bank of the river, just beyond the high water marks.

Colonel Jessup read Jonah 2:3-6, when the captain was laid in his grave:

For thou hadst cast me into the deep, in the midst of the seas; and the floods compassed me about: all thy billows and the waves passed over me. Then I said, I am cast out of thy sight; yet I will look again toward thy holy temple. The waters compassed me about, even to the soul: the depth closed me round about, the weeds were wrapped about my head. I went down to the bottom of the mountains; the earth with her bars was about me forever: yet hast thou brought up my life from corruption, O Lord my God.

My husband read the Bible passage with tenderness; it was obvious that he respected and liked Captain Levin.

Bif Cunningham played a sad lament on his bagpipe, and afterward, his Comanche daughter, Montana, sang a sad song about a Scottish Highlander, killed in a war. Her voice was rich and pure; many of us were crying.

My husband read the captain's will after the funeral:

> Colonel Jessup, if you are reading this document, it probably means I drowned in the Snake River, in a torrent of irony. I am the only man who has sailed the oceans and seas of the world and yet, it is I who drowns in this wee bit of fresh water. I accept my fate with dignity and plead no complaints.
>
> I have forgone earthly pleasures, to save and invest; consequently, I am a wealthy man with property and investments. I have no family, other than my Oregon Trail family, and through them, I have been enriched beyond measure. My friend Colonel Jessup is a man of honor and principle. I salute him. He has managed his financial affairs well, and needs no help from me. To my big friend from Texas, Ranger Captain Horn, who has a thirst for knowledge, I leave my personal library and a $100 a month stipend to attend school and read the law. After matriculation, he can have the designated plot of land for a home and law office. To the family of Bif Cunningham, I leave a downtown property for your trading business. To James, who, like my ancestors, was released from bondage to wander in the wilderness, I leave one third of my Asian Import Export Trading Company on the Columbia. Colonel Jessup and Sadie Jessup will be equal shareholders in the company, and the three of you will need to learn the business quickly.
>
> May I say, if I were a younger man, I would have stepped forward to take care of Sadie, much like Ranger Horn stepped forward to help Selena, and Bif stepped forward to help

Cougar. Thankfully, Colonel Jessup stepped forward for Sadie.

The world is a better place because of those I consider my Oregon Trail family, and I have gone to my grave thinking of you.

Do not grieve for old Captain Levin. He lived a full life and has seen the world, and he is grateful for having known all of you.

God Speed,

Captain Ezekiel Levin

Chapter 52

An Exotic Visitor

Seamus found Nancy's ancestry to be fascinating and published stories in segments as Nancy Larkin. He cared nothing for fame, but he thought Nancy deserved a few moments of recognition, and he was going to provide those moments. The stories received the most complimentary commentary he had ever read on the Internet, and Nancy Larkin had thousands of friends who loved her.

Seamus realized it wasn't right to publish under another person's identity, and reality was about to knock on his door and demand an explanation.

Seamus lived on two thousand acres northeast of San Luis Obispo. The gate was always locked, unless he was expecting a visitor. He almost never had visitors, but if someone arrived unannounced, they would honk their car horn and hope for the best. He was a loner and lived in the middle of nowhere for a reason.

This visitor was different; she had an expensive German car and was dressed for Madison Avenue. She had black hair and olive skin like you see on the ultra-rich women in the casinos on the French Rivera. Seamus could tell this rich woman was spoiled and her frustration was building. He was watching her from his window with binoculars and decided he better talk with her and cool her out, before she started pestering the neighbors.

He rode an old BMW motorcycle with a sidecar down to the gate and asked what the problem was.

"Are you Mr. Larkin?" She asked.

"No," Seamus said with a big grin. He didn't make the connection and figured she was lost and would soon be leaving. Although she was a beautiful woman, in her early to mid-twenties, with a striking figure, she had the look of a wealthy woman who was used to having things go her way.

"I am looking for Mrs. Nancy Larkin. She writes on the Internet from this ranch, and I need to speak to her. It's important."

Seamus heard Nancy's name, saw the Oregon plates, and said, *Oh-oh*, to himself. "You've come a long way. Come to the cabin, and I will fill you in." Seamus opened the gate and tried to charm her with his best smile.

"You don't understand, I am more than a fan of hers; we have similar DNA," the well-dressed lady said. "In other words, we are distant cousins."

"I see. It's getting late and we should talk. Come to the cabin; I will fix dinner and tell you all about Nancy."

"You don't understand. I already know all about Nancy. I want to *meet* her."

Seamus started the motorcycle and revved it up to drown out the woman's complaints. He headed for the cabin and figured she would leave or follow him. Seamus watched her in the mirror; she hesitated, shrugged her shoulders, and followed him to the cabin.

When she got out of her vehicle at the cabin, Seamus asked, "Are you hungry?"

"I am starving, but I want to meet Nancy."

"Come on in. I am a decent camp cook, and you can have a glass of wine before dinner."

She walked into the semi-luxurious cabin with high heels clicking across the plywood floor. Seamus pulled off his Western boots and took a good look at the expensive high heels; they were the first of their kind to walk across his floor, and they would probably be the last. He'd take a picture of them, but it would probably make her nervous.

"Make yourself comfortable. I have Chardonnay, Cabernet, or Pinot; which do you prefer?"

"I'll have a Cabernet, thank you."

"Excellent choice. Cabernet is my favorite; my best wines are Cabernets." Seamus opened a decent bottle and poured her a generous amount of wine.

She sipped the wine and said, "You don't seem like a wine connoisseur, but this is an excellent bottle of wine, Mr. ..."

"Excuse me, I am Seamus Seville, rancher and recluse. I am glad to meet you. I have known Nancy since I was a boy. You are?"

"Miss Tarzana, Miss Emily Tarzana, from just east of Portland; now, when can I meet Nancy?"

"I belong to a wine club and buy a case of wine a month. I buy the higher-end bottles and hope for the best. I almost never have visitors, so my wine collection continues to grow. It's my only indulgence.

"Now, what should I fix for dinner? I can make a nice steak with potatoes and onions, and a salad. How does that sound?"

"It was not my intention to impose or intrude."

"Don't even think about that. I love to cook, and I never get to cook for beautiful women."

She lifted her eyebrows and said, "You are a charmer, Mr. Seamus."

"No, not really, just honest."

She laughed, rolled her eyes, and began to relax.

She seemed to enjoy her steak, after cutting it into tiny pieces and eating slowly.

"The steak was exceptional, Mr. Seamus. I've never seen them cooked on a vertical grill next to the fire."

"It's the Gaucho method, from Argentina."

"Have you been to Argentina?" she asked.

"Of course. Every horseman goes to Argentina."

"Okay, Mr. Seamus, you are an excellent cook, and you have a good wine collection. Now, tell me about Nancy Larkin."

"Emily, you will never meet Nancy; she died three years ago in Northern British Columbia. I am her ghostwriter. I have carried on this charade because Nancy was a friend of mine, and she was kind to her horses. Life wasn't kind to her, but she had a few years of happiness, and I wanted to tell her story and the story of her family."

Seamus told Miss Emily the entire story, and she started sobbing uncontrollably.

"Did you ever stop to think that you could do real damage to the family by writing in her name after she died?"

"No. To be honest, I never considered the possibility of damaging the sensitivities of family members. I figured if she had a family who cared, they wouldn't have let her live like a nomadic horseman in the wilderness of Northern British Columbia. I am writing the history of a friend of mine, a woman who suffered through tragedy and misfortune, and lived in poverty for the last part of her life. I wanted the world to remember her like this; besides, she had no more living relatives on the reserve."

Miss Emily finished her second glass of wine and held out her glass for a refill. I poured out the rest of the bottle and said, "It's over fifty miles to the nearest motel. You can stay here tonight. You can have my bed. I'll sleep on the couch, or you can sleep in the bunkhouse. It's nice enough. There's a shower and an indoor toilet, but the coyotes often spook city people."

She asked, "Where is the bunkhouse?"

"It's about a quarter mile away, next to the barn. I can drive you down there in the sidecar, or you can drive it yourself."

The remoteness finally settled in on her, and the three glasses of liquid courage wasn't enough to sleep alone in a bunkhouse. She said quietly, "I'll sleep on the bed."

"Suit yourself. I'll get some towels."

"Seamus, would you be a sweetheart and bring in my suitcase from the trunk? If I walk outside in the gravel driveway, with these heels, in the dark, I might break an ankle."

"I'll get your duffel bag, but you better kick off those heels and relax, there's just the dogs and me."

She asked, "What dogs?"

Seamus opened the back door and whistled; his two Black Mouth Cur dogs bounded through the door and ran for Emily like they were going to kill her. She screamed, and the dogs were baying like they had a cougar treed. "Tiger, Blue, cool it. We have company. This is Emily. She's a dog lover. Be nice, you bad boys." The dogs changed their attitude, when they realized Emily posed no danger. They charmed her by staring into her eyes with their best loving dog look.

"They nearly scared me to death," Emily said.

"Oh, don't be too hard on them; they will kill to protect you tonight. I think they like you."

"I've never been around such big dogs. How much do they weigh?"

"The little one is seventy-five pounds, and the bigger one is ninety."

"What kind of dogs are they?"

"They are Black Mouth Curs. They work feral cattle and put the run on black bears and mountain lions. If something tries to come into the cabin, the dogs will stop it, whether it has two legs or four."

Seamus showed Emily his bunk and the bathroom, but when he turned to leave, she said, "I am scared."

"There's nothing to be afraid of. My dogs like you, and they will sleep next to your bed all night."

"Please sleep with me. I mean . . . sleep with me, but not in a sexual way."

Seamus could tell she was scared, and he'd much rather sleep in his own bed. "All right, but I need to get some sleep. Here on the ranch, we go to bed early and get up early."

Midway through the night, the dogs were whimpering next to the bed. Seamus let them out, and they got into a big fight in the yard. There was a family of raccoons who wanted to move into the cabin; it was probably them.

Emily asked, "Are you worried about the dogs?"

"No, they take care of themselves. If they need me, they'll let me know."

A few moments later, Emily snuggled up against Seamus' back and fell asleep.

Seamus had an internal alarm clock that woke him up, without fail, at five every morning. He cooked a hearty breakfast using the basic food groups: bacon, green onions, eggs, potatoes, beans, biscuits, and coffee. The bacon was cooked ranchero style with jalapeno pieces, and the beans were added after draining the bacon. He turned off the propane burners and let the flavors mingle. He planned to heat up a few tortillas once Emily sat down. He walked into the bedroom and said, "Breakfast is ready. Time to get up."

Emily showed up for breakfast in her pajamas and a pair of moccasins. "What time is it?" She asked.

"It's 5:30, the sun will be up soon, and the morning will be gone."

He could tell she wasn't a morning person.

Seamus served breakfast, and Emily ate like she was hungry. "This is delicious, very flavorful. Thank you for breakfast."

While Emily was finishing her breakfast, Seamus started washing the dishes. Emily again proved herself to be a slow, but enthusiastic eater.

Seamus told her, "I usually write after breakfast. The morning is yours. You can walk down to the barn and saddle up a horse, or you can take a nature hike, but I need to feed this passion of mine."

He sat down and began the steady tapping on the worn-out keys of his computer.

Emily curled up on the couch with a blanket and fell asleep as Seamus typed away for two hours, before realizing how late it was. He made another pot of coffee, sat at his desk, and watched a light rain falling.

Seamus was thinking of all the people with Nancy's DNA and how their lives had intertwined with history. He felt a pair of small hands on his shoulders, and Emily whispered in his ear, "Thanks again for breakfast." She kissed him lightly on the cheek, and he felt each of his balls click and lift up. His root thickened and began to rise for a possible romantic interlude, before he shut everything down. Seamus said to himself, *Emily is forty years younger than me; she is scared and lonely. Forget the sexual stuff. She is a young female friend, and she probably looks up to me as a father figure. I'm not going to ruin it by making a fool of myself.*

Seamus reached up and held her tiny hands in his and said, "What would you like to do today?"

"I've always wanted to ride a horse. Can you teach me how?"

Seamus smiled and lifted one eyebrow. "Learning to ride is a long journey; a lifetime is hardly enough time. Sitting on a horse with a leg on each side and a faraway look is easy. It's the communication that takes so long, and building the bonds of the heart and mind; these are the bonds that endear horses to humans and makes horses loyal. Children often develop the bonds without effort, and they lose the secrets after becoming adults and reality robs them of their innocence. Yes, I will start you on your journey with horses. Do you have a pair of jeans?"

Emily clapped her hands, "Yes, I will get dressed." She rushed off to the bedroom and reappeared wearing a flannel shirt, jeans, and sneakers. She looked cute and had the enthusiasm of a schoolgirl.

Seamus packed a few sandwiches with cheese and crackers for lunch.

They rode the sidecar to the barn. Seamus caught Barney for Emily. He was twenty years old and tolerant of beginners. Seamus showed Emily how to put on the saddle and bridle, took them off, and had her put them back on. She did well. Emily was a clever girl.

Seamus saddled a colt from Nancy's bunch for himself. They rode over the hill to a remote part of the ranch. There were several small deer, and Emily acted as if they were watching lions on safari.

The creek was deep and fast from the spring runoff. Seamus didn't think they should cross with a young horse and an old horse, and he made camp next to the creek. Seamus picketed the horses, spread a blanket on the ground, and built a small fire to make coffee.

Emily was excited about everything. After lunch, she asked if she could go swimming. Seamus laughed, "That water is cold and fast. It's runoff from the snowpack in the mountains. You are a grown woman, and you can make your own decisions."

Emily started taking off her clothes and said, "It's getting hot, and I am going swimming." She stripped down to a fancy purple pair of bra and panties, and said, "After reading your stories of early man bathing in cold streams, during the Ice Age, I think I can handle the cold water."

Seamus tried not to look at the tight, hard body as she tiptoed over the gravel to a creek that was running like a river, but he had to watch to make sure she didn't get into trouble.

She tested the water with her right foot, and Seamus thought she would give up the idea of swimming, but she leaped into the water and was immediately swept downstream. Seamus got his lariat and ran downstream.

Emily managed to hold on to a large rock sticking out of the water in the center of the creek. The water was about four feet deep, and Emily was so cold she was turning blue, and looked like she was in shock. Seamus threw the loop over her shoulders and yelled, "Put your arms through the loop." When she had both arms through the loop, Seamus took up the slack and pulled her away from the rock. She was swept downstream again, but the current and the rope brought her to shore. Seamus ran to her and carried her to the fire. Her lips were blue, her teeth were chattering, and her whole body was shivering.

Seamus had her sit on a saddle pad and wrapped the blanket around her. He dried her body by rubbing the blanket over her, but the cold water had her underwear soaked. He said, "Take off the underwear. You need to get dry as fast as possible." Her trembling fingers couldn't manage the bra snap, Seamus flicked open the catches for her, and she slid off the soaked panties.

Seamus squeezed the water out of the underwear and hung them on a tree branch to dry in the sun. He gathered enough firewood to make a hot fire, and in thirty minutes, she wanted to put on her clothes. Seamus helped her with her jeans, socks, and shirt. When she was dressed, she fell into a deep sleep for two hours. She wasn't shivering, and she seemed warm under the blanket.

She woke up with a raging appetite and asked if there was more food. Seamus laughed and said, "Luckily, I brought an extra sandwich." She ate the sandwich and drank a cup of coffee.

Seamus could tell Emily had something on her mind. He asked, "Were you scared?"

"I thought I was going to die."

"Emily, if you were by yourself, you would have died."

Emily had something else to think about, and she drifted off into silence again.

After several minutes of deep thought, she asked, "Can you take me to Canada, and show me Nancy's grave?"

"It's been three years. Those graves are not like the white man's graves. They deteriorate, and it isn't necessarily pretty."

"Can you take me to the cabin on the North Fork?"

Seamus hesitated and replied, "That wee creek almost killed you. Multiply everything times ten or twenty and you will have a feel for the creeks and rivers of northern BC at this time of year."

"Have you ever been in water that cold?"

"I've broken through the ice twice, when it was forty below."

"How did you survive?"

"I'm not sure."

"I have over two and a half weeks of vacation left. Is that enough time to drive to the North Fork Cabin and back?"

"Yes, we can drive up there and back, if there are no complications."

"What kind of complications?"

"Weather, vehicle, someone doing something foolish, like jumping into a raging flood of fast, cold water."

"What if I agree to listen to your advice?"

"That would be a step in the right direction," Seamus said.

"You know, you can be arrogant and mean at times."

Seamus looked at her with a cold green-eyed stare, and Emily said, "I'm sorry, that wasn't necessary." She hesitated and added, "I own the company. If I am a day or two late, it will be fine."

"How do you know you can trust me? I might be a Muslim slave trader, waiting to sell you to the highest bidder."

"It's the Western clothes—you don't fit the image. Besides, if you had evil intentions, you would have already made your move. We are alone, completely isolated."

"So, you think this is isolation? I am going to show you what isolation is all about."

They rode another half-mile toward the cabin, when Emily stopped. "I need my underwear. My jeans are chafing me in a sensitive area."

Seamus didn't say anything. He understood the problems of women. He reached into his saddlebag and handed Emily her panties.

"Don't watch," she said, with her cutest smile.

"Don't worry," Seamus replied.

She glanced up with a look between disappointment and shock. In his youth, Seamus guided several women hunters and had ridden with many women. He learned to respect a woman's privacy. That was his way of getting along with women: although women aren't usually concerned with a man's privacy.

Emily changed into her underwear, and Seamus pulled out a large piece of sheepskin with a slit near the border for the saddle horn. He placed it over Emily's saddle, and when she sat down, she said, "Oh, that's much better." He had ridden with enough women to understand their problems.

They planned the trip to the North Fork Cabin during the ride back. Seamus would drive his Dodge one-ton with a slide-in camper. They would leave at midnight, after a nap, and drive both vehicles to her condo and leave her car in Portland. In two or three days, they would cross the border at Sumas and continue north for two days.

At Emily's condo, she had a self-portrait on the wall, and Seamus thought it was really good. He noticed that wherever he stood, the portrait was looking at him. Seamus asked how she accomplished that, or if it was his guilty conscience.

"I borrowed the technique from Leonardo Da Vinci," Emily said with pride.

Seamus said, "He's been dead a long time."

Emily acted exasperated. "Are you familiar with the *Mona Lisa*?"

"Yes, my dad had a copy in his library. For years, she watched me do my homework."

"Exactly! Do you know how Da Vinci accomplished that, with a two-dimensional painting?" Emily asked.

"I could never figure it out, but he was good with math."

"He didn't use his math skills. When someone looks at you, the shoulders are open toward you. In this painting, my shoulders are turned to the right, but my face is looking straight ahead, and my eyes are looking to the left. No matter where you stand in my living room, you and your guilty conscience cannot escape my view."

"Well, I'll be; that's amazing and humbling. I studied the *Mona Lisa* when I was a boy, and I was never able to figure it out."

Emily stopped in Portland to buy designer long johns at a yuppie shop, and Seamus told her they would stop at Filson's in Seattle and she could shop at the best outdoor clothing store in the world. She was excited about the shopping excursion, until she saw clothing she would never wear to Starbucks or to a wine and cheese party. Filson made rugged clothing for the guys headed to Alaska during the Gold Rush of '98. It's still rugged, but the prices reflect upon the guys who found gold, not the ones who were prospecting. Seamus convinced Emily to buy two wool shirts and two pairs of canvas trousers, a parka, and a pair of serious boots. He told her the clothes would last her the rest of her life, if she didn't turn into a porker. Maybe the joke wasn't funny; Emily didn't even smile.

After crossing the border, it was ten minutes to Highway 1, and an hour and a half to Hope. From Hope, it was a short drive north to the Coquihalla Highway and on to Kamloops. Seamus wanted Emily to see the Canadian mountains in the daylight.

Seamus pulled off on the Coldwater Ranch exit and found a nice level spot to camp. The creek was roaring. Emily looked at the raging torrent and said, "I see what you mean about the creeks and rivers."

Seamus didn't say anything; he just smiled.

Seamus built a fire and was grilling steaks with the gaucho method, when a snowmobile came down the road. The driver pulled in behind the Dodge and introduced himself as Billy Two Bears. Seamus asked Billy if he could stay for dinner, and Billy was delighted. He said he had not eaten since early morning. Billy was intrigued by the gaucho style of cooking and asked many questions.

Emily climbed out of the camper and met Billy. She was charming, and he obviously thought she was beautiful. He asked if she was native. She said she was part native, but raised as a white girl.

Billy thought her comment was hilarious and smiled to show a mouth with about half its teeth. Billy asked many questions, and Emily answered them, according to her DNA analysis. Billy liked hearing about the different Indian tribes of the past. Emily knew history and was a good storyteller. It was dark after dinner, and Billy said thanks for the meal and the history lesson.

He couldn't believe Emily had never had elk or moose steaks and told the two of them not to leave before 7:00 the next morning. Seamus gave him some pork loin, bacon, and beefsteak for his family.

The next morning, Billy showed up with moose and elk steaks, and a brown paper sack for Emily. He was in a hurry and was gone before Emily was awake. Emily opened the sack to find a pair of beaded moose-hide mukluks with beaver tops that tied below the knee and a pair of moose-hide mitts with beaver on the top half. She was in a state of awe. The mukluks had an eagle swooping down on a salmon. The artwork and craftsmanship was excellent, and she asked who made them.

"His wife does the sewing, and he smokes the moose hide and traps the beaver."

"They look expensive," Emily said.

"Yes, each pair would sell for more than an expensive pair of Western boots."

"We must follow him and pay him. These gifts are too valuable," she said.

"Impossible. This truck can't go where he is headed, and besides, you would insult him, if you tried to pay him."

"But he didn't look like he had this kind of money to give away."

"Did you see that snowmobile? Billy does all right, but that's not the point. You talked to him as an equal and taught him a lot of history. Billy is a bright kid, and he absorbed everything. He thinks you are wonderful, and he figures these gifts will help you get back to your roots. It's also a matter of pride; you'll need to be around more Indians to understand pride."

Back on the Coquihalla, Emily kept the mitts and the moccasins on her lap. She was doing serious introspection during the drive north. They headed into the bush before reaching Mackenzie and camped one night, before arriving at the base camp.

Seamus was watching the time like a typical white man. He kept a calendar on the dash of the truck and was crossing off each day. His schedule didn't matter, but Emily had a business and a life back in Portland. Seamus didn't want to muddy up Emily's water.

With two people, and pulling a sled with supplies, Seamus figured they could make it to the North Fork cabin in two hours and be there before dark.

It was an easy trip, and Emily loved the snowmobile ride. Seamus built a fire, while Emily swept out the cabin. Seamus loaded a Dutch oven with a moose roast, turnips, and Bermuda onions, and started baking biscuits.

While dinner was cooking, Emily asked if they could go up on the Blueberry Hill. Seamus told her the plain truth: "We don't know what Nancy's grave is going to look like. It might not have been tampered with or the animals might have chewed through the shroud and the bones. We don't know. Nancy knew what might happen, but she was living in the moment, like she did with Charles. She would appreciate us coming here and gazing upon Blueberry Hill at sunset, but she doesn't want us looking at her bleached bones. Indians consider these old graveyards to be sacred, and I think that is why."

Emily had a few big tears roll down her cheeks and said, "I understand."

After dinner, Emily asked if she could take a bath. There was a washtub on the wall and a twenty-gallon water tank heating up above the stove. Seamus filled the washtub by opening a tap on the hot water tank and lowered the temperature of the bath water with snow. Seamus arranged the chairs between the bed and the washtub and draped a blanket over them, so Emily could bathe in private. She said she loved her old-time bath and climbed between the sheets wearing a cute pair of flannel pajamas.

Seamus didn't really fit in the washtub; he sat on one of the chairs and had a sponge bath without a sponge. Emily was asleep when he crawled in bed.

In the middle of the night, the wolves started howling from several different locations. Emily whispered, "What's that noise?"

Seamus chuckled. "It's the call of the wild. The wolves lost a pack member, and they are grieving."

"How do you know that?" she asked.

"A long time ago, I caused different packs to sing those same songs."

In a voice that betrayed her fear, she said, "I am scared. Will you hold me?"

Seamus had his back to her, his usual position, to avoid the problems of male arousal. He turned over on his back and said, "You realize, those wilderness movies are a bunch of hokum. Wolves don't terrorize people. The only danger we face is me falling asleep on my back and snoring."

"I've heard you. It's impressive."

He held her tight with his right arm. Her tiny body wrapped onto him like a little animal. Her right leg was over his hip, and the inevitable happened. She could feel his male hardness with her knee and said, "Oh my, excuse me."

Emily reached over to grasp his cock. "Do you mind?" She asked.

"No, I don't mind." Seamus answered.

Emily squeezed it and waved it back and forth. She began to tell Seamus of her previous sexual experiences. "In college, I had sex with four guys; at least, I think I did. Each time was nearly the same. We'd have a few beers and get naked. I could feel their dinks probing, but I wasn't sure whether we were having sex or not. Suddenly, they would pull back, and I was covered with a sticky mess. Afterward, they'd ask if it was good for me."

"What did you tell them?" Seamus asked.

"I told them, people get better with time."

"That was diplomatic. Did it help their self-esteem?" Seamus asked.

"Each of them told me, in different ways, they were worried about being gay."

"If you are worried about being gay, quit worrying, because you *are* gay. Emily, straight guys don't worry about being gay. How did you end up with four rump rangers?"

"Maybe it was because I majored in journalism with a minor in art. Now, I have my own fashion line and work with gay men all the time."

"Forget the wolves. I'd be scared of journalism and art majors."

Seamus wanted to lighten the mood with humor, but Emily ignored his effort. She sounded distracted, when she said, "You sometimes remind me of those cavemen you write about." Emily laid her head on his chest, while she continued to test the rigidity of his cock. Seamus wondered if she really thought of him as a caveman, and if that was an insult.

She rose up to kiss him. At this point, it was impossible to resist. He could feel Emily pushing her pajama bottoms off her hips and down her legs. She rose up over him, and carefully positioned his cock in the breech. She was slowly lowering herself and easing his cock into her most intimate part. Suddenly, she slipped and instantaneously absorbed the full length. She made a hissing sound and remained still. Emily leaned forward and put her hands on his shoulders and began a hinge-like movement of her hips. It was slow at first, but she increased the tempo of her movements, until she was in a state of abandonment. She spoke aloud as if she were alone, "Yes, yes, I am really fucking. Oh God, don't stop. Please, don't stop, uh, uh—"

Seamus didn't figure she was talking to him; he wasn't moving, and he doesn't normally join in on the conversation, when people are speaking to God.

In a few minutes, she made up for years of frustration. She pulled forward to the tip of his cock, to kiss Seamus, and slipped back again the hinge-like movement of her hips again. Seamus felt her body quivering as she inundated his cock with a hot, oily tribute. She laid her head on his chest. Emily's deep rhythmic breathing indicated that she was sleeping with his rigid cock still imbedded. Seamus usually needed to be directing the orchestra to achieve orgasm, and Emily was sleeping, he would wait.

Seamus rolled out from under Emily and looked at her sleeping form. He admired her beauty while smiling at how she had changed from acting like a bored and bitter rich woman to become an animated, carefree girl who found everything to be interesting and exciting. Seamus thought of how Emily was the end result of fifty thousand years of love, tragedy, and artistic creativity, since the time of Ariel and the exodus from North Africa. These women walked the world, from the Indus River and the adventures of Lavender to the Oregon Trail, when several of them headed to Portland. This evening, in a land of snow and ice, Seamus became a small part of the story.

The End

Epilogue

There should be a hall of fame for every student who loved history in spite of the professors and teachers who claim to be historians. Oh, these guardians of facts, names, and dates have their purpose, if for nothing else but to train the next generation of historians. Sadly, they have driven away millions from the fascinating world of our ancestors. Ask your friends and neighbors how they view the study of history. Most will tell you of the boring rhetoric of teachers and textbooks.

Plato recognized the problem and wrote, “Poetry is nearer to vital truth than history.” To avoid philosophical discussions of rhetoric versus poetry, it is easier to assume he is referring to the Iliad and the Odyssey, written by Homer, 8th Century BC. These epic poems have captured the imaginations of millions ever since. Would anyone know of the Trojan War or the return of Odysseus, without the poems? Almost everyone has a vague idea who Helen and Achilles were, and yet, they walked the earth almost three thousand years ago.

We won’t find a modern audience willing to listen to 12,000 line poems in this era, but if readers are interested in a good story with occasional bits of history and science, learning becomes interesting and exciting.

One of the rarely mentioned points of the Odyssey and the Iliad is that women and slaves were making decisions. Homer was the earliest feminist and a civil rights advocate.

Hopefully this book will give a few women and girls confidence to face life and its trials. The story doesn't provide the answers; however, the story portrays women facing problems and adversity with courage and ingenuity; rather than pleading through a prism of weakness and defeatism, while pointing fingers at an often-hapless villain, man.

Glossary

Prologue:

Glacial Maximum: A period or pulse of extreme cold during an ice age. This book begins during a glacial maximum, Fifty Thousand years ago. There were several glacial maximums to follow, along with countless regional glacial maximums around the world.

The last glacial period is commonly referred to as the 'Ice Age.' It began 125,000 years BP (before present), and began a warming phase between 19,000 years BP and 9,500 years BP. Technically, because of the earth's glaciers, Greenland, and the polar ice caps, we are in the final stages of the Ice Age.

The Mammoth Steppe was the earth's largest biome. This unique grassland was just south of the ice and stretched from Spain eastward, across Eurasia, across Asia, to Siberia, and across the continental land bridge between Siberia and Alaska, and continuing east to the Yukon. The Wisconsin glacial ice sheet was the eastern border.

Beringia, the land bridge between Siberia and Alaska and Alaska extended one thousand miles North to South and facilitated the migration of animals and humans from Asia to North America until 11,000 BP, when it disappeared because of melting ice and rising sea levels.

The weight of the ice on the earth's surface produced warm springs, lakes, and streams that were protein rich hunting and fishing grounds. Life was thriving near the ice. During the summers, warm temperatures created massive runoff and this created the great river systems of the Northern Hemisphere.

Mitochondrial DNA: is present in both men and women, but it is one component of DNA that can only be passed on from mother to daughter, and since it does not recombine from the input of both parents, it remains unchanged for eons, until there is an infrequent mutation and a unique strain of mitochondrial DNA begins. Every man has his mother's mitochondrial DNA, but he can't pass it on. This story is predicated on the strength of a line of women having creative and artistic abilities through their mitochondrial DNA.

Mitochondrial DNA is found in the mitochondria of all eukaryotic organisms. It is a double membrane bound, self-replicating double organelle, functioning as an organ within a cell. It is sometimes called a cell compartment. Eukaryotic cells convert food into chemical energy for other cells. Most DNA is found in the nucleus of cells, but mitochondrial has its own DNA. Every cell has mitochondrial cells except for red blood cells. The rest of the cells have varying amounts of mitochondrial cells; liver cells have the most mitochondrial cells with over 2,000 per molecule.

The DNA of the nucleus and mitochondrial DNA evolved independently. Mitochondrial DNA evolved from bacteria with its circular genomes, of the early eukaryotic cells. Nuclear DNA is inherited from both parents and the genes are rearranged through recombination. Mitochondrial DNA recombines, but uses copies of itself within the mitochondrion and there is no change from parent to child. The incidence of mutation of the mitochondrial DNA is infrequent; therefore, mitochondrial DNA is used as a powerful tool to trace maternal ancestry.

Neanderthal: A close relative of humans, was much closer than we realized. The human DNA genome from Northern Europe and Asia has proven the Neanderthal and humans were close enough to breed and reproduce, most Northern Europeans carry Neanderthal DNA.

Chapter 1: Omineca/Peace: An Arctic river drainage system in Northeastern British Columbia.

Williston Lake: A large man made lake, formed when the Peace River was dammed with a hydroelectric dam.

Government trap line: Trap lines in Canada are leased from the crown and the queen receives a percentage for all the fur harvested.

Trap cabins: A trapper is allowed to build cabins on crown land and live on his trap line year round.

Training horses: There are many ways to train horses. Mountain horses are often trained without fences and over a hundred miles from the nearest road. This requires different techniques. They learn to cross fast and dangerous rivers, to negotiate steep grades, and to remain cool when a grizzly walks out on the trail or when a bull moose is in the rut and on a rampage.

Chapter 2: In North America, ninety percent of riders are women. In Europe, Argentina, and Mexico, these figures are reversed.

Moccasin Telegraph: Natives in the North have a curious way of knowing inside information on many things. No one knows whether they are psychic or just good guessers.

Panniers: The pack boxes a packhorse carries attached to the packsaddle.

Moose Roast: Moose is the staple of most people who live in the Northern Canadian bush country.

Chapter 3: Putting a horse down with a rifle, by a skilled shot, is often considered more humane and quicker than the euthanasia shot.

Chapter 4: Early Man in North America: Early man began exploring North America about twenty thousand years ago and possibly earlier. They utilized Beringia, the continental landmass connecting Alaska and Siberia, which appeared when the ocean was shallower. Early man probably came by boat as well, since more islands appeared in the Pacific and more fresh water sources would have been available. Crossing the North Atlantic, with increased landfall, was also within the boating technology of early man.

Chapter 5: When the supermen hunted the mammoth and mastodon with a spear; early man's cave art had spectacular realism. With the invention of the bow, every man was a hunter of smaller game and potentially dangerous. The realism of his previous art gave way to crude impressionism and man began to depict the murder of other men.

Chapter 6: Sylvie: Born with a mutation within her mitochondrial DNA, Sylvie was able to sculpt magnificent tools from flint. These creative and artistic skills were encoded in her DNA and were passed on to her daughter and many more daughters.

Phenotypical traits are observable features expressed by genetic and environmental influences.

Chapter 7: The Knife: Man's most basic tool is the knife. Today, our knives are made of iron, but the Stone Age takes us back before metallurgy. If you needed a tool, you carved it from stone by using another stone as a striker.

Today's house maker should think of how difficult it is to carve a turkey or a steak with a sharp knife, and then imagine walking into the yard to find a rock and sharpening it enough to butcher a twenty thousand pound mammoth.

Chapter 8: Musth is an Urdu word that indicates drunkenness. The East Indian uses this word to describe the rut of the bull elephant.

H1W1: Is a fictional designation for Lavender's DNA, after a mutation of her DNA has made her resistant to certain diseases.

Diseases of the Stone Age: The flu viruses were far more deadly when people had primitive shelters or no shelter. Cholera is a great killer among people without basic hygiene. The hunter-gatherer tribes were fortunate if they were always migrating. In winter, the cold helped reduce the incidence of the disease. Hygiene improved with the gradual advent of culture and civilization.

Neanderthal Influence: Camel Track and other members of the Mammoth Hunters show Neanderthal features. In this story, the Neanderthals are portrayed as blue-eyed fair-haired beings; instead of being brutish, they are kind and gentle.

Traps: A few decades ago, college anthropology classes taught that early men tricked the mammoths and mastodons into falling into large holes, where they were speared. There are problems with this scenario. Any trapper will tell you the animals can sense when there is a hole beneath a layer of brush. Also the prospect of digging such a large hole without shovels to build a dubious trap is impractical. The killing machines described in the book are far easier and faster to build, and far more likely to work than a hole in the ground.

Chapter 9: Mushrooms: The science of hunting wild mushrooms has been developed over the eons. Learning the poisonous types could only be observed by watching the results of those who ate a specific type. Apparently, when a poisonous mushroom has been picked and put with others, before being recognized as a poisonous mushroom, and thrown away, the microscopic spoors of the poisonous mushroom will poison the mushrooms it has been in contact with..

Cooking Technology: Cooking during the Stone Age was difficult. The so-called gaucho-method of cooking on a vertical wooden spit was probably one of the technologies adopted through necessity by early man.

Chapter 10:

Chapter 11:

Chapter 12: Paints of the cave artists were formulated from naturally occurring ingredients; most were derived from minerals found in the ground. The reds, yellows, and browns were often derived from different clay ochre (clay with iron oxide). Limonite is the main ingredient of ochre. It contains iron hydroxide and when heated, converts to red colors. Iron hydroxide is the main ingredient of yellow ochre. Manganese provides the coloring for brown ochre. Black was obtained from both charcoal and manganese dioxides. Iron oxide and manganese were used to lighten or darken the pigments. Increasing the manganese concentration, yielded darker colors. The raw pigments were ground to a fine powder and mixed with different combinations of animal fats, blood, urine, vegetable extracts, ground quartz, calcium carbonate (typically found in cave water), and calcium phosphate (derived from crushing heated bone). The closest source for the minerals used at Lascaux are in an area 250 kilometers from the cave.

Tadpole's cave is in southwestern France, near the village Montignac, of Dordogne.

Chapter 13: The Cave Lion (*Panthera leo)* was one of the more deadly threats to early man in Europe. Sub-species of the modern lion, the Cave Lion earned its name by its habit of feeding on hibernating Cave Bears. The Cave lion didn't live in caves; it raided caves. One of the largest cats to have ever existed, it did not go extinct until 2,000 years ago. It is assumed humans regarded the Cave lion with reverence and awe, since the cave art of early man is often dominated with portrayals of this huge cat. A litter of kittens was found in the permafrost of Siberia. They are in an excellent state of preservation and there is a good chance of replicating these predators through their DNA.

The Eurasian Wolf was and is the largest European wolf. The size varied regionally. The largest ones were 152 to 176 pounds. The howl of the Eurasian is melodious and protracted, compared to its cousin the Grey wolf.

The Grey Wolf or Timber Wolf was spread widely over Europe, Eurasia, Asia, and North America. It is the most common wolf and averages about 85 pounds.

Chapter 14:

Chapter 15: The Mammoth Steppe was a grassland that extended from Spain to Siberia, across Beringia to Alaska, and Yukon. It provided excellent grazing for the mammoth, rhinoceros, camels, horses, caribou, moose and many other animals, including the predators and man.

Chapter 16: The ice sheets of North America and Europe created anticyclones (clockwise winds in the northern hemisphere) above them. These anticyclones produced a colder, high-pressure area, of dry winds that created drought and desertification. Despite having similar temperatures as the glaciated areas, East Asia was not glaciated (except at higher elevations) because of the dry winds. Rainfall was calculated at 90% less than the current levels. These dry winds prevented Manchuria, Siberia, Beringia, Alaska, and Yukon from glaciating and facilitated the migration of humans and animals by providing enough precipitation to create great grasslands.

The deserts and the winds created an atmosphere of dust, leaving foreign deposits of dust all over the world. Australia had shifting sand dunes cover half the continent

Exceptions existed in western North America, where changes in the jet stream brought heavy rainfall to areas that are now desert, creating large pluvial lakes, i.e. Lake Bonneville.

Chapter 17: During the Pliocene, the auroch or feral cattle roamed the steppe from Spain to Asia and south as far as North Africa. The progenitor of modern cattle, the last auroch cattle died in the Jaktorow forest of Poland in 1627.

Fish fermentation occurs when fish is sealed off from microorganisms (contaminants) and the enzymes are rendered inactive. The fish flesh can remain stable for extended periods of time, because the wet complex molecules are broken down into simpler molecules that remain stable at certain temperatures. The addition of salt helps ensure preservation. The process can preserve fish in their original structure or reduced to a paste or a liquid. Temperature and salt are the two main variables, although, gutting the fish also alters the product.

Chapter 18: The bow is now being dated at 70,000 years ago, in South Africa. The tool design for the points is ambiguous and the dating is subjective. Of course these are the same academics, two generations later, who claimed early man trapped the mammoth in dug holes and speared the trapped animals. The author maintains that the invention of the bow was much later, as the archaeological and artistic evidence supports. The bow changed culture by making every human a dangerous adversary. Attacking with a spear or two leaves a smaller man vulnerable much quicker; once he has thrown his spear. Warfare was recorded in the caves, after the bow came into use.

Oral history can be altered in a generation by the young minds listening to the legends and myths. Those who became historians or storytellers were left to their own devices to improve or detract from the stories, even without devious political motives.

Early man surely used the stars as visual aids to reinforce the messaging of their stories; consequently, the children grew up with a greater knowledge of the night sky and the navigational aids it provides.

Chapter 19: The domestication of the horse and the development of a horse culture or horsemanship have intrigued horsemen for generations. Unfortunately, few modern horsemen are familiar with packing the horse or the complex nature of migration. However, nomads would see a great advantage to carrying hundred pound packs on the backs of horses, and everyone who has packed seriously in the mountains, knows it is easy to train a tired packhorse to ride. When a tired vagabond climbed on the back of a tired packhorse, the horse world began to change rapidly.

Chapter 20: The distance from the Korean peninsula and the island of Tsushu is estimated to have been 50 kilometers, and another 50 kilometers to the main island of Kyushu. It is a fairly short sail for a competent sailor of the day, if the winds and weather are favorable.

Beringia is the landmass exposed during the Ice Age, due to lowered sea levels. It was an extension of the Mammoth Steppe. Measuring one thousand miles from North to South it extended the savannah from Asia through Alaska to the Yukon, allowing the migration of many animals and humans over thousands of years.

Cholera is a bacterial infection of the gut, vibrio cholera. An infection may display mild or no symptoms. Approximately ten percent of infections are severe and these victims will display watery diarrhea, vomiting, and leg cramps. The rapid loss of bodily fluids leads to dehydration and shock;

without treatment, death occurs within a few hours. Treatment is relatively simple and effective: rehydration with salts and sugars. Antibiotics are often used, but rehydration is the most effective treatment. The bacterium is usually ingested with contaminated water or food, from feces of an infected individual.

Inadequate sewage disposal or contaminated water are warning signs for the possibility of cholera infection. The migrating hunters often avoided transmission because of their nomadic lifestyle. The colder temperatures of winter helped reduce the incidence and transmission of disease.

Chapter 21: Cabu's speech problem was probably a speech impediment. The descent of the human hyoid bone within the throat seems to have occurred in Africa, 50,000 to 75,000 years BP. This is the phenomenon we attribute to man's ability to use complex speech capabilities. The Neanderthal hyoid bone descended earlier than the human hyoid. Comparison of Neanderthal's hyoid to modern man's hyoid indicates similar capabilities of complex speech. It is being accepted that Neanderthal had the ability to utilize complex speech. The use of complex speech appears to be a component of or a coincidental occurrence to man's great intellectual awakening.

Neanderthals were burying their dead and performing complex funerals before modern man, and they were producing tools that required hierarchical planning (requiring 50 steps) before modern man, and they were creating exceptional realistic art in the caves, before modern man. They may have produced shoes and many other objects that don't survive the test of time. It was wrong to portray the Neanderthal as brutes with limited intelligence; indeed, some of our ancestors considered them worthy bedmates and produced many children with them. This is indisputable; since many of us carry one to four percent of Neanderthal's DNA.

Chapter 22: A leader who follows, *"The moral law causes the people to be in complete accord with their leader, so that they will follow him regardless of their lives, undismayed by any danger."* Sun Tzu, The Art of War

Chapter 23: The Salmon People were defeated. Like many people after them, they moved on to find a new home or stayed on to live as a slave class, if they were allowed to live.

Chapter 24: Evidence of habitation by Neanderthal at Gibraltar goes back 125,000 years BP. Gibraltar is one of the last known sites of the Neanderthal, as recently as 24,000 years BP. The Straits of Gibraltar refers to the 7.7 nautical miles between Gibraltar and Morocco. In ancient literature, it is referred to as the Pillars of Hercules.

Chapter 25: The Chesapeake was destined to form after a bolide or asteroid landed on the tip of the Delmarva Peninsula 35 million years ago. The impact created the Exmore Crater; it is estimated to have been as wide as Rhode Island and as deep as the Grand Canyon. Chesapeake Bay formed from the Susquehanna River drainage during a thawing of the Ice Age, 18,000 BP.

Chapter 26: During the Ice Age, people without boating technology could walk to Sicily from Italy. New rich land was exposed offering opportunities for humans to exploit.

Evaporative forces were continuing to take away more water from the Mediterranean than could be replaced and leaving a salt deposit layer on the lake floors.

Chapter 27: The Cumberland Gap was originally a game trail, used by deer and buffalo for thousands of years before Native Americans found the trail. It connects Virginia to Kentucky and Tennessee. Dr. Thomas Walker, a British naturalist and scientist, explored the trail in 1750, after hearing of the trail through Native Americans. He named the trail the Cave Gap and he named a river to the North, the Cumberland River, in respect to his sponsor, the Duke of Cumberland, son of King George II.

In 1775, Daniel Boone passed through the gap and blazed a 200-mile trail into Kentucky's Blue Grass Country; it was called Boone's Path or Boone's Road. By 1796, over 200,000 people had passed over the trail, including Abraham Lincoln's grandparents; there was two-lane traffic at this time, because Kentuckians were driving herds of horses and cattle to the markets on the Eastern Seaboard. The trail was widened at this time to accommodate the Conestoga Wagons heading west. By 1830, the Wilderness Road and several other trails opened up and the Cumberland Gap's popularity began to wane.

Chapter 28: Phoenicia is a word from the Greeks, referring to an ancient Semitic thalassocracy ('Greek,' a maritime people or empire that relies on a navy) with no known origin. Centered on the coastal area of the Fertile Crescent, known as the Canaanite port cities, they colonized the Mediterranean coasts and the Atlantic coasts between 1500 BC and 300 BC. Their cities were independent city-states and were the first nation to be involved in international maritime trade. They produced a purple dye from the Murex mollusk. Through archaeology, we know there was a remarkably similar culture to the rest of Canaan. The most prominent city was Carthage, before its destruction by the Romans. The Phoenicians were the first to use an alphabet and brought this advancement to Anatolia, North Africa, and Europe. The Greeks adopted the alphabet and bequeathed the technology to the Romans, and Western Civilization was born.

There are a multitude of CO2 theories that try to explain the melting of the ice sheets, but none of them address the sufficient accumulation of green house gases needed to produce the relatively rapid melting of the ice sheets. During the rapid melting of the Ice Age, glaciers retreated and sea levels rose. Animal species adapted or became extinct.

The Mediterranean is a basin surrounded by continents. During the Ice Age, the microclimate of this rich valley with its marshes and grasslands supported a large human and animal population. The rising water forced animals and humans to higher ground in Eastern Europe and Eurasia. The mass migration of refugees caused conflict among the residents of the river valleys and the newcomers. Some groups were dominant and others were destroyed. The human pressures exerted on the coastal communities forced the development of new technologies: agriculture, urban communities, and animal husbandry.

In Europe, Asia, and North America this concentration of human population didn't occur. Thus the melting of the ice was a major factor in the development of Western Civilization.

Chapter 29: The Phoenicians were the first international mercantile power in the world.

Chapter 30: Alexander destroyed Tyre, and the wealthy escaped the carnage. They settled in Carthage and became the new economic power in the Mediterranean.

Chapter 31: One of the major factors in the breakdown of society is immorality. When an individual accepts the loss of morality, he becomes a loss to himself, and a loss to society, becoming a negative influence within society. When large numbers of people embrace immorality or the leaders become immoral, the society is vulnerable to collapse.

Chapter 32: The Tarahumara are a tribe of high altitude runners from the northwest corner of Mexico. They are known for great feats of running, like running down deer and hazing them back into their village with a switch.

Chapter 33: The original Spanish horses produced the mustangs (a derivative of the Spanish word *mesteno,* wild and unclaimed sheep) of the mounted Indian and the ranchers of the West. However these strains of Spanish horses were diluted with horses from the east and from Canada. The dilution of the mustang causes a loss of the qualities that endeared them to early horsemen. The Kiger Mustang is the closest to the original Spanish mustang, after analysis of the DNA and observation of the spirit and physical abilities of the horses.

Chapter 34: The equestrian bullfighter incorporates dressage movements into his performance, but he must execute the movements at the speed of a charging bull.

Chapter 35: The Llano Estacado or Staked Plain of northwestern Texas and eastern New Mexico is one of the largest mesas or tablelands of North America. The elevation increases From 3,000 feet in the southeast to 5,000 in the northwest, with a uniform grade of 10 feet per mile. The Canadian River is the northern boundary and separates the Llano Estacado from the Great Plains of North America.

Francisco Coronado was the first European to traverse this "Sea of grass" in 1541. He described the Llano Estacado: "I reached some plains so vast, I did not find their limit; although I traveled over 300 leagues... there was not a stone, nor bit of rising ground, nor a tree, nor a shrub, nor anything to go by."

The Comanche was a tribe of mounted Indians, who hunted buffalo as their primary staple. They lived in tribal bands on their homeland, the Comancheria, occupying large portions of Texas, New Mexico, Colorado, Oklahoma, and Texas. The annihilation of the buffalo herds and European diseases; cholera, smallpox, and measles reduced the Comanche population from 20,000 during the mid-nineteenth century to a few thousand by 1880.

Chapter 36: The Spanish Conquest of Mexico made Spain one of the richest countries of Europe. Although some of the gold shipments were captured by British pirates and some were lost at sea due to storms and there were many poor investments. One of the worst was the Spanish Armada, launched against Britain to reestablish a Roman Catholic country, and depose Queen Elizabeth. Phillip, king of Spain, believed he had a claim to the English throne and planned to liberate Mary, Queen of Scots. This plan fell through when Mary was executed.

Despite the death of Mary, Phillip continued with the building of ships. Sir Francis Drake raided and destroyed some of the ships while they were still in harbor at Cadiz.

The fleet sailed in May of 1588 with over 100 ships. The plan was to meet the Duke of Parma, Phillip's nephew, from the Netherlands, and sail to England. The Brits were waiting, and when the armada was sighted, beacons were lighted on the hillsides and the message was sent throughout the country, "The Spanish are coming."

Elizabeth rode among her soldiers and sailors on a white horse, endearing her to the troops. In the English Channel, the weather was horrible. The Spanish relied on obsolete naval tactics of releasing a single salvo before using grappling hooks to board an enemy vessel. The Brits had more modern ships and were firing at the water line of the Spanish ships. The Spanish were ill prepared to stand up to the superior sailing, gunnery, and fighting tactics of the Brits.

The Spanish lost approximately half their ships to storms, while they sailed to the north around the coast of Scotland and the west coast of Ireland. Several of the ships were wrecked by storms off the west coast of Ireland, and British troops hanged the survivors.

Phillip imposed new taxation to recoup the losses incurred by the ill-fated expedition and he had investigations as to why the mission failed. Eventually it was decided that they had waited too long to expel the Moors almost a hundred years earlier.

Chapter 37: The one glaring weakness of Cortes was his womanizing.

Chapter 38: The term Moor is an ambiguous term, often used in a derogatory manner to describe Muslims, particularly Berber and Arab people who occupied the Iberian Peninsula, Sicily, and Malta during the Middle Ages. The Moors crossed the Strait of Gibraltar in 711 to conquer the Visigoths in Christian Spain. The Muslim conquest included most of Spain except for the northwest, parts of Portugal, and the Basque in the Pyrenees. The Moors raided as far north as Tours where they were defeated by Charles Martel. The Moors were confined to Granada for the last 300 years, when they were expelled in 1491.

Chapter 39: Gonzalo Guerrero is one of the most interesting characters of the Spanish conquest of the Americas; sadly, he is overlooked by the white western world as a historical figure. Surviving against the odds, he became a war chief among the Maya. He was obviously a bold warrior, but his prowess in war was overshadowed by his betrayal of the Spanish myth of invincibility.

The native armies often fled in terror upon seeing the horses, war dogs, and early firearms. Guerrero was the one who convinced the Maya that the Spanish and their animals were mortal and devised strategies to kill them. He also explained that the arquebus was not a magic weapon and how it could be rushed immediately after firing the first round. The Spanish hated the man who exposed their vulnerabilities and this prejudicial view is probably why Guerrero is virtually unknown in the white historical view of history. Of course it is also hard for indigenous Americans to recognize a white man as a hero in a struggle against white suppression.

The European diseases were decimating the native populations of North America, but the children of Guerrero, the first Mestizo children of Mexico, had immunity to the diseases and helped establish the Mexican people as a hardy race.

Chapter 40: Cortés actually trained his army, instead of leading a mob like traditional conquistador armies. This is one fact that helped him achieve his victories.

Malinche is one of the more curious personalities of the Spanish subjugation of Mexico. She served as an interpreter for Cortés and as his mistress. She gave birth to his son and was a powerful influence in winning over native tribes that might have fought Cortés. She is credited with being instrumental in the success of Cortés. Unfortunately, the Mexicans use a derogatory term,"Malinchista" to designate someone who turns their back on their own people; yet she is regarded with honor as one of the first mothers of the Mestizo race.

Chapter 41: Cortés was incredibly lucky to survive his own audacity and become a rich and powerful man.

Chapter 42: The principal economic activity of Zacatecas was mining until recently; cattle ranching and farming now represent over 10% of the state's GDP.

Chapter 43: The conquistador was typically a desperate man and probably not among the most stable personalities. They sailed to the New World in ships that were often not seaworthy, and arrived to spend years in tropical jungles and frosty mountains, while hunger, fatigue, disease, and violent natives were trying to kill them. The conquistador Lope Aguirre could only maintain his sanity for so long; he was known for having a violent disposition when he joined an expedition to search the jungles of South America to find the legendary El Dorado. While in the jungle, he went mad and began killing his own companions.

Chapter 44: The Comanchero was a group of traders who profited from trading with the Comanche and Kiowa. Coming from eastern New Mexico, they brought in food and manufactured goods to trade for stolen cattle, horses, buffalo robes, and captive women and children. They were active until 1875, when the Comanche and Kiowa were defeated and forced upon reservations in Oklahoma.

Chapter 45: The secret to survival in the wilderness is to be aware of what nature provides and have the resourcefulness to exploit those resources.

Chapter 46: The Iberian Peninsula, particularly Toledo, has been recognized as an exceptional manufacturer of weapons since 500 BC. During the Punic Wars, the weapons from Toledo, carried by Hannibal's army, came to the attention of Rome. After the Punic Wars, Toledo was supplying the weapons of the Roman Legions.

Chapter 47: The journals of those who survived the trip provide an accurate portrayal of the trail and the Indians they encountered on the trail.

Chapter 48: It is a curious fact that intelligent people of the 19th Century took pride in mastering several trades and our modern intellectuals take a perverse pride in being incapable of working with their hands.

Chapter 49: The young hunter who killed the bull had never had a horseback lesson or read the books on equitation, but he accomplished something that few modern riders could hope to accomplish: he ran alongside a running buffalo and buried arrows into the heart area. Shooting a bow requires both hands, and the reins were either tucked into the boy's belt or tied above the horse's neck. Few people who have ridden horses at speed will be willing to give control to the horse while they are riding alongside a running buffalo and discharging a bow. The bull turns to gore his pursuers, while the boy and his pony jump out of the way to avoid the horns. It is this simple act of riding that should make all of those who study riding and equitation wonder about the advanced skills of these nomadic horsemen of the past.

Chapter 50: Cholera or the bacterium Vibrio cholera causes an infection of the small intestine. The infections cause symptoms of watery diarrhea, with leg cramps and vomiting. Symptoms can last a few hours or a few days. The diarrhea can be severe enough to cause dehydration and electrolyte imbalance. This results in cold, bluish skin, wrinkling of the hands and feet, a decrease of skin elasticity, and sunken eyes.

The vectors of infection are water and food contaminated with human feces containing the Vibrio cholera bacterium. Humans are the only organisms affected by the disease. Treatment consists of rehydration with minerals and sugars. The risk of death is less than 5%; without treatment, the death ratio is closer to 50%. Poverty and poor hygiene often indicate the presence of the disease. The disease is currently prevalent in Africa and Southeast Asia

Chapter 51: Three Island Crossing is located at the town of Glenns Ferry in Southern Idaho. The town has an interpretive center and a festival every summer. The tracks of the wagons are cut deep into the hardpan on the hills to the south of the Snake River and are visible to the casual observer.

Chapter 52: Lavender brought the Digger method of cooking steaks to the rest of the world, and the Argentine gaucho appropriated this ancient method of cooking.

The Author

Dylan Casa del Lobos has been a professional horseman for 50 years and has worked throughout the United States, Canada, and Europe. There have been countless adventures, and he has known thousands of horsemen and well over a hundred thousand horses. He uses this vast resource of horse people and horses to create his cast of characters.

Hopefully the reader will find them as interesting as Dylan did during his career. There were some wonderful characters and some renegades, but most of them were somewhere in between.

There are three books that are nearly finished and should be on Amazon in a few months. Here are a few sample chapters. There will be further updates on my website.

http://natural2thman.wixsite.com/author-blog

Roughing It- In Style

Chapter 1

The Liquor Store

"There are indeed certain Liquors, which being applied to our Passions, or to Fire, produce Effects the very Reverse of those produced by Water… Among these the generous Liquor called Punch is one."

Henry Fielding: Tom Jones ~ 1749

My Friend Barb Wire Johnny kept a 1940 Chevrolet pickup at the home ranch. I don't think he ever drove or had a license, but his mother drove before her dementia began to set-in. After that, Johnny couldn't trust her to be alone while he trained horses, guided hunters, or went out on the trap line; he was forced to have her committed to the old folks home in Dawson Creek.

I inherited the job of chauffeur, a fifteen year old, unpaid, and unlicensed (no driver's license, it was a different era) chauffeur. Every three or four months, I would drive Johnny to mile One-O-One on the Alaska Highway, turn South towards Fort St John, and continue South on the Alaska Highway to Mile Zero at Dawson Creek, so Johnny could visit his mother. It wasn't really a chore, I enjoyed being with Johnny; he was a magician with a horse. He taught me many of the mystical and spiritual relationships that can exist between men and horses, things I still use on a daily basis.

My dad, a taciturn man who seldom showed emotion, had a soft spot for Johnny and his mother. They were handsome people who had wandered off the Reservation years earlier.

I often wondered whether my departed mother, a beautiful Indian

Princess type, who made men stumble over each other, and push each other out of the way, to be the one to open a door for her or hold a chair for her, was related to Johnny and his mother. All the local natives called each other cousin and they might have been, for all I know.

The soft black flowing hair, the eyes and complexion were similar among Johnny, his mother, and my mother. Most natives in the area had coarse straight hair. When you considered the physical similarities and the fact that my dad would have the battery charged, the tires pumped up with spare tires and rims in the back, and a full tank of gas, I figured Johnny and I were probably real cousins. My dad didn't maintain a vehicle for me or anyone else; it was a special deal for Johnny and his mother.

This was going to be Johnny's Christmas visit, I made my specialty, Captain's Punch, and had it stored behind the seat in three Mason jars. My dad gave me $50.00 and specific instructions: don't drive over 40 mph, don't let Johnny get too drunk, stop by the junk yard and see if they have any good tires for the ranch trucks, but don't pay over three dollars for a tire without a rim. I was to get a room at the Mile Zero Hotel and make sure that none of the oil field roughnecks beat Johnny up. I was to drag him out of the bar by 10:30, no matter what was happening.

He knew I would only have a glass or two of the Captain's Punch, Liquor has never been a part of my life, unlike the rest of my family. Today, I like a glass or two of red wine with dinner, but only for medicinal reasons.

Soon, Johnny and I were off like a herd of turtles. The old truck would barely pull some of the hills at 20 mph, going down I'd pump the brakes and keep us under 40 mph. On the steep down hill grades, Johnny would pull his Western hat down with his right hand, and flash a big grin, like he was going for a fast gallop on a colt. We were laughing and having a great time when Johnny saw an Indian woman walking along the road about a mile ahead. He pointed to her and said, "It's Clarice my cousin, pull over and we'll give her a ride."

I never doubted Johnny's instincts or tracking ability, but this woman was a speck on the horizon, how could he know who it was?

We pulled up along side of her, and Johnny jumps out, "Clarice, hop in, we're going to town, where ya headed?"

In the thick native brogue, she replied, "Goin Licka Storr."

She was glad to see Johnny, the native women all thought Johnny was special, even the ones who were three times bigger than him. Let's say Johnny never lacked for female companionship; especially, when he needed attention or a new moose hide jacket or trousers.

She climbed in between us and Johnny said, "Clarice, this is Dylan, they call him Skook at the ranch. He's Ida Faye's boy."

She looked at me in disbelief with her head held back and said, "Heard, Ida had boy." Clarice was underwhelmed.

Her shocked expression was understandable; when the genetic dice were rolled, I came up with auburn hair, a white hide, and green eyes. Consequently, I have been able to witness bigotry and racism through a special prism, a prism viewed from both directions.

Johnny decided to break out the Captain's Punch so that he and Clarice could have a drink for old times. They rattled on in bits and pieces of three languages; English, French, and their Native tongue, while I concentrated on the gravel road.

After three drinks from the Punch Jar, Johnny fell asleep, and it was just Clarice and I. Suddenly she reached down and grabbed the inside of my thigh. She turned toward me, and from a few inches away, whispered with a raspy voice and breath like turpentine, "You pashinate!"

My right foot nearly pushed the throttle through the rusty floorboard. The engine was roaring, but thankfully, the truck wasn't going any faster. I stammered in desperation, "I don't think I am interested; no, I don't want too."

She pushed her bosom hard against me, gripped my thigh harder and higher, while pleading with a desperate, voice, "You pashinate!"

This time I jumped off the seat and smashed my Western hat on the roof of the cab. In a high-pitched teenage voice, I cried out, "I have a girl friend."

With a frustrated voice that betrayed an inner anger, she yelled in my face, "You pashin Damn Likka Storr."

I made a 'U' turn on the Alaska Highway and felt an enormous sense of relief as I pulled up to the liquor store. It was still against the law to sell liquor to Indians, but at 15, I could walk in and buy a bottle of whiskey.

Johnny asked Clarice if she wanted to go to Dawson Creek with us. She said, “Hell no! That damn Dylan boy, he’s bad damn driver.”

The Slaver

Everyone is aware of the plight of the African, who was sold into slavery, but only a few of us are aware of the transgressions against the Irish and the untold numbers who were sold into slavery.

The New World required slaves who would work until they died. It was the possibility of great profit that fueled this desire for slave labor, but it was the indifference to human suffering and misery that facilitated the trans-Atlantic slave trade.

Most of us were taught that whites from Ireland came to the New World as indentured servants; who were expected to serve an indenture of 7 to 12 years to pay for their transport. An indenture was a binding contract for labor over a specific period of time. A few Irish were transported as indentured servants before 1625, but from then on, all the Irish except for those who had the funds to emigrate, were sold as lifetime slaves to the highest bidder.

Without argument, until the 18th Century, North America imported more Irish slaves than African slaves. Why would there be a concerted effort to conceal these intriguing facts of history? Too often political agendas influence the writing of historians and teachers; the story of slavery is no exception.

If it is politically expedient to concentrate on African slavery and ignore the bondage of the Irish, the educational system will sacrifice the truth for a politically correct message.

White guilt is politically correct, but asking people whose ancestors were also in bondage to feel guilty is humorous in a macabre sense. The fact that Irish slaves outnumbered Africans is an inconvenient fact of history.

The countryside Northwest of Dublin was locked in a feudal system of injustice and cruelty in 1840. Since the Norman Invasion, the laws were written to give the British landlord complete power and control over the land, which was complete control over the Irish serf (a polite word for slave). The landlord's word was law.

Rebellion or resistance meant death or banishment, the homeless and beggars were exiled, but the system was far worse than the peasant could imagine, for no Irish man or woman had ever returned from banishment to tell of the horrors.

If the Irish peasant had a small plot of land and a hovel, it was in his best interests to maximize profits for the landlord, while he tried to feed his family on scraps.

Bob Larkin was luckier than most. He leased an acre of ground and conducted his blacksmith trade on that one-acre. He had a one room stone house that measured 8 X 12, with a thatch roof and a three-sided stone shed to conduct his business.

Rob Roy, Bob's 18-year-old son and apprentice, was carrying on an animated conversation with Melissa, the raven haired, blue-eyed enchantress of the county. At the age of sixteen, she knew how to lead men on and have them begging like puppies for attention, but Rob Roy was different.

He was treating her as an equal, with an innocent smile and a formal, polite way of speaking; this young Irishman charmed her.

It was unseemly for an English girl from the aristocratic classes to be interacting with an Irish tradesman; he was one step up from an Irish peasant, who was one step down from a good stock dog.

Melissa's father owned vast acreages and leased those acreages to landlords, who subleased ten-acre parcels to Irish peasants. The peasant had the right to build a home or a hovel and to plant a small garden to feed his family. The crop was split with the landlord receiving a disproportionate larger percentage. Turning a profit was key to survival of both the peasant and the landlord, but poor crop years and crop failures were not unusual.

The peasant's one room hovel was usually shared with a pig and whatever farm animals they owned; the animals provided warmth and they had to be protected against theft. It was a narrow margin that separated the Irish peasant from survival and starvation. The landlord could evict his tenants at anytime for any reason, and the tenant and his family were soon beggars or thieves.

It was a harsh system based heavily on a tuber from the New World. The potato soon became a staple of the Western Europe, but in Ireland, the potato was keeping the peasant population alive.

The potato planting was timed so it could be harvested from early fall, until late spring. The months of mid-summer were known as the months of starvation, because no potatoes were harvested during the summer season.

In the winter of 41-42, blight struck the potato crop and there was famine in Ireland, Scotland, and the countries of Northeastern Europe, but the suffering of Ireland was the worst. Over a million people died of starvation. The Irish who could afford passage left for America in a mass migration.

However, in the spring of 1840, Melissa and Rob Roy were falling in love. It was an impossible love, every young Englishman wanted to marry Melissa, not only to have the most beautiful girl in Ireland, but also to control an unimaginable wealth that would someday be hers.

Melissa usually rode over with one or more of her friends to ask Rob Roy's opinion of one of her dad's racehorses or foxhunters. The young girls were curious to see the handsome Irishman, Melissa spoke so well of, but the men only wanted to show their contempt, and to belittle him in front of the girls.

On this particular day, Icarus rode with Melissa's group to the Black Water Forge; the shop where father and son plied their trade as blacksmiths, farriers, wheelwrights, and horse doctors. Icarus was a second cousin of Melissa, and he had come to the realization, if he didn't find a wife with money, he would be reduced to poverty. He and his family were wastrels, they considered work beneath their station and thought that a life of sloth and decadence was their birthright. Unfortunately, without money there is no birthright. Reality was closing in on Icarus. However, if Melissa became his wife, he could laugh at his creditors and be the envy of every man in Ireland, but Melissa wasn't interested in him. Somehow, he had to get her attention and make her consider him a serious suitor.

Icarus was not a handsome lad, he was thin and bowlegged, not from riding, he was born with legs that angled outward at the knees. He was a fastidious type, who liked to impress people with how busy he was with business affairs that were a personal fantasy. He spoke with a high-pitch nasal voice that sounded effeminate, especially to people who knew of men who were different or odd. Icarus was especially known for being abnormally cruel to destitute girls who sold themselves, for a penny or two, to avoid starvation. Icarus earned his reputation honestly, when a poor girl offered sexual favors to Icarus and his friends, who were riding along a country road. She was a cute girl about thirteen years old, with a dirty face and dressed in rags. Icarus dismounted and told his friends he would only be a few minutes. He walked the girl behind some brush to be out of sight.

His friends looked at each other in disbelief and made jokes about Icarus needing his ashes hauled, but they soon heard the girl screaming. Suspecting foul play, the young men rode around the brush to see what the problem was.

Icarus had his trousers around his ankles, and he was flogging the girl with his whip. The girl was naked, rolling on the ground, and screaming in agony. Icarus was reciting scripture, and his whip met the girl's flesh to emphasize every punctuation pause.

"Therefore be imitators of God, as beloved children. And walk in love, as Christ loved us and gave himself up for us, a fragrant offering and sacrifice to God. But sexual immorality and all impurity or covetousness must not even be named among you, as is proper among saints. Let there be no filthiness nor foolish talk nor crude joking, which are out of place, but instead let there be thanksgiving. For you may be sure of this, that everyone who is sexually immoral or impure, or who is covetous (that is, an idolater), has no inheritance in the kingdom of Christ and God."

Ephesians 5:1-33

Her hands were protecting her face and her body was becoming a mass of red welts oozing blood.

The young men were bewildered at the bizarre spectacle, and sat on their horses in disbelief and silence. Although, one young man, wasn't caught up in this scene of depravity; he yelled out, "Icarus, she has had enough."

Icarus stopped suddenly; he seemed lost and bewildered, as if he was returning from another dimension. He watched the young girl writhing in pain, and began to smile warmly, before he remembered his trousers were around his ankles and his flaccid manhood was on display to all his friends.

After attending to his clothing, Icarus mounted his horse and said with humor in his voice, "The little bitch should thank me for showing her the error of her ways and saving her eternal soul. Now, she will find an Irish husband, and have a litter of kids. It makes a man feel good to help people." The men laughed, as they cantered down the road.

Unfortunately this wasn't an isolated event, it was repeated many times and Icarus became bolder and more sadistic with each incident. He didn't limit his victims to the Irish; any woman or girl who was desperate enough to offer sexual favors to Icarus was eligible to be humiliated and beaten with a cane or a whip.

He told his friends, after leaving a girl naked and bleeding, he felt like Jesus, and since he helped girls turn their life around, he should receive a remittance from the Catholic Church for his good work. Icarus admitted that Jesus was good at what he did, but he believed his method made a more lasting impression. His friends howled with laughter.

On a cool September morning, Icarus was with Melissa and several of her friends when they rode over to the blacksmith's shop to see if Rob Roy could help one of her father's steeple chasers. The horse had a front hoof out of balance with a pronounced flare to the outside.

Rob Roy looked at the horse and was explaining the problem and how it could be corrected with careful trimming and a slightly different shoe, while he heated a length of bar stock in the coal forge.

There were nine young people from Melissa's aristocratic class. The girls wanted to see the strapping young lad Melissa spoke so well of, and the young men wanted to see the lad they hated. They were contemptuous of an Irish peasant who could captivate a young girl's attention by talking about a horse's hoof.

The young men were bored with talk of horse anatomy, they gathered outside to talk of gambling and whoring. With loud voices and animated laughter, they hoped to entice the girls outside and impress them with their worldliness.

Inside the shop, Melissa and her friends were intrigued with rasping and shaping the hoof to the desired form. Melissa asked Rob Roy if she could try to shape the hoof.

Rob Roy laughed, and said, "I don't know of any reason why you can't."

Yet, the young Rob Roy was crossing a line of social convention that was hundreds, if not thousands of years old. Women didn't do this type of work on horses, especially young aristocratic British women, and an Irish peasant would never instruct them.

Melissa's friends watched in disbelief as Rob Roy put the hoof on a hoof stand that was the height of a human knee and showed Melissa how to guide the rasp smoothly with a light touch, to cut cleanly through the hoof. His hands touched and guided hers, and their bodies were dangerously close, at times they seemed to be touching.

Rob Roy kept everything on a professional level, but the girls were fascinated with the proceedings and the confident manner of Rob Roy.

Icarus walked in to see Melissa and Rob Roy next to each other working on the hoof. Rob Roy straightened up and said, "You are gifted with your hands Miss Melissa, you could probably do anything with your hands, if you set your heart to it.

Rob Roy was serious about Melissa's abilities. The girls were intrigued and rolling their eyes and smiling at one another. Men didn't compliment young ladies on their ability to perform work, especially work meant for a man.

Icarus took offense and flew into a rage, "How dare you speak to Melissa in such a condescending manner you insolent Irish knave."

"She asked if she could try her hand at the work, and I said, yes," Rob Roy replied with an indifferent attitude.

"You'll say, sir, when you speak to your betters, you Irish pig," Icarus said, just before hitting Rob Roy across the face with a violent slash from his riding crop.

The cruel leather cut a deep gash beneath Rob's left eye. Even Icarus was surprised at the violence of his reaction, but then he realized, this is exactly what he needs to get the attention of his cousin, the beautiful Melissa.

Rob Roy put his hand to his cheek to stop the blood and ease the pain.

He looked up to see Icarus raising his arm to deliver another cut with the whip and reached out to grab the wrist of Icarus with a grip of iron.

Rob Roy placed the hand on the anvil, and with a three-pound hammer, smashed the three middle fingers of Icarus' right hand.

Icarus screamed in pain, and his friends rushed in to find Icarus on his knees, holding his broken hand. They picked him up, dragged him outside, and put him on his horse. As they were leaving, one of them said, "We'll have you flogged, and then hanged, Irish. We'll be back."

Melissa walked over to Rob Roy and said, "It will be best if you leave Ireland, immediately. They will hunt you down and kill you."

"Missy, it takes money to leave," Rob Roy said.

"Go to the Dublin docks, look for the Black Wench. Tell Captain De Wolf, I sent you and that you want to apply as a midshipman. They will sail with the tide. I suggest you be on that ship if you value your life. Next year, I will attend Miss Livingston's Finishing School in Boston. Please stop there to visit, when you have learned the sailing trade. I want to see you again. Here are a few pieces of silver to help you make the trip to Dublin. Now go before they have time to figure out your plans."

She pulled his head down and said, 'Let me see that wound."

When he pulled his hand away, she reached up and kissed him on the mouth and turned to leave. At the door, she turned to say, "Remember, Miss Livingston's in Boston."

She left and the most life-changing five minutes of his life were over. He walked into his house to explain his desperate situation and say goodbye to his parents. He packed his few belongings into an old carpetbag his mother had made. His parents didn't want him to leave, but Rob Roy no longer had a future in Ireland.

His father gave him a small sack of silver coins. "Beware of the highwayman son, he will rob you and cut your throat to watch you die," was the warning he offered his son. Rob Roy was a good lad and could avoid most problems, instinctively.

He caught a coach on the Dublin Pike and booked a ride next to the driver for two pennies. In six hours, he was on the docks looking for the Black Wench and Captain De Wolf.

Rob Roy met a sailor guarding a small sailing ketch with Black Wench written across the bow. "Can you tell me where I can find Captain De Wolf?" Rob Roy asked.

"Aye, mate, he will be at the Friar's Comfort, until tomorrow morning," the sailor said, "unless, he runs out of money or pulls a belly muscle."

"Can you tell me where I can find the Friar's Comfort?" Rob Roy asked.

"You'll be a country lad; there's not a red-blooded lad who stands to piss, who doesn't know of the Friar's Comfort. It's a mile due West on State St," the young sailor answered and looked away as if he were bored.

Rob Roy was anxious to see what the Friar's Comfort was all about.

It was a short walk for Rob Roy. There was a small sign overhead, but once he stepped into the foyer, there was a large wooden carving of a naked woman from the waist up.

He was staring at the carving when a small, well-formed Chinese lady approached Rob Roy and pulled his arm against a body that had just a few more clothes on than the carving. She looked up into his eyes, and asked, "Did you come to see a wooden woman or did you come to see real girls?"

"Actually, I came to see, Captain De Wolf, of the Black Wench," Rob Roy answered awkwardly, feeling humiliated over staring at a wooden woman.

The young woman made a pouting face and said, "Oh, too bad, I thought we might be naughty together. Come into the parlor and I will tell Captain De Wolf, you are here to see him. What is your name handsome boy?"

"Rob Roy, mam, Rob Roy Larkin," he answered.

"Oh, I see, have a seat Mr. Larkin, make yourself at home. The Captain will see you when he is not, indisposed," the girl said, with a smile and a wink.

Rob Roy was out of his element, but he was fairly certain, this was a house of ill repute. For the next two hours, several girls approached Rob Roy. He was appealing and looked innocent; an interesting conquest for professional girls who were bored with the typical rich customers, but he insisted that he was here to see the Captain.

A huge man walked into the parlor as if he owned the building. The girls all acted as if he was an intimate friend and the men cowered and stepped back to give him room. He ignored them all, and walked up to Rob Roy.

Rob Roy stood awkwardly and the Captain said, “I am Captain De Wolf. What is your business with me?”

“I am Rob Roy Larkin. Melissa suggested I talk to you about being a midshipmen on the Black Wench, I have mastered several skills, I am literate, and I can tally numbers better than most men.”

The captain seemed mad, until he heard Melissa’s name. He had walked in like a savage, capable of killing a man with his hands, but now, he smiled and asked, “Is Melissa a friend of yours?”

“Yes, sir, I help her with her horses, and we enjoy each other’s company,” Rob Roy replied.

“What skills do you have?” the Captain asked.

“I am a wheelwright, but I am good with working iron in the forge, and working wood as well. It is all part of the trade. I can also shoe horses, and have a natural knack for doctoring wounds on horses and dogs.”

The captain was quiet for a minute, while feeling his short gray and black beard. “You realize, a midshipman is the first step in becoming an officer. Your skills will be useful aboard ship, but your job is teaching and overseeing the crew while they perform those tasks. In an emergency, you are expected to perform the tasks. My surgeon got drunk in Haiti and never made it back to the ship. If you can perform surgical duties you will rise through the ranks much faster. Your pay is based on a percentage of the profit of a voyage. We sail from the British Isles, to Europe, to Africa, to the New World and back. If we have fair winds and trade well, we can make a handsome profit three times a year. I expect the ship to be run well and efficiently, but that isn’t my job; it is the responsibility of my officers. We face many dangers on the high seas; two of the worst are storms and pirates. Do you still want to sign on?”

“Yes, sir.”

“We sail in the morning with the tide. You can stay here, this is my place of business or you can walk back to the ketch and wait, but I suggest you wait here and ride back with me in a coach. These streets are dangerous at night. One of the girls will find a bunk for you, and someone will wake you in the morning any questions?”

“No sir, I have no questions,” Rob Roy answered.

The captain called over Rita, the young girl who met Rob Roy in the foyer. "Rita, this is Rob Roy. Prepare that small room in the back and draw bath water for him, oh and get him something to eat as well." The captain looked at Rob Roy and said, "I'll expect to see you well-rested in the morning."

"Yes sir, thank you sir," Rob Roy replied, but the captain was already preoccupied with the women and other business.

Rita told Rob Roy to wait a few minutes while she prepared his room and bed.

She came back and motioned Rob Roy to follow her. She walked down a narrow hallway of many rooms and opened the door of the last room. She walked into the room and told Rob to sit down next to a copper bathtub with steaming water. She took off his shoes and began undressing him. He resisted when she started to take off his trousers, but she said, "You don't expect to take a bath with your clothes on, do you?"

Soon Rita was helping Rob Roy into his first real bathtub. She admired his naked body and her fingertips touched his back and butt as he settled in to the tub. He was muscular and his body was proportional. She knew how to judge the masculine form.

She bathed him as if he were a child and complimented his body to give him confidence as she progressed. Once the slow bath was nearly over she said, "Oops, we forgot something". She reached down into the water and grasped his intimate manly parts, "We need to wash your baby. We don't want to forget him."

Her smile and gentle hands made him forget about being self-conscious and he was enjoying his time with this knowing woman who put him to ease. He was stepping out of the tub, when a young woman walked into the room with a plate of food. She looked at Rob Roy and glanced at Rita, before saying, "You are lucky, this looks really good." The woman put the plate next to the bed on a table and winked at Rob Roy as she was leaving.

Rita dried Rob Roy and sat him in a chair at the table. "Go ahead and eat, some things are better hot." Rita massaged his shoulders while he ate the best meal he had ever been served. When he was finished, Rita tucked him into bed. She asked if he was comfortable and warm, and he replied that he felt wonderful, she kissed him on the cheek and slipped out of the room. The night was still early, but he fell asleep almost immediately.

After the Charge of the Light Brigade

Edward, it's time I told you about my life. This beautiful country and its energetic people take my mind away from my troubles. My father, your uncle, was in the diplomatic service of the crown and served in many countries, but he met and married my beautiful mother, Patricia Zavaleta, in Buenos Aries, and I was born 18 months later.

My mother's family owns a large hacienda, about thirty miles south of the city on the pampas and there, my cousins have untold numbers of cattle and horses. They have the leisure to dedicate their lives to polo and the seduction of maidens. I was fortunate to spend my teenage years on the hacienda and enjoy the decadent life; until my father decided it was time to accept the responsibilities of a young British aristocrat, before I became like my polo-playing cousins. He gave me the options of joining the church, but that was not a real option, or I could follow my father in the diplomatic corps, but that was intensely boring, or I could choose the military, the cavalry to be precise. Here was adventure and travel.

As you well know, commissions are purchased; although, after Balaclava this system is being changed, and you will probably be among the last officers to purchase a commission. Officers provide their own horses and equipment, and receive very little in pay. It is a depository for elitists who have nothing to do or those who love the military or God forbid, war.

This was the life I chose, but sometimes I wonder what life would have been like as a diplomat or as an employee of the Hudson Bay or East India Trading companies. My problem was I loved my horses as much as I loved the young girls and their flirting smiles and flashing eyes. The cavalry gave me the opportunity to be in the saddle everyday and the young ladies are always fascinated with a man in uniform who can ride a horse well. Thus the life of a young cavalry officer suited my lifestyle and I enjoyed the travel, but my good life was destined to change in the year 1854, on a remote corner of the world called Crimea.

France, Turkey, and Britain formed an alliance against Russia; negotiations broke down and we were destined for war, and we of the Light Brigade were ordered to illustrate the folly of valor without reason or substance. Yes, we rode into the valley of death, at Balaclava on the 25th of October 1854.

On that fateful day, our commanding officer, Lord Raglan, wanted us to pursue, harass and capture, a retreating enemy artillery battery. Unfortunately, the order was not concise, and its accuracy was compromised as the order was passed through the chain of command. The last officer, to deliver the order, a Captain Nolan, during a desperate and critical moment, pointed to the wrong battery, with a sweep of his hand, during a verbal consultation, with our brigade commander, Lord Cardigan. This battery was not retreating; indeed, it was in a secure redoubt, at a distance of about a mile and a half, and down-valley from our position. Attacking this battery along the valley floor would have been formidable, but on the heights above the valley floor, were multiple artillery batteries and infantry emplacements.

A moment of sanity might have questioned the validity of the order, but we were anxious to prove our valor and loyalty; questioning an order was considered an act of cowardice in those days. In fairness to Captain Nolan, he seemed to realize the mistake and joined the charge, without orders and bolted ahead of our commanding officer, Lord Cardigan, but he was cut down by cannon fire during the first moments of the charge. His true intent and whether he wanted to make the correction or join in the glorious charge will never be known.

Six hundred sixty men on horses rode into the valley of death. A valley defended by 5,240 Russian infantry and three artillery batteries. You know the poem:

Alfred, Lord Tennyson/Battle of Balaclava, October 25, 1854

The Charge of the Light Brigade

Half a league half a league,
Half a league onward,
All in the valley of Death
Rode the six hundred:
'Forward, the Light Brigade!
Charge for the guns' he said:
Into the valley of Death
Rode the six hundred.

'Forward, the Light Brigade!'
Was there a man dismay'd ?
Not tho' the soldier knew
Some one had blunder'd:
Theirs not to make reply,
Theirs not to reason why,
Theirs but to do & die,

Edward said, "I was honored to hear you recite those words."

"Edward, it is my epitaph of dishonor. I saw the mistake early on and should have overtaken Lord Cardigan and told him of the utter insanity of such a hopeless charge." The field grade officers argue over what went wrong, but I saw what happened. We had 110 killed and another 161 wounded. Several men who had their horses shot out from under them were killed as they tried to crawl back to our lines. I should have stopped the insanity, but I did nothing."

I requested 18 months off and Edward is awaiting an official billet. He will be a captain, when a position opens up, despite his inexperience. Our military is a rigid class system, preserved by the purchase of commissions for young men. If you desire a higher rank, your family must be willing to pay more. Edward will be the same rank as me, when a berth opens up in the cavalry. Until then he will remain a subaltern, theoretically acquiring the skills needed to serve as an officer.

Edward is an intelligent lad, filled with hope and excitement for the future. He is tall, strong, and handsome, and I dread the thought of training a fine young man to be a cavalry officer. Like the common man who signs a twenty-one year enlistment for a penny a day, we sign because there are no options. An enlistment is usually considered a lifetime and there is no pension. The options are limited for aristocrats as well. Some of us join the church and settle down with a fat wife and a brood of kids to fleece the flock for decades or become merchants or manage tenant farmers, but some of us are hopeless romantics and want to see the world.

Unfortunately, there is a fly in the pudding. I am known, throughout the realm, as a hero. I am considered a hero because of performing a heroic act. I am a hero because I survived a cavalry charge. It was one of the biggest mistakes of British military history, but because I wasn't killed, while the Russian artillery and infantry had target practice, I am a hero.

I plan to teach Edward about being a leader, and of the tactics of the Cossack and the Bedouin horsemen, but secretly, I hope he develops other interests. I realize my role, as a cavalry captain is to be a strong-arm man or thug for the mercantile interests of the British trading companies; if the profits are being threatened, we ride in to threaten, punish, or kill those who threaten the ledger books.

We'll spend four or five weeks crossing the Atlantic and plan to spend the next year crossing North America, before catching a ship bound for India. Hopefully, Edward and I will find a means to live our lives in a more meaningful pursuit.

Edward can ride well enough; he spent a great part of his youth chasing foxes with the hounds. However, he will need to learn to survive in the wilderness, with a horse, like a Cossack. If we survive the trip, Edward will have gone way beyond riding a horse on the parade ground or chasing the elusive fox. Those are worthy endeavors, but they wont prepare you for the Cossack's lance or the Bedouin's sword.

The Crimean War was the first war to have correspondents from the newspapers. Every literate person knew about the war, the massive carnage, and the dreadful Charge of the Light Brigade.

Edward and I had long discussions about life, Britain, the empire, horses, women, and what we expected to see in America, during long walks on the deck. We both agreed, sailing was nice for a few days, but the prospect of living on the ocean for months and years seemed to be condemnation to a life of perpetual boredom.

We arrived in Baltimore Inner Harbor a few days ahead of schedule, and we were fascinated with the dynamic economic energy of Baltimore. We decided to tour the city for a few days, before taking the Baltimore & Ohio to Wheeling, Virginia. We found a hotel on Pratt Street, a short walk from the harbor, and toured the foundries that were building locomotives around the clock. Not only were they trying to keep up with orders for the United States, but they were also building locomotives for Russia and China, and many countries around the world. We learned a new appreciation for the economic might of the United States.

For dinner, we chose a nice restaurant near the hotel, without realizing it served the community as a bordello as well. We were in uniform and the women were dressed elegantly in evening dresses. They were attractive women, who knew how to smile and flirt with their eyes. They left small cards on our table with their names written in flowery script.

Edward was overwhelmed with the songs of the sirens, and believed they were attracted to him. I decided to insert myself, "Edward, they may find you attractive, but this is their business. When they have exhausted you or your money, they will find someone else. He may not have your boyish good looks and charm, but he will have money and that, my young cousin, is why they are here. There will be many opportunities for romance and feminine companionship, as we follow the sun across this great continent. Here we have an increased chance of catching the venereal diseases that are associated with women of compromised virtue. These are not the country lasses that hang out at the hunt club, who are ready to play 'hide the sausage,' in the forlorn hope of snagging a rich man before settling down with a red-faced farmer to have a brood of kids and live in the same house with their cows and chickens. These women are pros and every man represents a possible cash transaction."

Edward's passion cooled and he was lost in thought. A young red-haired wench bent over his shoulder, exposing an ample bosom, she hugged Edward, kissed his cheek, and asked, "Captain Handsome, can we spend time together, to become bosom buddies?"

With his boyish smile, he reached in his pocket for a silver coin and placed it in her bodice, between her breasts. He looked in her eyes and said, "There's no time tonight, but when we return, I will look for you." He winked and she looked disappointed..

She said, "Don't be too long soldier boy. A girl gets lonely." She walked away with her fingertips lingering as long as possible on Edward's shoulder.

Moments later, Edward looked at me to say, "My goodness."

I laughed at his innocence, and we walked down Pratt Street to see the sights. We passed a courtyard and noticed black men in cages. Many of the men looked feral and some had nasty wounds. A well-dressed man walked up to us and said, "They are bound for the slave market in New Orleans, but if you would like a semi-civilized slave, I will make you a good deal. I am Martin Luther, I own these pens and their contents."

The introductions were made and I asked, "Sir, why do you say semi-civilized?"

"These are recalcitrant slaves and runaways. They have proven themselves difficult and unreliable. My men retrain them with the lash and the club, but where they are going, there are slave trainers who have no pity for slaves with bad attitudes.

We walked among the cages, until we came to a cage of women of various ages and sizes. Mister Luther continued to tell us about the slave trade, "Most of these slaves will be sold to the sugar and rice plantations, in Mississippi, Louisiana, and Texas. They will live two or three years before they are worked to death or succumb to the tropical diseases associated with the climate and stale air. These Africans, from the homeland, need to be worked hard to keep them submissive; unfortunately, the planters work them too hard and they often die early, before they begin turning a profit. It's a hard business, gentlemen, but it is a business where demand is always greater than the supply."

Edward saw a woman who caught his eye. "Mister Luther, tell me about the light colored woman."

Luther laughed, "She's Black Irish and a comely bitch if there ever was one."

I smiled at Luther and said, "Sir, I have a farm in Ireland, and I can assure you, there are no blackamoors in Ireland."

Mister Luther smiled, showing irregular teeth yellowed by chewing tobacco, "Captain, you have a lot to learn about the slave trade. Her mother was an Irish wench, gathered up by you English as a homeless peasant or beggar or possibly a fomenter of rebellion. They brought the undesirable Irish to the West Indies by the hundreds of thousands and sold them into slavery, during the 17th and 18th Centuries. The Bahamas has traditionally been a lucrative slave-breeding source, but when someone came up with the idea of crossing the Irish wench with the African buck, a new breed of slave was created, the mulatto or Black Irish. The Irish men are difficult, but much easier and safer than the African. The Black Irish were so popular, the African market was depressed, and your parliament made it illegal to breed for the Mulatto, to protect the African slave trade, in 1690. Later on, you English stopped the trans-Atlantic slave trade in 1807, conveniently making your Irish insurrectionists and homeless peasants more valuable. Thus putting an end to the African slave trade was a humanitarian gesture, but your Irish slave trade became more profitable, and the Irish influx was increased. The plantations in North America and South America were crying out for more black slaves, but only a few were getting out of Africa, and those were the Yankee Clippers owned by abolitionists in New England. Their ships were so fast, Lord Nelson himself couldn't catch them.

Luther yelled to one of his black workers, "Jojo, bring us the mulatto, Lucia."

Jojo went into the pen and proceeded to put wrist irons on the young woman and a pair of leather hobbles that kept her from walking a full stride. Luther explained, "She is fairly civilized, but I don't want to be running down the city streets of Baltimore chasing a mulatto wench like a farm boy chasing a black split tail down a cornrow.

He laughed at his own joke, and didn't seem to notice that we weren't laughing. When she was standing in front of us, Luther had her turn around. He used a stockman's cane to pick up the hem of her loose fitting dress above her hips. She had on no underclothing and her figure was a perfect feminine form. He lifted the dress higher to reveal her back and ran his hand over the flawless skin. "No whip has ever cut this back." He reached downward to grasp a buttock in his hand, he looked at us to say, "Have a feel, she is round and firm like an apple."

She protested and Jojo pulled hard on a leather strap tied to her hobbles and she hit the dirt hard. Luther lost his temper and yelled at her, "You stand, you high yeller bitch or Jojo will take the whip to you. Now, get back on your feet and act like you have some manners."

Luther turned to us with a smile, "She's not dangerous. She just needs a little discipline. A young husband bought her, and his wife went crazy with jealousy. She waited until her husband was gone for a few days, brought me the wench and told me to sell her to a brothel in New Orleans or as far away as possible. It's kind of funny when you think about it."

Luther reached down with his stockman's cane and pulled her dress up slowly, until her whole body was exposed. She trembled in fear, but she didn't move.

Luther looked at the two of us and said, "I can make you a good deal if you are interested."

I was about to say, no thanks, when Edward asked, "How much for the wench?"

Luther answered immediately, "Six thousand Yankee Dollars."

"I'll give you $2,500 U.S., drawn on a bank note from the Bank of England," Edward said.

Luther said, "Sold," and spit in his hand and reached out to shake hands with Edward, "You bought yourself a mulatto, son."

The papers were drawn up and signed and in no time, my young cousin owned a woman. I didn't know what he had planned, but our trip was becoming more interesting. Mr. Luther asked if Edward wanted to buy the shackles and hobbles and Edward replied, "No, Mr. Luther, if she runs, I will hunt her down, sell her back to you, and you can sell her to a brothel down in New Orleans."

We left with a light colored woman with exotic features and raven black hair. Her dress barely hid her womanly charms and she was barefoot. Edward and I attracted attention in our uniforms, but with Lucia, we were a sensation.

The clerk at our hotel created a scene when we came in with the girl, but quickly forgot his problems, when Edward laid a two dollar gold piece on the counter. Edward pulled the clerk across the counter by his shirt and said, "Be a good sport and bring us a pair of sheets and an extra blanket, and heat up some water for a bath. I may have another coin if you cooperate."

A copper bathtub was brought into the room and 20 gallons of warm water was used to fill it up. Edward asked me to make sure no one disturbed Lucia while she bathed, and I told him I would read at the desk while she was bathing. He left and said he had an errand to run.

Edward stopped at the bordello, and asked to speak to the red haired woman. She walked into the lobby, a few minutes later, "Soldier boy, you are back!"

"Yes, but I need help, of a different type, and I am willing to pay you for your time," Edward smiled and winked at the woman.

Her curiosity was aroused and she liked the naïve rascal in his fancy uniform, "OK soldier boy, what's the deal?"

"I bought a mulatto woman tonight, and she needs new clothes. I am hoping to buy an outfit from you, since you are of a similar body shape. Tomorrow, I will pay you to take her shopping for new clothing and the things a woman needs. In fact, you can buy yourself a new outfit as well."

She thought for a few minutes and said, "Come with me, to my private room and I will find something for her." She led Edward out the back door and into an adjacent shed in the back yard. "No man has ever been to my private room. I will expect you behave yourself like a gentleman."

Edward grinned and said, "I am harmless."

She opened the door stepped inside and held the door for Edward as he walked through the door, "You are not harmless. I think you have broken many hearts in your travels."

Edward smiled to say, "This is my first trip, away from home, and I have never been in a woman's bedroom in my life."

She moaned and put her hand on her lower abdomen, as if she was in pain. "Where have you been all my life, handsome? She opened a drawer and placed some clothes on the table. "These will make her presentable and she can wear them while we buy her some nice things. Now, tell me your name, and why you feel you need to buy a woman."

"My name is Edward. I didn't buy her to own her; I bought her to give her a new life. I can afford to help her, and that is what I am doing.

Here is a twenty dollar gold piece. I will expect you to be at the hotel room tomorrow at noon. I will give you another gold coin to use for buying the clothes. If things go well, I will have more money for you at the end of the day. Now, you must tell me your name."

She leaned forward and pulled Edward's head to her shoulder and whispered in his ear, "My name is Sissy. Now kiss me, Edward."

He turned to look at her and Sissy's mouth covered his as if she was starving. He kissed her with innocence and Sissy was overwhelmed with passion. His voice quaked with fear, "I think … we should stop. I am not ready."

Sissy opened his trousers and grasped his cock with her hand, "You are ready, handsome." She pushed him backwards on the bed and pulled up her skirt. She pushed her tongue deep into his mouth and leaned back to impale herself on his rock hard cock. She kissed his neck and cheeks, while her hips began a steady up and down movement on his cock. She felt his hot maiden tribute flooding deep in her vagina and her own orgasm began radiating outward from the core of her being.

She drifted away from her body for a few moments and when she returned, she smiled to feel the young Edward breathing deeply beneath her while his cock was still hard in her vagina. She slowly rose up and back down several times, increasing the speed slightly with each thrust until she kept up a steady precise movement and suddenly another orgasm rocked her body as she felt the young cock in her vagina spill forth another lighter load against her womb.

When she recovered, she was still lying on Edward and his semi-deflated cock was gripped tightly in her vagina. She wondered, *why did I climax so hard? Why did I even climax? What is it about this virgin boy that pushed me so far over the edge? He is handsome, but she had been with many handsome men and none of them affected her like this. Oh my, if she had met him a few years ago, she would do anything for a young man like Edward. They just don't make men like him, very often. He was waking up; the magic time is nearly over.*

Edward stood up and straightened his uniform, "I am sorry. I was not expecting … I hope we still have our arrangement for tomorrow."

"We better have our arrangement. I am taking the rest of the evening off. I am tired and I don't want to be late, to take your new woman shopping. You can stay here with me, if you want. I have never asked a man to stay with me, through the night, that is a rare compliment."

"No, I better get back or my cousin will worry; besides, I left him with my acquisition, and he is always at odds with morality. I would love to spend the evening with you, but I am obligated to my cousin."

Sissy was intrigued, "He seems old enough and capable enough to take care of himself."

Edward replied, "You don't understand, he is a war hero who carries around a tremendous load of guilt."

Sissy asked, "Why does he carry so much guilt?"

Edward answered, "Because, he is alive and many of his men are dead."

Sissy stood up from the bed and loosened her dress, so it fell to the floor. She stood naked a few inches in front of Edward, "I want you to remember me, like this." She kissed him once more, before they parted for the evening.

Edward found Carlos reading at a small desk, and Lucia asleep in his bed. He waved at his cousin and placed the borrowed outfit on the bed. He pulled a chair next to his cousin and Carlos asked him, "Edward, are you in control of your faculties?"

Edward thought for a minute, "Yes, indeed; I know what I am doing, and I think we can make a difference in the life of a fellow human being."

"Edward, owning a slave, is not a humanitarian gesture." Carlos said with skepticism.

"I didn't buy her to own a slave. I bought her to give her a new life. Somewhere between here and San Francisco, we will find her a home and hopefully, a husband. In the interim, I want to educate her to serve as a wife." There was a soft knocking at the door.

Edward answered the door to find a maid with the sheets and a blanket. He gave her a copper coin and turned to Carlos, "I guess I will be the one sleeping on the floor."

The next morning, the three of them walked to the Baltimore & Ohio train station at Camden Yards to inquire about tickets West. The Baltimore & Ohio ran to Wheeling and from there they could book passage on a riverboat to Saint Louis. They bought three tickets to Wheeling for the next morning and met Sissy at the hotel for lunch. She took Lucia shopping and the men visited some of the horse traders.

They met for dinner; Lucia had acquired some of the mannerisms of Sissy and she seemed to be breaking free of a shell she had formed around herself. Sissy asked Edward to accompany her on a walk through the city. Edward offered his elbow, and they walked into the evening.

Sissy began the conversation, "Edward, Lucia told me of your plans for her and she said, the two of you are perfect gentlemen."

Edward said, "We are expected to be gentlemen, but not perfect."

"Close enough for me," Sissy said, "I have saved some money and I want to go west to start a new life, but a woman can't travel alone. I was wondering if you would allow me to travel with you to St Louis. I think I could start a legitimate business there or maybe find a husband. I need to leave Baltimore; while I am still young and have a chance at starting over."

Edward stopped and turned to face Sissy, "If you pay your own way, there is no reason why you can't travel with us for security. I will need to convince Carlos, but you must remember, he is a private person. He will object at first, but he is a kindhearted soul.

You will need a ticket."

"I bought one this afternoon, and I withdrew my money from my account. I have no reason to go back to my, place of employment. I am ready to leave with you tomorrow."

Edward thought for a few minutes and said, "You took a lot for granted, Sissy. I hope Carlos doesn't pull rank on me and ruin your plans."

“I have my ticket and I am going on that train, with you or without you. You two can teach Lucia to read and cypher, but you can’t teach her how to be a lady. I know how to conduct myself as a lady and I will be a lady, from the moment I leave Baltimore.”

43679895R00213

Made in the USA
Middletown, DE
27 April 2019